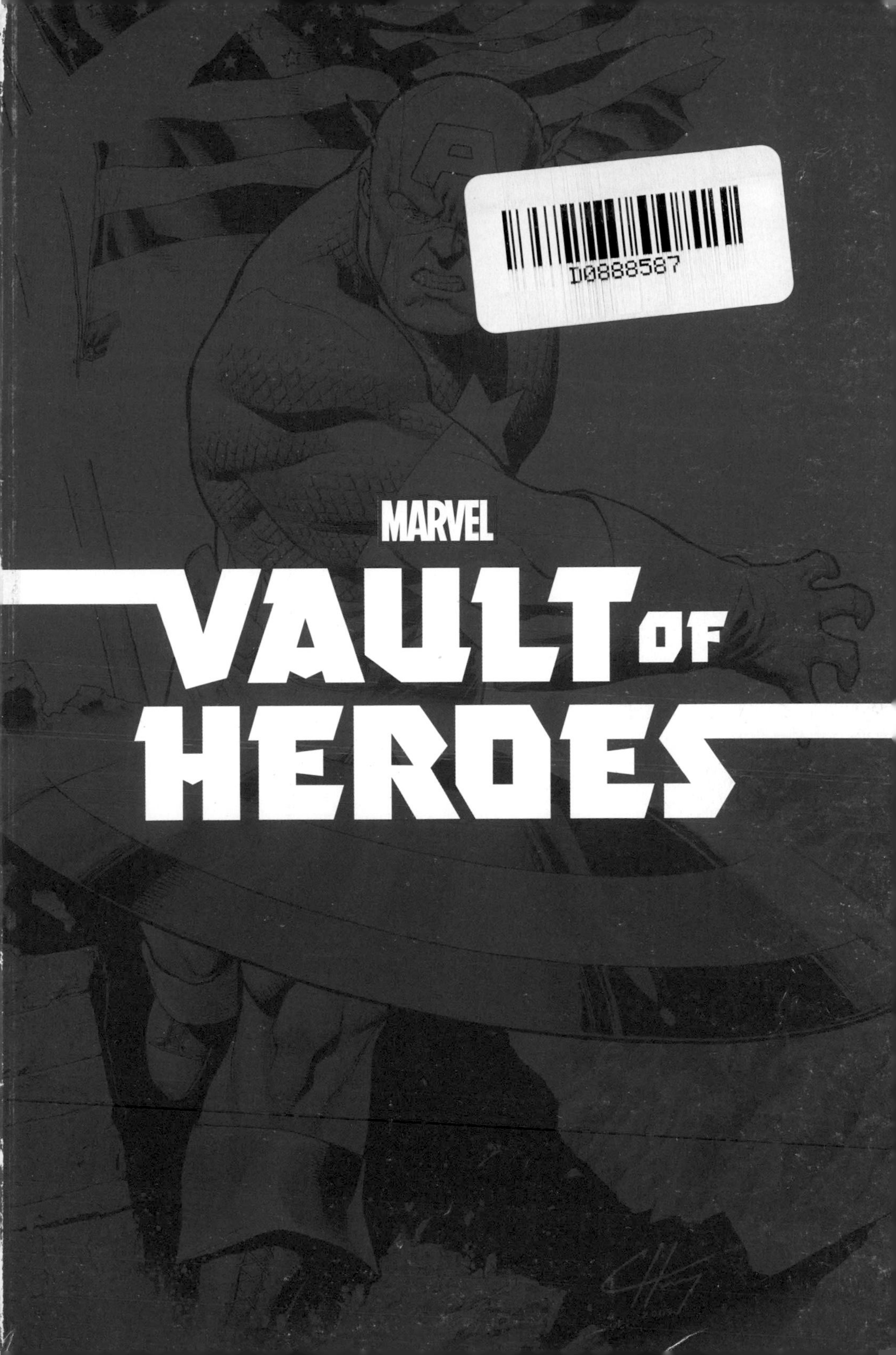
MARVEL
VAULT OF
HEROES

ISBN: 978-1-68405-678-1     23  22  21  20     1 2 3 4

Originally published by MARVEL as MARVEL ADVENTURES SUPER HEROES (2008) issues #8 and 12
and MARVEL ADVENTURES SUPER HEROES (2010) issues #3, 5, 15, 16, and 21.

Cover Art by
**Clayton Henry**

Cover Colors by
**Guru-eFX**

Collection Edits by
**Alonzo Simon** and
**Zac Boone**

Collection Design by
**Jeff Powell**

Chris Ryall, President & Publisher/CCO
Cara Morrison, Chief Financial Officer
Matthew Ruzicka, Chief Accounting Officer
David Hedgecock, Associate Publisher
John Barber, Editor-in-Chief
Justin Eisinger, Editorial Director, Graphic Novels and Collections
Scott Dunbier, Director, Special Projects
Jerry Bennington, VP of New Product Development
Lorelei Bunjes, VP of Technology & Information Services
Jud Meyers, Sales Director
Anna Morrow, Marketing Director
Tara McCrillis, Director of Design & Production
Mike Ford, Director of Operations
Shauna Monteforte, Manufacturing Operations Director
Rebekah Cahalin, General Manager

Ted Adams and Robbie Robbins, IDW Founders

Marvel Publishing:

VP Production & Special Projects: Jeff Youngquist

Editor, Juvenile Publishing: Lauren Bisom

Assistant Editor, Special Projects: Caitlin O'Connell

VP Licensed Publishing: Sven Larsen

SVP Print, Sales & Marketing: David Gabriel

Editor In Chief: C.B. Cebulski

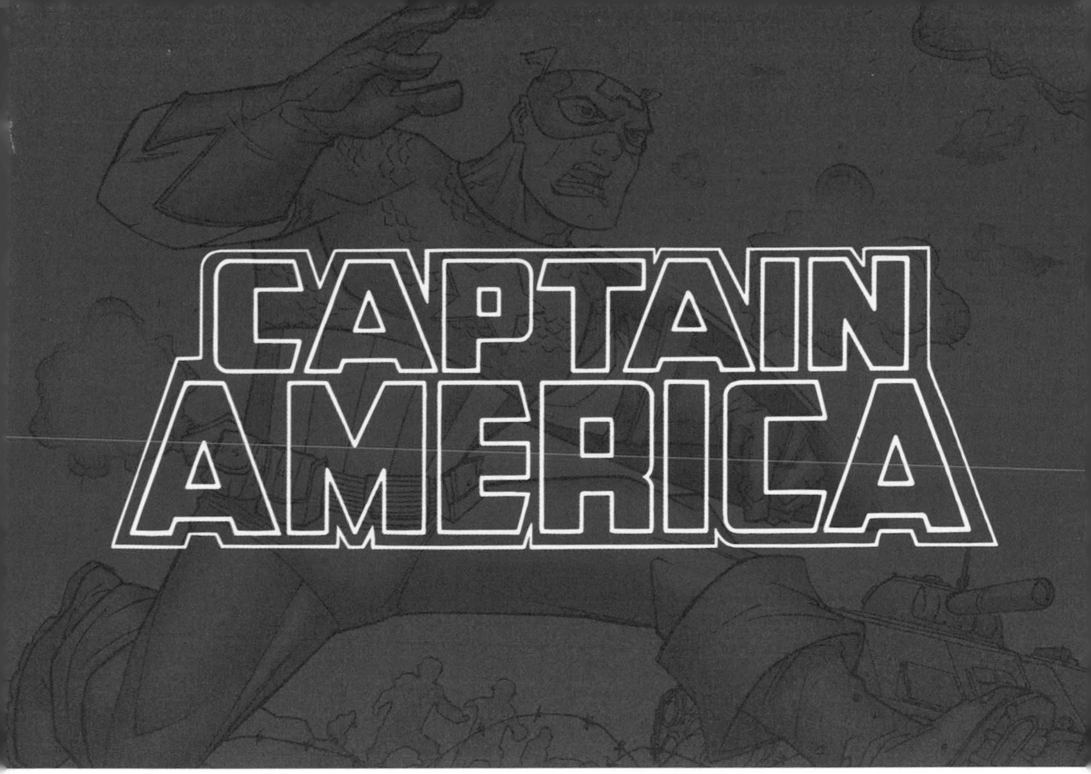
CAPTAIN AMERICA

**• ISSUE 01**

*The Legend Reborn*
WRITTEN BY **SCOTT GRAY**
ART BY **CRAIG ROUSSEAU**
COLORS BY **CHRIS SOTOMAYOR**
LETTERS BY **DAVE SHARPE**

*Spy for the Cameras!*
WRITTEN BY **ROGER LANGRIDGE**
ART BY **CRAIG ROUSSEAU**
COLORS BY **CHRIS SOTOMAYOR**
LETTERS BY **DAVE SHARPE**

**• ISSUE 02**

*Web of Deceit*
WRITTEN BY **SCOTT GRAY**
PENCILS BY **MATTEO LOLLI**
INKS BY **CHRISTIAN VECCHIA**
COLORS BY **SOTOCOLOR**
LETTERS BY **DAVE SHARPE**

*If This Be P.R.O.D.O.K!*
WRITTEN BY **ROGER LANGRIDGE**
ART BY **CRAIG ROUSSEAU**
COLORS BY **SOTOCOLOR**
LETTERS BY **DAVE SHARPE**

**• ISSUE 03**

*Marvel Adventures Super Heroes #3*
WRITTEN BY **PAUL TOBIN**
PENCILS BY **RONAN CLIQUET**
INKS BY **AMILTON SANTOS**
COLORS BY **SOTOCOLOR**
LETTERS BY **DAVE SHARPE**

**• ISSUE 04**

*Marvel Adventures Super Heroes #5*
WRITTEN BY **PAUL TOBIN**
PENCILS BY **CHRIS CROSS**
INKS BY **RICK KETCHAM**
COLORS BY **SOTOCOLOR**
LETTERS BY **DAVE SHARPE**

**• ISSUE 05**

*Back In Time*
WRITTEN BY **PAUL TOBIN**
PENCILS BY **RONAN CLIQUET**
INKS BY **AMILTON SANTOS**
COLORS BY **SOTOCOLOR**
LETTERS BY **DAVE SHARPE**

**• ISSUE 06**

*Stars, Stripes, and Spiders!*
WRITTEN BY **TODD DEZAGO**
PENCILS BY **LOU KANG**
INKS BY **PAT DAVIDSON**
COLORS BY **DIGITAL RAINBOW**
LETTERS BY **DAVE SHARPE**

**• ISSUE 07**

*The Big Idea*
WRITTEN BY **J.M. DMATTEIS**
PENCILS BY **WELLINTON ALVES**
INKS BY **NELSON PEREIRA**
COLORS BY **BRUNO HANG**
**HARPE**

01

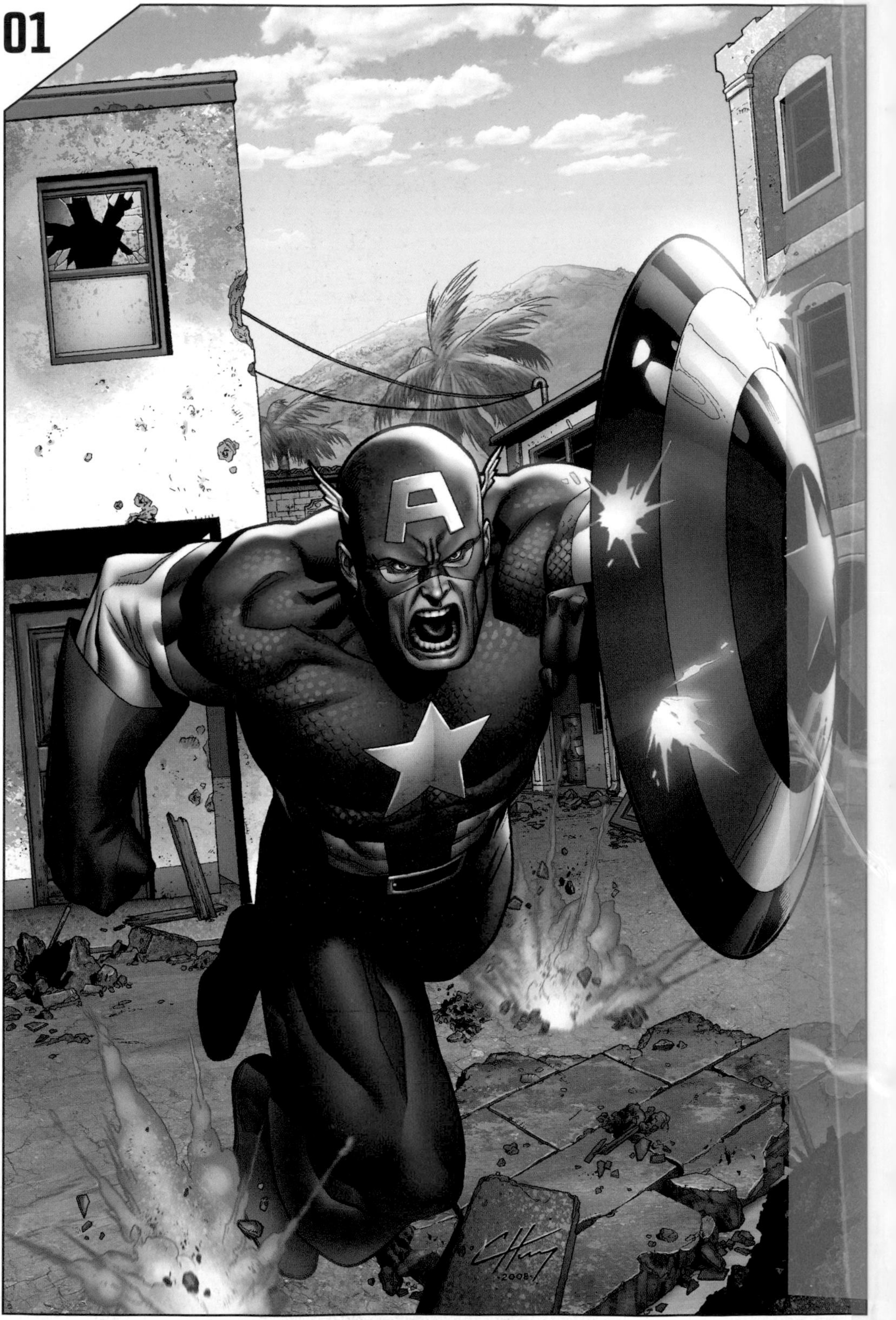

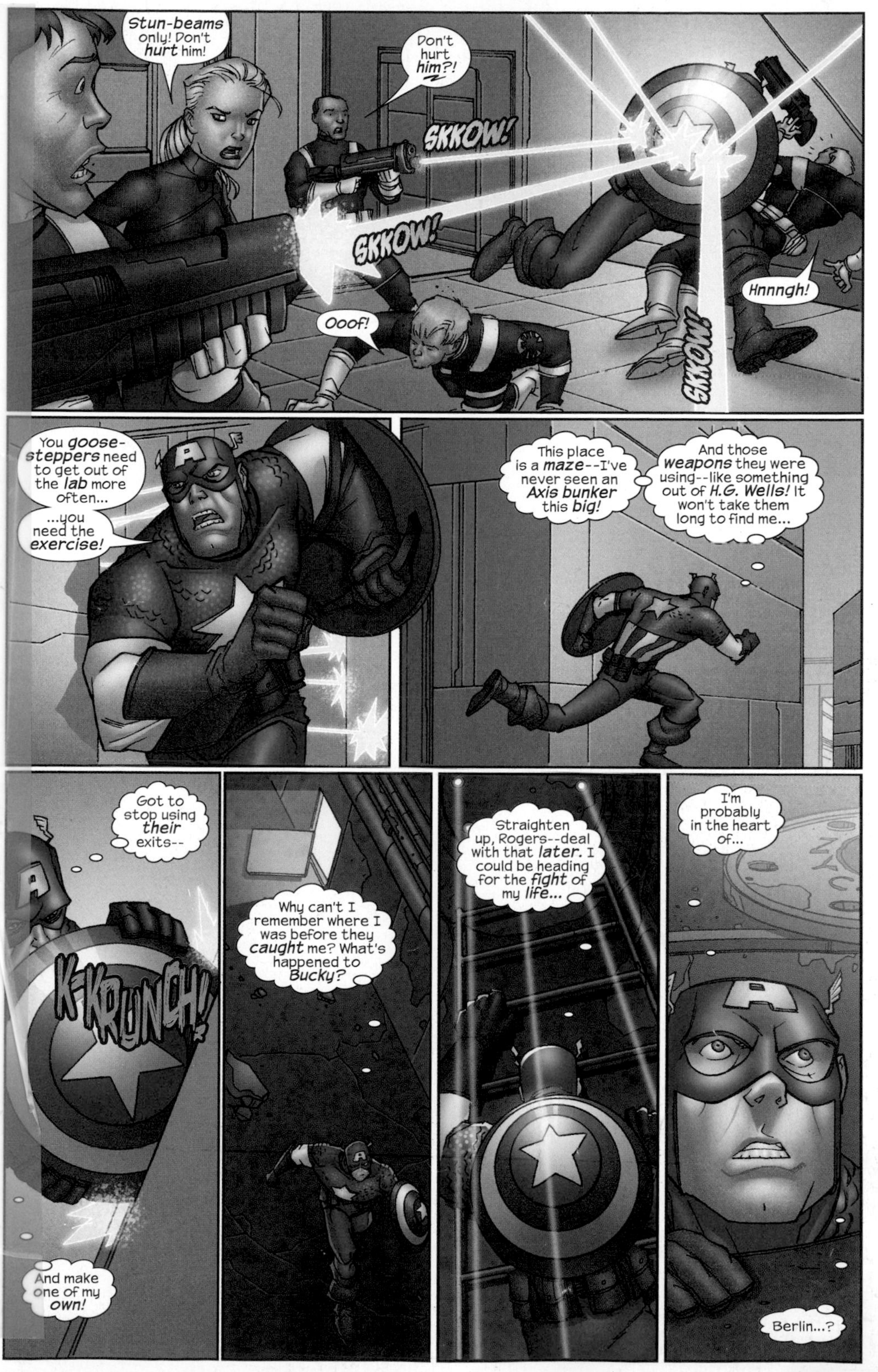
Stun-beams only! Don't hurt him!
Don't hurt him?!
SKKOW!
SKKOW!
SKKOW!
Ooof!
Hnnngh!
You goose-steppers need to get out of the lab more often...
...you need the exercise!
This place is a maze--I've never seen an Axis bunker this big!
And those weapons they were using--like something out of H.G. Wells! It won't take them long to find me...
Got to stop using their exits--
K-KRUNCH!
And make one of my own!
Why can't I remember where I was before they caught me? What's happened to Bucky?
Straighten up, Rogers--deal with that later. I could be heading for the fight of my life...
I'm probably in the heart of...
Berlin...?

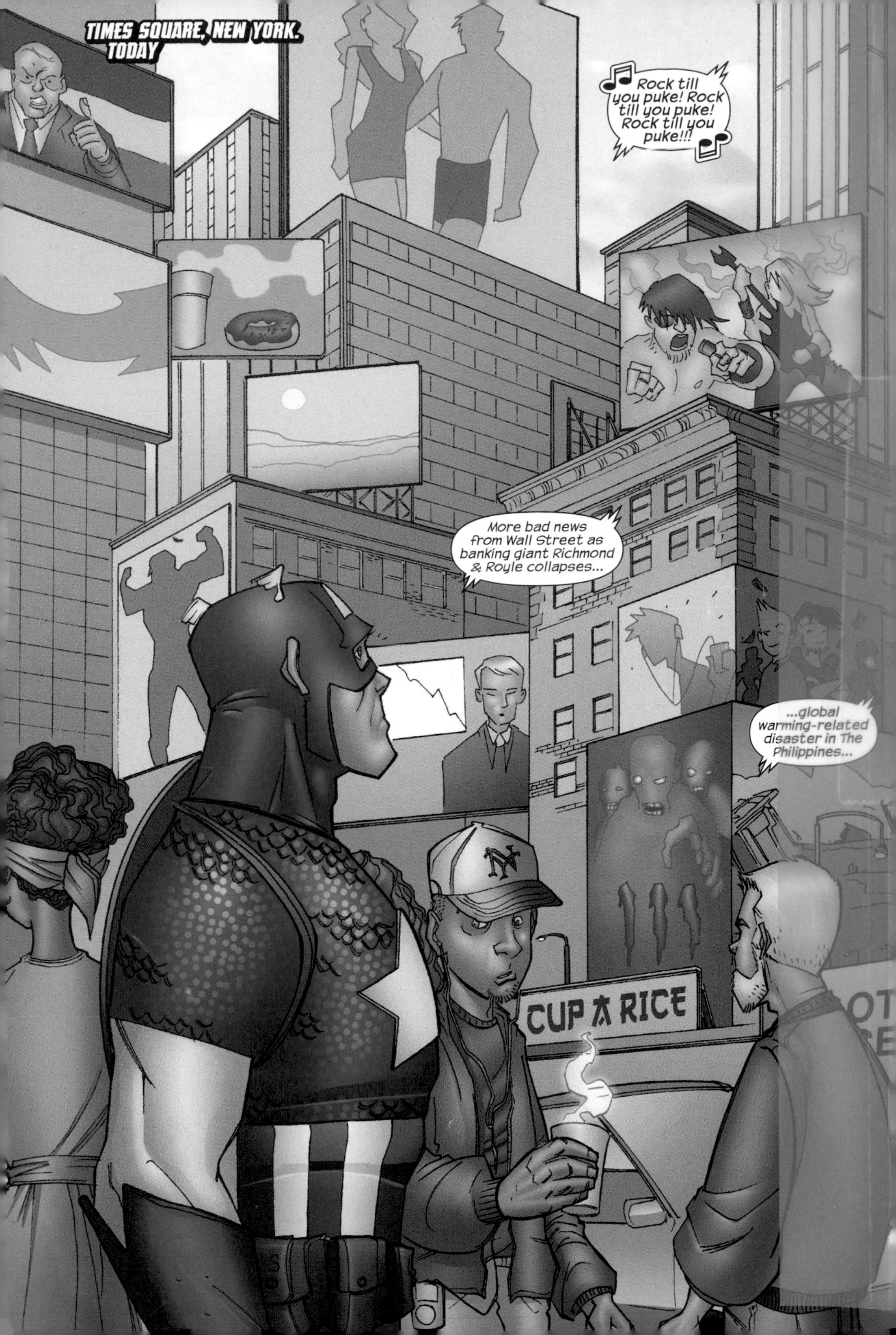
TIMES SQUARE, NEW YORK. TODAY
Rock till you puke! Rock till you puke! Rock till you puke!!!
More bad news from Wall Street as banking giant Richmond & Royle collapses...
...global warming-related disaster in The Philippines...
CUP A RICE

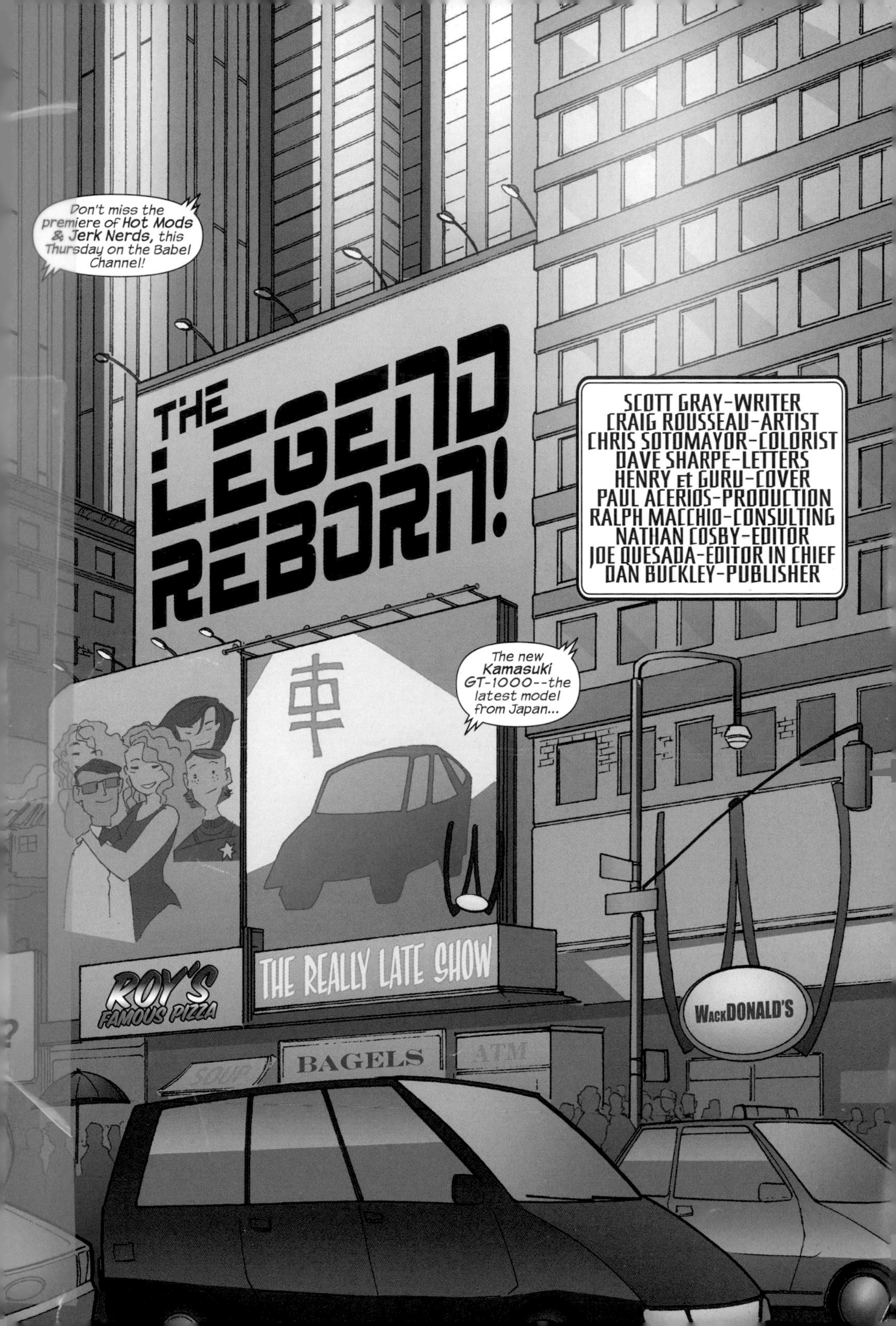

Don't miss the premiere of Hot Mods & Jerk Nerds, this Thursday on the Babel Channel!
THE LEGEND REBORN!
SCOTT GRAY-WRITER
CRAIG ROUSSEAU-ARTIST
CHRIS SOTOMAYOR-COLORIST
DAVE SHARPE-LETTERS
HENRY et GURU-COVER
PAUL ACERIOS-PRODUCTION
RALPH MACCHIO-CONSULTING
NATHAN COSBY-EDITOR
JOE QUESADA-EDITOR IN CHIEF
DAN BUCKLEY-PUBLISHER
The new Kamasuki GT-1000--the latest model from Japan...
車
THE REALLY LATE SHOW
ROY'S FAMOUS PIZZA
WACKDONALD'S
SOUP
BAGELS
ATM

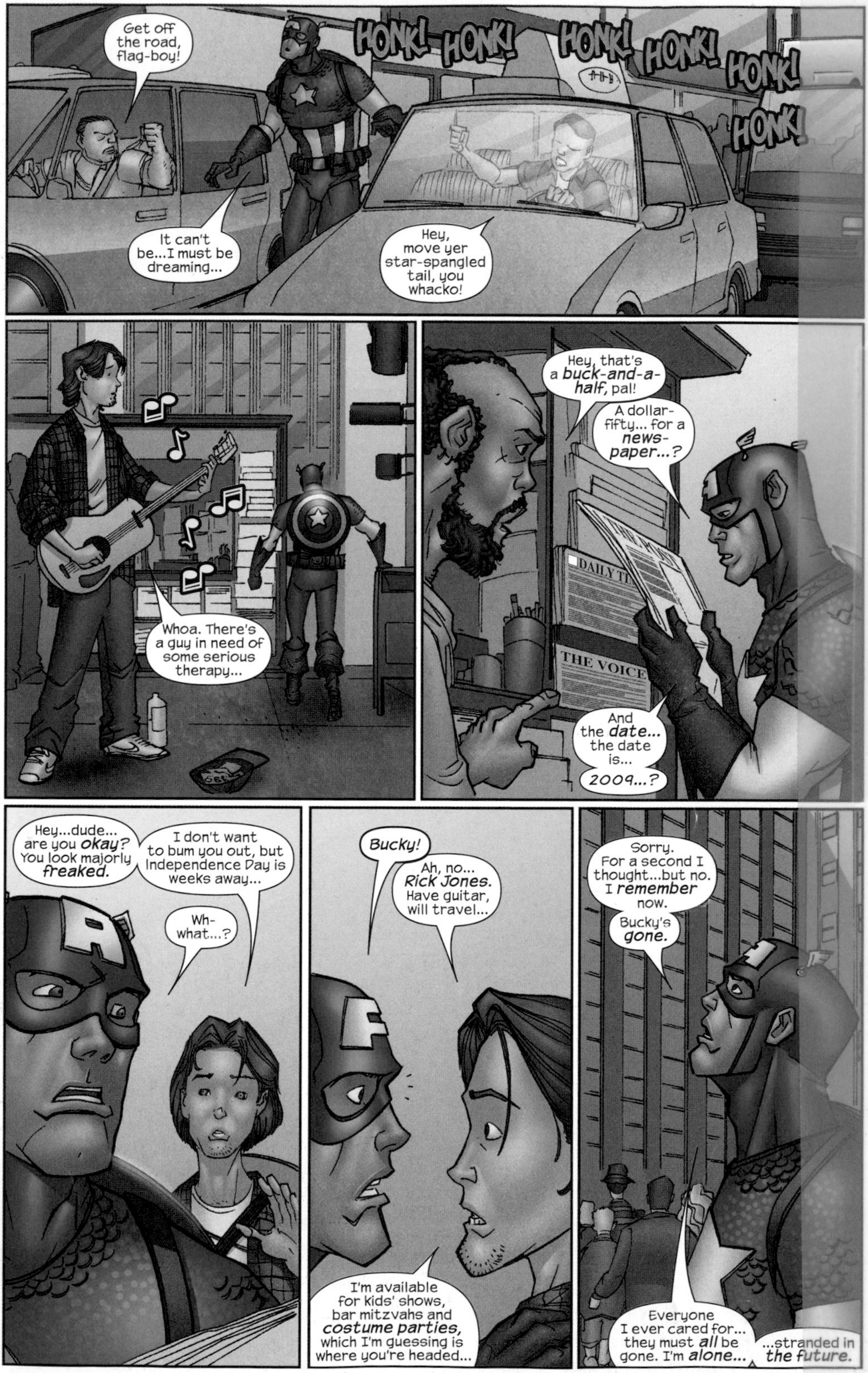
Get off the road, flag-boy!
HONK! HONK! HONK! HONK! HONK! HONK!
It can't be...I must be dreaming...
Hey, move yer star-spangled tail, you whacko!
Whoa. There's a guy in need of some serious therapy...
Hey, that's a buck-and-a-half, pal!
A dollar-fifty... for a news-paper...?
DAILY TI
THE VOICE
And the date... the date is...
2009...?
Hey...dude... are you okay? You look majorly freaked.
I don't want to bum you out, but Independence Day is weeks away...
Wh-what...?
Bucky!
Ah, no... Rick Jones. Have guitar, will travel...
I'm available for kids' shows, bar mitzvahs and costume parties, which I'm guessing is where you're headed...
Sorry. For a second I thought...but no. I remember now.
Bucky's gone.
Everyone I ever cared for... they must all be gone. I'm alone...
...stranded in the future.

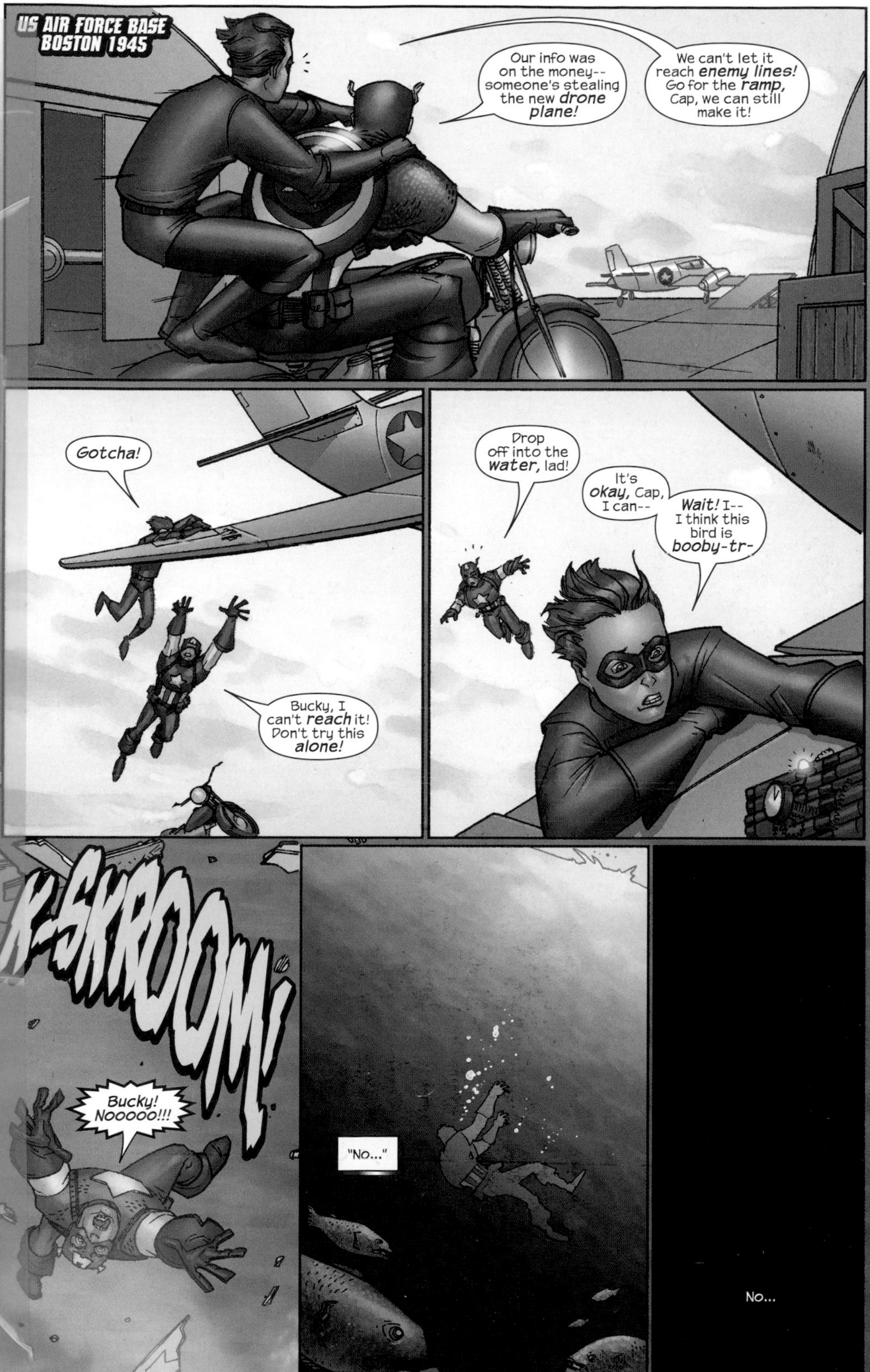
US AIR FORCE BASE
BOSTON 1945
Our info was on the money-- someone's stealing the new drone plane!
We can't let it reach enemy lines! Go for the ramp, Cap, we can still make it!
Gotcha!
Bucky, I can't reach it! Don't try this alone!
Drop off into the water, lad!
It's okay, Cap, I can--
Wait! I-- I think this bird is booby-tr-
K-SKROOM!
Bucky! Nooooo!!!
"No..."
No...

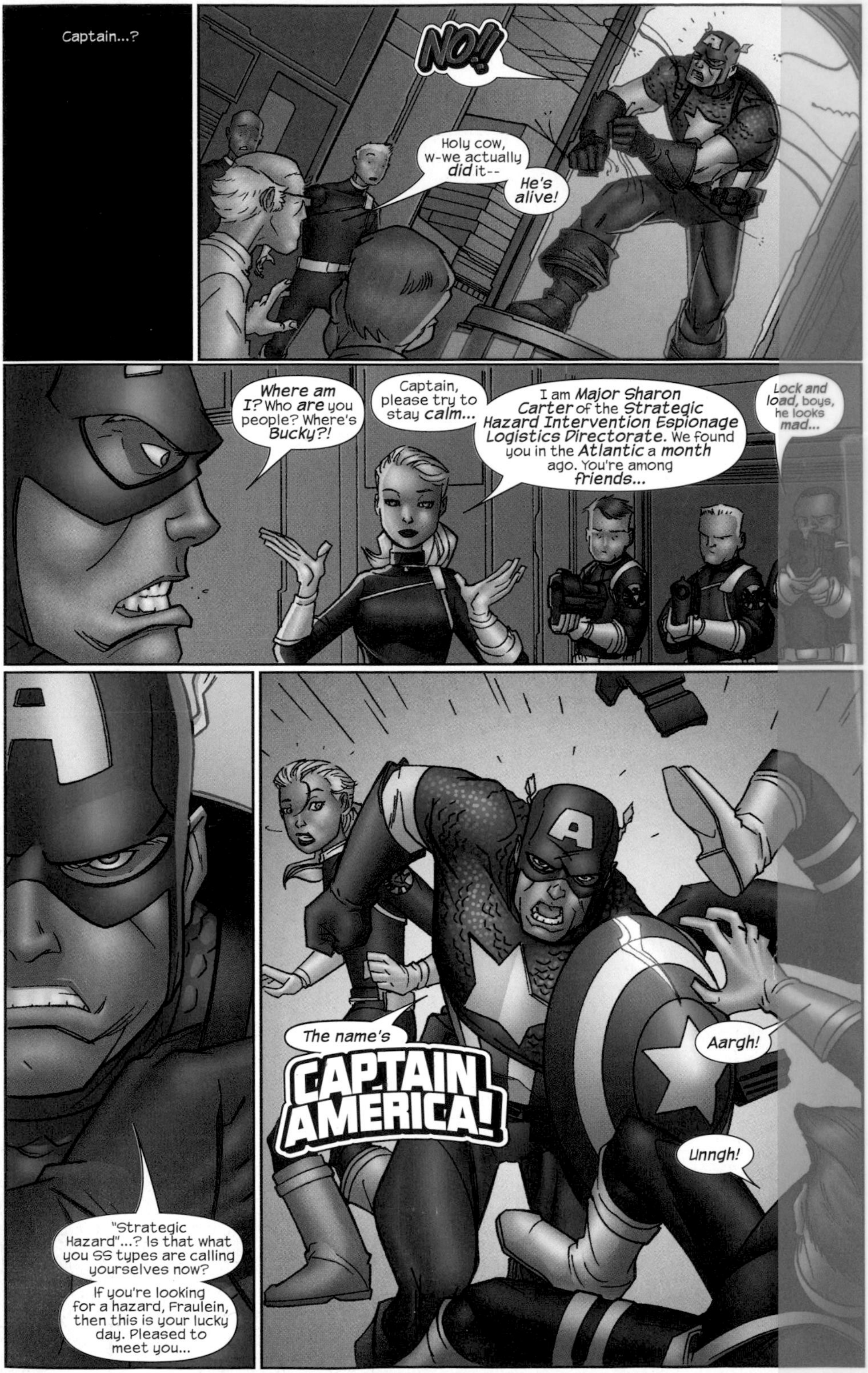
Captain...?
NO!!
Holy cow, w-we actually did it--
He's alive!
Where am I? Who are you people? Where's Bucky?!
Captain, please try to stay calm...
I am Major Sharon Carter of the Strategic Hazard Intervention Espionage Logistics Directorate. We found you in the Atlantic a month ago. You're among friends...
Lock and load, boys, he looks mad...
"Strategic Hazard"...? Is that what you SS types are calling yourselves now?
If you're looking for a hazard, Fraulein, then this is your lucky day. Pleased to meet you...
The name's
CAPTAIN AMERICA!
Aargh!
Unngh!

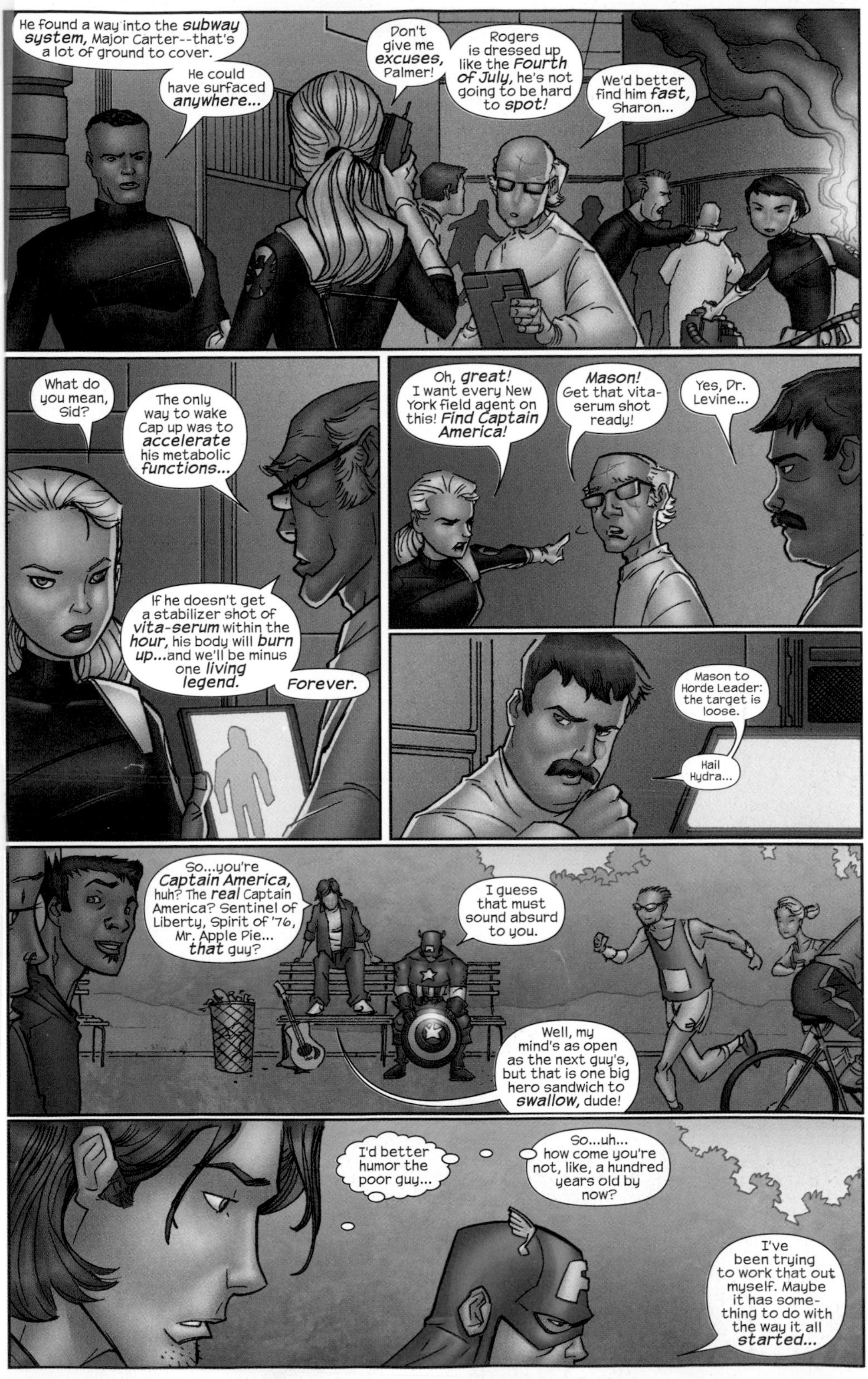
He found a way into the subway system, Major Carter--that's a lot of ground to cover.
He could have surfaced anywhere...
Don't give me excuses, Palmer!
Rogers is dressed up like the Fourth of July, he's not going to be hard to spot!
We'd better find him fast, Sharon...
What do you mean, Sid?
The only way to wake Cap up was to accelerate his metabolic functions...
If he doesn't get a stabilizer shot of vita-serum within the hour, his body will burn up...and we'll be minus one living legend.
Forever.
Oh, great! I want every New York field agent on this! Find Captain America!
Mason! Get that vita-serum shot ready!
Yes, Dr. Levine...
Mason to Horde Leader: the target is loose.
Hail Hydra...
So...you're Captain America, huh? The real Captain America? Sentinel of Liberty, Spirit of '76, Mr. Apple Pie... that guy?
I guess that must sound absurd to you.
Well, my mind's as open as the next guy's, but that is one big hero sandwich to swallow, dude!
I'd better humor the poor guy...
So...uh... how come you're not, like, a hundred years old by now?
I've been trying to work that out myself. Maybe it has something to do with the way it all started...

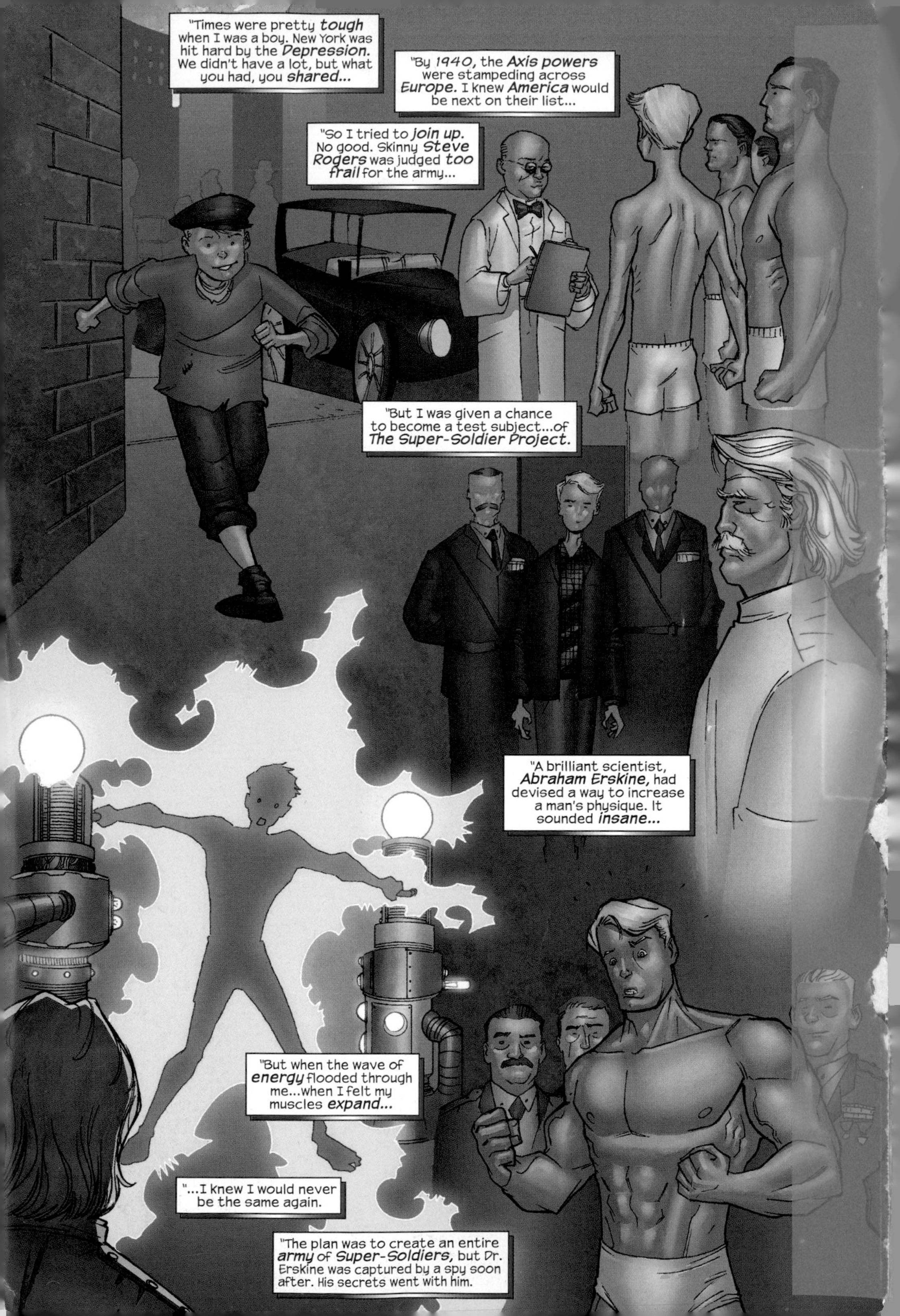
"Times were pretty tough when I was a boy. New York was hit hard by the Depression. We didn't have a lot, but what you had, you shared...
"By 1940, the Axis powers were stampeding across Europe. I knew America would be next on their list...
"So I tried to join up. No good. Skinny Steve Rogers was judged too frail for the army...
"But I was given a chance to become a test subject...of The Super-Soldier Project.
"A brilliant scientist, Abraham Erskine, had devised a way to increase a man's physique. It sounded insane...
"But when the wave of energy flooded through me...when I felt my muscles expand...
"...I knew I would never be the same again.
"The plan was to create an entire army of Super-Soldiers, but Dr. Erskine was captured by a spy soon after. His secrets went with him.

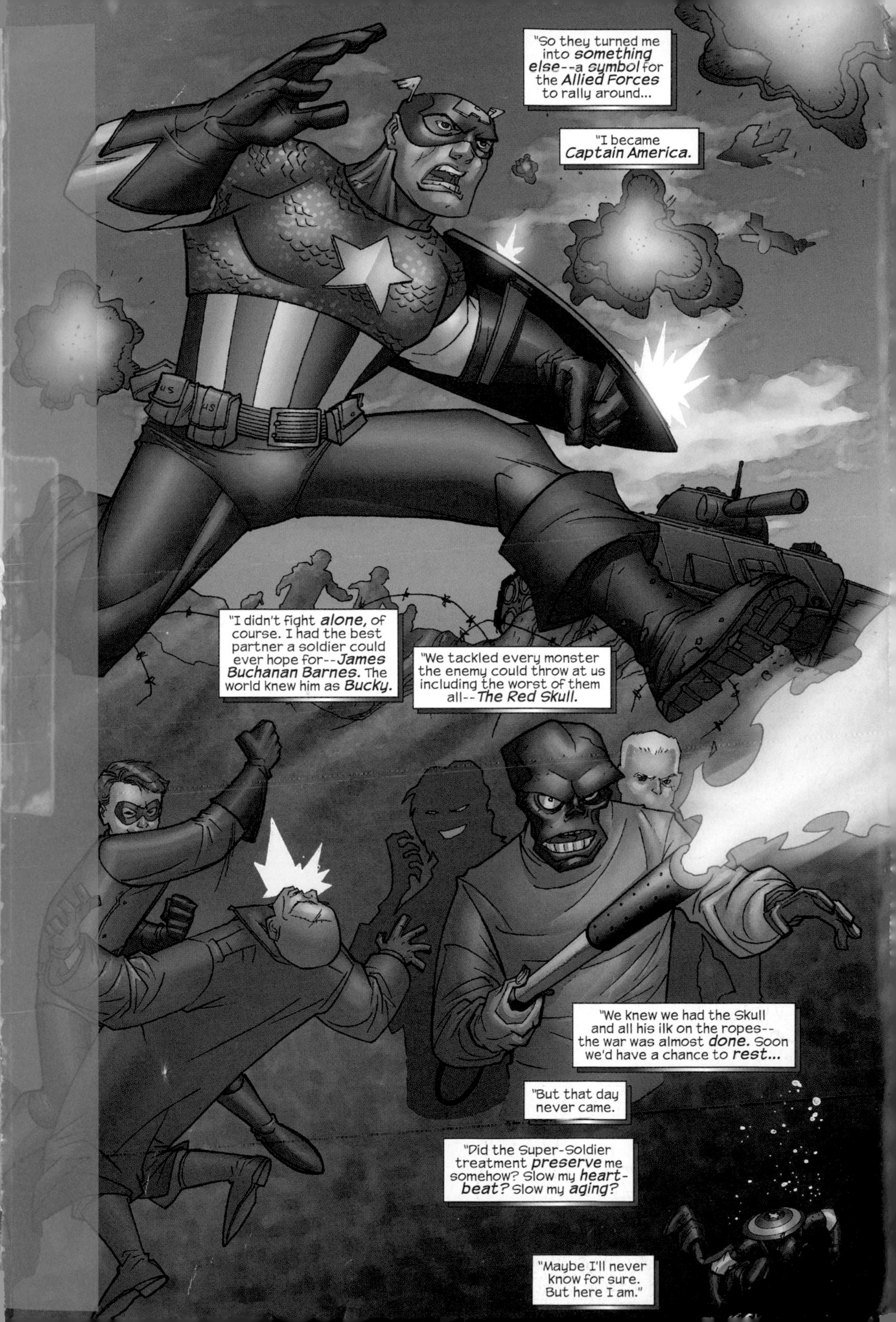
"So they turned me into something else--a symbol for the Allied Forces to rally around...
"I became Captain America.
"I didn't fight alone, of course. I had the best partner a soldier could ever hope for--James Buchanan Barnes. The world knew him as Bucky.
"We tackled every monster the enemy could throw at us including the worst of them all--The Red Skull.
"We knew we had the Skull and all his ilk on the ropes--the war was almost done. Soon we'd have a chance to rest...
"But that day never came.
"Did the Super-Soldier treatment preserve me somehow? Slow my heart-beat? Slow my aging?
"Maybe I'll never know for sure. But here I am."

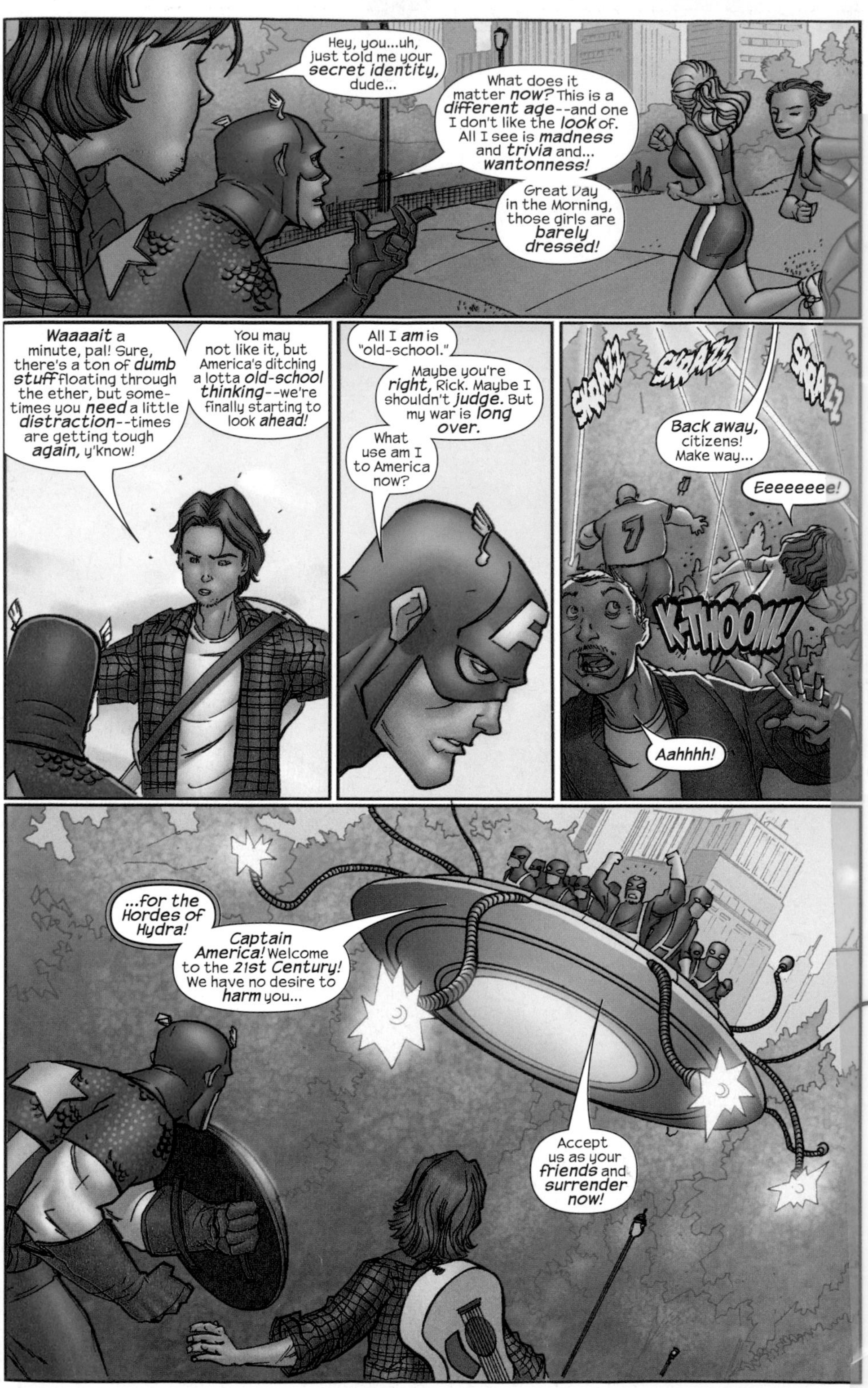
Hey, you...uh, just told me your secret identity, dude...
What does it matter now? This is a different age--and one I don't like the look of. All I see is madness and trivia and... wantonness!
Great Day in the Morning, those girls are barely dressed!
Waaaait a minute, pal! Sure, there's a ton of dumb stuff floating through the ether, but some-times you need a little distraction--times are getting tough again, y'know!
You may not like it, but America's ditching a lotta old-school thinking--we're finally starting to look ahead!
All I am is "old-school."
Maybe you're right, Rick. Maybe I shouldn't judge. But my war is long over.
What use am I to America now?
SKRAZZ
SKRAZZ
SKRAZZ
Back away, citizens! Make way...
Eeeeeeee!
K-THOOM!
Aahhhh!
...for the Hordes of Hydra!
Captain America! Welcome to the 21st Century! We have no desire to harm you...
Accept us as your friends and surrender now!

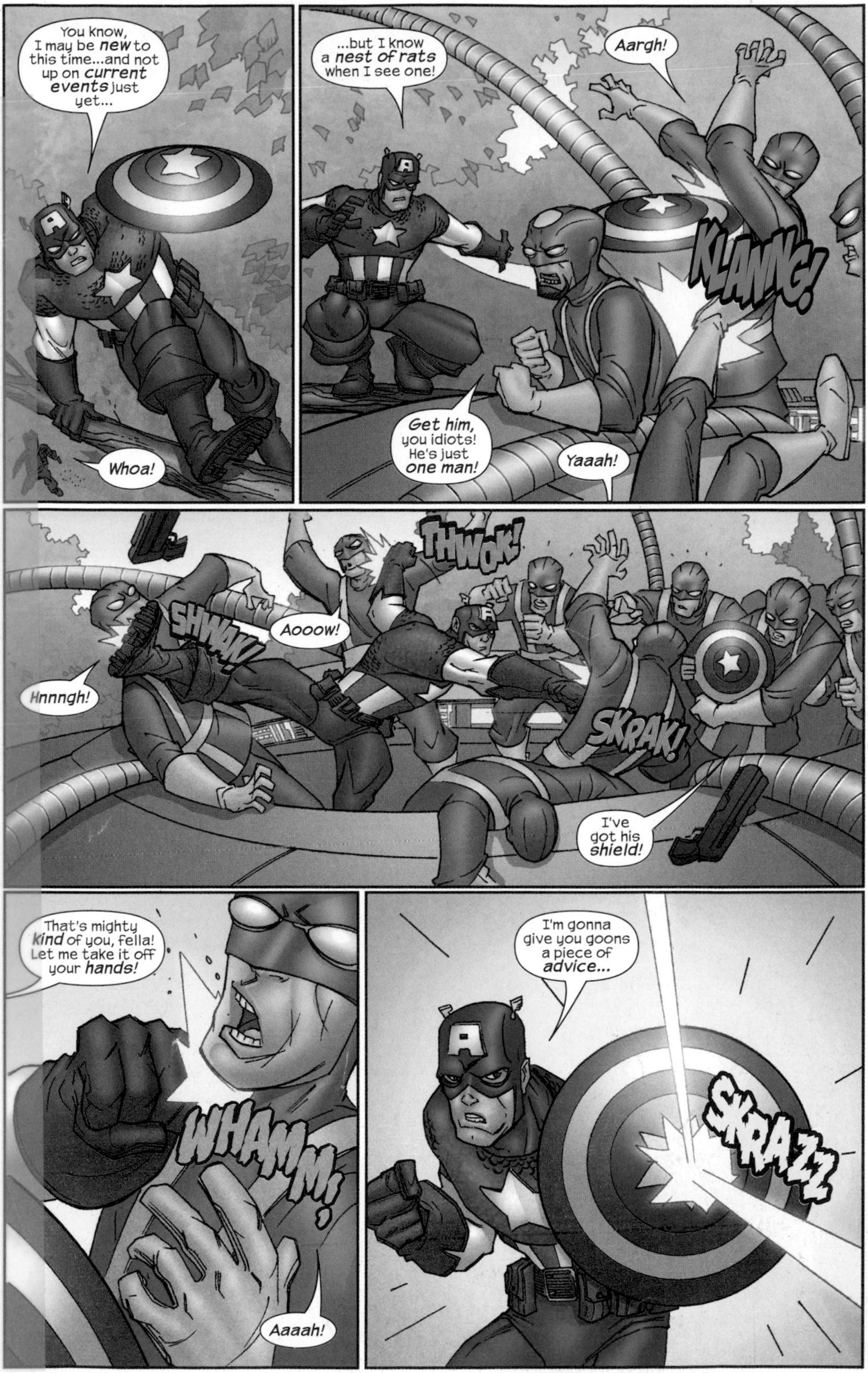
You know, I may be new to this time...and not up on current events just yet...
Whoa!
...but I know a nest of rats when I see one!
Aargh!
KLANNG!
Get him, you idiots! He's just one man!
Yaaah!
THWOK!
SHWAK!
Aooow!
Hnnngh!
SKRAK!
I've got his shield!
That's mighty kind of you, fella! Let me take it off your hands!
WHAMM!
Aaaah!
I'm gonna give you goons a piece of advice...
SKRAZZ

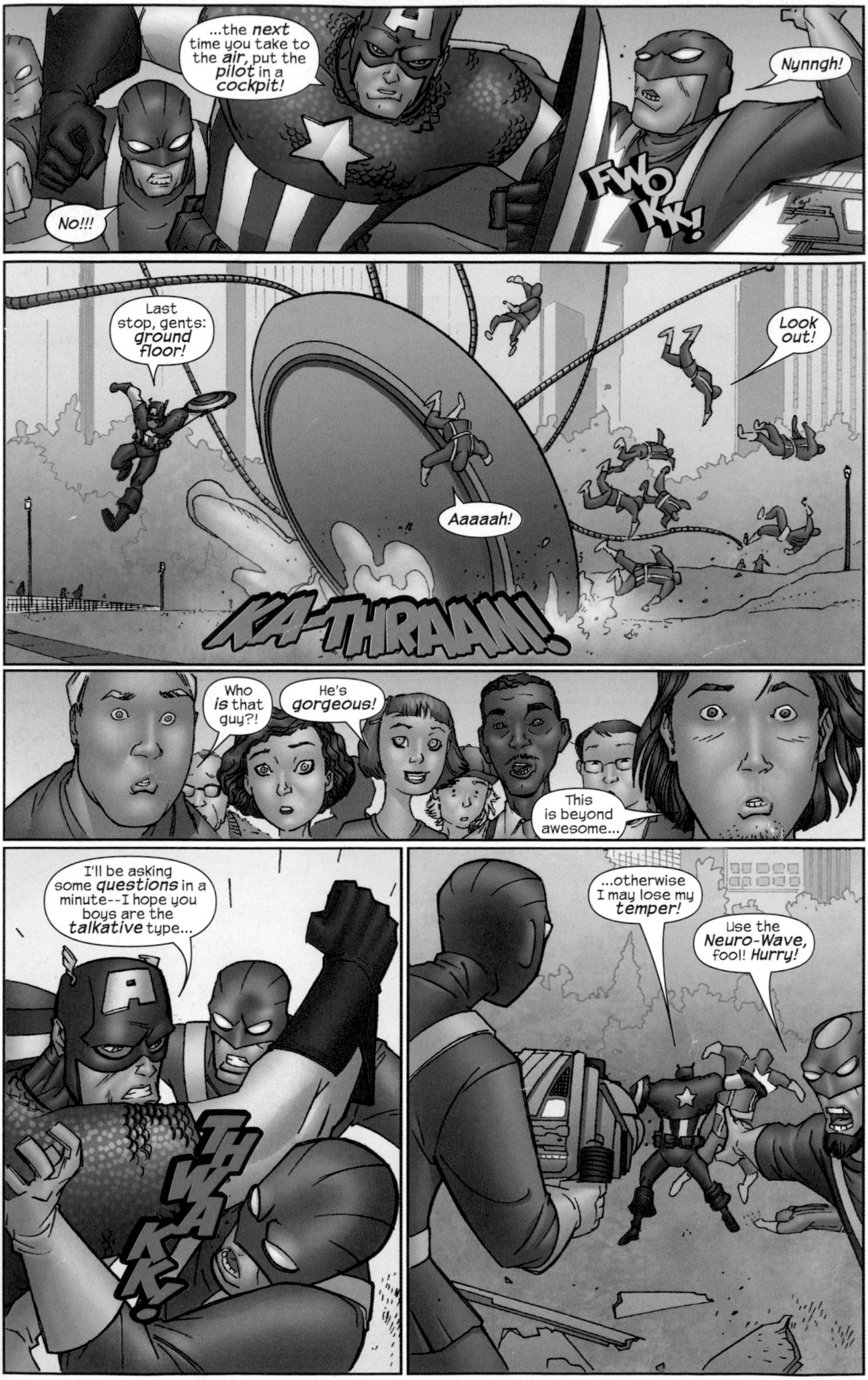
...the next time you take to the air, put the pilot in a cockpit!
Nynngh!
No!!!
FWOKK!
Last stop, gents: ground floor!
Look out!
Aaaaah!
KA-THRAAM!
Who is that guy?!
He's gorgeous!
This is beyond awesome...
I'll be asking some questions in a minute--I hope you boys are the talkative type...
THWAKK!
...otherwise I may lose my temper!
Use the Neuro-Wave, fool! Hurry!

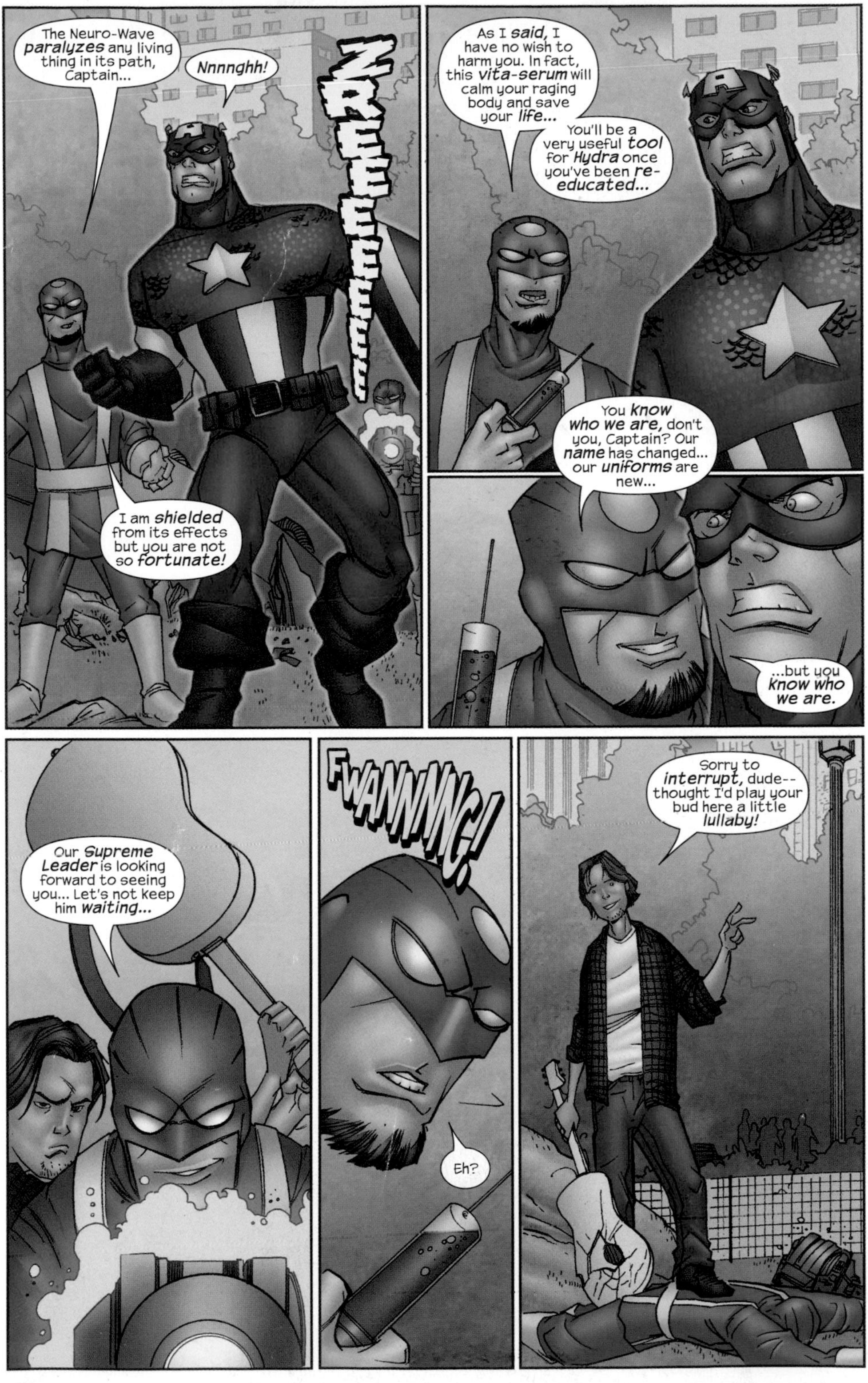
The Neuro-Wave paralyzes any living thing in its path, Captain...
Nnnnghh!
ZREEEEEEEE
I am shielded from its effects but you are not so fortunate!
As I said, I have no wish to harm you. In fact, this vita-serum will calm your raging body and save your life...
You'll be a very useful tool for Hydra once you've been re-educated...
You know who we are, don't you, Captain? Our name has changed... our uniforms are new...
...but you know who we are.
Our Supreme Leader is looking forward to seeing you... Let's not keep him waiting...
FWANNNNG!!
Eh?
Sorry to interrupt, dude-- thought I'd play your bud here a little lullaby!

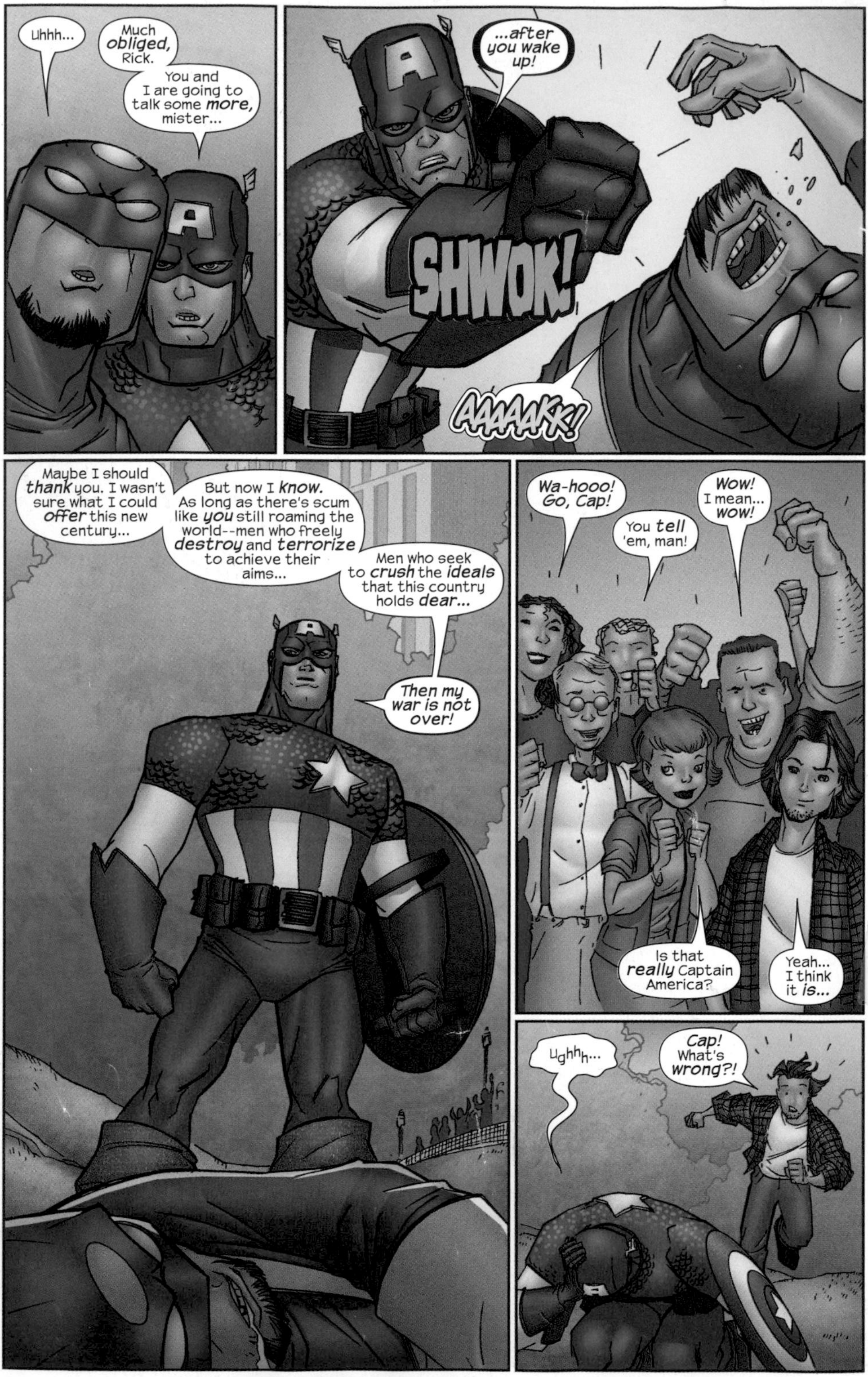

Uhhh...
Much obliged, Rick.
You and I are going to talk some more, mister...
...after you wake up!
SHWOK!
AAAAAKK!
Maybe I should thank you. I wasn't sure what I could offer this new century...
But now I know. As long as there's scum like you still roaming the world--men who freely destroy and terrorize to achieve their aims...
Men who seek to crush the ideals that this country holds dear...
Then my war is not over!
Wa-hooo! Go, Cap!
You tell 'em, man!
Wow! I mean... WOW!
Is that really Captain America?
Yeah... I think it is...
Ughhh...
Cap! What's wrong?!

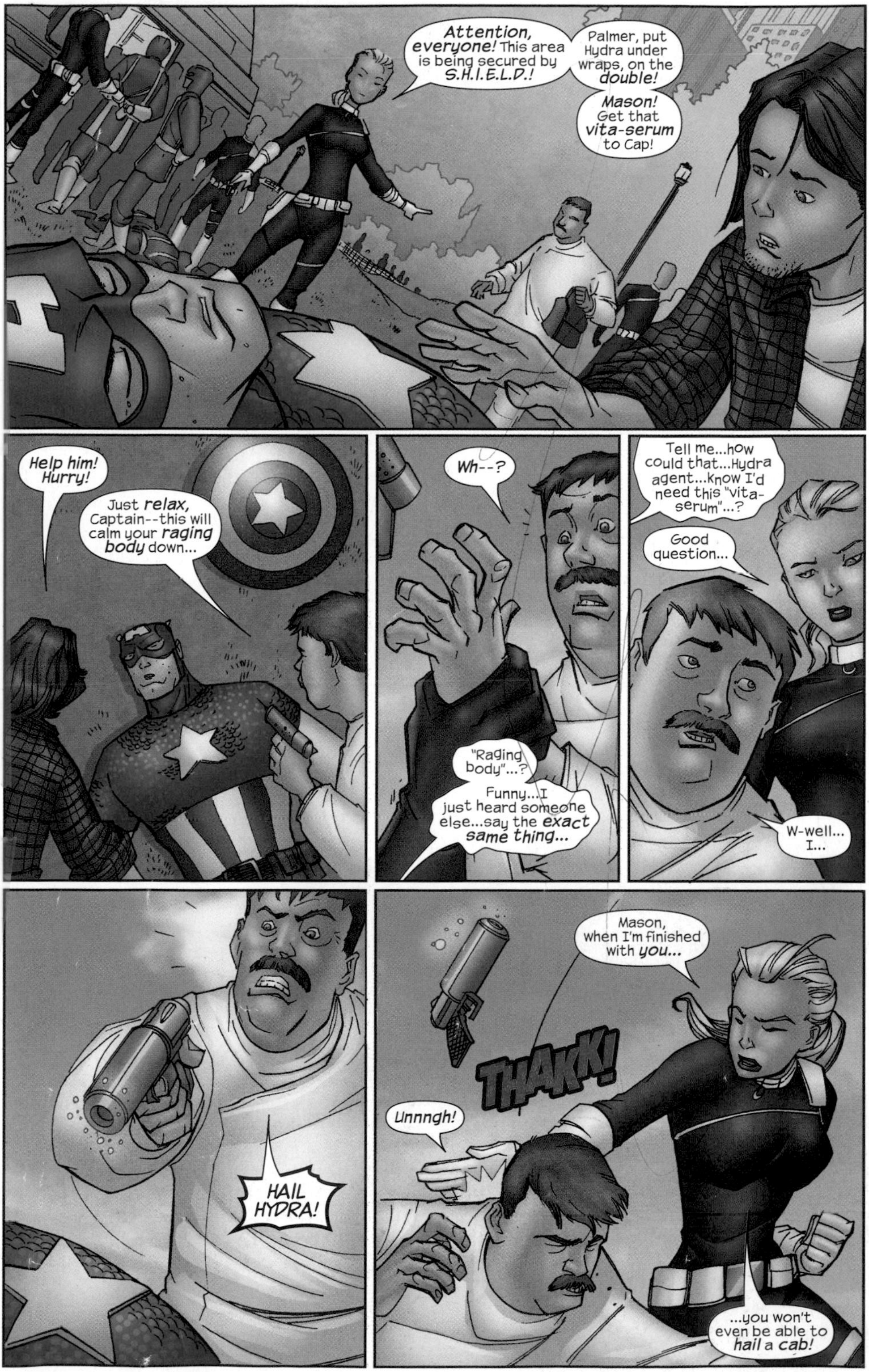

Attention, everyone! This area is being secured by S.H.I.E.L.D.!
Palmer, put Hydra under wraps, on the double!
Mason! Get that vita-serum to Cap!
Help him! Hurry!
Just relax, Captain--this will calm your raging body down...
Wh--?
"Raging body"...?
Funny...I just heard someone else...say the exact same thing...
Tell me...how could that...Hydra agent...know I'd need this "vita-serum"...?
Good question...
W-well... I...
HAIL HYDRA!
Mason, when I'm finished with you...
THAKK!
Unnngh!
...you won't even be able to hail a cab!

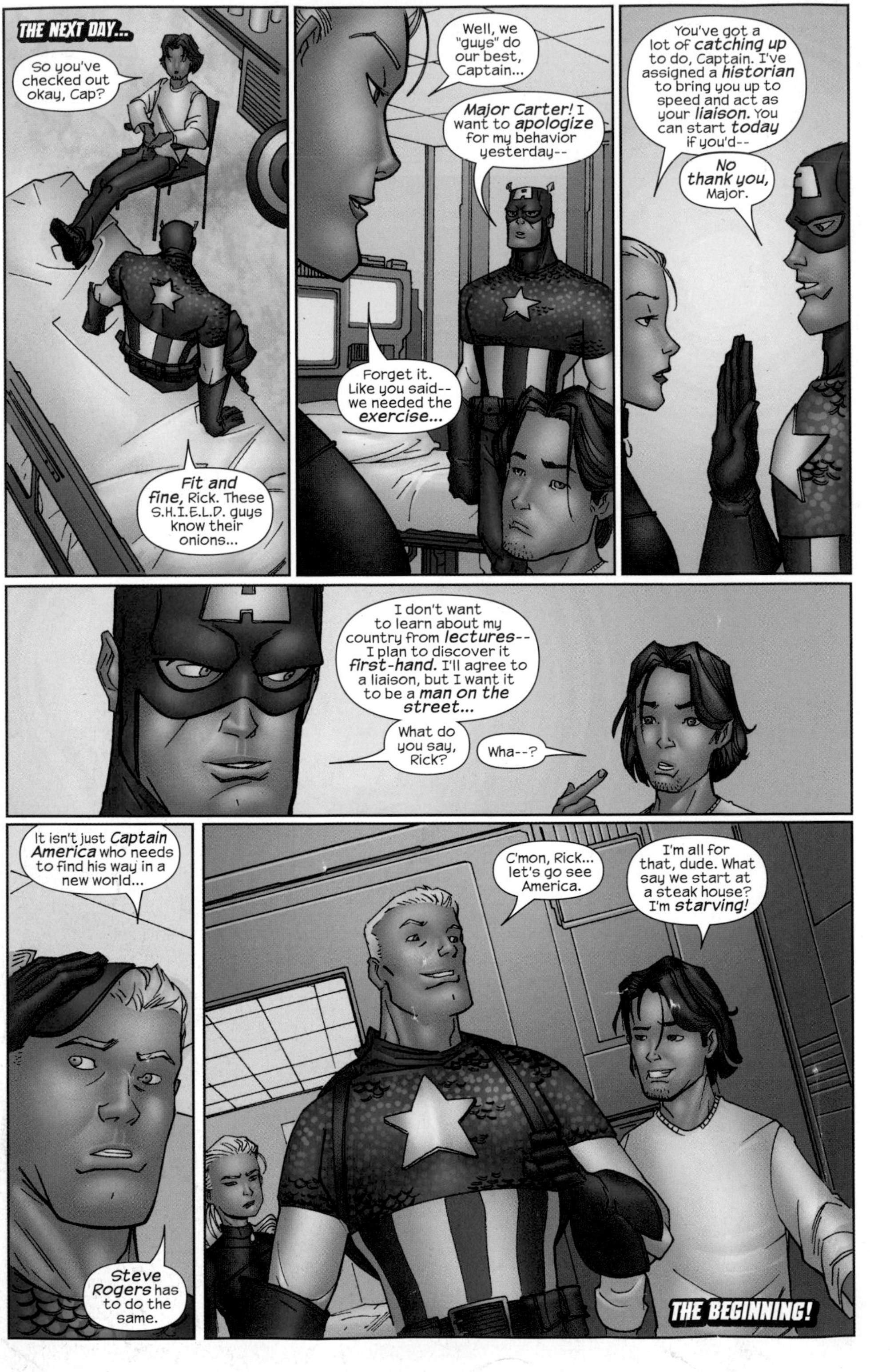
THE NEXT DAY...
So you've checked out okay, Cap?
Fit and fine, Rick. These S.H.I.E.L.D. guys know their onions...
Well, we "guys" do our best, Captain...
Major Carter! I want to apologize for my behavior yesterday--
Forget it. Like you said-- we needed the exercise...
You've got a lot of catching up to do, Captain. I've assigned a historian to bring you up to speed and act as your liaison. You can start today if you'd--
No thank you, Major.
I don't want to learn about my country from lectures-- I plan to discover it first-hand. I'll agree to a liaison, but I want it to be a man on the street...
What do you say, Rick?
Wha--?
It isn't just Captain America who needs to find his way in a new world...
Steve Rogers has to do the same.
C'mon, Rick... let's go see America.
I'm all for that, dude. What say we start at a steak house? I'm starving!
THE BEGINNING!

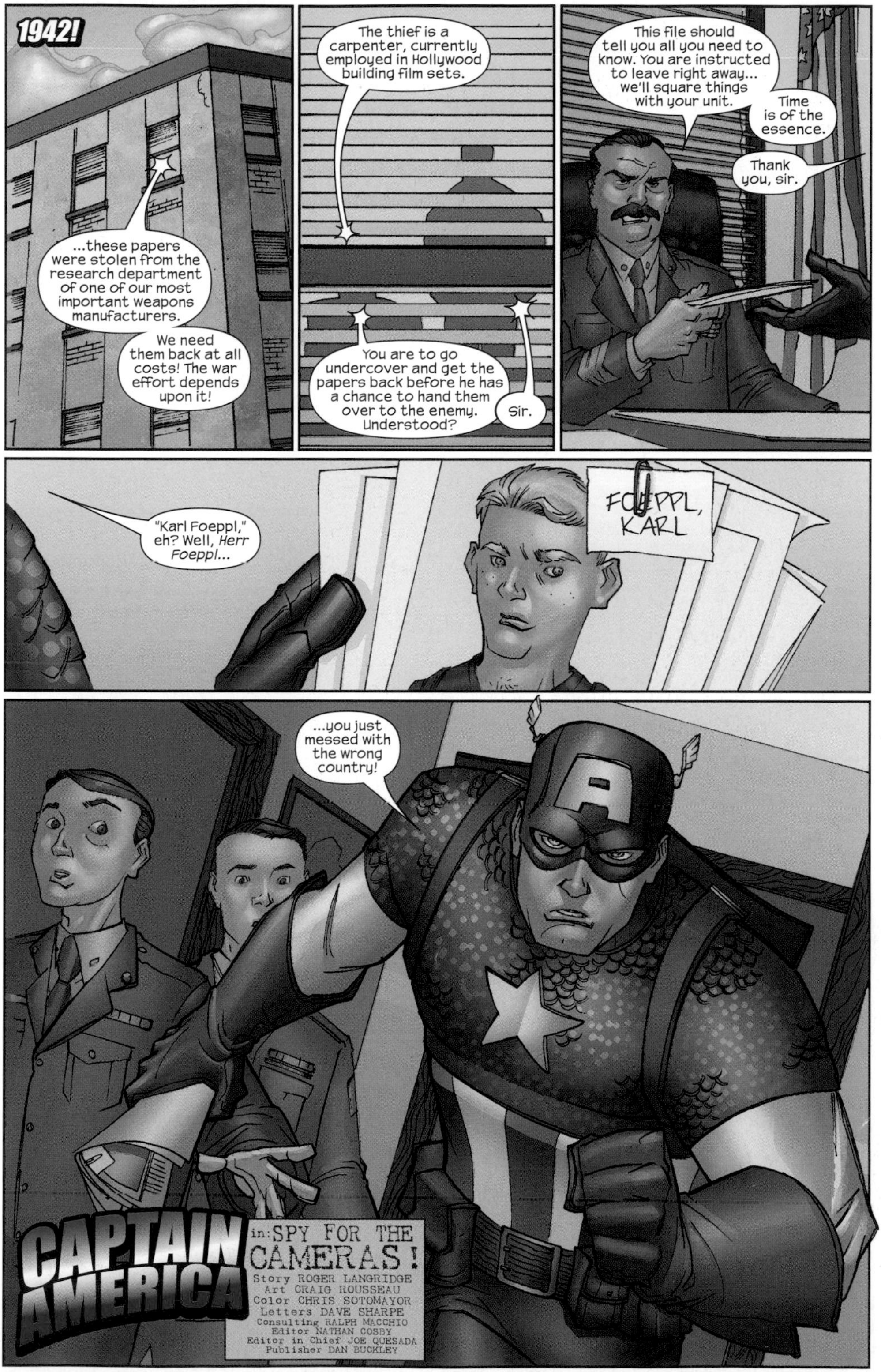
1942!
...these papers were stolen from the research department of one of our most important weapons manufacturers.
We need them back at all costs! The war effort depends upon it!
The thief is a carpenter, currently employed in Hollywood building film sets.
You are to go undercover and get the papers back before he has a chance to hand them over to the enemy. Understood?
Sir.
This file should tell you all you need to know. You are instructed to leave right away... we'll square things with your unit.
Time is of the essence.
Thank you, sir.
"Karl Foeppl," eh? Well, *Herr Foeppl*...
FOEPPL, KARL
...you just messed with the wrong country!
CAPTAIN AMERICA
in: SPY FOR THE CAMERAS!
Story ROGER LANGRIDGE
Art CRAIG ROUSSEAU
Color CHRIS SOTOMAYOR
Letters DAVE SHARPE
Consulting RALPH MACCHIO
Editor NATHAN COSBY
Editor in Chief JOE QUESADA
Publisher DAN BUCKLEY

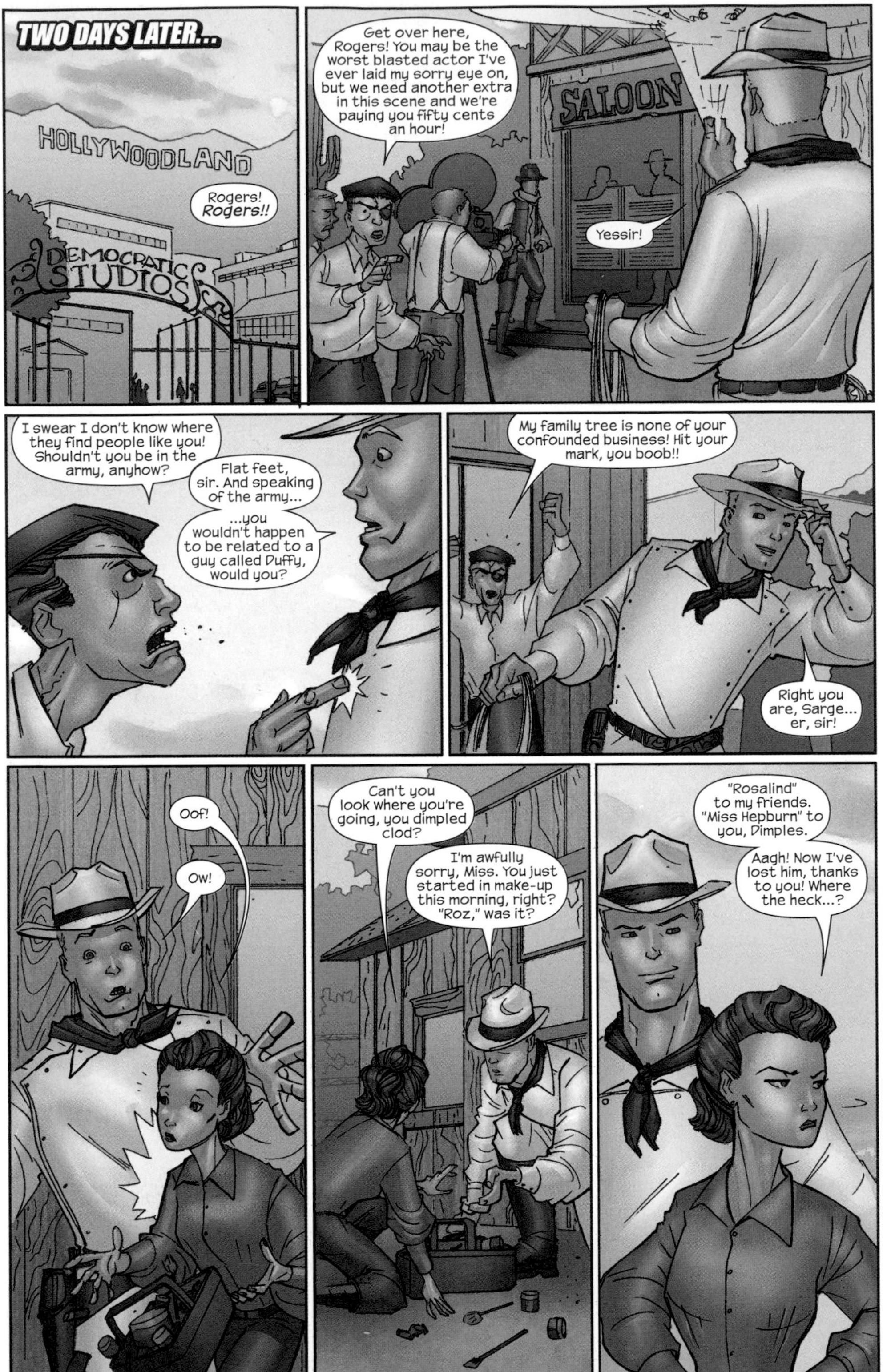

TWO DAYS LATER...
HOLLYWOODLAND
DEMOCRATIC STUDIOS
Rogers! *Rogers!!*
SALOON
Get over here, Rogers! You may be the worst blasted actor I've ever laid my sorry eye on, but we need another extra in this scene and we're paying you fifty cents an hour!
Yessir!
I swear I don't know where they find people like you! Shouldn't you be in the army, anyhow?
Flat feet, sir. And speaking of the army...
...you wouldn't happen to be related to a guy called Duffy, would you?
My family tree is none of your confounded business! Hit your mark, you boob!!
Right you are, Sarge... er, sir!
Oof!
Ow!
Can't you look where you're going, you dimpled clod?
I'm awfully sorry, Miss. You just started in make-up this morning, right? "Roz," was it?
"Rosalind" to my friends. "Miss Hepburn" to you, Dimples.
Aagh! Now I've lost him, thanks to you! Where the heck...?

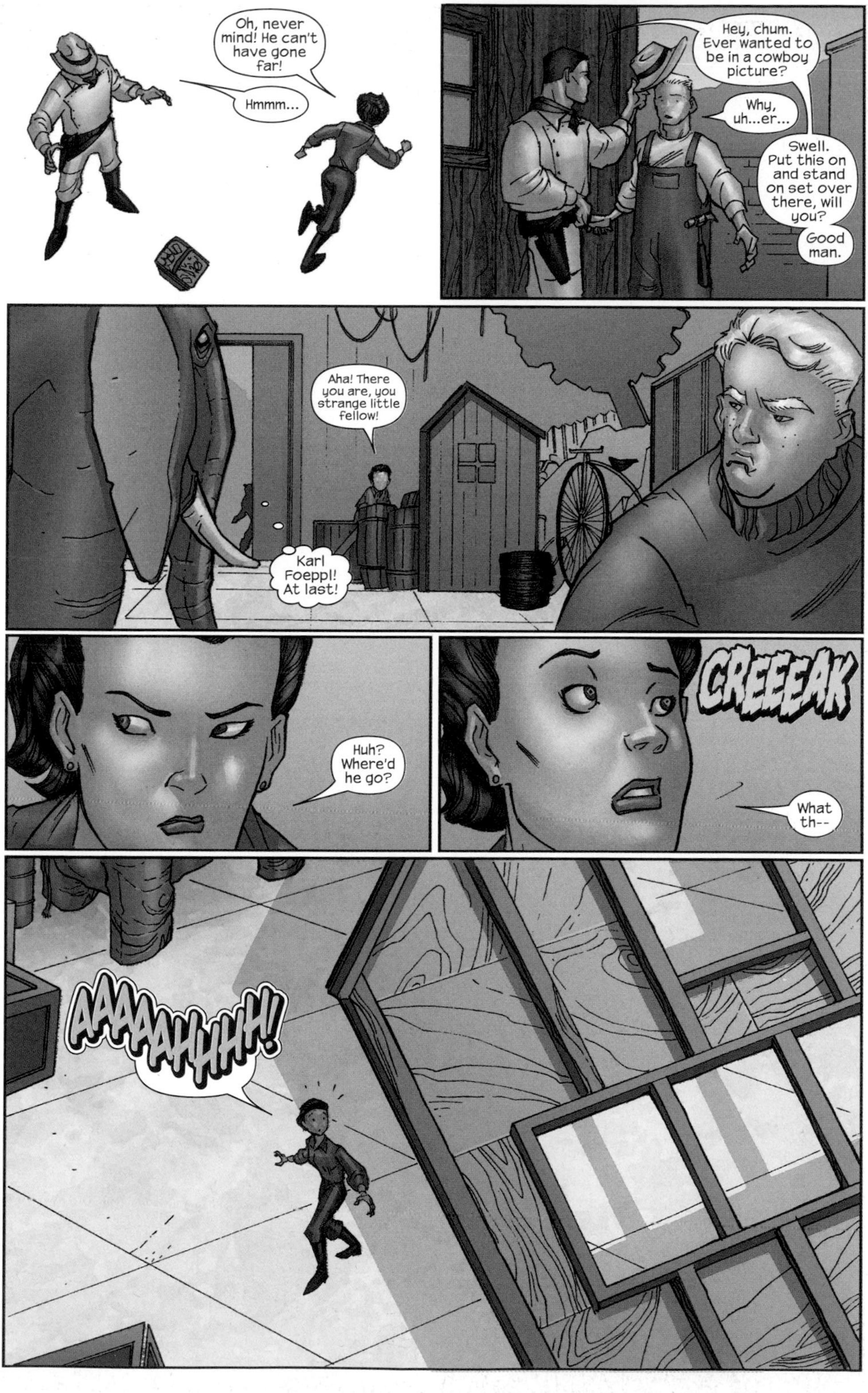
Oh, never mind! He can't have gone far!
Hmmm...
Hey, chum. Ever wanted to be in a cowboy picture?
Why, uh...er...
Swell. Put this on and stand on set over there, will you?
Good man.
Aha! There you are, you strange little fellow!
Karl Foeppl! At last!
Huh? Where'd he go?
CREEEAK
What th--
AAAAAHHHH!

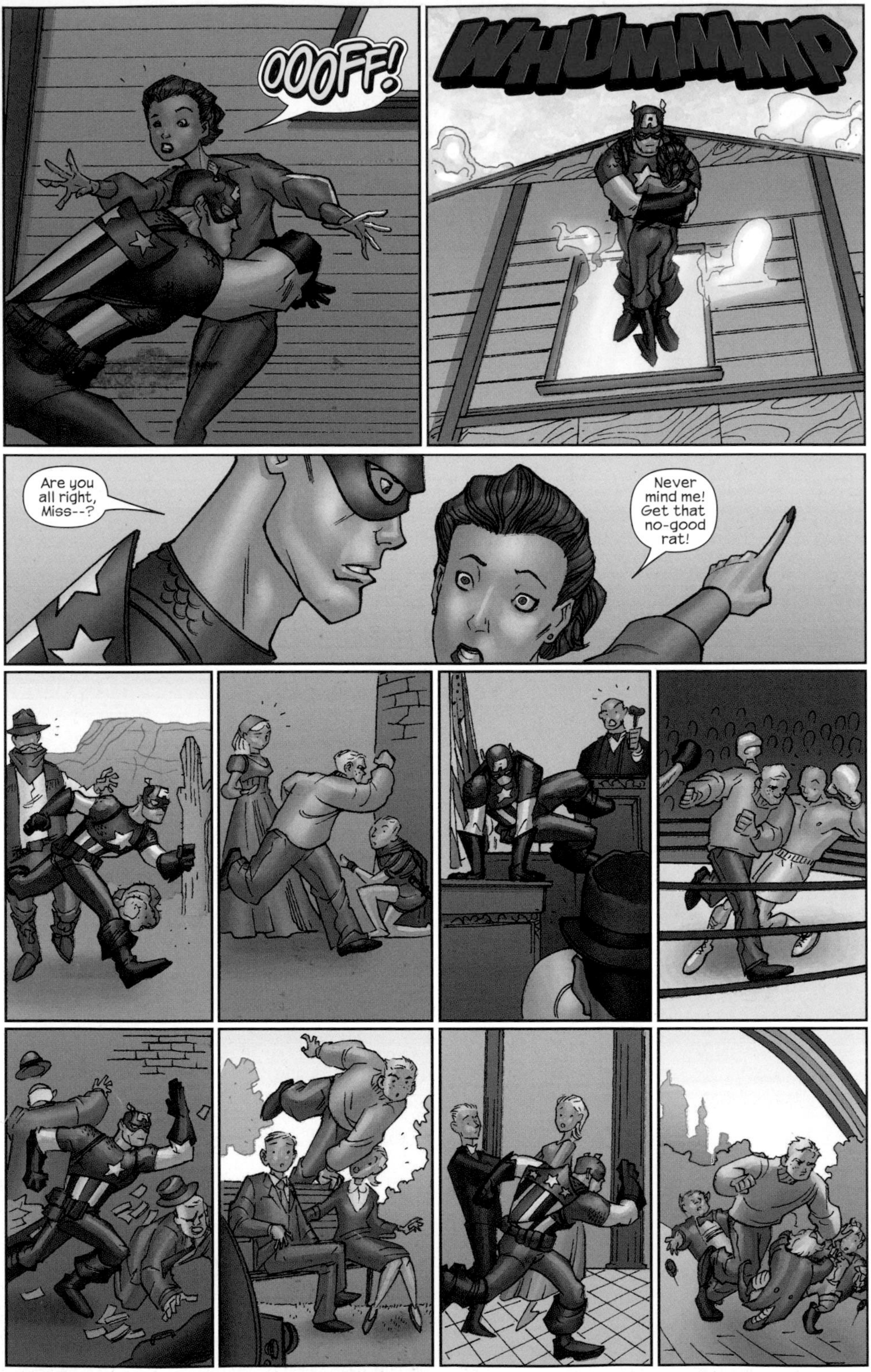
OOOFF!
WHUMMMMP
Are you all right, Miss--?
Never mind me! Get that no-good rat!

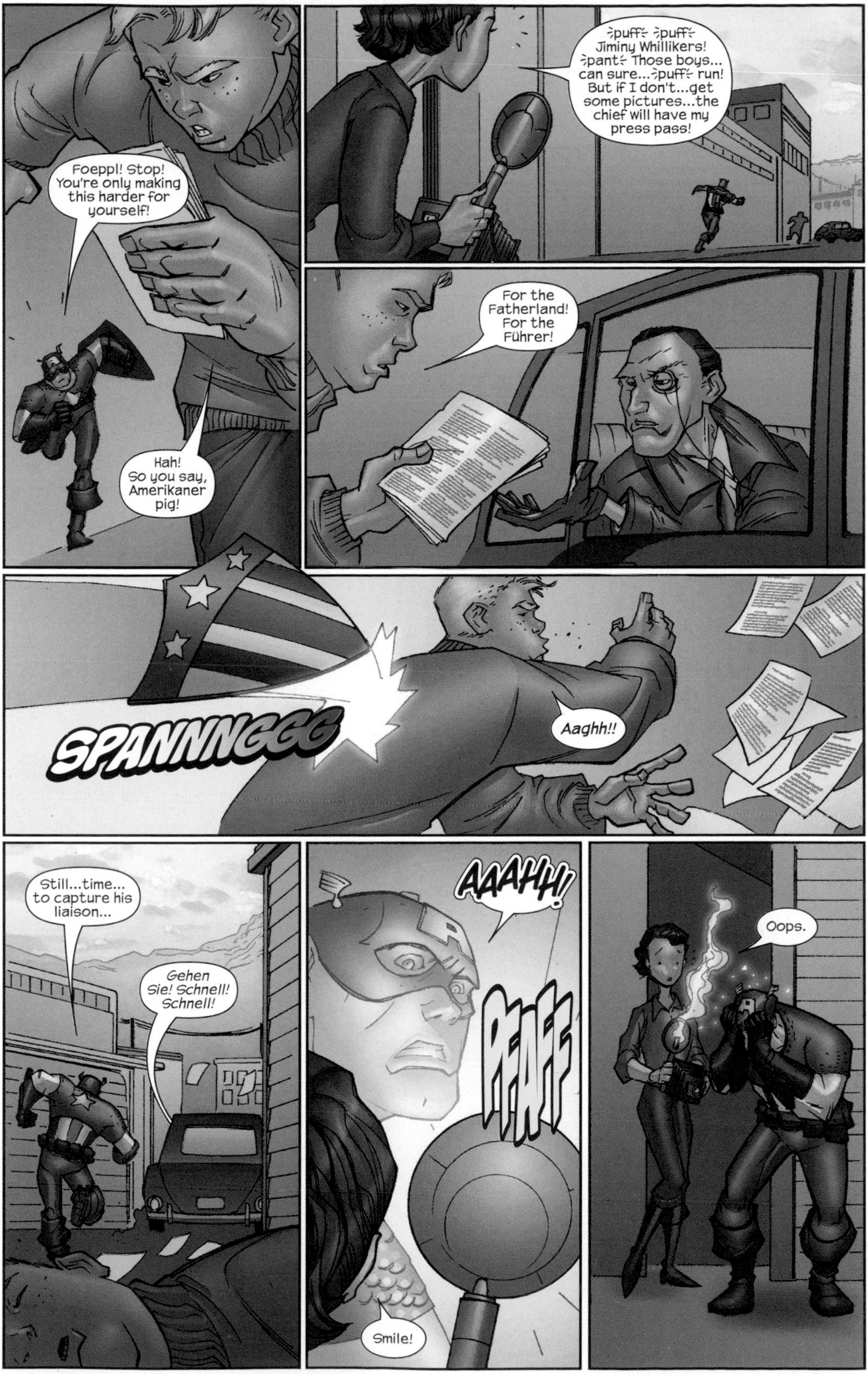
Foeppl! Stop! You're only making this harder for yourself!
Hah! So you say, Amerikaner pig!
⊰puff⊱ ⊰puff⊱ Jiminy Whillikers! ⊰pant⊱ Those boys... can sure... ⊰puff⊱ run! But if I don't...get some pictures...the chief will have my press pass!
For the Fatherland! For the Führer!
SPANNNGGG
Aaghh!!
Still...time... to capture his liaison...
Gehen Sie! Schnell! Schnell!
AAAHH!
PFAFF
Smile!
Oops.

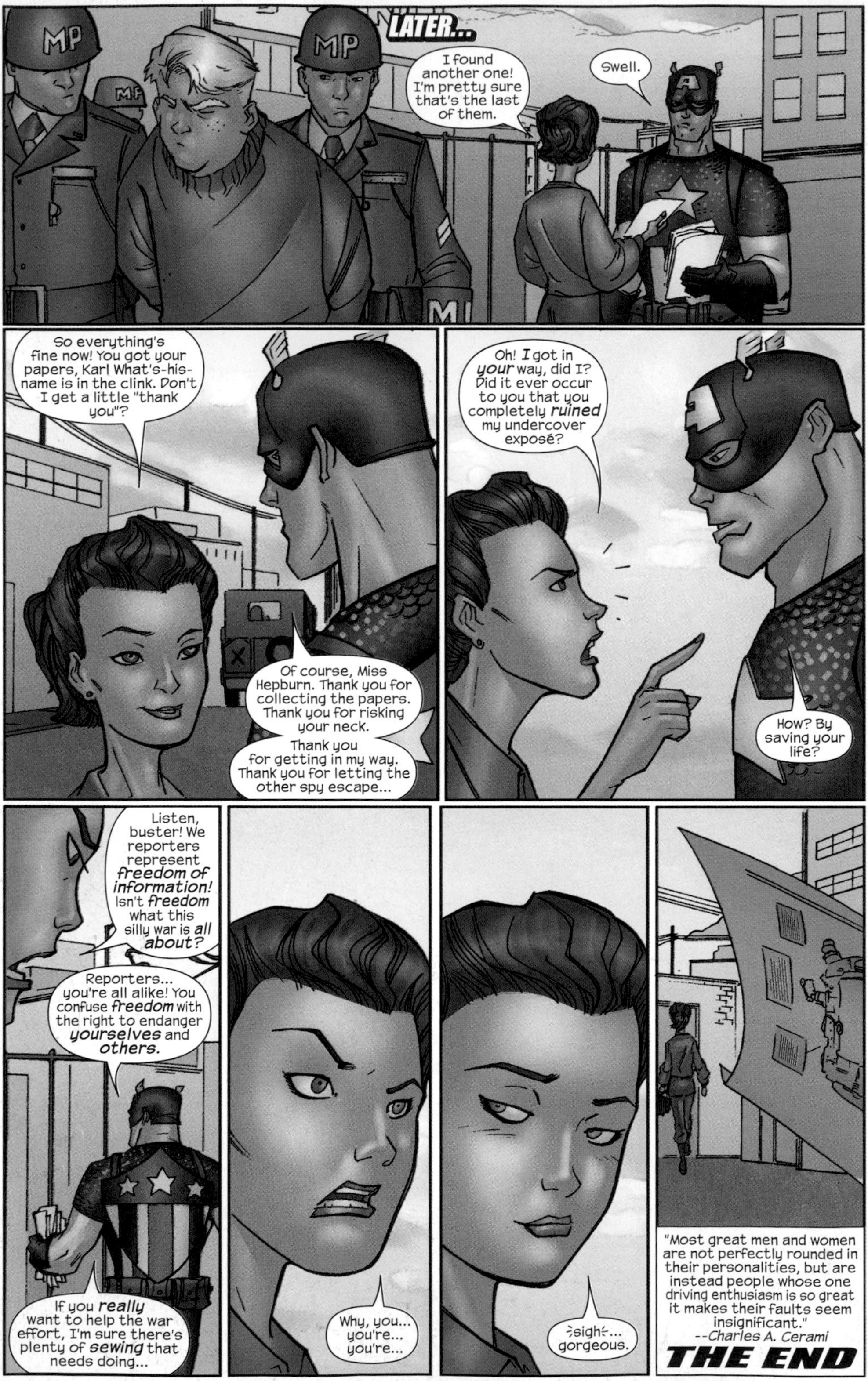
LATER...
I found another one! I'm pretty sure that's the last of them.
Swell.
So everything's fine now! You got your papers, Karl What's-his-name is in the clink. Don't I get a little "thank you"?
Of course, Miss Hepburn. Thank you for collecting the papers. Thank you for risking your neck.
Thank you for getting in my way. Thank you for letting the other spy escape...
Oh! I got in your way, did I? Did it ever occur to you that you completely ruined my undercover exposé?
How? By saving your life?
Listen, buster! We reporters represent freedom of information! Isn't freedom what this silly war is all about?
Reporters... you're all alike! You confuse freedom with the right to endanger yourselves and others.
If you really want to help the war effort, I'm sure there's plenty of sewing that needs doing...
Why, you... you're... you're...
sigh... gorgeous.
"Most great men and women are not perfectly rounded in their personalities, but are instead people whose one driving enthusiasm is so great it makes their faults seem insignificant."
--Charles A. Cerami
THE END

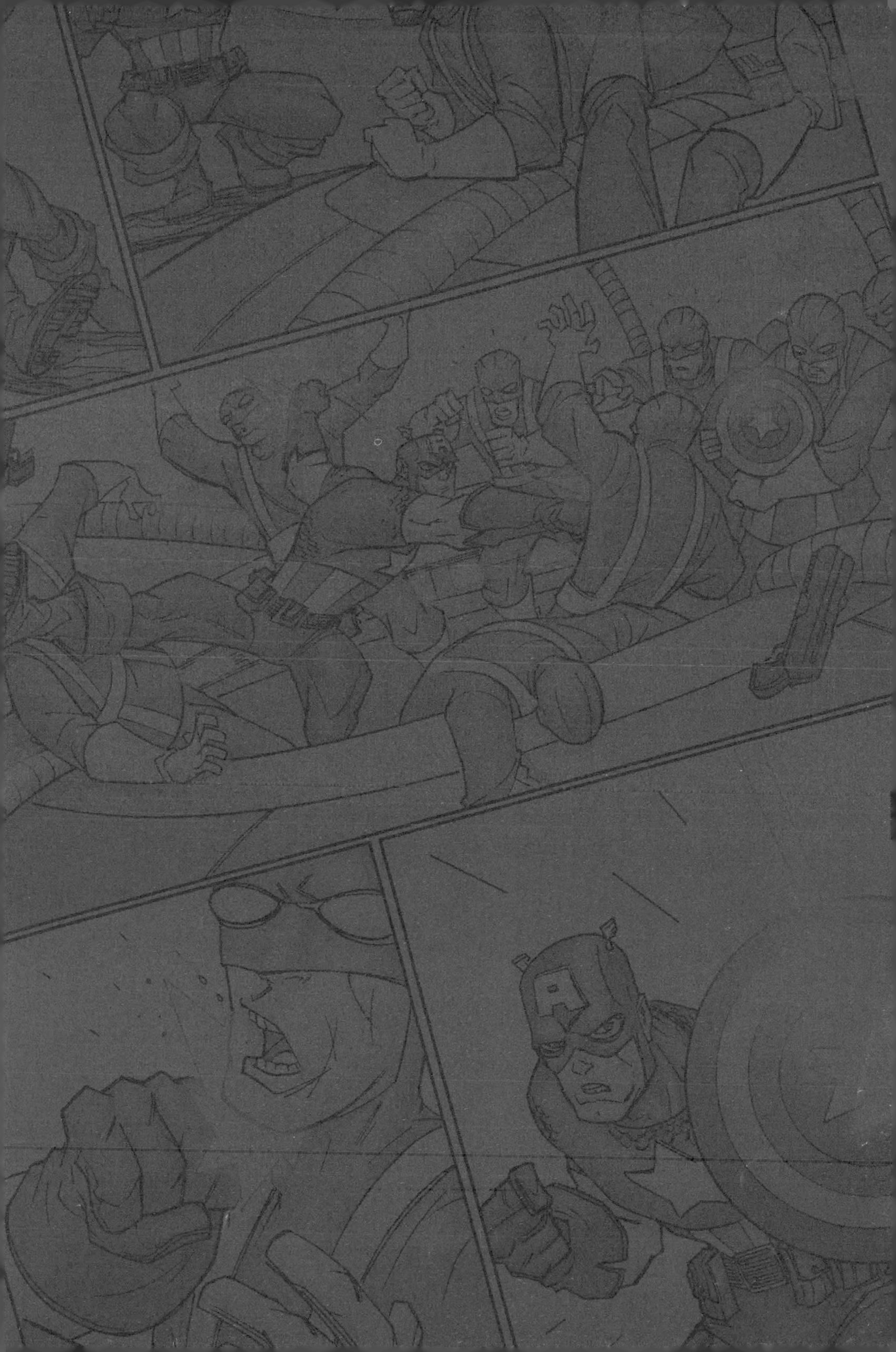

# 02

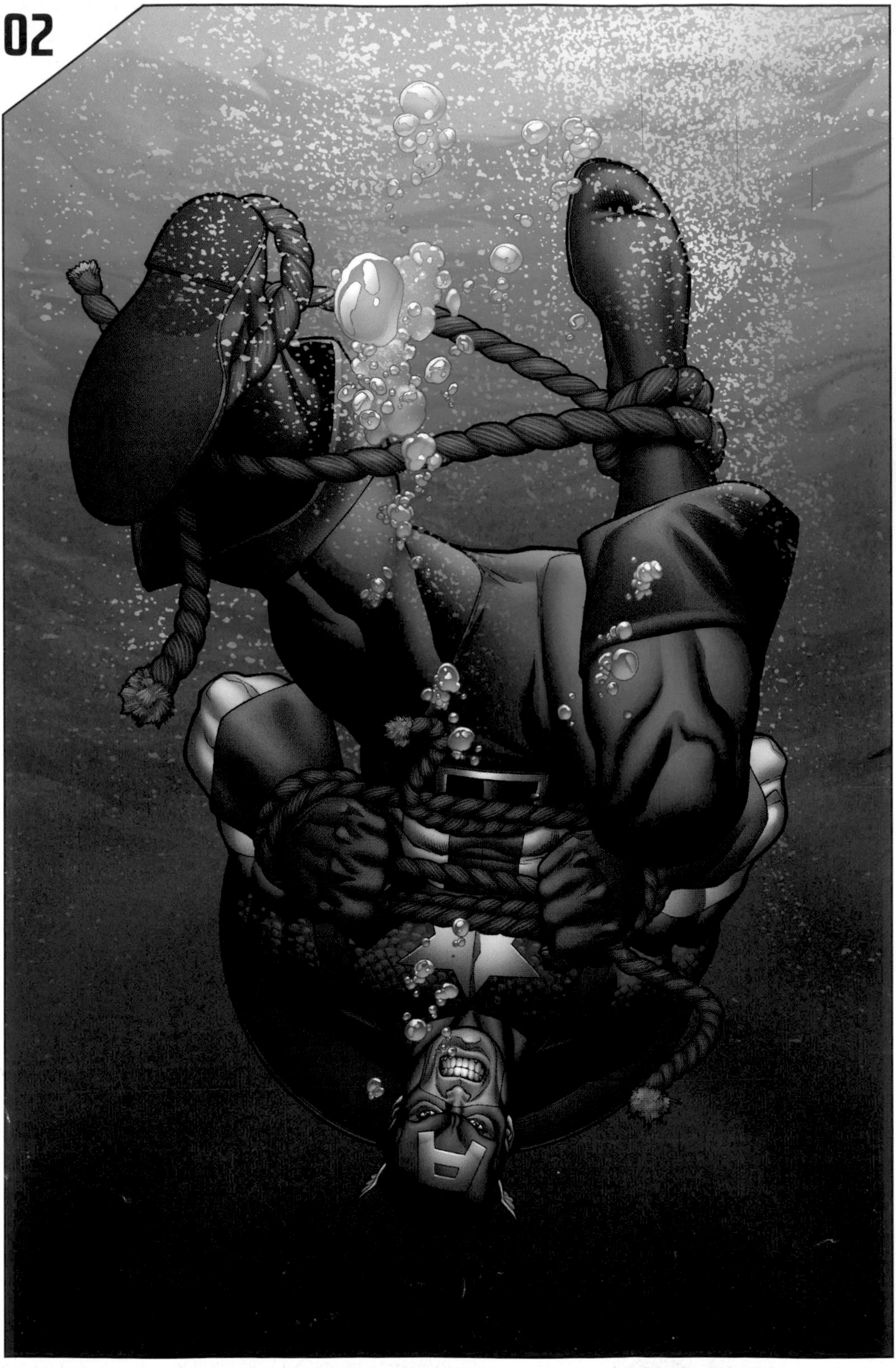

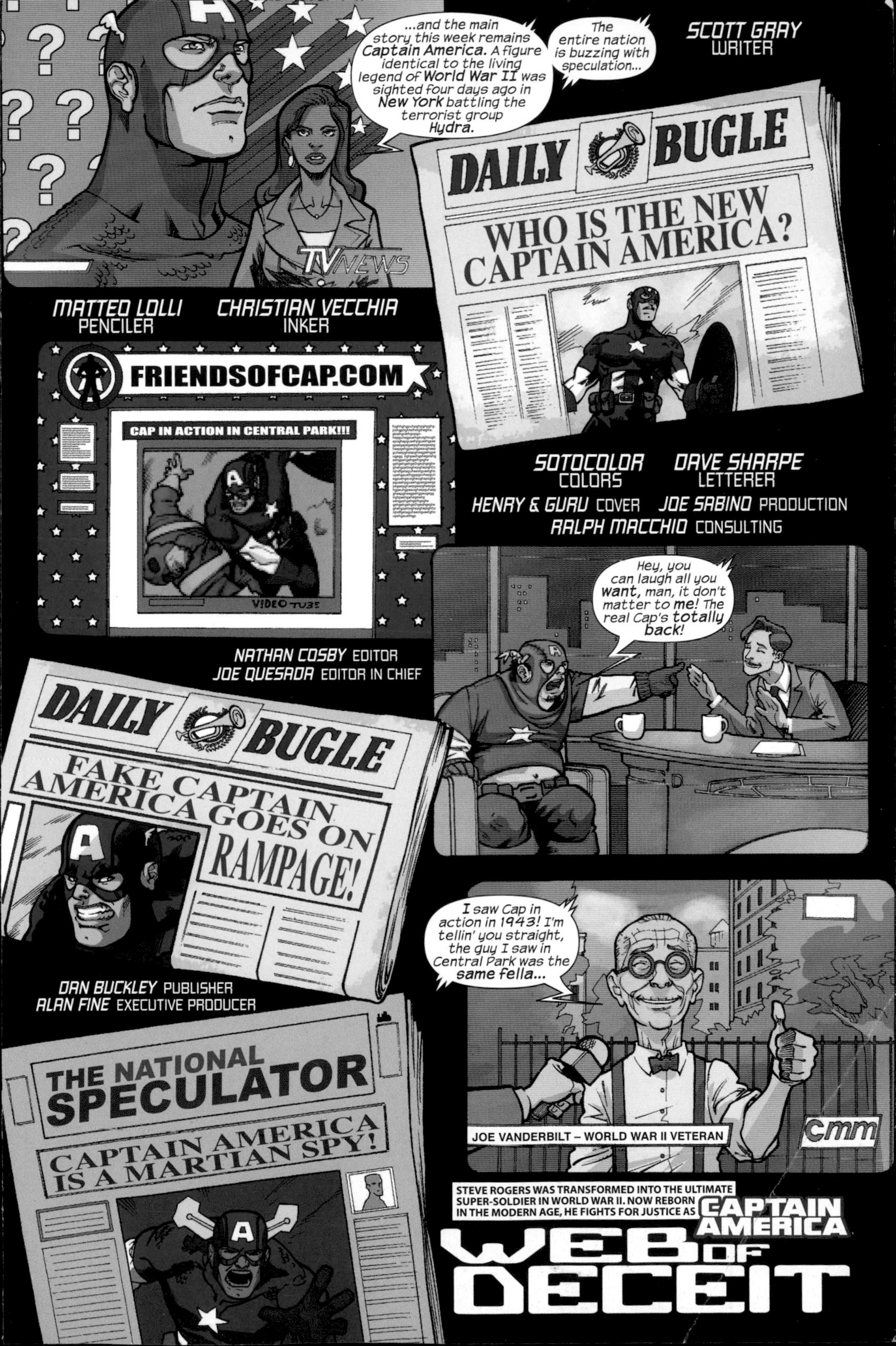
...and the main story this week remains Captain America. A figure identical to the living legend of World War II was sighted four days ago in New York battling the terrorist group Hydra.
The entire nation is buzzing with speculation...
TV NEWS
SCOTT GRAY WRITER
DAILY BUGLE
WHO IS THE NEW CAPTAIN AMERICA?
MATTEO LOLLI PENCILER
CHRISTIAN VECCHIA INKER
FRIENDSOFCAP.COM
CAP IN ACTION IN CENTRAL PARK!!!
VIDEO TUBE
SOTOCOLOR COLORS
DAVE SHARPE LETTERER
HENRY & GURU COVER
JOE SABINO PRODUCTION
RALPH MACCHIO CONSULTING
Hey, you can laugh all you want, man, it don't matter to me! The real Cap's totally back!
NATHAN COSBY EDITOR
JOE QUESADA EDITOR IN CHIEF
DAILY BUGLE
FAKE CAPTAIN AMERICA GOES ON RAMPAGE!
I saw Cap in action in 1943! I'm tellin' you straight, the guy I saw in Central Park was the same fella...
JOE VANDERBILT – WORLD WAR II VETERAN
cmm
DAN BUCKLEY PUBLISHER
ALAN FINE EXECUTIVE PRODUCER
THE NATIONAL SPECULATOR
CAPTAIN AMERICA IS A MARTIAN SPY!
STEVE ROGERS WAS TRANSFORMED INTO THE ULTIMATE SUPER-SOLDIER IN WORLD WAR II. NOW REBORN IN THE MODERN AGE, HE FIGHTS FOR JUSTICE AS
CAPTAIN AMERICA
WEB OF DECEIT

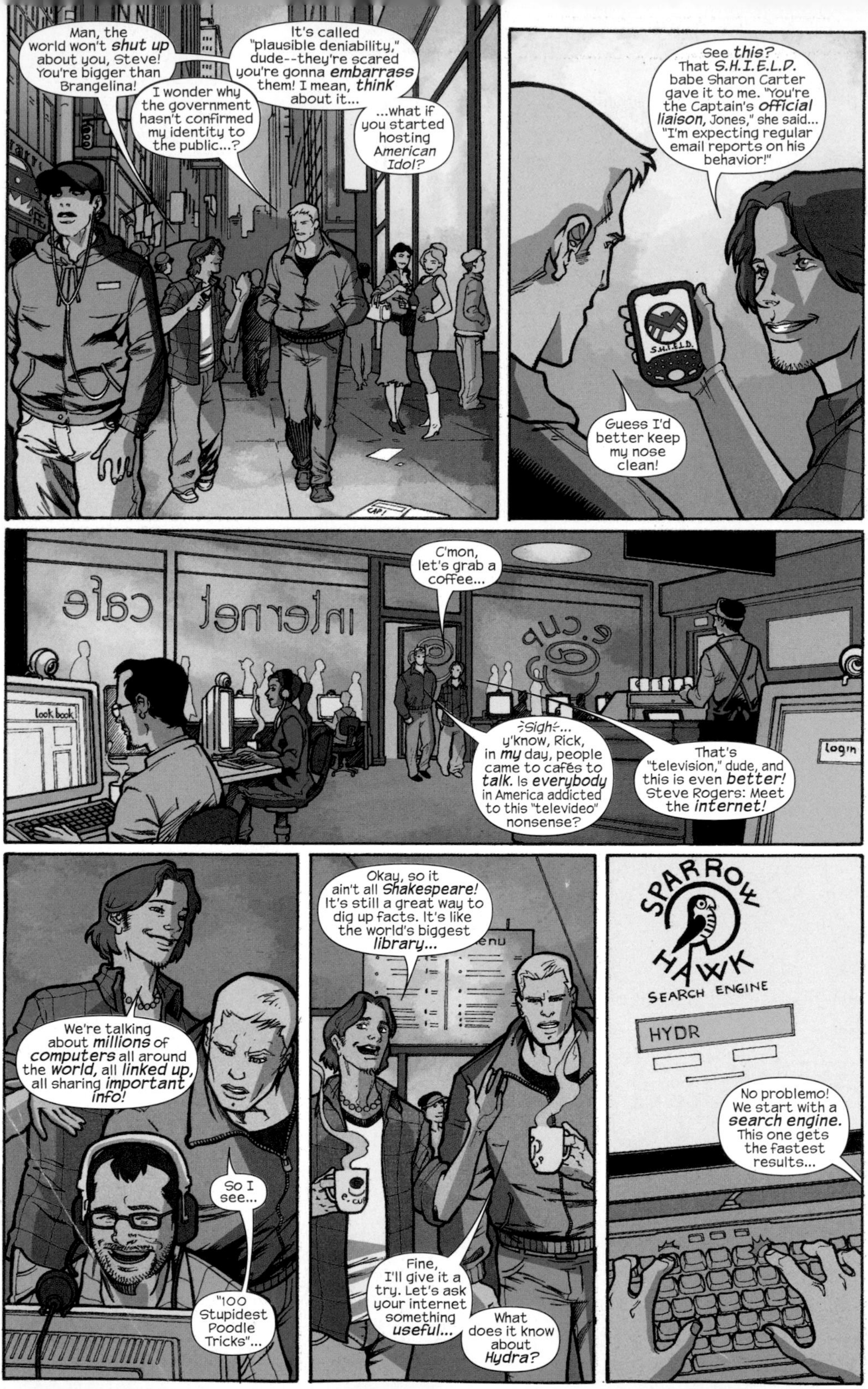

Man, the world won't *shut up* about you, Steve! You're bigger than Brangelina!
I wonder why the government hasn't confirmed my identity to the public...?
It's called "plausible deniability," dude--they're scared you're gonna *embarrass* them! I mean, *think* about it...
...what if you started hosting *American Idol?*
See *this?* That *S.H.I.E.L.D.* babe Sharon Carter gave it to me. "You're the Captain's *official liaison,* Jones," she said... "I'm expecting regular email reports on his behavior!"
S.H.I.E.L.D.
Guess I'd better keep my nose clean!
internet cafe
e.cup
C'mon, let's grab a coffee...
look book
*sigh*... y'know, Rick, in *my* day, people came to cafés to *talk.* Is *everybody* in America addicted to this "televideo" nonsense?
That's "television," dude, and this is even *better!* Steve Rogers: Meet the *internet!*
login
We're talking about *millions* of *computers* all around the *world,* all *linked up,* all sharing *important info!*
So I see...
"100 Stupidest Poodle Tricks"...
Okay, so it ain't all *Shakespeare!* It's still a great way to dig up facts. It's like the world's biggest *library...*
Fine, I'll give it a try. Let's ask your internet something *useful...*
What does it know about *Hydra?*
SPARROW HAWK
SEARCH ENGINE
HYDR
No problemo! We start with a *search engine.* This one gets the fastest results...

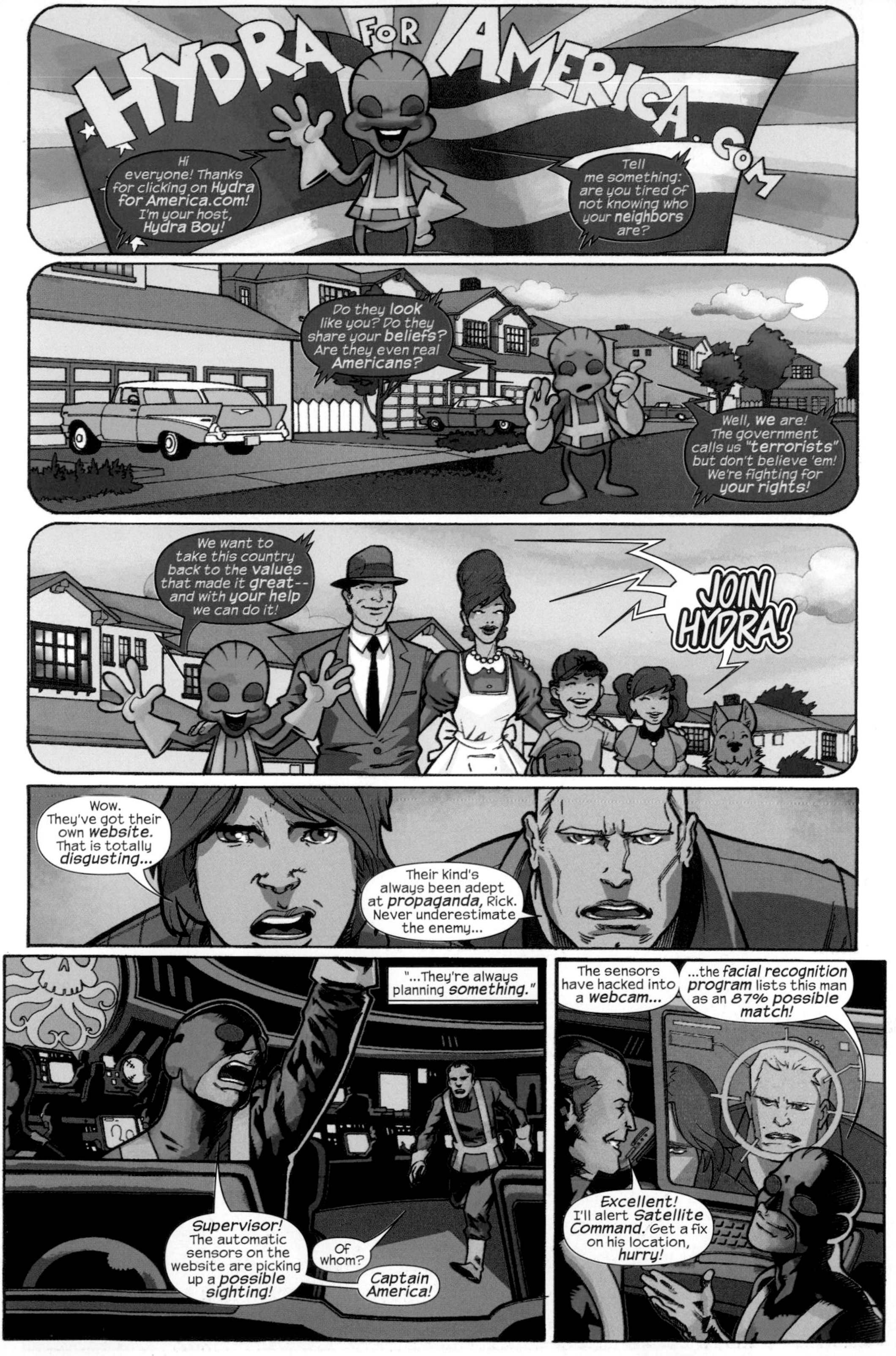
HYDRA FOR AMERICA.COM
Hi everyone! Thanks for clicking on Hydra for America.com! I'm your host, Hydra Boy!
Tell me something: are you tired of not knowing who your neighbors are?
Do they look like you? Do they share your beliefs? Are they even real Americans?
Well, we are! The government calls us "terrorists" but don't believe 'em! We're fighting for your rights!
We want to take this country back to the values that made it great--and with your help we can do it!
JOIN HYDRA!
Wow. They've got their own website. That is totally disgusting...
Their kind's always been adept at propaganda, Rick. Never underestimate the enemy...
"...They're always planning something."
Supervisor! The automatic sensors on the website are picking up a possible sighting!
Of whom?
Captain America!
The sensors have hacked into a webcam...
...the facial recognition program lists this man as an 87% possible match!
Excellent! I'll alert Satellite Command. Get a fix on his location, hurry!

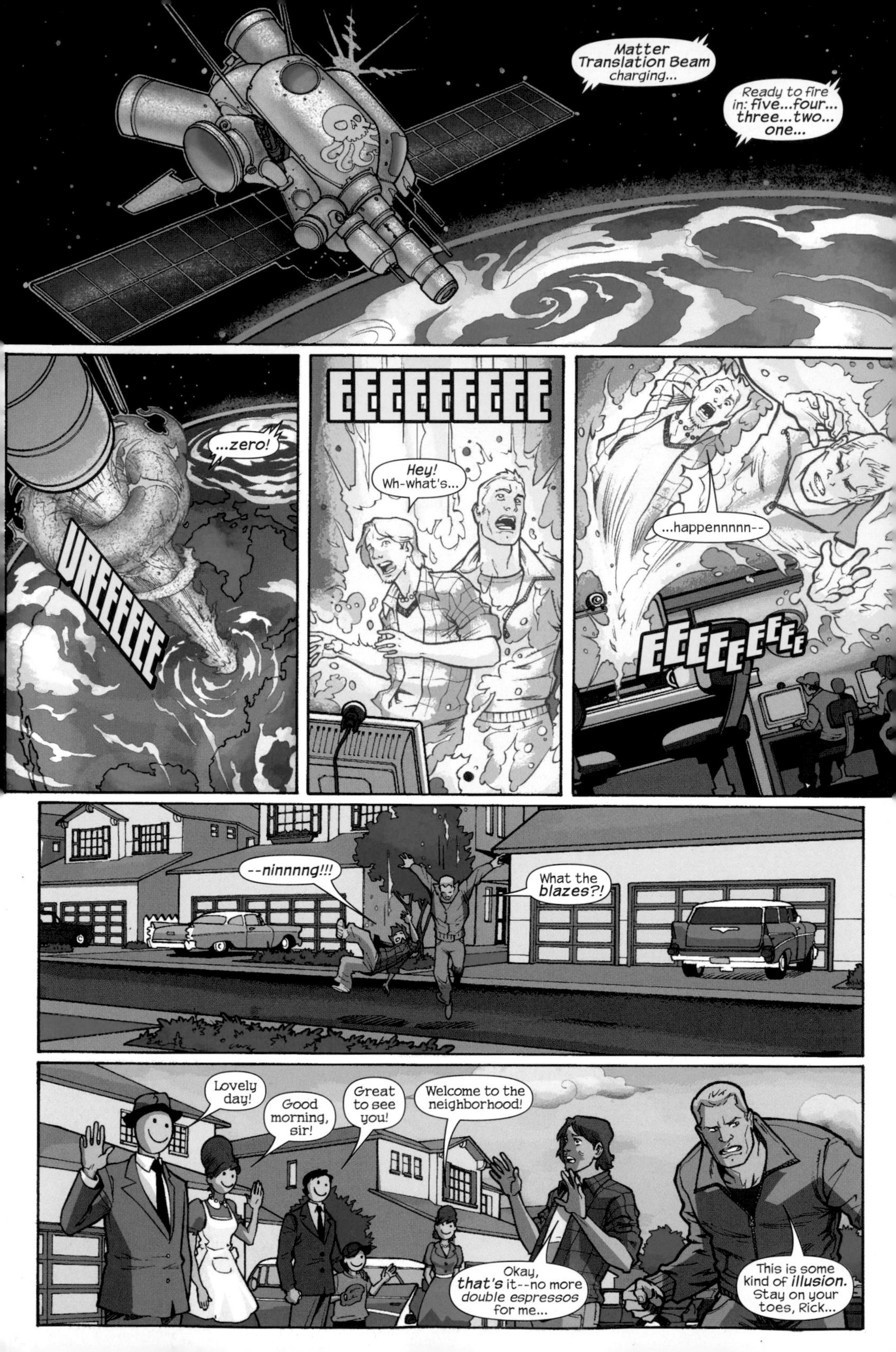

Matter Translation Beam charging...
Ready to fire in: five...four... three...two... one...
...zero!
UREEEEEE
EEEEEEEEE
Hey! Wh-what's...
...happennnnn--
EEEEEEEEE
--ninnnng!!!
What the blazes?!
Lovely day!
Good morning, sir!
Great to see you!
Welcome to the neighborhood!
Okay, that's it--no more double espressos for me...
This is some kind of illusion. Stay on your toes, Rick...

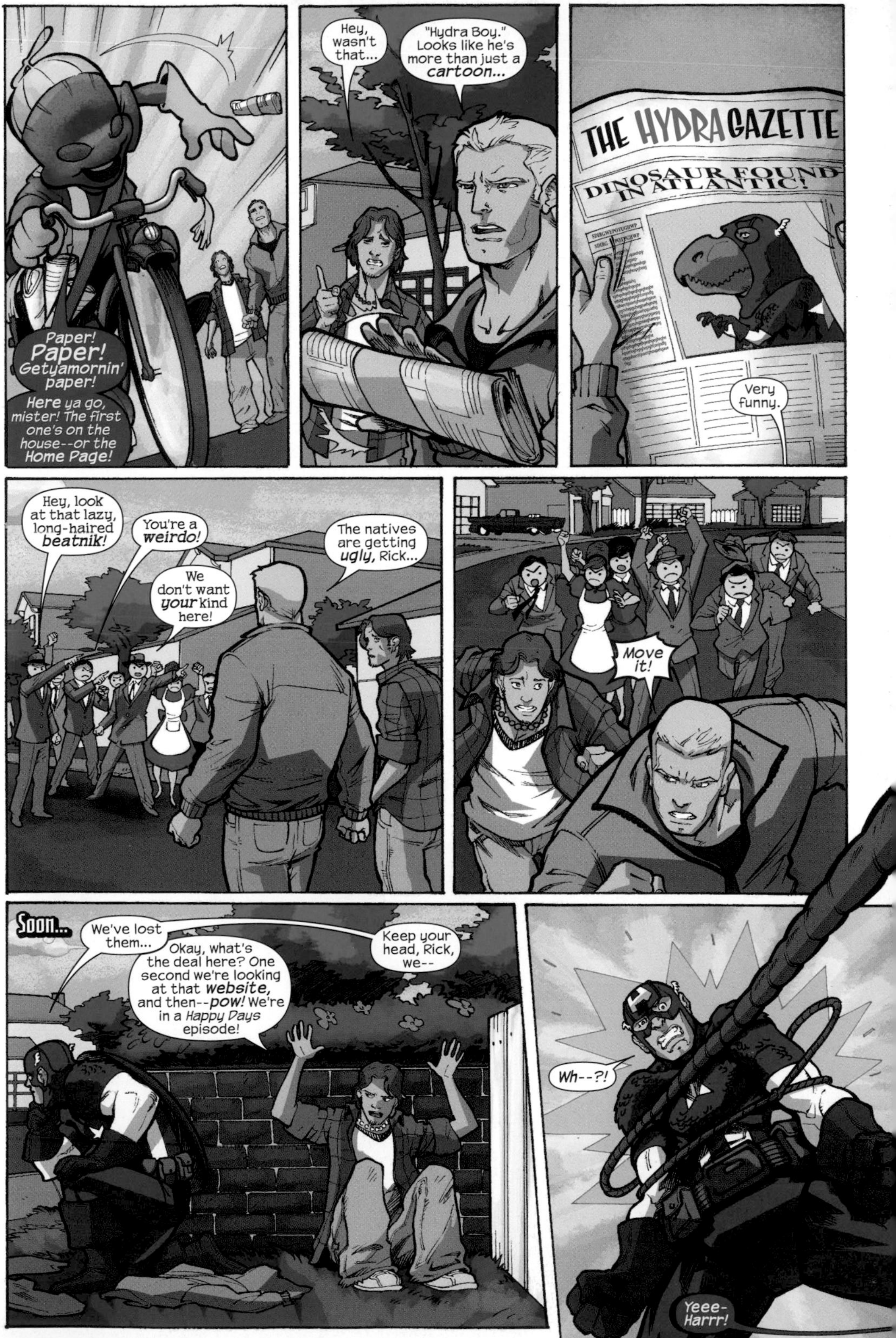
Paper! Paper! Getyamornin' paper!
Here ya go, mister! The first one's on the house--or the Home Page!
Hey, wasn't that...
"Hydra Boy." Looks like he's more than just a cartoon...
THE HYDRA GAZETTE
DINOSAUR FOUND IN ATLANTIC!
Very funny.
Hey, look at that lazy, long-haired beatnik!
You're a weirdo!
We don't want your kind here!
The natives are getting ugly, Rick...
Move it!
Soon...
We've lost them...
Okay, what's the deal here? One second we're looking at that website, and then--pow! We're in a Happy Days episode!
Keep your head, Rick, we--
Wh--?!
Yeee-Harrr!

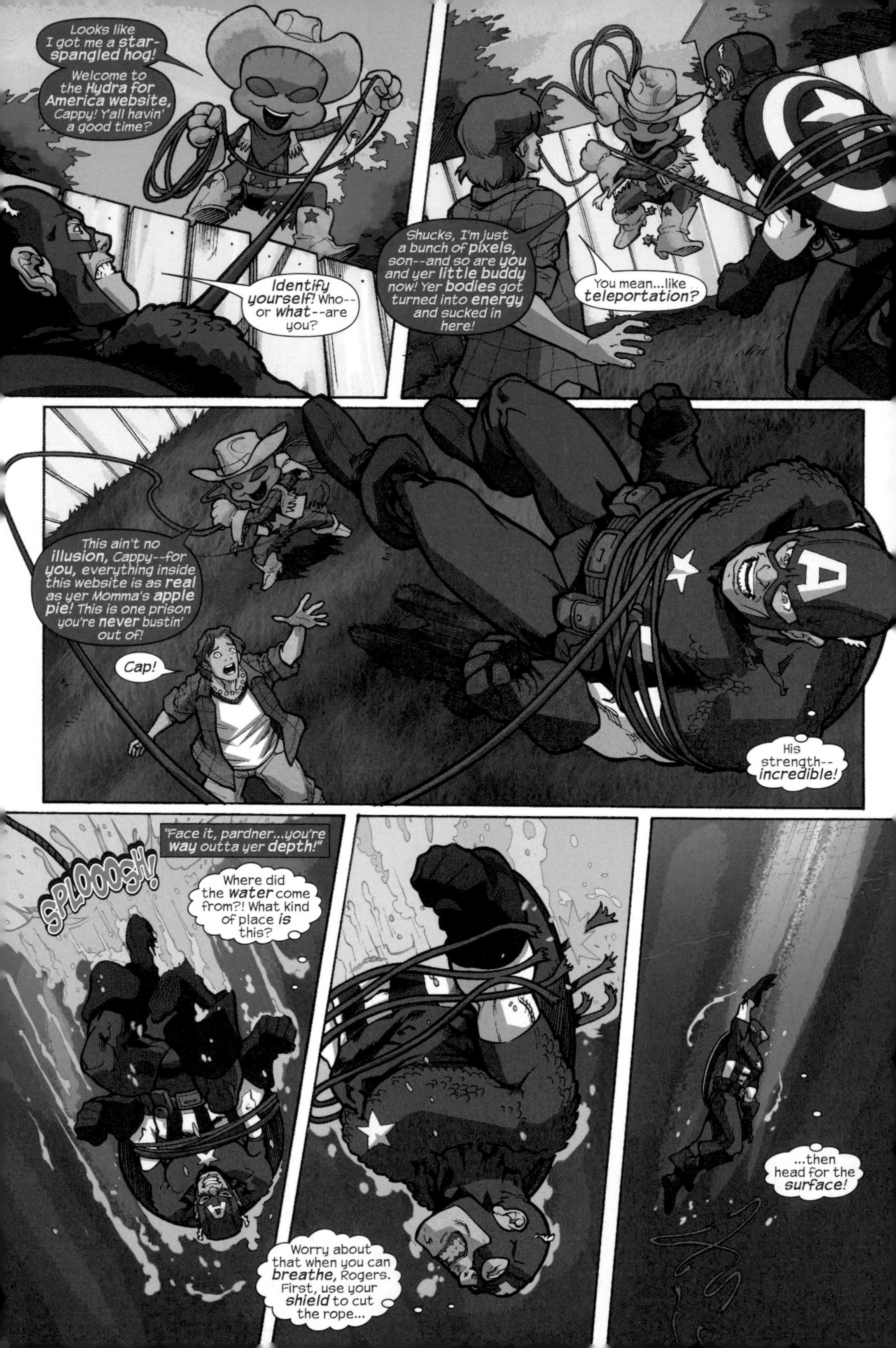

Looks like I got me a star-spangled hog!
Welcome to the Hydra for America website, Cappy! Y'all havin' a good time?
Identify yourself! Who--or what--are you?
Shucks, I'm just a bunch of pixels, son--and so are you and yer little buddy now! Yer bodies got turned into energy and sucked in here!
You mean...like teleportation?
This ain't no illusion, Cappy--for you, everything inside this website is as real as yer Momma's apple pie! This is one prison you're never bustin' out of!
Cap!
His strength--incredible!
"Face it, pardner...you're way outta yer depth!"
SPLOOOSH!
Where did the water come from?! What kind of place is this?
Worry about that when you can breathe, Rogers. First, use your shield to cut the rope...
...then head for the surface!

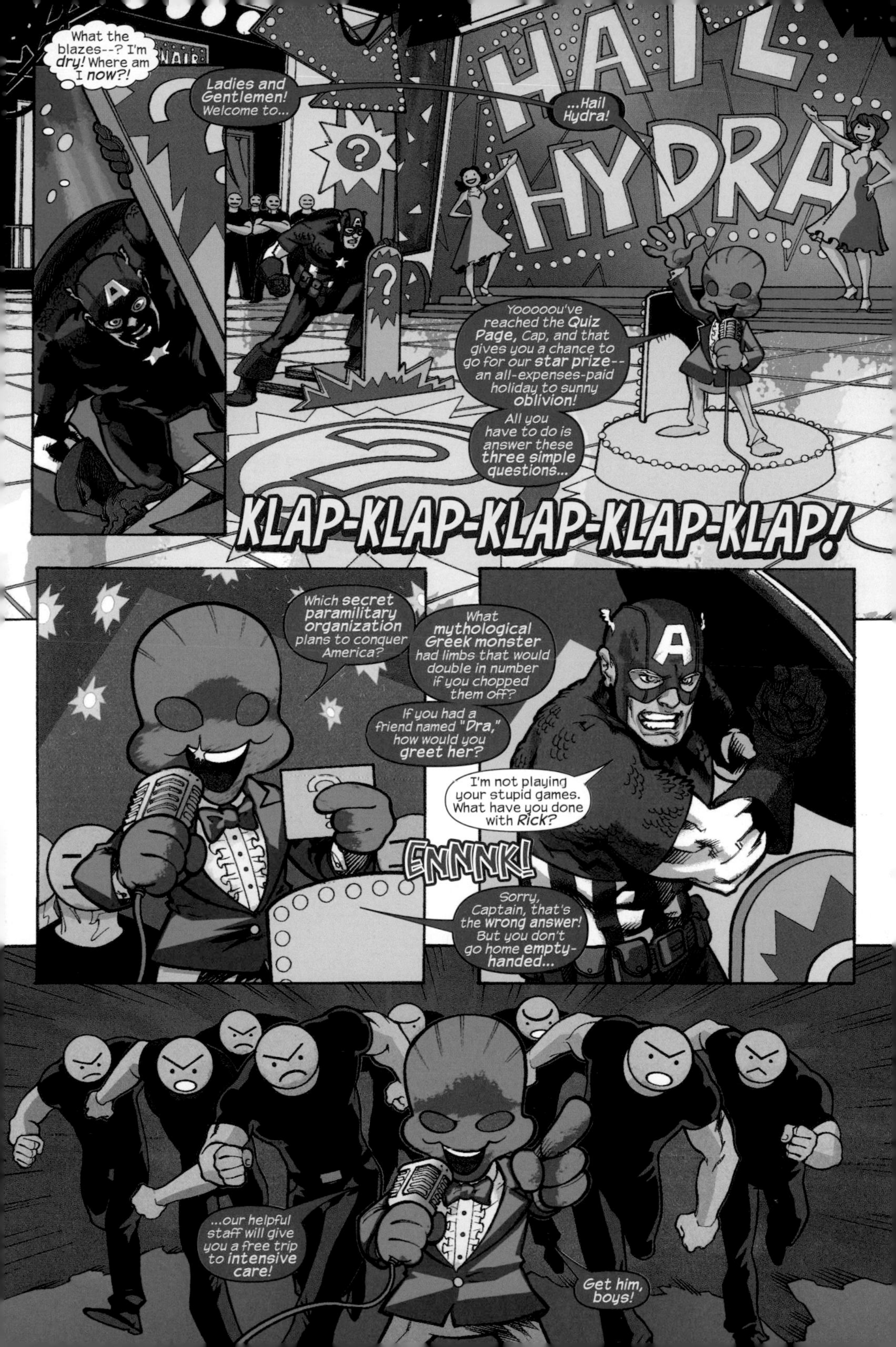
What the blazes--? I'm dry! Where am I now?!
Ladies and Gentlemen! Welcome to...
...Hail Hydra!
HAIL HYDRA
Yooooou've reached the Quiz Page, Cap, and that gives you a chance to go for our star prize--an all-expenses-paid holiday to sunny oblivion!
All you have to do is answer these three simple questions...
KLAP-KLAP-KLAP-KLAP-KLAP!
Which secret paramilitary organization plans to conquer America?
What mythological Greek monster had limbs that would double in number if you chopped them off?
If you had a friend named "Dra," how would you greet her?
I'm not playing your stupid games. What have you done with Rick?
ENNNK!
Sorry, Captain, that's the wrong answer! But you don't go home empty-handed...
...our helpful staff will give you a free trip to intensive care!
Get him, boys!

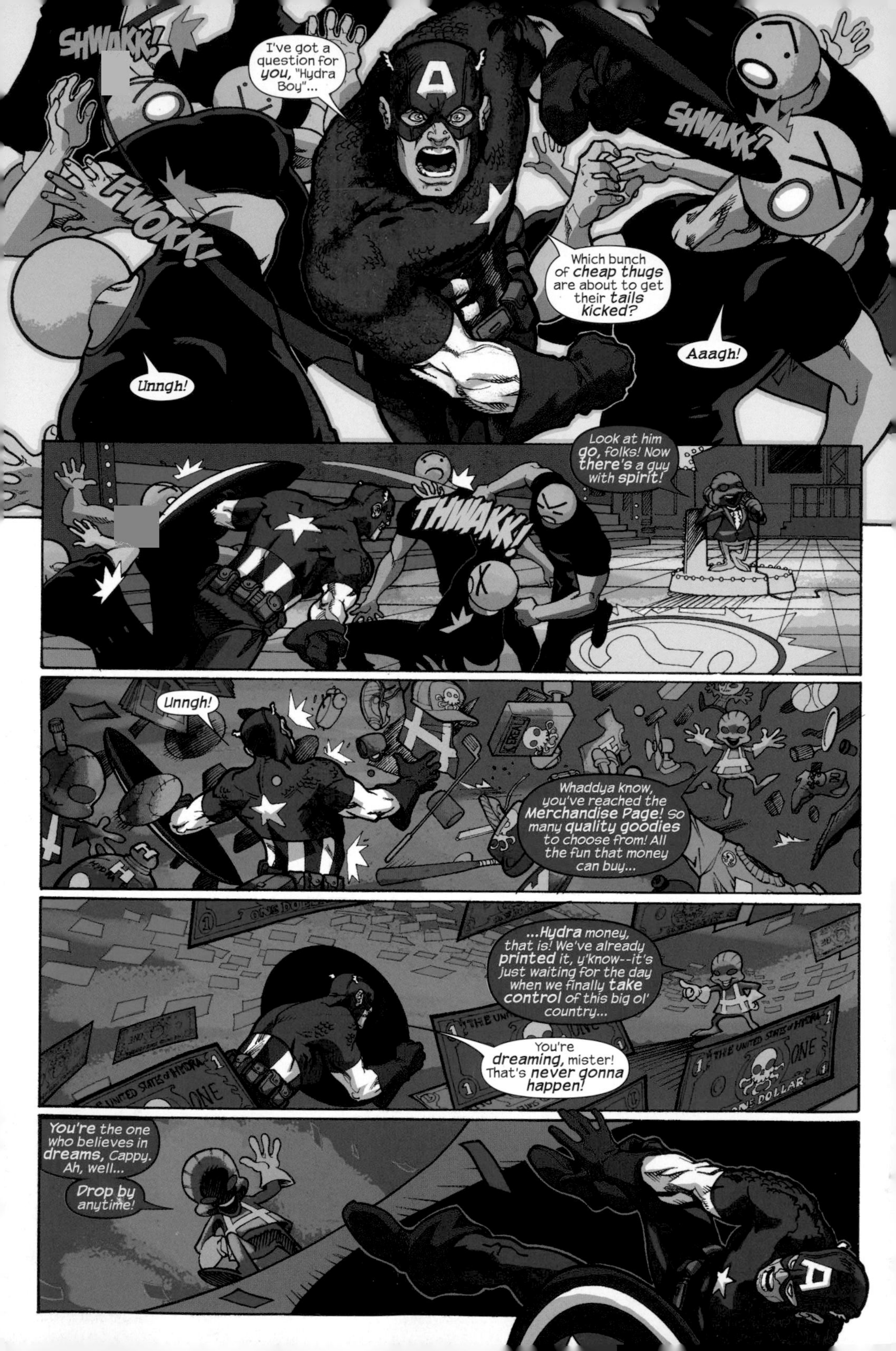
SHWAKK!
I've got a question for you, "Hydra Boy"...
SHWAKK!
FWOKK!
Which bunch of cheap thugs are about to get their tails kicked?
Unngh!
Aaagh!
Look at him go, folks! Now there's a guy with spirit!
THWAKK!
Unngh!
Whaddya know, you've reached the Merchandise Page! So many quality goodies to choose from! All the fun that money can buy...
...Hydra money, that is! We've already printed it, y'know--it's just waiting for the day when we finally take control of this big ol' country...
You're dreaming, mister! That's never gonna happen!
You're the one who believes in dreams, Cappy. Ah, well...
Drop by anytime!

Looks like Hydra Punk decided I wasn't gonna be a *problem*--he's left me *alone*. *Big mistake,* kid--nobody knows the web better than *Rick Jones!*

Okay, if everything inside this website is *real,* then I'll have to *navigate* the *pages.* That means I need...

...a *menu,* please!

Here ya go, honey!

It all looks *great,* babe--I think I'll start with the *Message Board...*

HOUSE OF H

HOME
QUIZ
MERCHANDISE
SPORTS
GALLERY
F.A.Q.
LINKS
MESSAGE BOARD

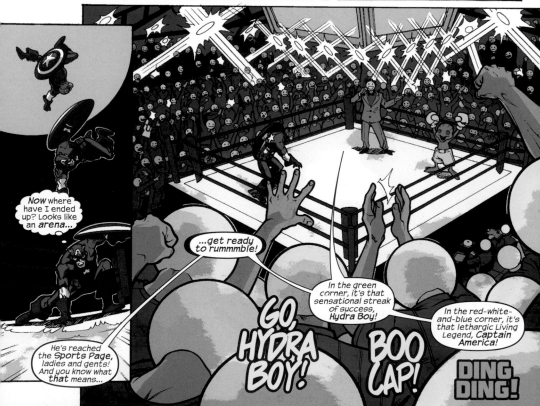

*Now* where have I ended up? Looks like an *arena...*

He's reached the *Sports Page,* ladies and gents! And you know what *that* means...

...get ready to *rummmble!*

In the green corner, it's that sensational streak of success, *Hydra Boy!*

In the red-white-and-blue corner, it's that lethargic Living Legend, *Captain America!*

GO, HYDRA BOY!

BOO CAP!

DING, DING!

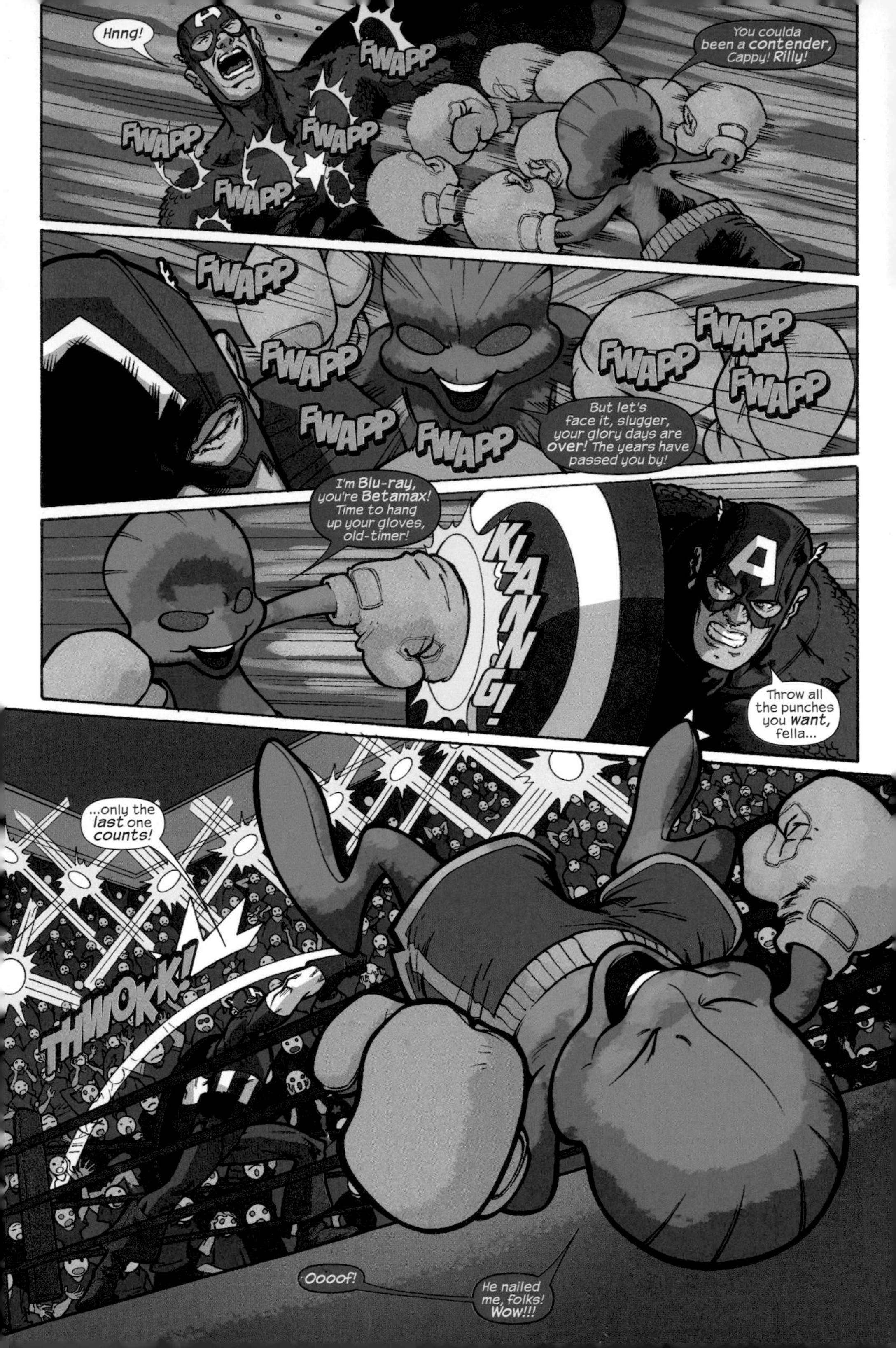
Hnng!
FWAPP
You coulda been a contender, Cappy! Rilly!
FWAPP
FWAPP
FWAPP
FWAPP
FWAPP
FWAPP
FWAPP
FWAPP
FWAPP
But let's face it, slugger, your glory days are over! The years have passed you by!
I'm Blu-ray, you're Betamax! Time to hang up your gloves, old-timer!
KLANNG!
Throw all the punches you want, fella...
...only the last one counts!
THWOKK!
Oooof!
He nailed me, folks! Wow!!!

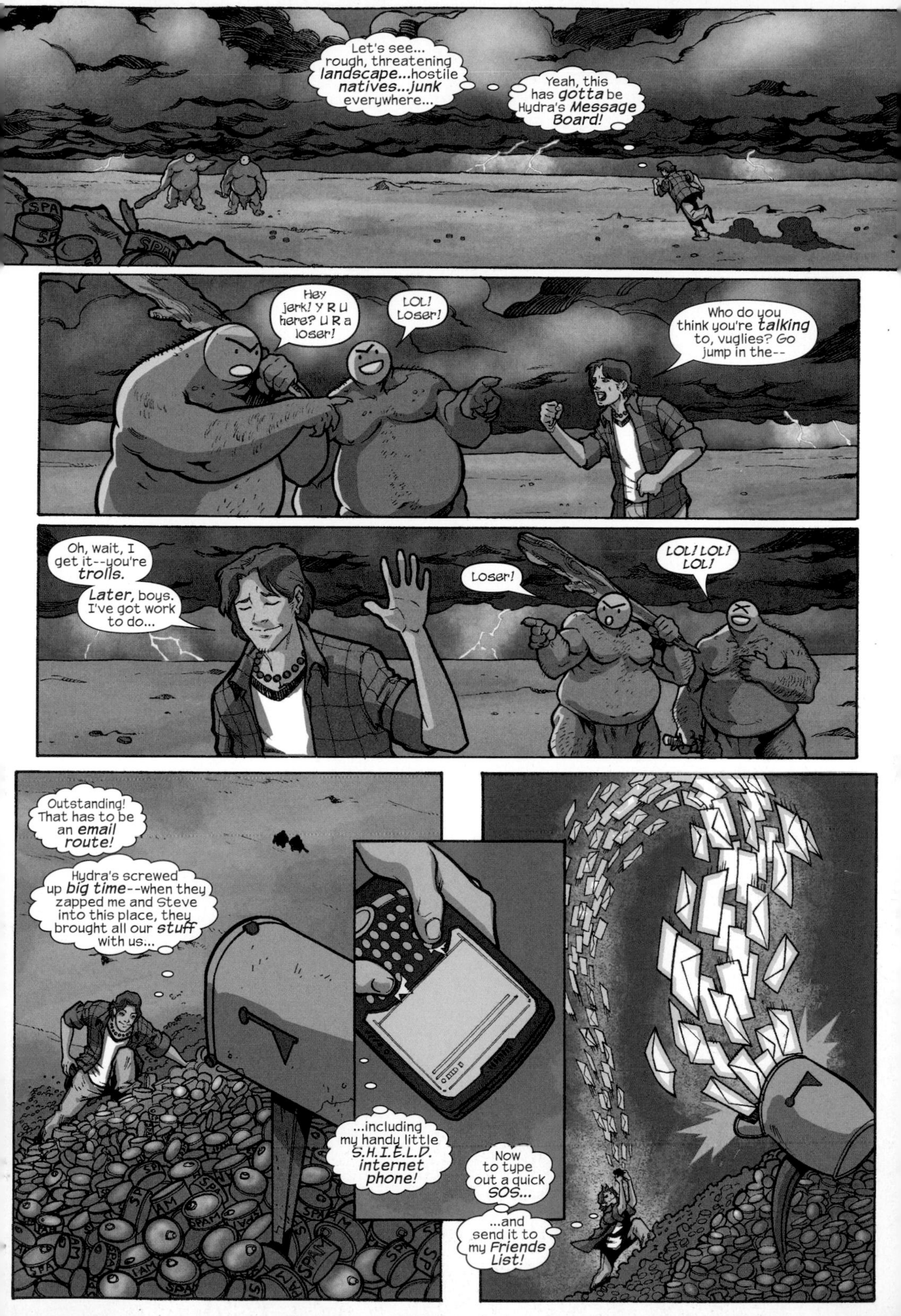
Let's see... rough, threatening landscape...hostile natives...junk everywhere...
Yeah, this has gotta be Hydra's Message Board!
Hey jerk! Y R U here? U R a loser!
LOL! Loser!
Who do you think you're talking to, vuglies? Go jump in the--
Oh, wait, I get it--you're trolls.
Later, boys. I've got work to do...
Loser!
LOL! LOL! LOL!
Outstanding! That has to be an email route!
Hydra's screwed up big time--when they zapped me and Steve into this place, they brought all our stuff with us...
...including my handy little S.H.I.E.L.D. internet phone!
Now to type out a quick SOS...
...and send it to my Friends List!
SPAM

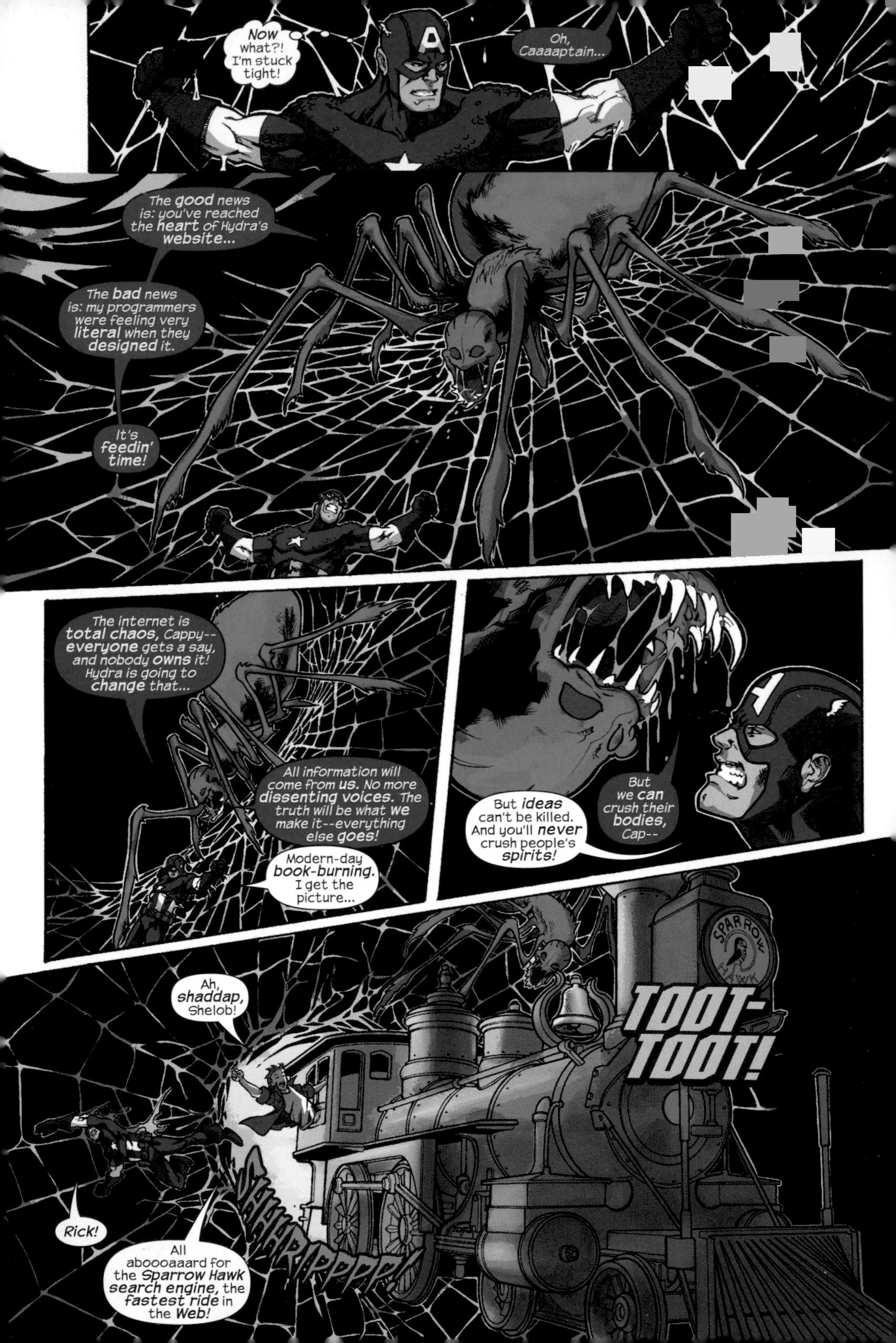
Now what?! I'm stuck tight!
Oh, Caaaaptain...
The good news is: you've reached the heart of Hydra's website...
The bad news is: my programmers were feeling very literal when they designed it.
It's feedin' time!
The internet is total chaos, Cappy-- everyone gets a say, and nobody owns it! Hydra is going to change that...
All information will come from us. No more dissenting voices. The truth will be what we make it--everything else goes!
Modern-day book-burning. I get the picture...
But we can crush their bodies, Cap--
But ideas can't be killed. And you'll never crush people's spirits!
Ah, shaddap, Shelob!
TOOT-TOOT!
SPARROW HAWK
Rick!
All aboooaaard for the Sparrow Hawk search engine, the fastest ride in the Web!

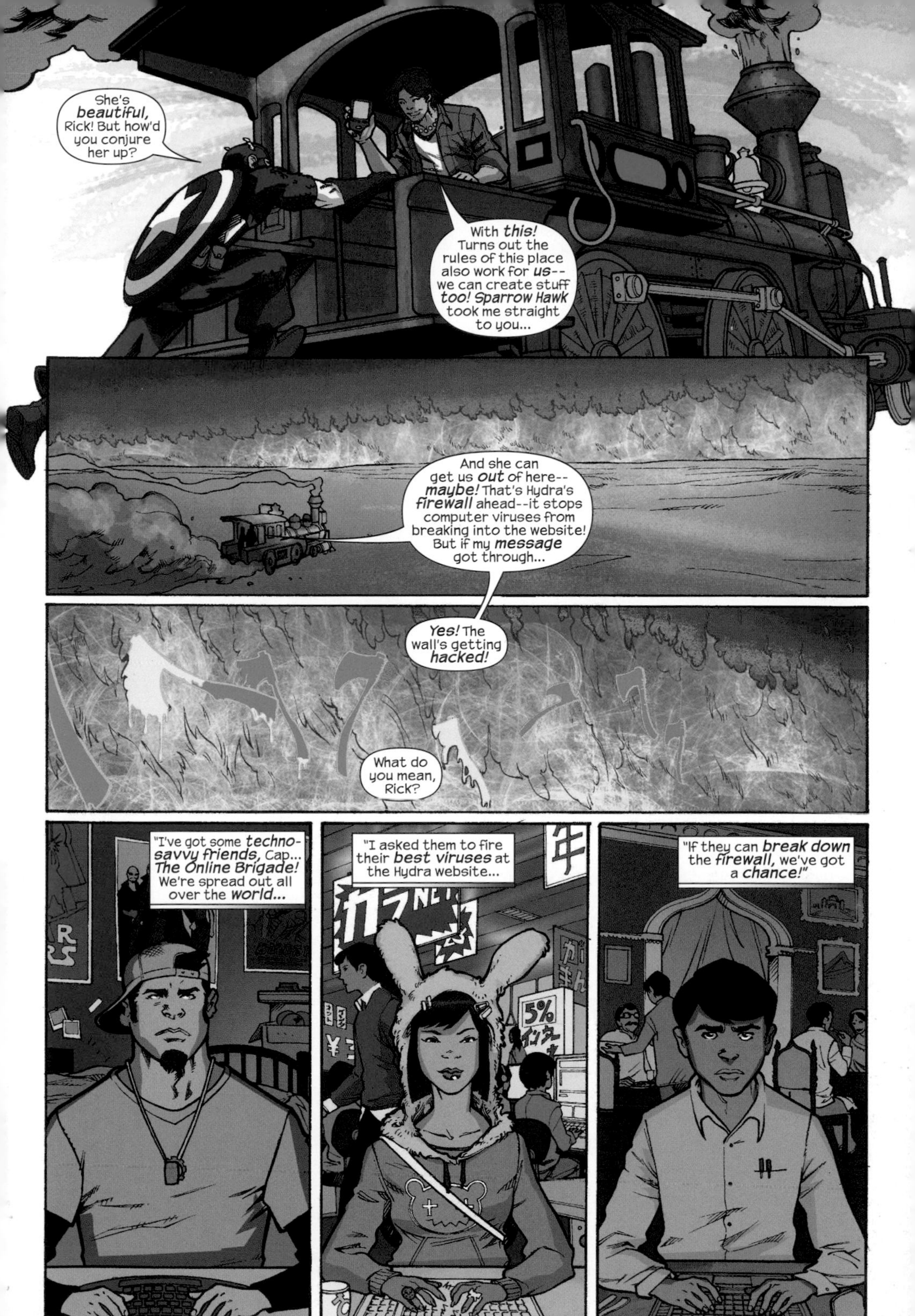
She's *beautiful,* Rick! But how'd you conjure her up?
With *this!* Turns out the rules of this place also work for *us*-- we can create stuff *too! Sparrow Hawk* took me straight to you...
And she can get us *out* of here-- *maybe!* That's Hydra's *firewall* ahead--it stops computer viruses from breaking into the website! But if my *message* got through...
*Yes!* The wall's getting *hacked!*
What do you mean, Rick?
"I've got some *techno-savvy friends,* Cap... *The Online Brigade!* We're spread out all over the *world*...
"I asked them to fire their *best viruses* at the Hydra website...
"If they can *break down* the *firewall,* we've got a *chance!*"
5%

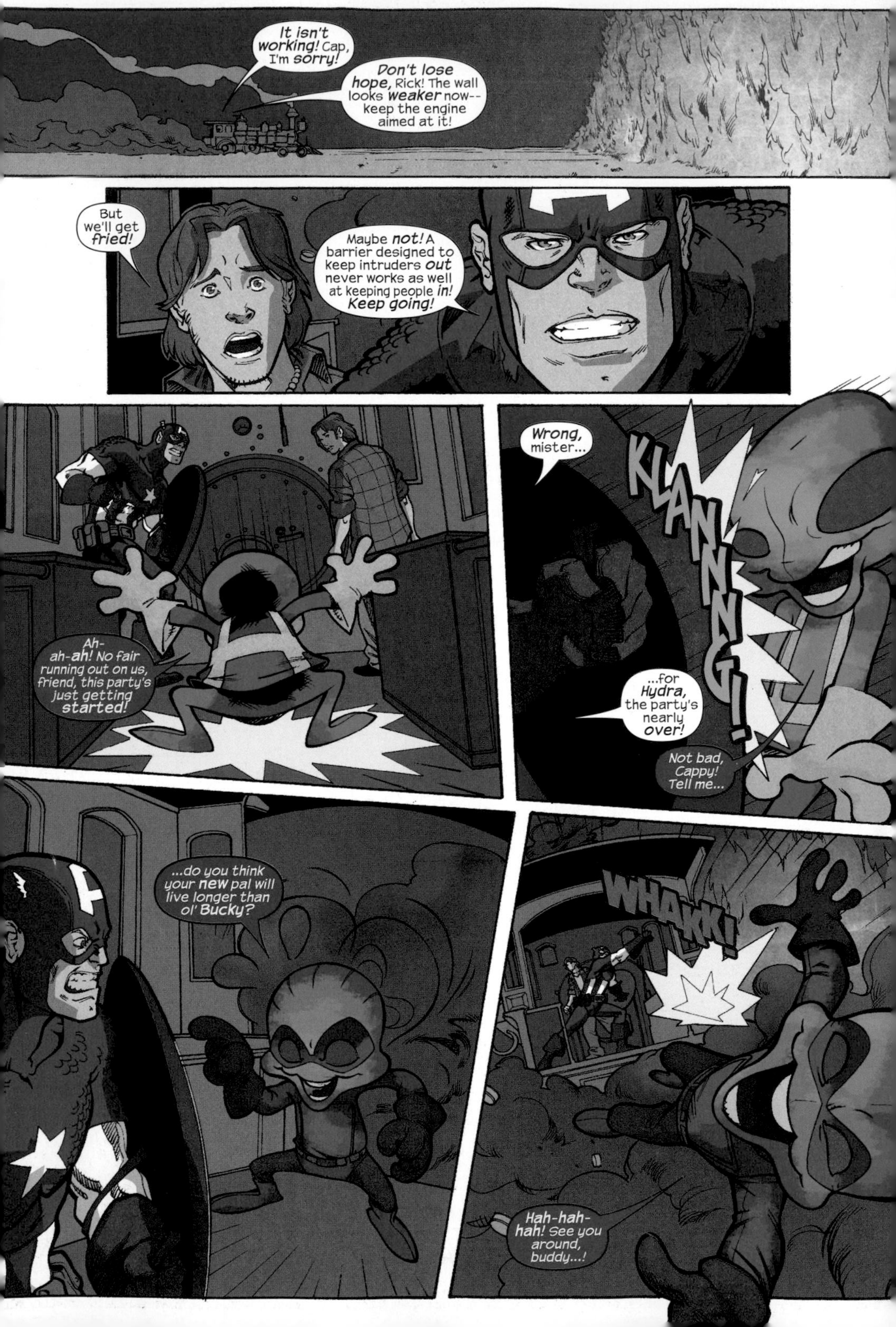
It isn't working! Cap, I'm sorry!
Don't lose hope, Rick! The wall looks weaker now-- keep the engine aimed at it!
But we'll get fried!
Maybe not! A barrier designed to keep intruders out never works as well at keeping people in! Keep going!
Ah-ah-ah! No fair running out on us, friend, this party's just getting started!
Wrong, mister...
KLANNNG!
...for Hydra, the party's nearly over!
Not bad, Cappy! Tell me...
...do you think your new pal will live longer than ol' Bucky?
WHAKK!
Hah-hah-hah! See you around, buddy...!

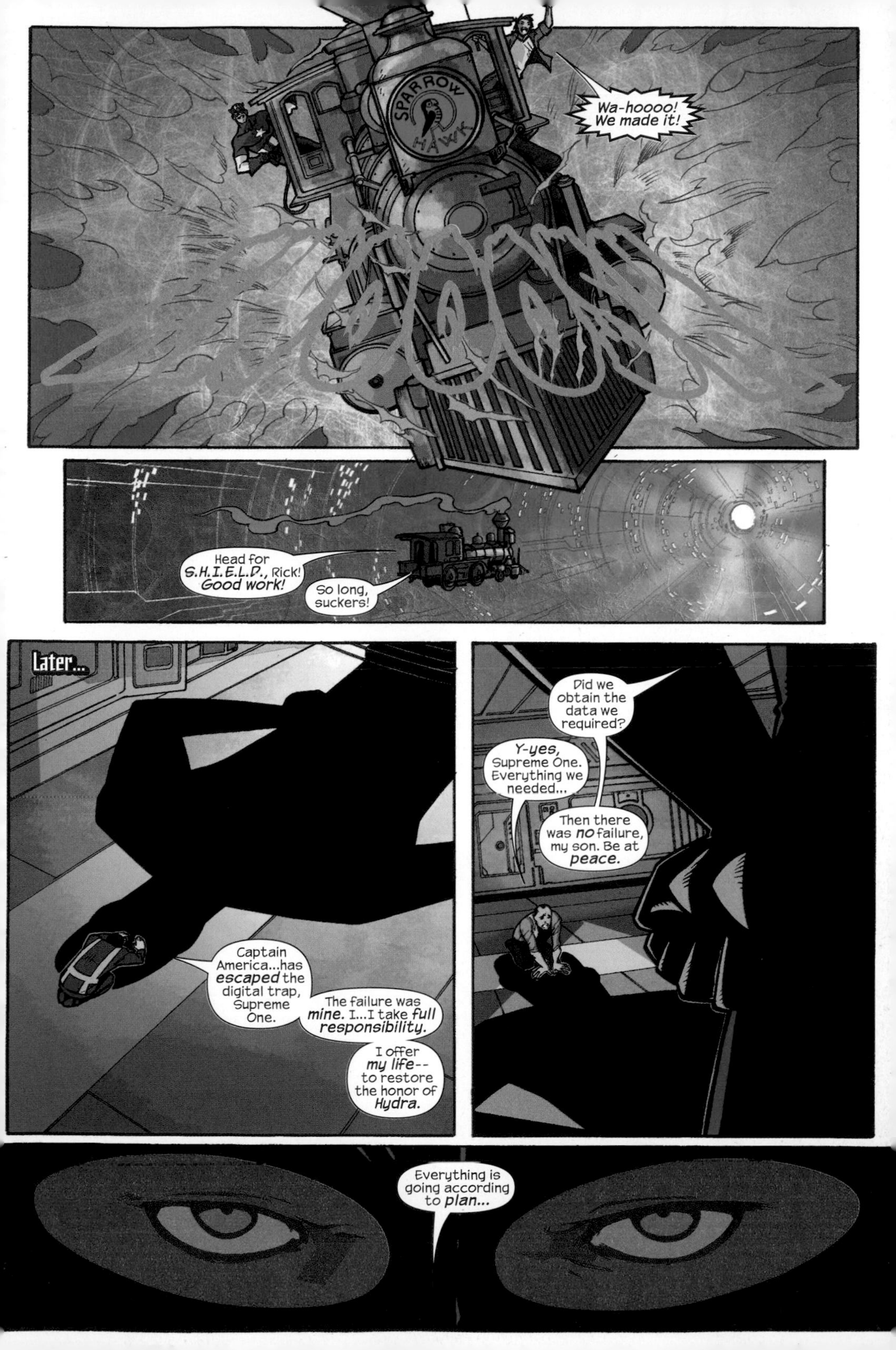
SPARROW HAWK
Wa-hoooo! We made it!
Head for S.H.I.E.L.D., Rick! Good work!
So long, suckers!
Later...
Captain America...has escaped the digital trap, Supreme One.
The failure was mine. I...I take full responsibility.
I offer my life-- to restore the honor of Hydra.
Did we obtain the data we required?
Y-yes, Supreme One. Everything we needed...
Then there was no failure, my son. Be at peace.
Everything is going according to plan...

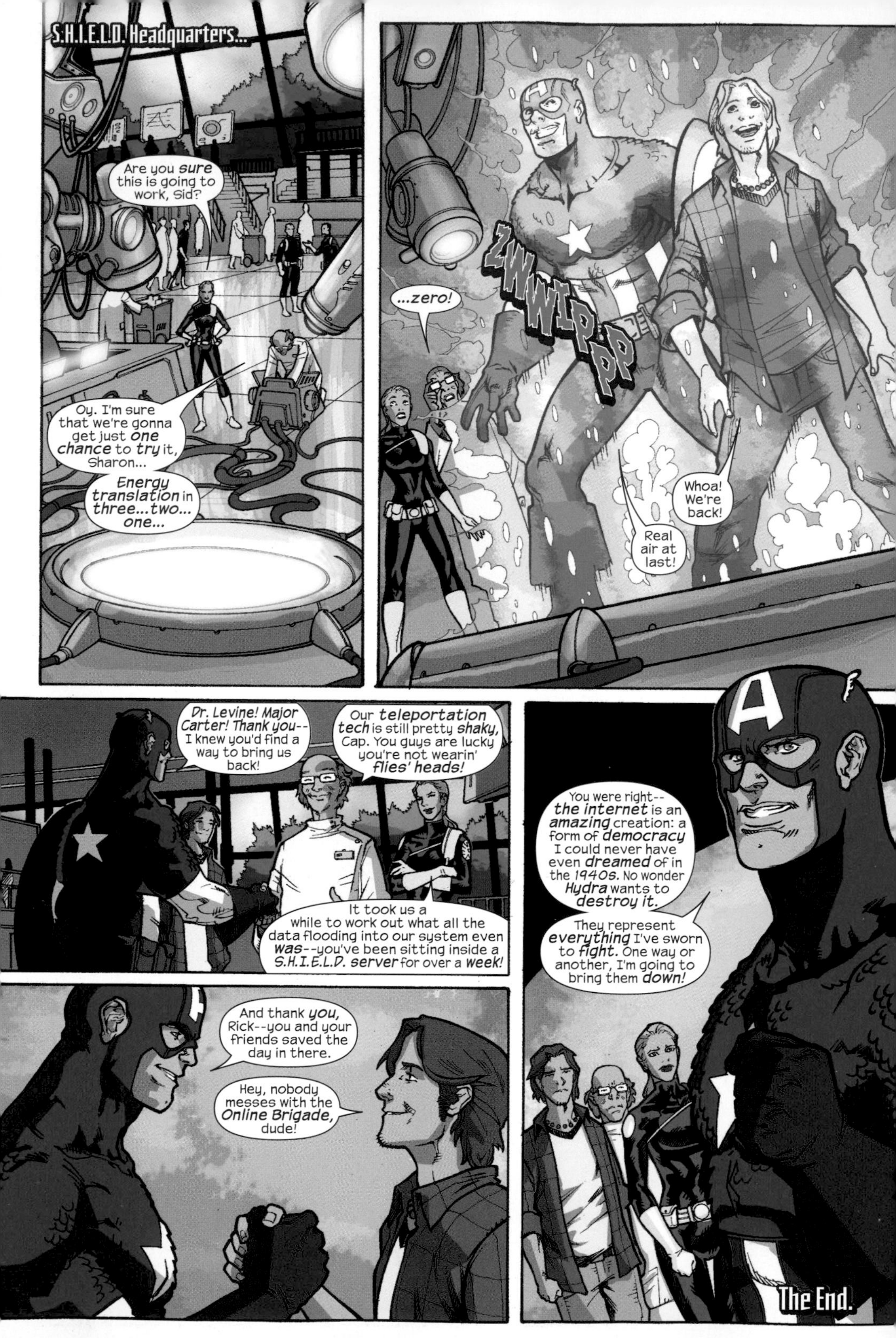
S.H.I.E.L.D. Headquarters...
Are you sure this is going to work, Sid?
Oy. I'm sure that we're gonna get just one chance to try it, Sharon...
Energy translation in three...two... one...
...zero!
ZWWIPPP
Whoa! We're back!
Real air at last!
Dr. Levine! Major Carter! Thank you-- I knew you'd find a way to bring us back!
Our teleportation tech is still pretty shaky, Cap. You guys are lucky you're not wearin' flies' heads!
It took us a while to work out what all the data flooding into our system even was--you've been sitting inside a S.H.I.E.L.D. server for over a week!
And thank you, Rick--you and your friends saved the day in there.
Hey, nobody messes with the Online Brigade, dude!
You were right-- the internet is an amazing creation: a form of democracy I could never have even dreamed of in the 1940s. No wonder Hydra wants to destroy it.
They represent everything I've sworn to fight. One way or another, I'm going to bring them down!
The End.

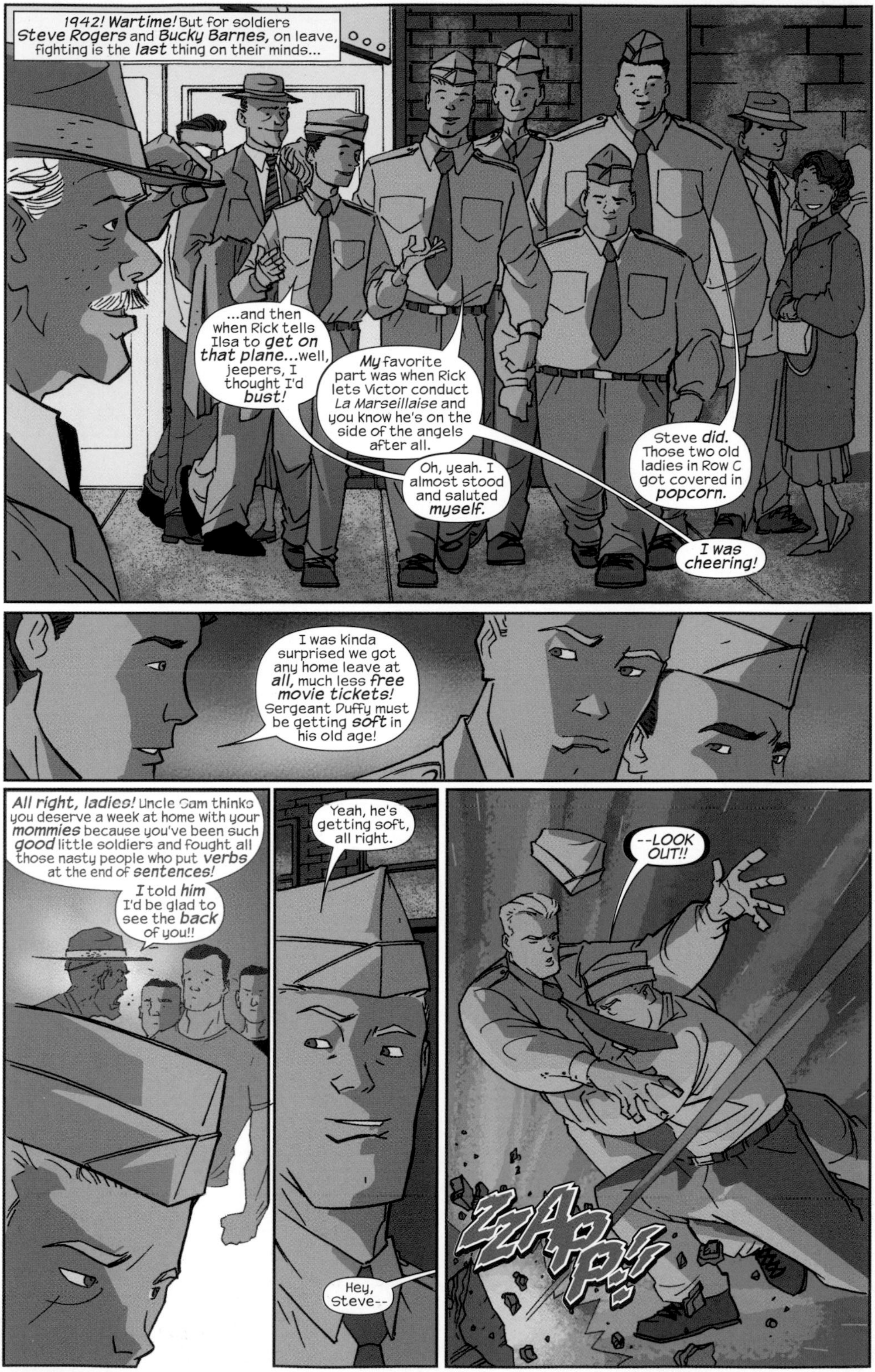
1942! Wartime! But for soldiers Steve Rogers and Bucky Barnes, on leave, fighting is the last thing on their minds...
...and then when Rick tells Ilsa to get on that plane...well, jeepers, I thought I'd bust!
My favorite part was when Rick lets Victor conduct La Marseillaise and you know he's on the side of the angels after all.
Oh, yeah. I almost stood and saluted myself.
I was cheering!
Steve did. Those two old ladies in Row C got covered in popcorn.
I was kinda surprised we got any home leave at all, much less free movie tickets! Sergeant Duffy must be getting soft in his old age!
All right, ladies! Uncle Sam thinks you deserve a week at home with your mommies because you've been such good little soldiers and fought all those nasty people who put verbs at the end of sentences!
I told him I'd be glad to see the back of you!!
Yeah, he's getting soft, all right.
Hey, Steve--
--LOOK OUT!!
ZZAPP!!

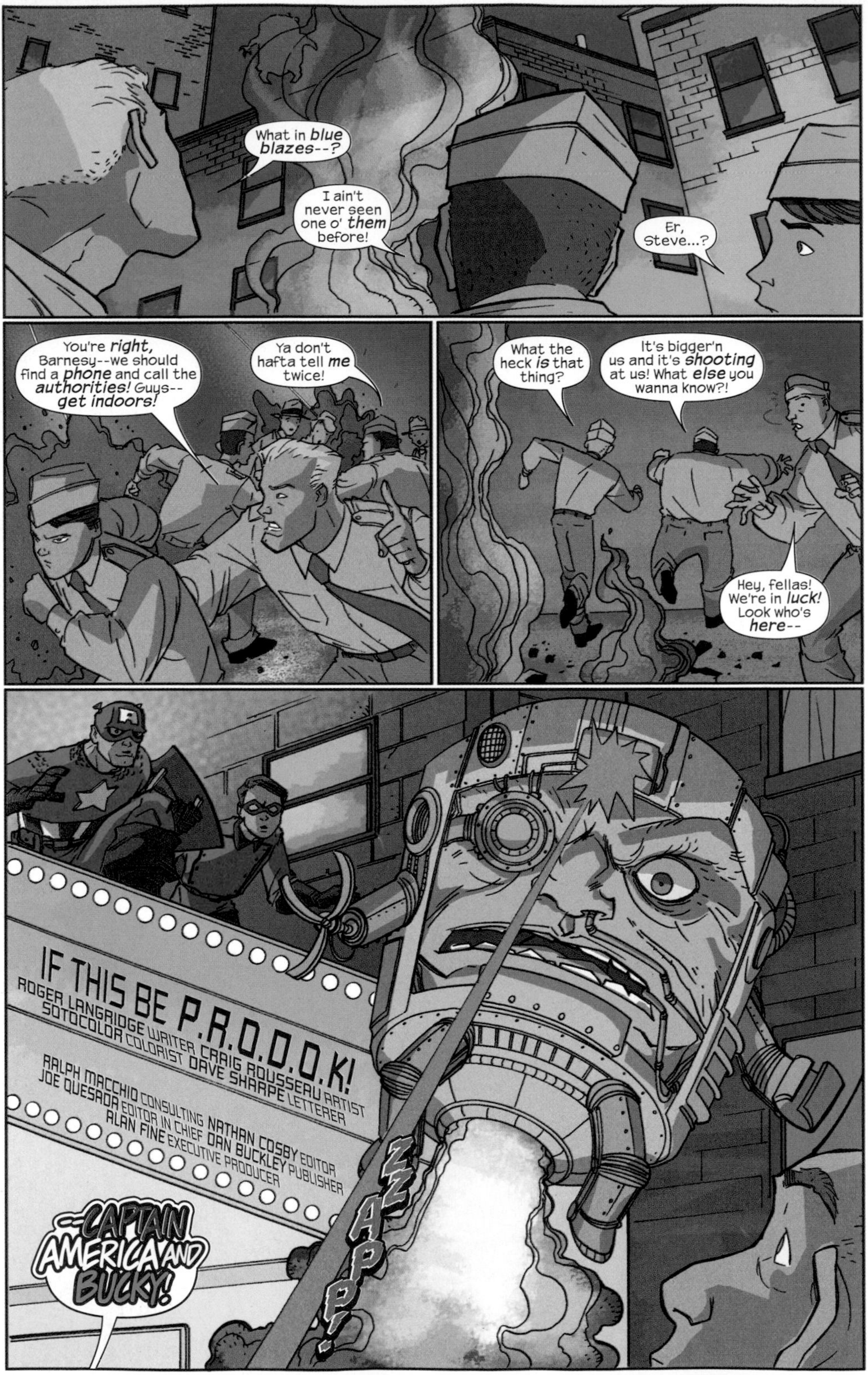
What in blue blazes--?
I ain't never seen one o' them before!
Er, Steve...?
You're right, Barnesy--we should find a phone and call the authorities! Guys-- get indoors!
Ya don't hafta tell me twice!
What the heck is that thing?
It's bigger'n us and it's shooting at us! What else you wanna know?!
Hey, fellas! We're in luck! Look who's here--
IF THIS BE P.R.O.D.O.K!
ROGER LANGRIDGE WRITER CRAIG ROUSSEAU ARTIST
SOTOCOLOR COLORIST DAVE SHARPE LETTERER
RALPH MACCHIO CONSULTING NATHAN COSBY EDITOR
JOE QUESADA EDITOR IN CHIEF DAN BUCKLEY PUBLISHER
ALAN FINE EXECUTIVE PRODUCER
ZZAPP!
--CAPTAIN AMERICA AND BUCKY!

Now *that* has got to be one of the *strangest* things I have ever seen.

Hey, Cap-- I don't think it's after the guys! Did you notice how it's blasting kind of *randomly*?

Randomly... or at something we haven't *noticed* yet! Let's take it down! Maneuver 29-B!

Right behind you!

*Durchlauf! Laufen Sie für Ihre Leben, kleine Flöhe!*

ZZARR!

Get that, Chalky! This is *dynamite!*

Nawww! I only do babies, weddings and *bar mitzvahs!*

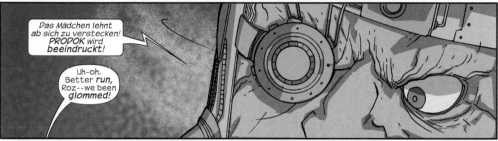

*Das Mädchen lehnt ab sich zu verstecken! PRODOK wird beeindruckt!*

Uh-oh. Better *run*, Roz--we been *glommed!*

*Jetzt laufen Sie! Jetzt Sie Fell!*

K-CHOW!!

Nice knowing you, Chalky!

Pleasure's all mine.

Surprise.

*Was geschieht--?*

SMASSH!

*NEIN!!*

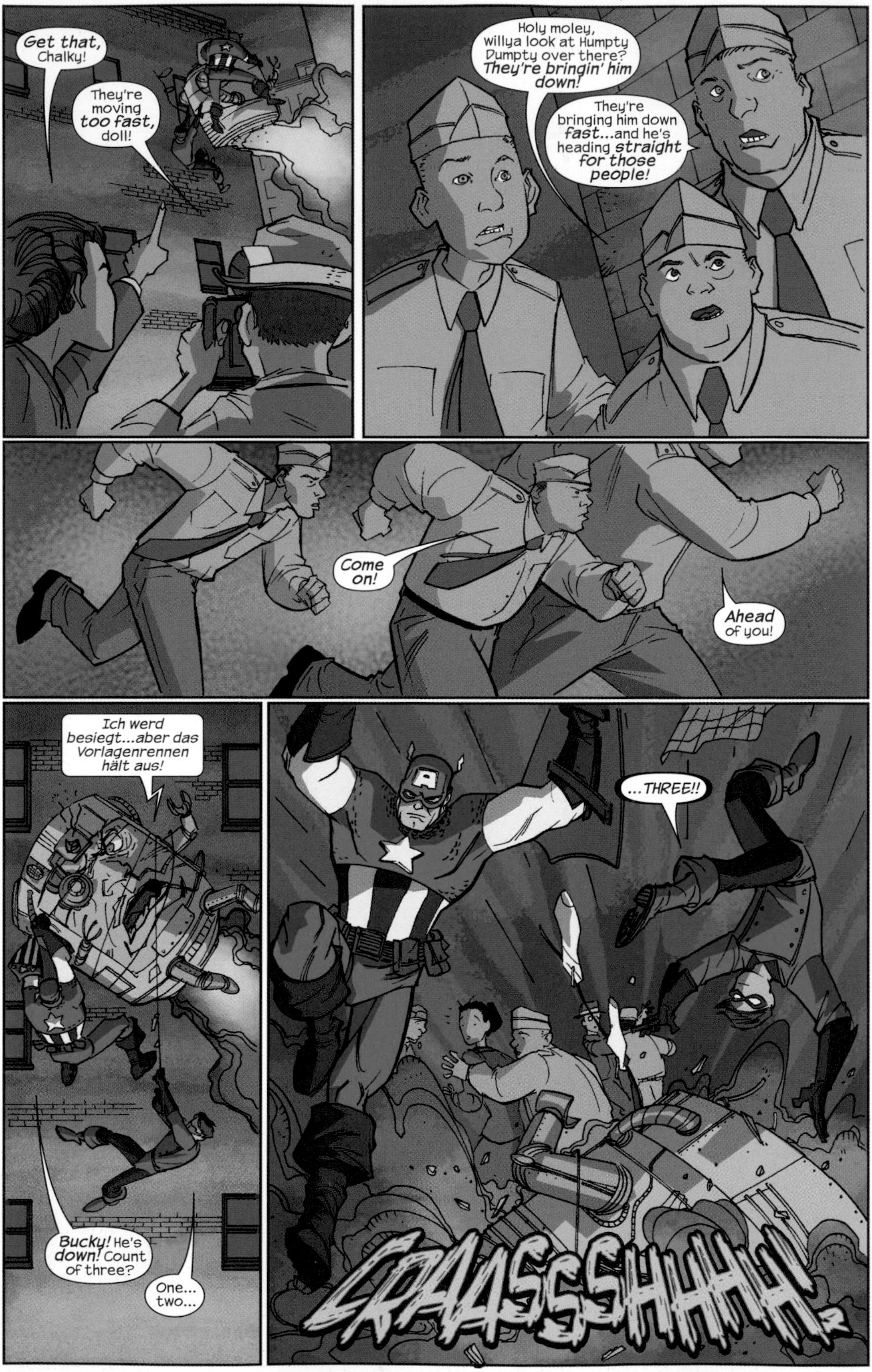

Get that, Chalky!
They're moving too fast, doll!
Holy moley, willya look at Humpty Dumpty over there? They're bringin' him down!
They're bringing him down fast...and he's heading straight for those people!
Come on!
Ahead of you!
Ich werd besiegt...aber das Vorlagenrennen hält aus!
Bucky! He's down! Count of three?
One... two...
...THREE!!
CRAASSSHHHH!

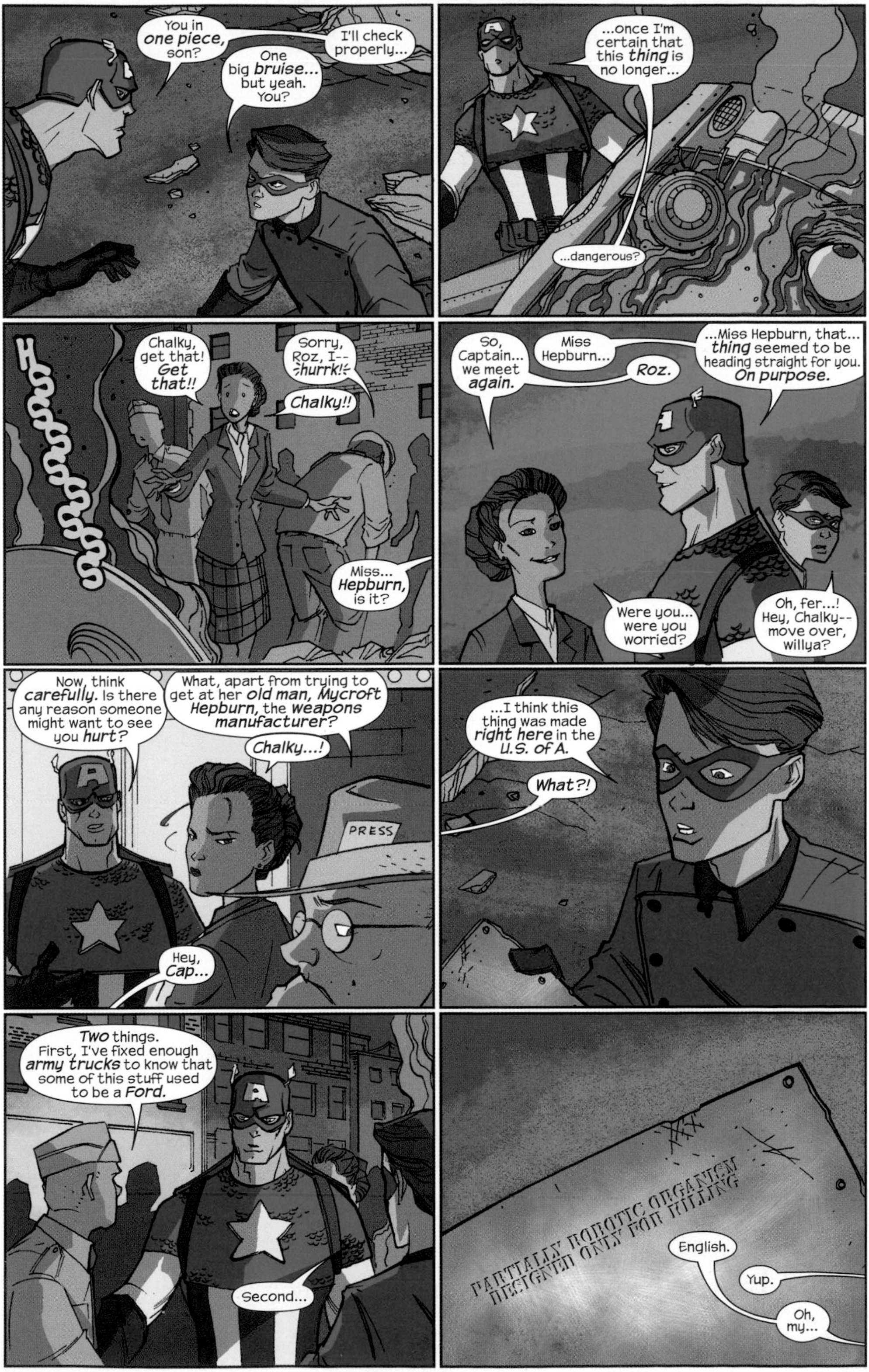
You in one piece, son?
I'll check properly...
One big bruise... but yeah. You?
...once I'm certain that this thing is no longer...
...dangerous?
Chalky, get that! Get that!!
Sorry, Roz, I-- hurrk!
Chalky!!
Miss... Hepburn, is it?
So, Captain... we meet again.
Miss Hepburn...
Roz.
...Miss Hepburn, that... thing seemed to be heading straight for you. On purpose.
Were you... were you worried?
Oh, fer...! Hey, Chalky-- move over, willya?
Now, think carefully. Is there any reason someone might want to see you hurt?
What, apart from trying to get at her old man, Mycroft Hepburn, the weapons manufacturer?
Chalky...!
PRESS
Hey, Cap...
...I think this thing was made right here in the U.S. of A.
What?!
Two things. First, I've fixed enough army trucks to know that some of this stuff used to be a Ford.
Second...
PARTIALLY ROBOTIC ORGANISM
DESIGNED ONLY FOR KILLING
English.
Yup.
Oh, my...

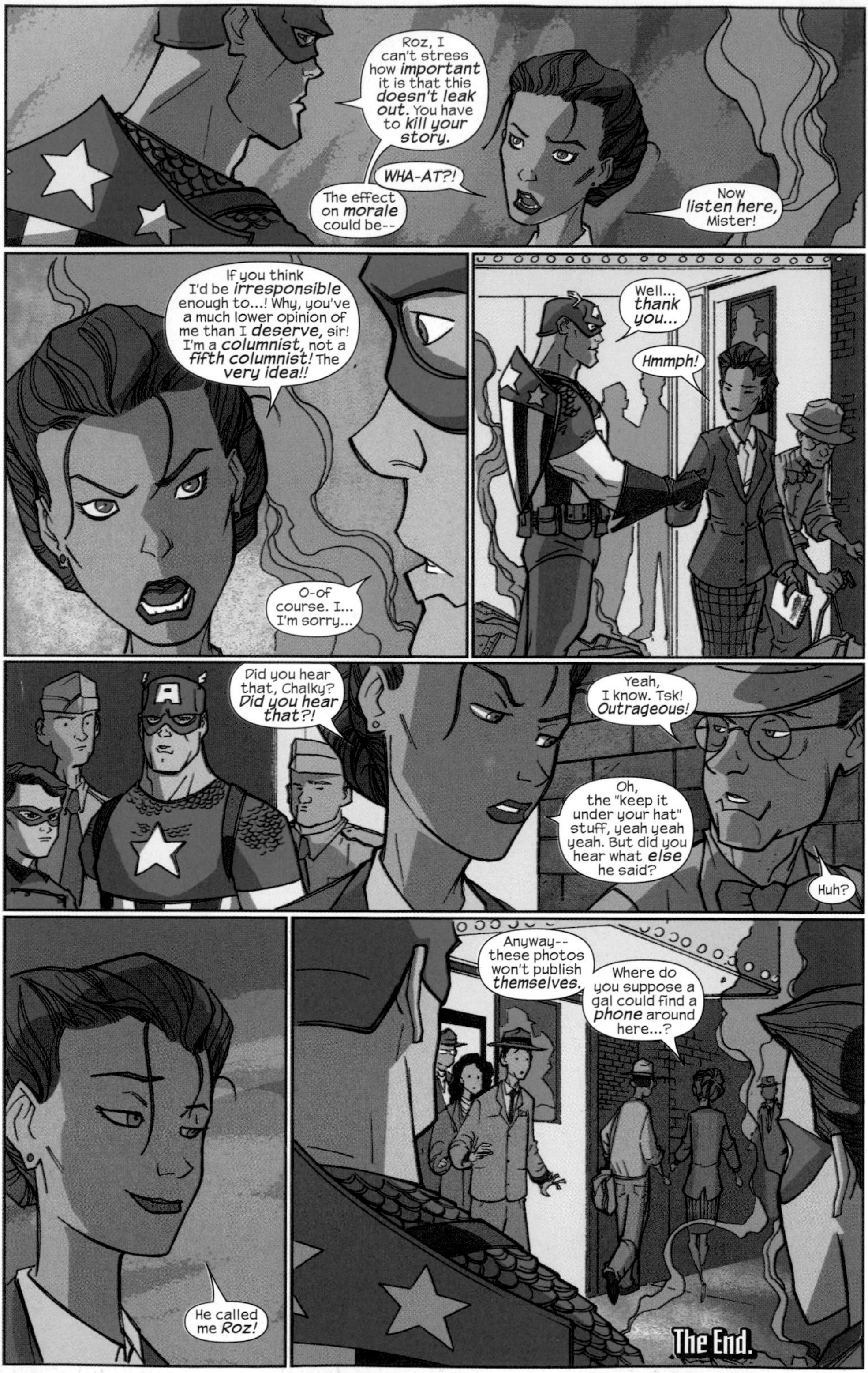
Roz, I can't stress how *important* it is that this *doesn't leak out.* You have to *kill your story.*
WHA-AT?!
The effect on *morale* could be--
Now *listen here,* Mister!
If you think I'd be *irresponsible* enough to...! Why, you've a much lower opinion of me than I *deserve,* sir! I'm a *columnist,* not a *fifth columnist!* The *very idea!!*
O-of course. I... I'm sorry...
Well... *thank you...*
*Hmmph!*
Did you hear that, Chalky? *Did you hear that?!*
Yeah, I know. Tsk! *Outrageous!*
Oh, the "keep it under your hat" stuff, yeah yeah yeah. But did you hear what *else* he said?
Huh?
He called me *Roz!*
Anyway-- these photos won't publish *themselves.*
Where do you suppose a gal could find a *phone* around here...?
The End.

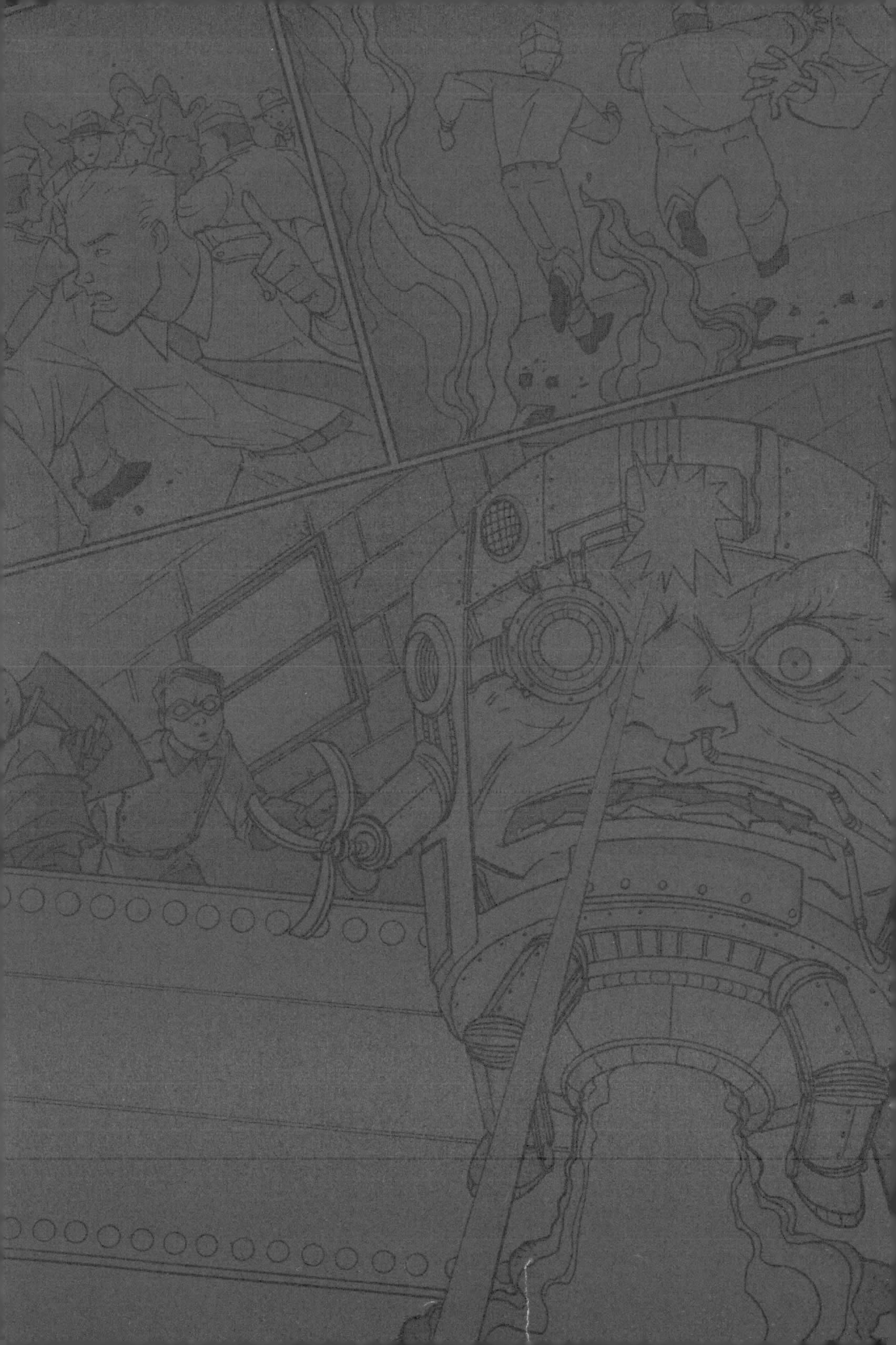

03

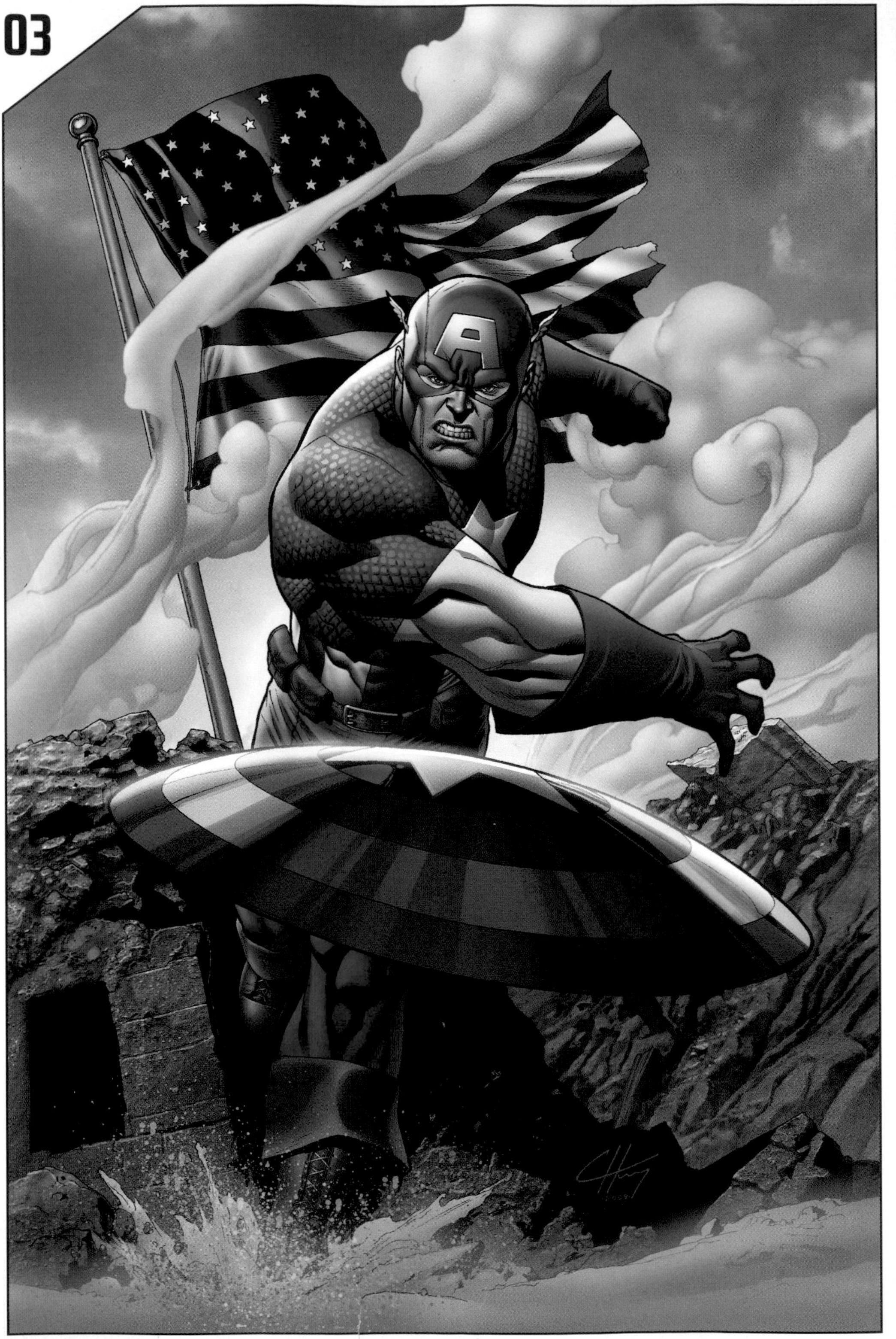

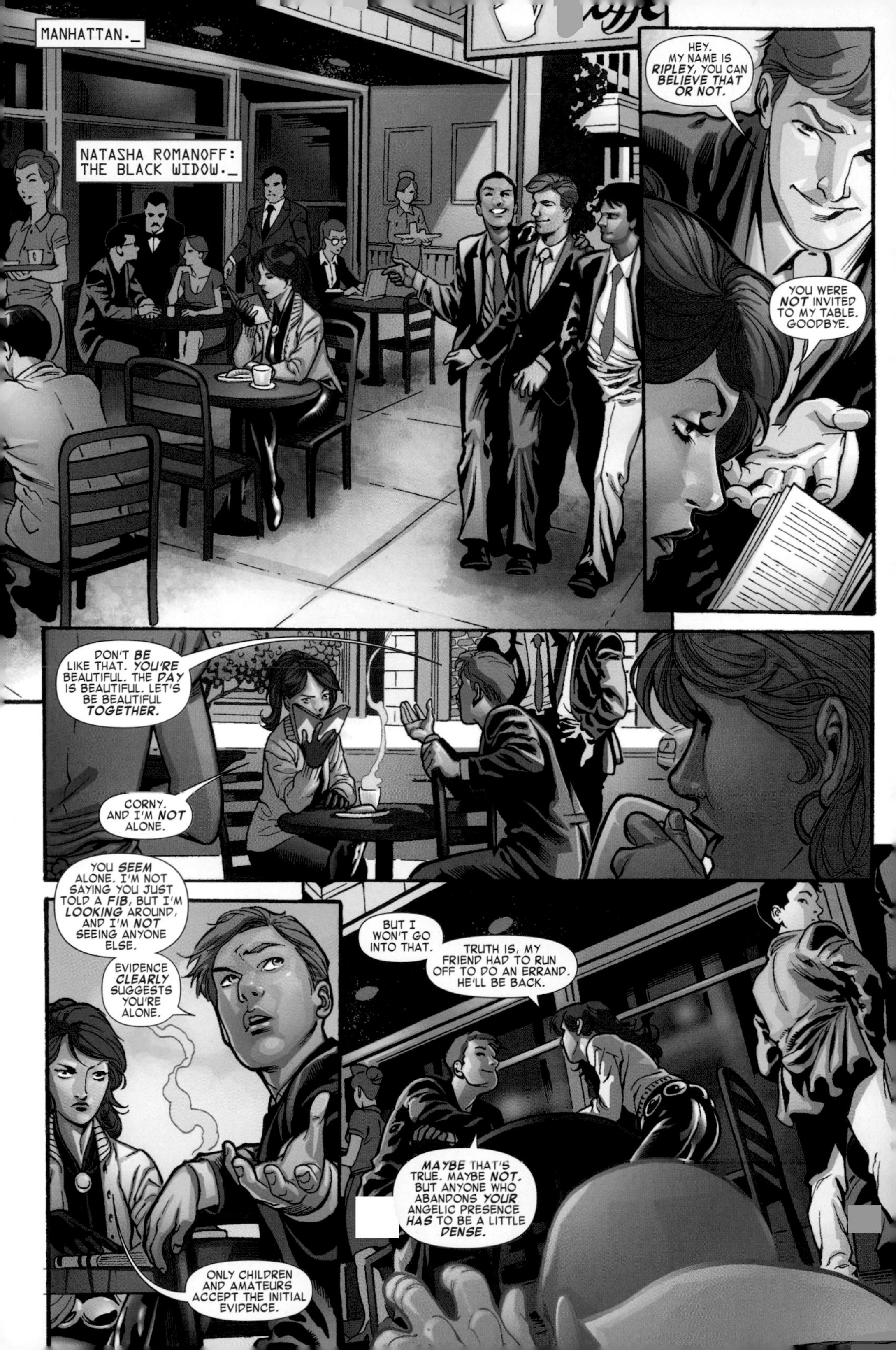
MANHATTAN._
NATASHA ROMANOFF: THE BLACK WIDOW._
HEY. MY NAME IS RIPLEY, YOU CAN BELIEVE THAT OR NOT.
YOU WERE NOT INVITED TO MY TABLE. GOODBYE.
DON'T BE LIKE THAT. YOU'RE BEAUTIFUL. THE DAY IS BEAUTIFUL. LET'S BE BEAUTIFUL TOGETHER.
CORNY. AND I'M NOT ALONE.
YOU SEEM ALONE. I'M NOT SAYING YOU JUST TOLD A FIB, BUT I'M LOOKING AROUND, AND I'M NOT SEEING ANYONE ELSE.
EVIDENCE CLEARLY SUGGESTS YOU'RE ALONE.
ONLY CHILDREN AND AMATEURS ACCEPT THE INITIAL EVIDENCE.
BUT I WON'T GO INTO THAT.
TRUTH IS, MY FRIEND HAD TO RUN OFF TO DO AN ERRAND. HE'LL BE BACK.
MAYBE THAT'S TRUE. MAYBE NOT. BUT ANYONE WHO ABANDONS YOUR ANGELIC PRESENCE HAS TO BE A LITTLE DENSE.

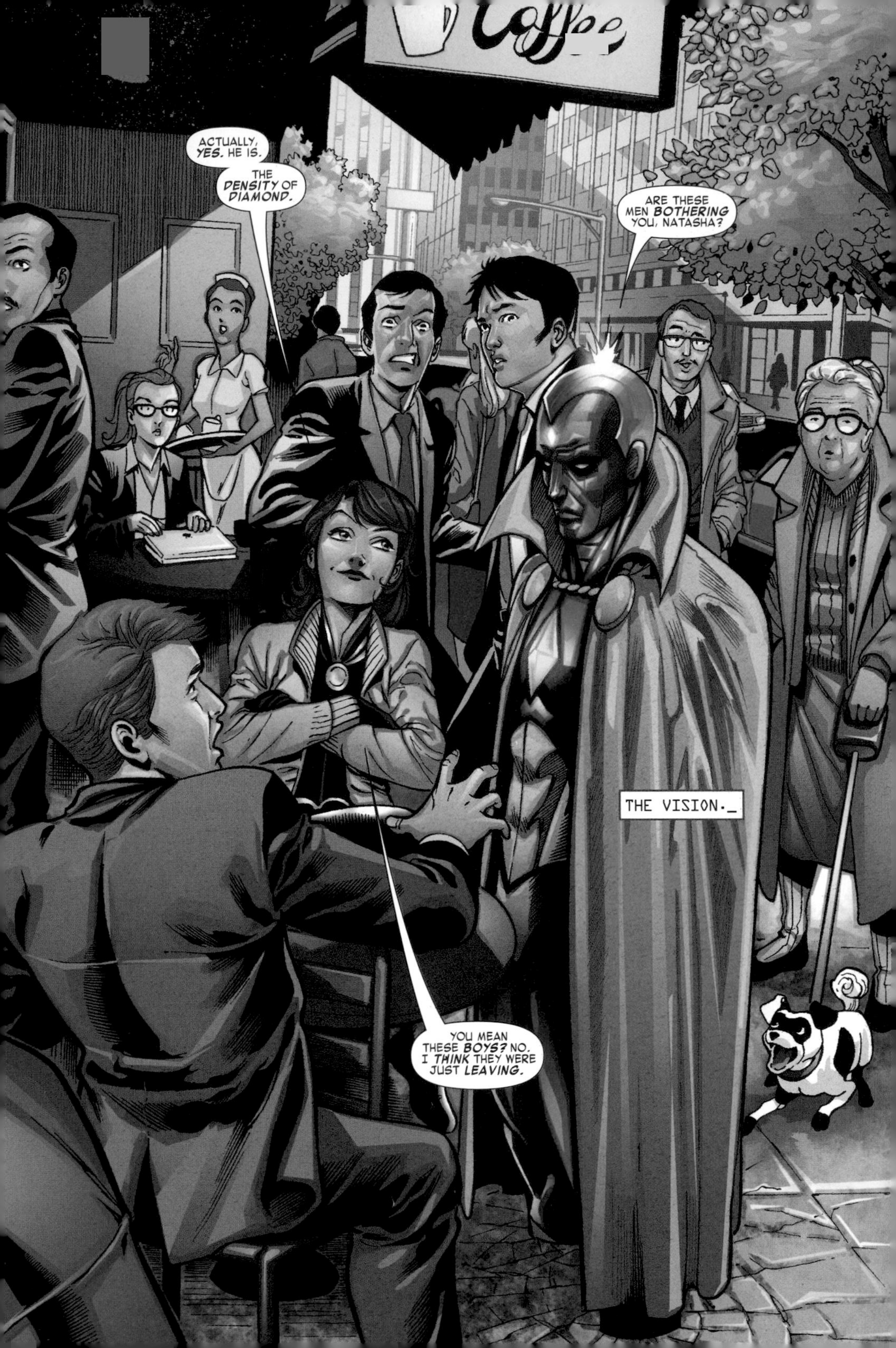
ACTUALLY, YES. HE IS.
THE DENSITY OF DIAMOND.
ARE THESE MEN BOTHERING YOU, NATASHA?
THE VISION._
YOU MEAN THESE BOYS? NO. I THINK THEY WERE JUST LEAVING.

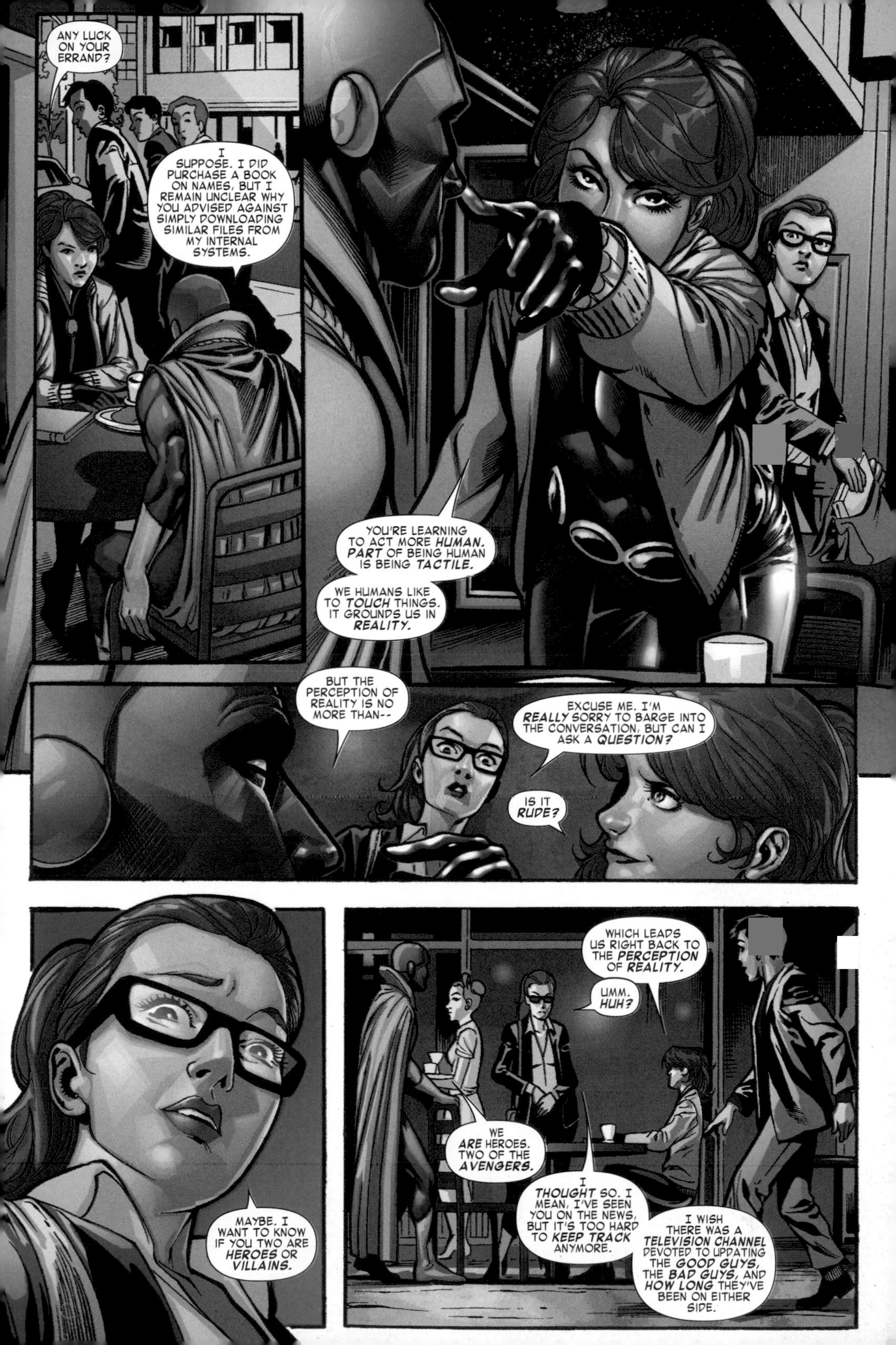
ANY LUCK ON YOUR ERRAND?
I SUPPOSE. I DID PURCHASE A BOOK ON NAMES, BUT I REMAIN UNCLEAR WHY YOU ADVISED AGAINST SIMPLY DOWNLOADING SIMILAR FILES FROM MY INTERNAL SYSTEMS.
YOU'RE LEARNING TO ACT MORE HUMAN. PART OF BEING HUMAN IS BEING TACTILE.
WE HUMANS LIKE TO TOUCH THINGS. IT GROUNDS US IN REALITY.
BUT THE PERCEPTION OF REALITY IS NO MORE THAN--
EXCUSE ME. I'M REALLY SORRY TO BARGE INTO THE CONVERSATION, BUT CAN I ASK A QUESTION?
IS IT RUDE?
MAYBE. I WANT TO KNOW IF YOU TWO ARE HEROES OR VILLAINS.
WHICH LEADS US RIGHT BACK TO THE PERCEPTION OF REALITY.
UMM. HUH?
WE ARE HEROES. TWO OF THE AVENGERS.
I THOUGHT SO. I MEAN, I'VE SEEN YOU ON THE NEWS, BUT IT'S TOO HARD TO KEEP TRACK ANYMORE.
I WISH THERE WAS A TELEVISION CHANNEL DEVOTED TO UPDATING THE GOOD GUYS, THE BAD GUYS, AND HOW LONG THEY'VE BEEN ON EITHER SIDE.

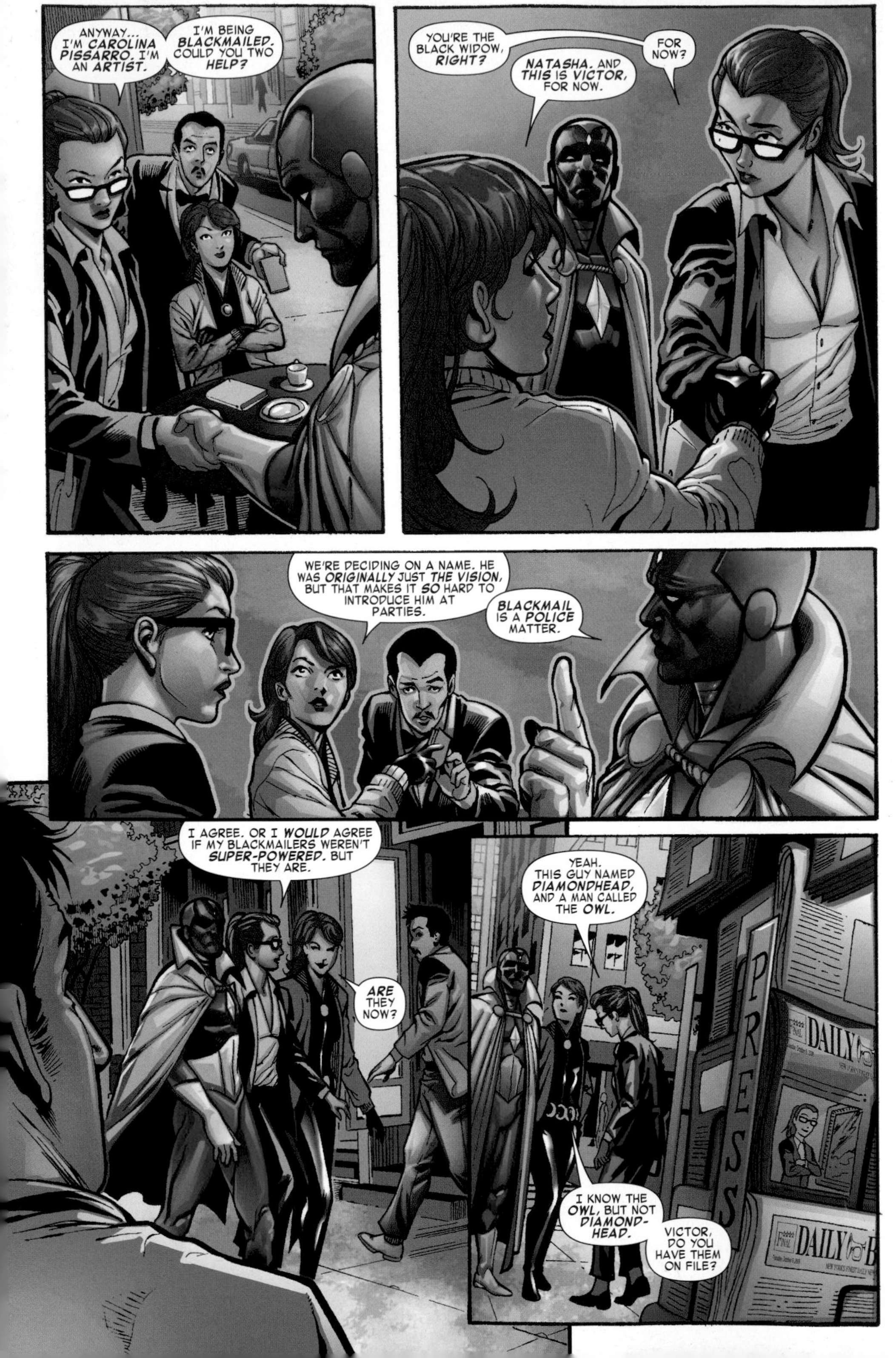
ANYWAY... I'M CAROLINA PISSARRO. I'M AN ARTIST.
I'M BEING BLACKMAILED. COULD YOU TWO HELP?
YOU'RE THE BLACK WIDOW, RIGHT?
NATASHA. AND THIS IS VICTOR, FOR NOW.
FOR NOW?
WE'RE DECIDING ON A NAME. HE WAS ORIGINALLY JUST THE VISION, BUT THAT MAKES IT SO HARD TO INTRODUCE HIM AT PARTIES.
BLACKMAIL IS A POLICE MATTER.
I AGREE. OR I WOULD AGREE IF MY BLACKMAILERS WEREN'T SUPER-POWERED. BUT THEY ARE.
ARE THEY NOW?
YEAH. THIS GUY NAMED DIAMONDHEAD, AND A MAN CALLED THE OWL.
PRESS
DAILY
I KNOW THE OWL, BUT NOT DIAMOND-HEAD.
VICTOR, DO YOU HAVE THEM ON FILE?

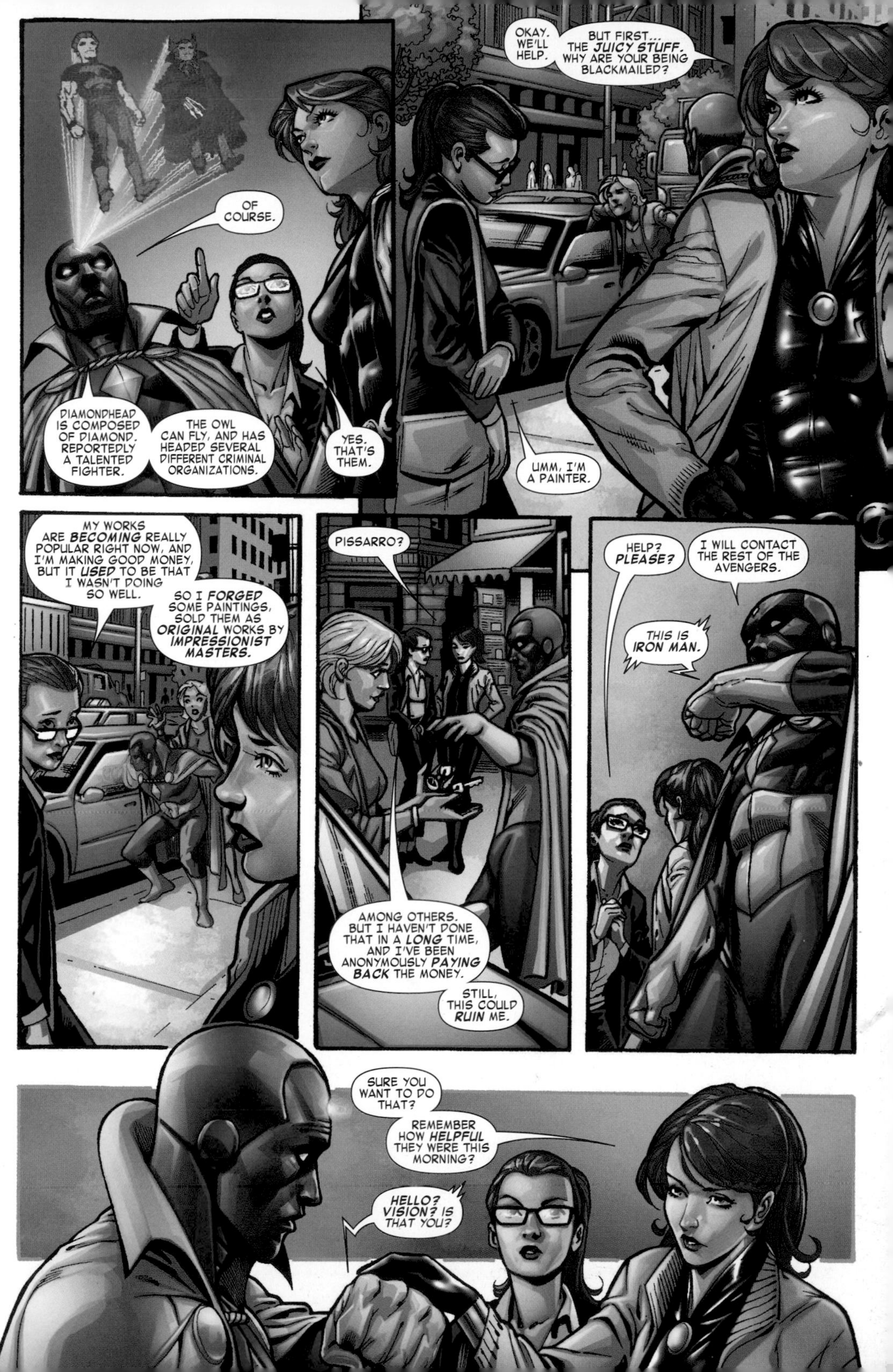
OF COURSE.
DIAMONDHEAD IS COMPOSED OF DIAMOND. REPORTEDLY A TALENTED FIGHTER.
THE OWL CAN FLY, AND HAS HEADED SEVERAL DIFFERENT CRIMINAL ORGANIZATIONS.
YES. THAT'S THEM.
OKAY. WE'LL HELP.
BUT FIRST... THE JUICY STUFF. WHY ARE YOUR BEING BLACKMAILED?
UMM, I'M A PAINTER.
MY WORKS ARE BECOMING REALLY POPULAR RIGHT NOW, AND I'M MAKING GOOD MONEY, BUT IT USED TO BE THAT I WASN'T DOING SO WELL.
SO I FORGED SOME PAINTINGS, SOLD THEM AS ORIGINAL WORKS BY IMPRESSIONIST MASTERS.
PISSARRO?
AMONG OTHERS. BUT I HAVEN'T DONE THAT IN A LONG TIME, AND I'VE BEEN ANONYMOUSLY PAYING BACK THE MONEY.
STILL, THIS COULD RUIN ME.
HELP? PLEASE?
I WILL CONTACT THE REST OF THE AVENGERS.
THIS IS IRON MAN.
SURE YOU WANT TO DO THAT?
REMEMBER HOW HELPFUL THEY WERE THIS MORNING?
HELLO? VISION? IS THAT YOU?

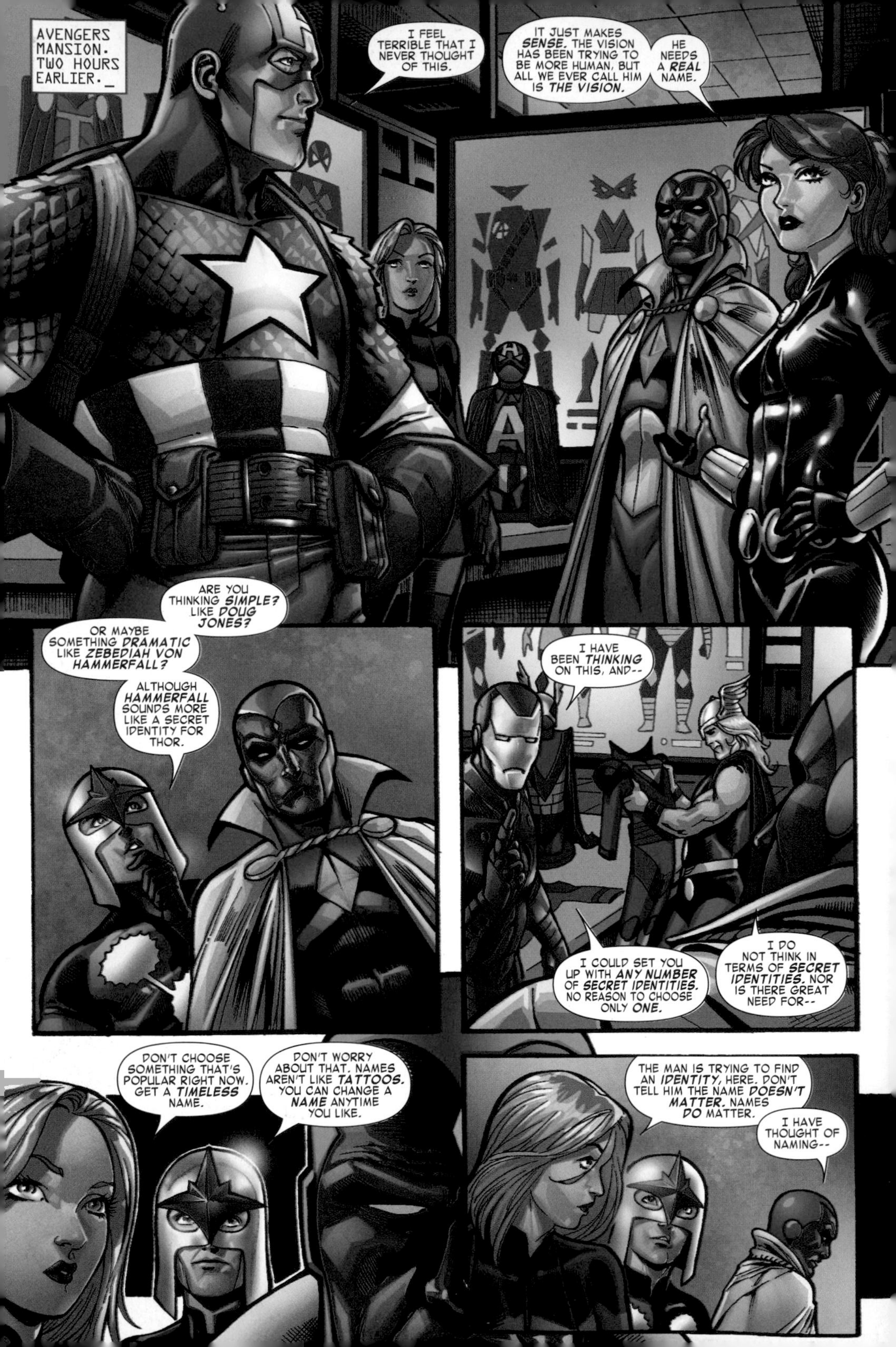
AVENGERS MANSION. TWO HOURS EARLIER._
I FEEL TERRIBLE THAT I NEVER THOUGHT OF THIS.
IT JUST MAKES SENSE. THE VISION HAS BEEN TRYING TO BE MORE HUMAN, BUT ALL WE EVER CALL HIM IS THE VISION.
HE NEEDS A REAL NAME.
ARE YOU THINKING SIMPLE? LIKE DOUG JONES?
OR MAYBE SOMETHING DRAMATIC LIKE ZEBEDIAH VON HAMMERFALL?
ALTHOUGH HAMMERFALL SOUNDS MORE LIKE A SECRET IDENTITY FOR THOR.
I HAVE BEEN THINKING ON THIS, AND--
I COULD SET YOU UP WITH ANY NUMBER OF SECRET IDENTITIES. NO REASON TO CHOOSE ONLY ONE.
I DO NOT THINK IN TERMS OF SECRET IDENTITIES. NOR IS THERE GREAT NEED FOR--
DON'T CHOOSE SOMETHING THAT'S POPULAR RIGHT NOW. GET A TIMELESS NAME.
DON'T WORRY ABOUT THAT. NAMES AREN'T LIKE TATTOOS. YOU CAN CHANGE A NAME ANYTIME YOU LIKE.
THE MAN IS TRYING TO FIND AN IDENTITY, HERE. DON'T TELL HIM THE NAME DOESN'T MATTER. NAMES DO MATTER.
I HAVE THOUGHT OF NAMING--

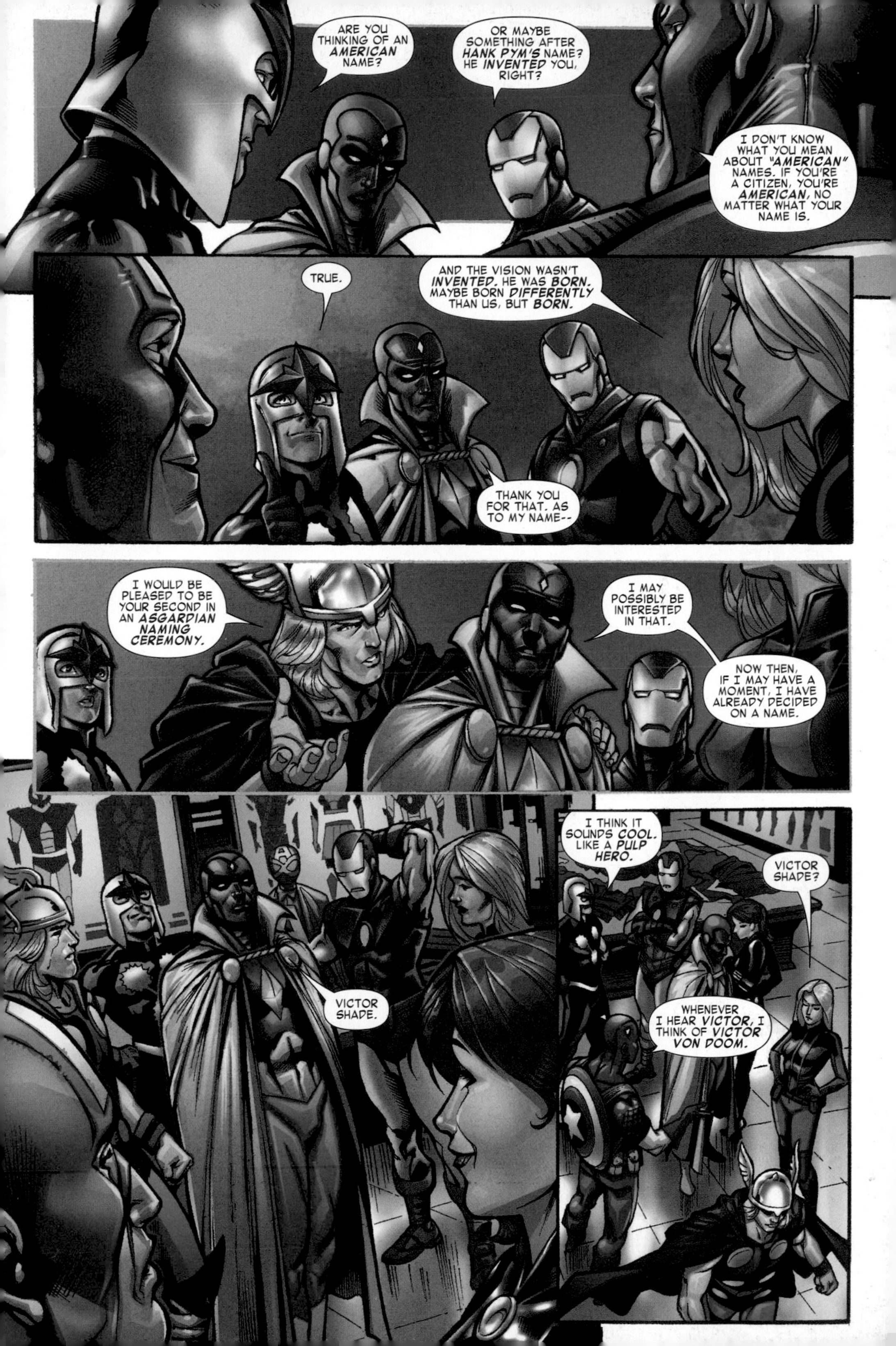

ARE YOU THINKING OF AN AMERICAN NAME?
OR MAYBE SOMETHING AFTER HANK PYM'S NAME? HE INVENTED YOU, RIGHT?
I DON'T KNOW WHAT YOU MEAN ABOUT "AMERICAN" NAMES. IF YOU'RE A CITIZEN, YOU'RE AMERICAN, NO MATTER WHAT YOUR NAME IS.
TRUE.
AND THE VISION WASN'T INVENTED. HE WAS BORN. MAYBE BORN DIFFERENTLY THAN US, BUT BORN.
THANK YOU FOR THAT. AS TO MY NAME--
I WOULD BE PLEASED TO BE YOUR SECOND IN AN ASGARDIAN NAMING CEREMONY.
I MAY POSSIBLY BE INTERESTED IN THAT.
NOW THEN, IF I MAY HAVE A MOMENT, I HAVE ALREADY DECIDED ON A NAME.
VICTOR SHADE.
I THINK IT SOUNDS COOL. LIKE A PULP HERO.
VICTOR SHADE?
WHENEVER I HEAR VICTOR, I THINK OF VICTOR VON DOOM.

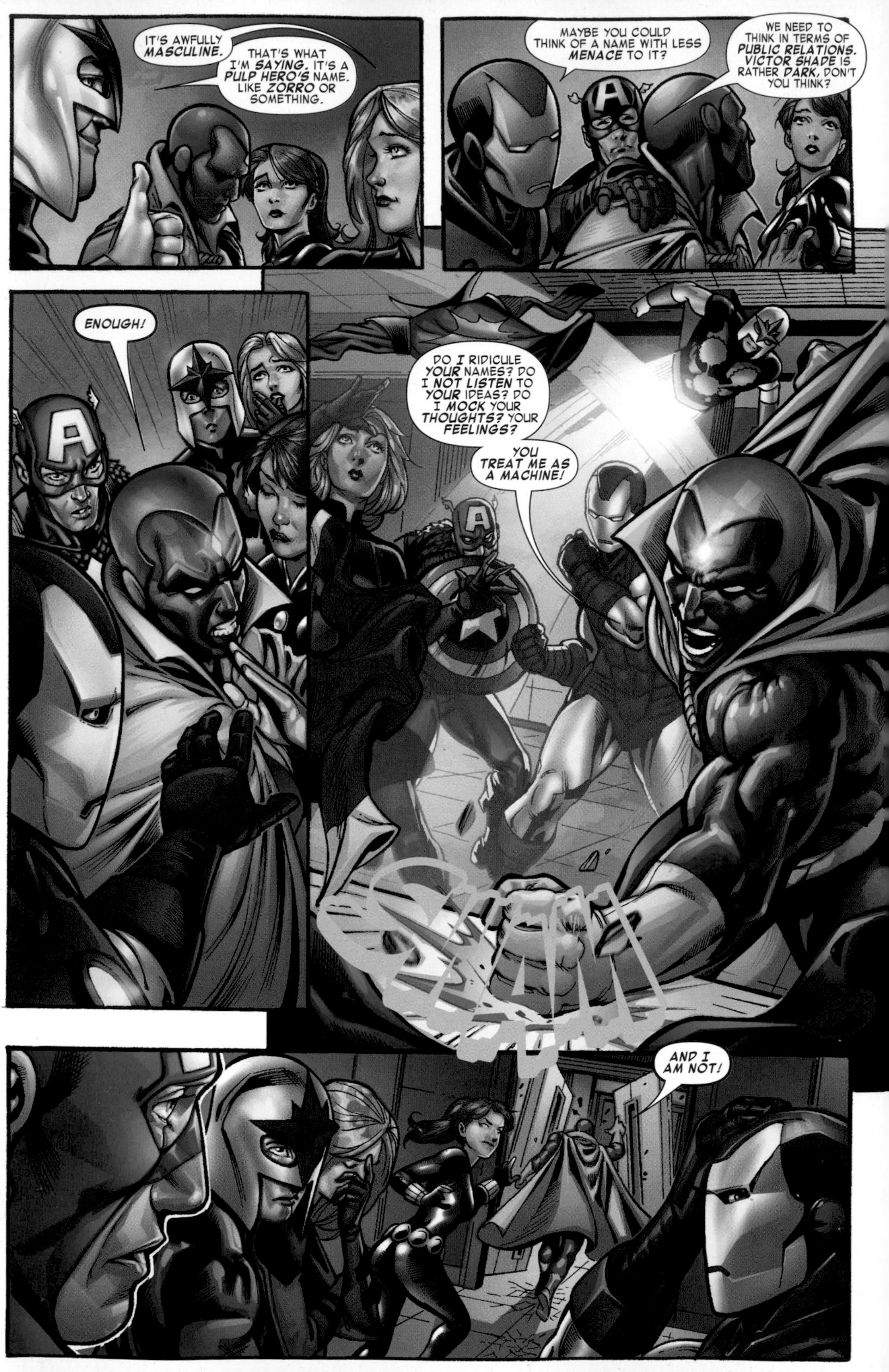
IT'S AWFULLY MASCULINE.
THAT'S WHAT I'M SAYING. IT'S A PULP HERO'S NAME. LIKE ZORRO OR SOMETHING.
MAYBE YOU COULD THINK OF A NAME WITH LESS MENACE TO IT?
WE NEED TO THINK IN TERMS OF PUBLIC RELATIONS. VICTOR SHADE IS RATHER DARK, DON'T YOU THINK?
ENOUGH!
DO I RIDICULE YOUR NAMES? DO I NOT LISTEN TO YOUR IDEAS? DO I MOCK YOUR THOUGHTS? YOUR FEELINGS?
YOU TREAT ME AS A MACHINE!
AND I AM NOT!

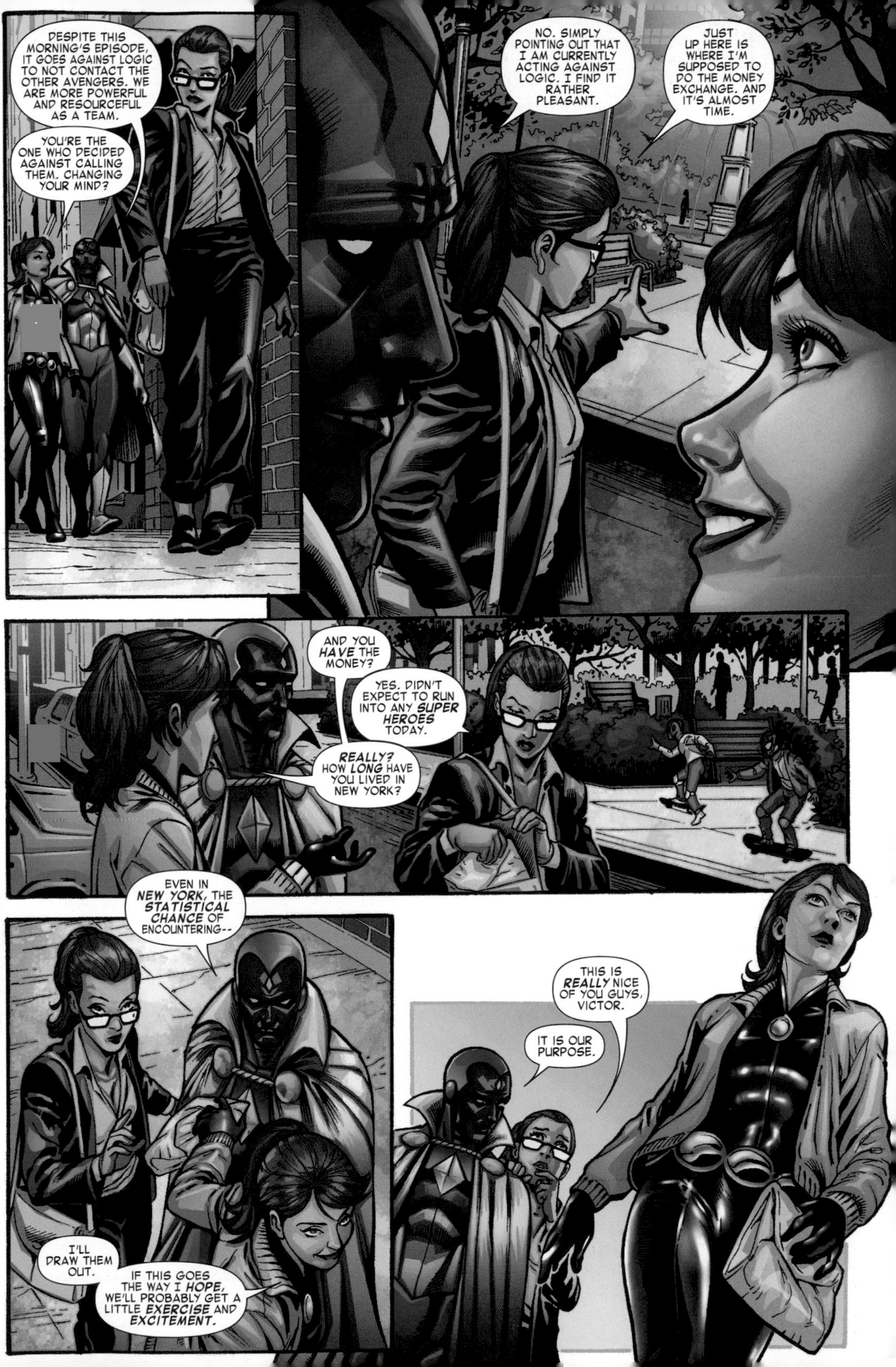

DESPITE THIS MORNING'S EPISODE, IT GOES AGAINST LOGIC TO NOT CONTACT THE OTHER AVENGERS. WE ARE MORE POWERFUL AND RESOURCEFUL AS A TEAM.
YOU'RE THE ONE WHO DECIDED AGAINST CALLING THEM. CHANGING YOUR MIND?
NO. SIMPLY POINTING OUT THAT I AM CURRENTLY ACTING AGAINST LOGIC. I FIND IT RATHER PLEASANT.
JUST UP HERE IS WHERE I'M SUPPOSED TO DO THE MONEY EXCHANGE. AND IT'S ALMOST TIME.
AND YOU HAVE THE MONEY?
YES. DIDN'T EXPECT TO RUN INTO ANY SUPER HEROES TODAY.
REALLY? HOW LONG HAVE YOU LIVED IN NEW YORK?
EVEN IN NEW YORK, THE STATISTICAL CHANCE OF ENCOUNTERING--
I'LL DRAW THEM OUT.
IF THIS GOES THE WAY I HOPE, WE'LL PROBABLY GET A LITTLE EXERCISE AND EXCITEMENT.
THIS IS REALLY NICE OF YOU GUYS, VICTOR.
IT IS OUR PURPOSE.

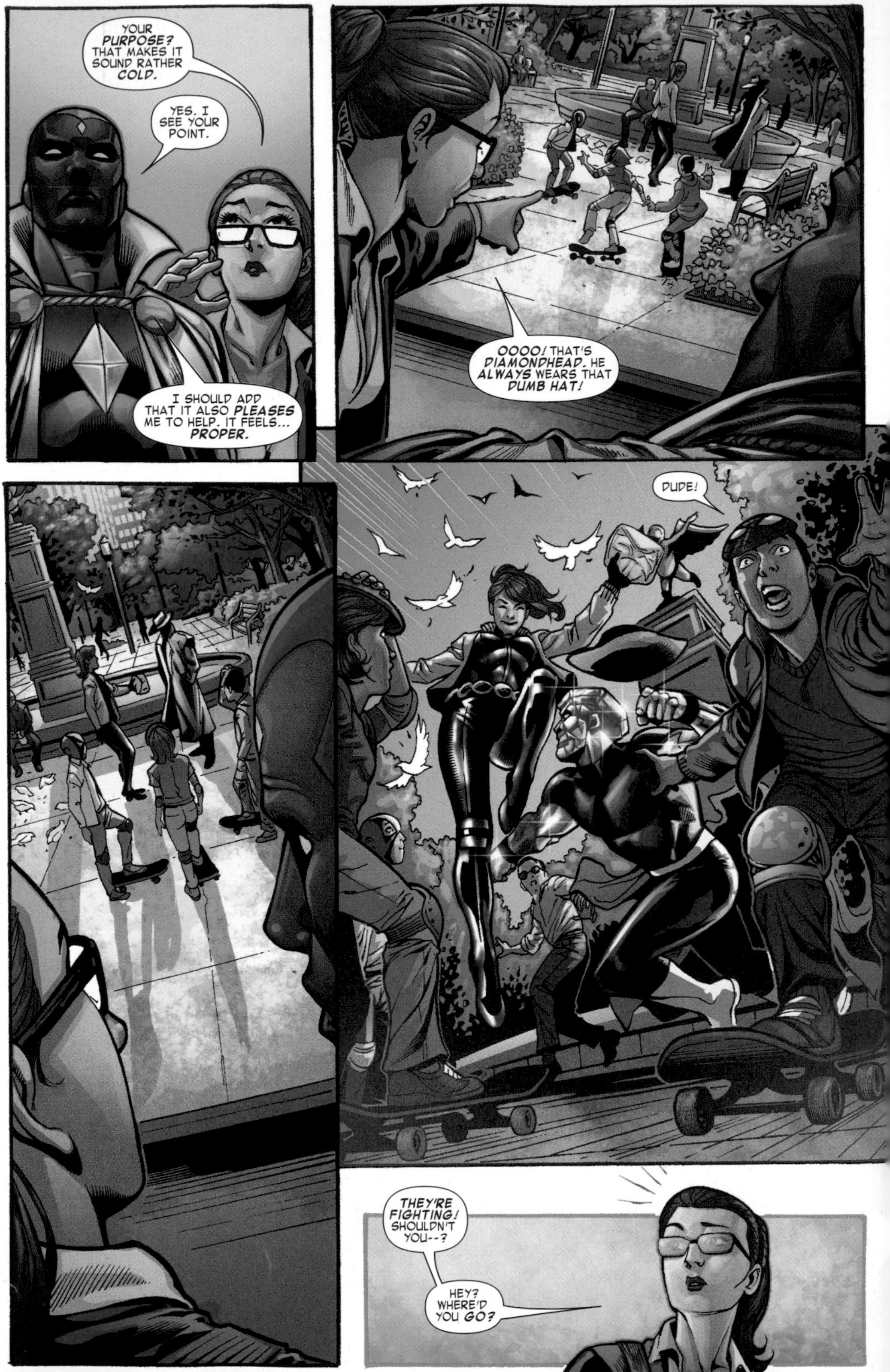
YOUR PURPOSE? THAT MAKES IT SOUND RATHER COLD.
YES. I SEE YOUR POINT.
I SHOULD ADD THAT IT ALSO PLEASES ME TO HELP. IT FEELS... PROPER.
OOOO! THAT'S DIAMONDHEAD. HE ALWAYS WEARS THAT DUMB HAT!
DUDE!
THEY'RE FIGHTING! SHOULDN'T YOU--?
HEY? WHERE'D YOU GO?

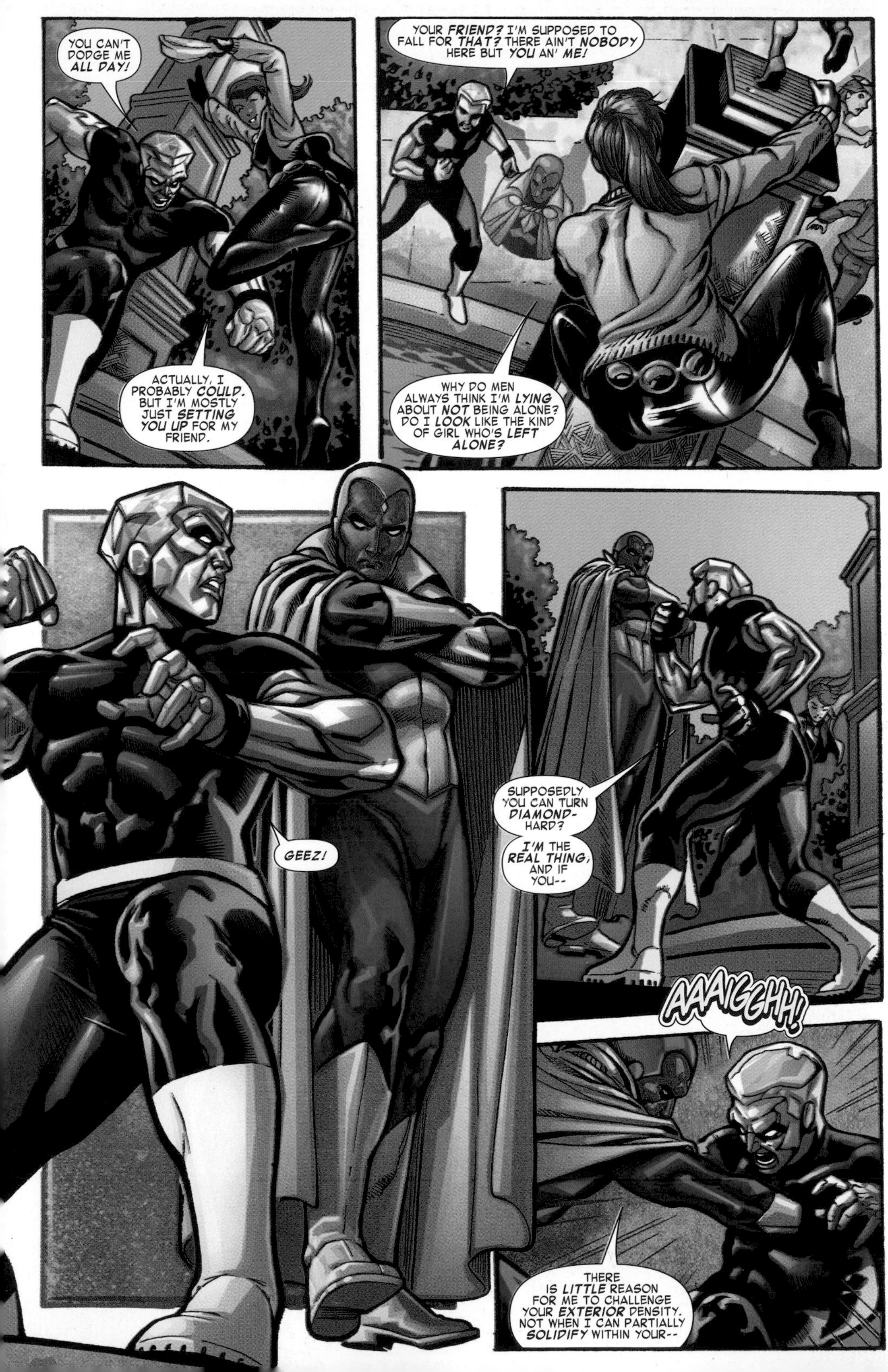
YOU CAN'T DODGE ME ALL DAY!
ACTUALLY, I PROBABLY COULD. BUT I'M MOSTLY JUST SETTING YOU UP FOR MY FRIEND.
YOUR FRIEND? I'M SUPPOSED TO FALL FOR THAT? THERE AIN'T NOBODY HERE BUT YOU AN' ME!
WHY DO MEN ALWAYS THINK I'M LYING ABOUT NOT BEING ALONE? DO I LOOK LIKE THE KIND OF GIRL WHO'S LEFT ALONE?
GEEZ!
SUPPOSEDLY YOU CAN TURN DIAMOND-HARD?
I'M THE REAL THING, AND IF YOU--
AAAIGGHH!
THERE IS LITTLE REASON FOR ME TO CHALLENGE YOUR EXTERIOR DENSITY. NOT WHEN I CAN PARTIALLY SOLIDIFY WITHIN YOUR--

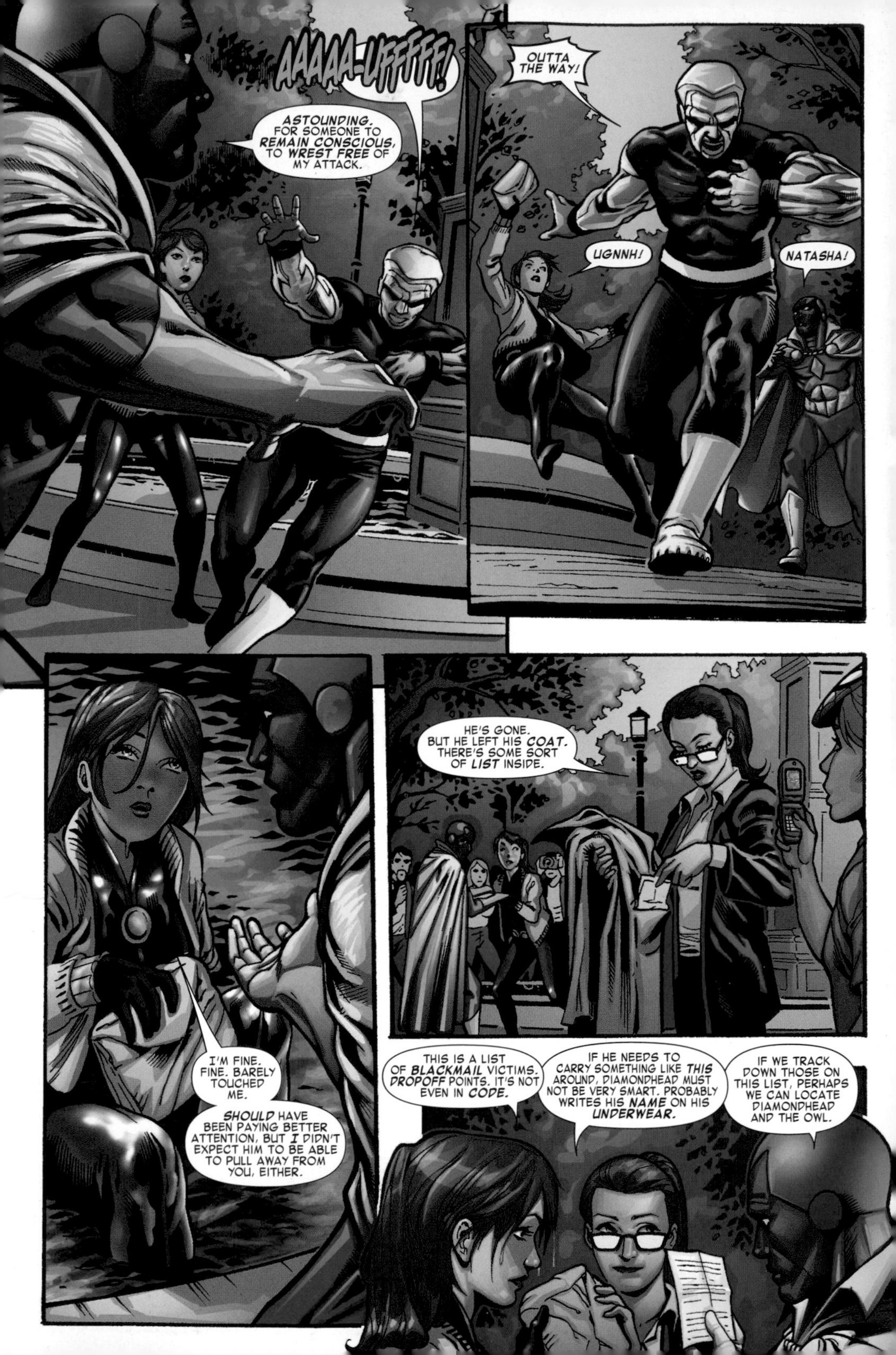
AAAAA-UFFFFF!
ASTOUNDING. FOR SOMEONE TO REMAIN CONSCIOUS, TO WREST FREE OF MY ATTACK.
OUTTA THE WAY!
UGNNH!
NATASHA!
I'M FINE. FINE. BARELY TOUCHED ME.
SHOULD HAVE BEEN PAYING BETTER ATTENTION, BUT I DIDN'T EXPECT HIM TO BE ABLE TO PULL AWAY FROM YOU, EITHER.
HE'S GONE. BUT HE LEFT HIS COAT. THERE'S SOME SORT OF LIST INSIDE.
THIS IS A LIST OF BLACKMAIL VICTIMS. DROPOFF POINTS. IT'S NOT EVEN IN CODE.
IF HE NEEDS TO CARRY SOMETHING LIKE THIS AROUND, DIAMONDHEAD MUST NOT BE VERY SMART. PROBABLY WRITES HIS NAME ON HIS UNDERWEAR.
IF WE TRACK DOWN THOSE ON THIS LIST, PERHAPS WE CAN LOCATE DIAMONDHEAD AND THE OWL.

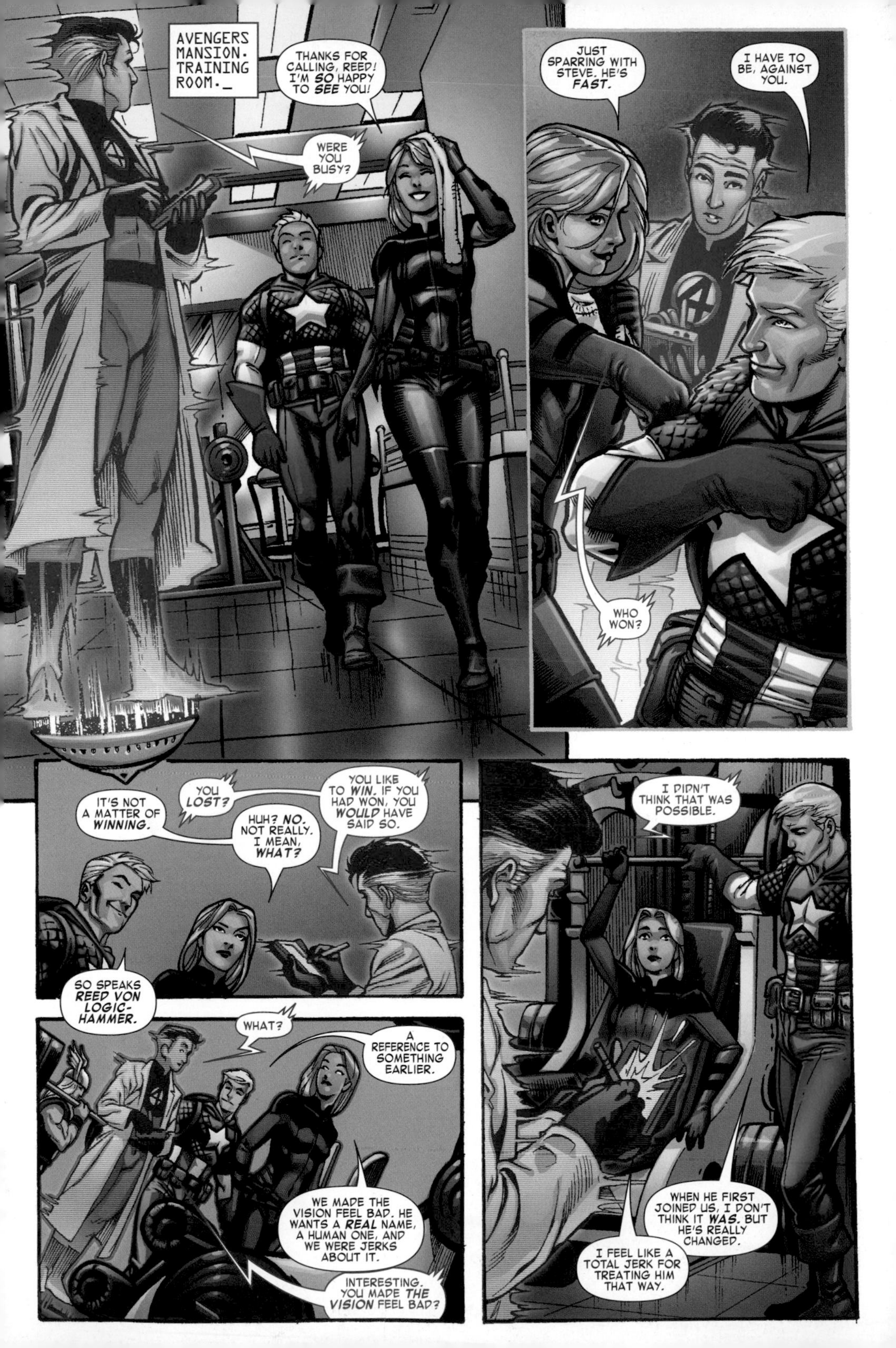

AVENGERS MANSION. TRAINING ROOM.
THANKS FOR CALLING, REED! I'M *SO* HAPPY TO *SEE* YOU!
WERE YOU BUSY?
JUST SPARRING WITH STEVE. HE'S *FAST.*
I HAVE TO BE, AGAINST YOU.
WHO WON?
IT'S NOT A MATTER OF *WINNING.*
YOU *LOST?*
HUH? *NO.* NOT REALLY. I MEAN, *WHAT?*
YOU LIKE TO *WIN.* IF YOU HAD WON, YOU *WOULD* HAVE SAID SO.
SO SPEAKS *REED VON LOGIC-HAMMER.*
WHAT?
A REFERENCE TO SOMETHING EARLIER.
WE MADE THE VISION FEEL BAD. HE WANTS A *REAL* NAME, A HUMAN ONE, AND WE WERE JERKS ABOUT IT.
INTERESTING. YOU MADE *THE VISION* FEEL BAD?
I DIDN'T THINK THAT WAS POSSIBLE.
WHEN HE FIRST JOINED US, I DON'T THINK IT *WAS.* BUT HE'S REALLY CHANGED.
I FEEL LIKE A TOTAL JERK FOR TREATING HIM THAT WAY.

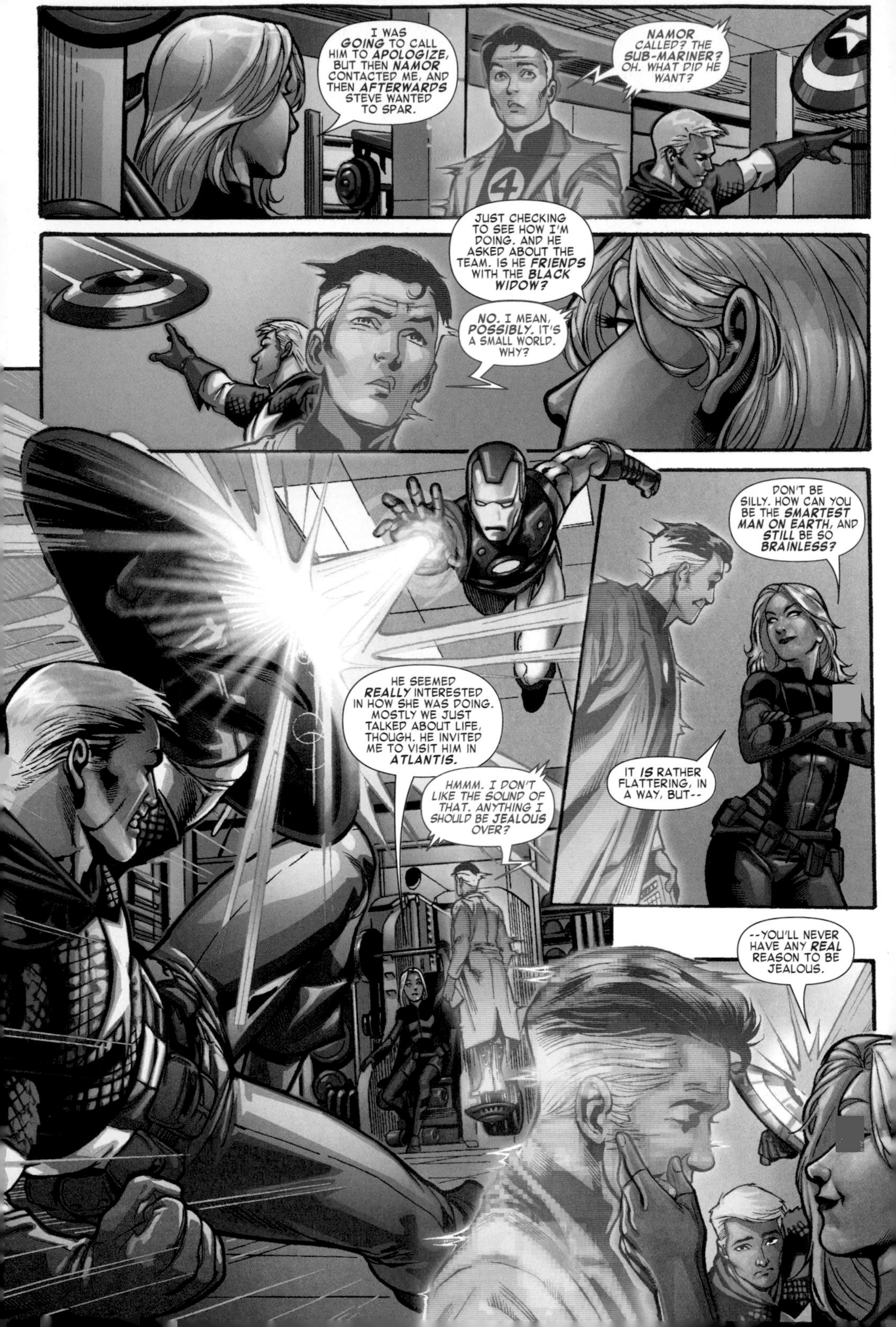
I WAS GOING TO CALL HIM TO APOLOGIZE, BUT THEN NAMOR CONTACTED ME, AND THEN AFTERWARDS STEVE WANTED TO SPAR.
NAMOR CALLED? THE SUB-MARINER? OH. WHAT DID HE WANT?
JUST CHECKING TO SEE HOW I'M DOING. AND HE ASKED ABOUT THE TEAM. IS HE FRIENDS WITH THE BLACK WIDOW?
NO. I MEAN, POSSIBLY. IT'S A SMALL WORLD. WHY?
HE SEEMED REALLY INTERESTED IN HOW SHE WAS DOING. MOSTLY WE JUST TALKED ABOUT LIFE, THOUGH. HE INVITED ME TO VISIT HIM IN ATLANTIS.
HMMM. I DON'T LIKE THE SOUND OF THAT. ANYTHING I SHOULD BE JEALOUS OVER?
DON'T BE SILLY. HOW CAN YOU BE THE SMARTEST MAN ON EARTH, AND STILL BE SO BRAINLESS?
IT IS RATHER FLATTERING, IN A WAY, BUT--
--YOU'LL NEVER HAVE ANY REAL REASON TO BE JEALOUS.

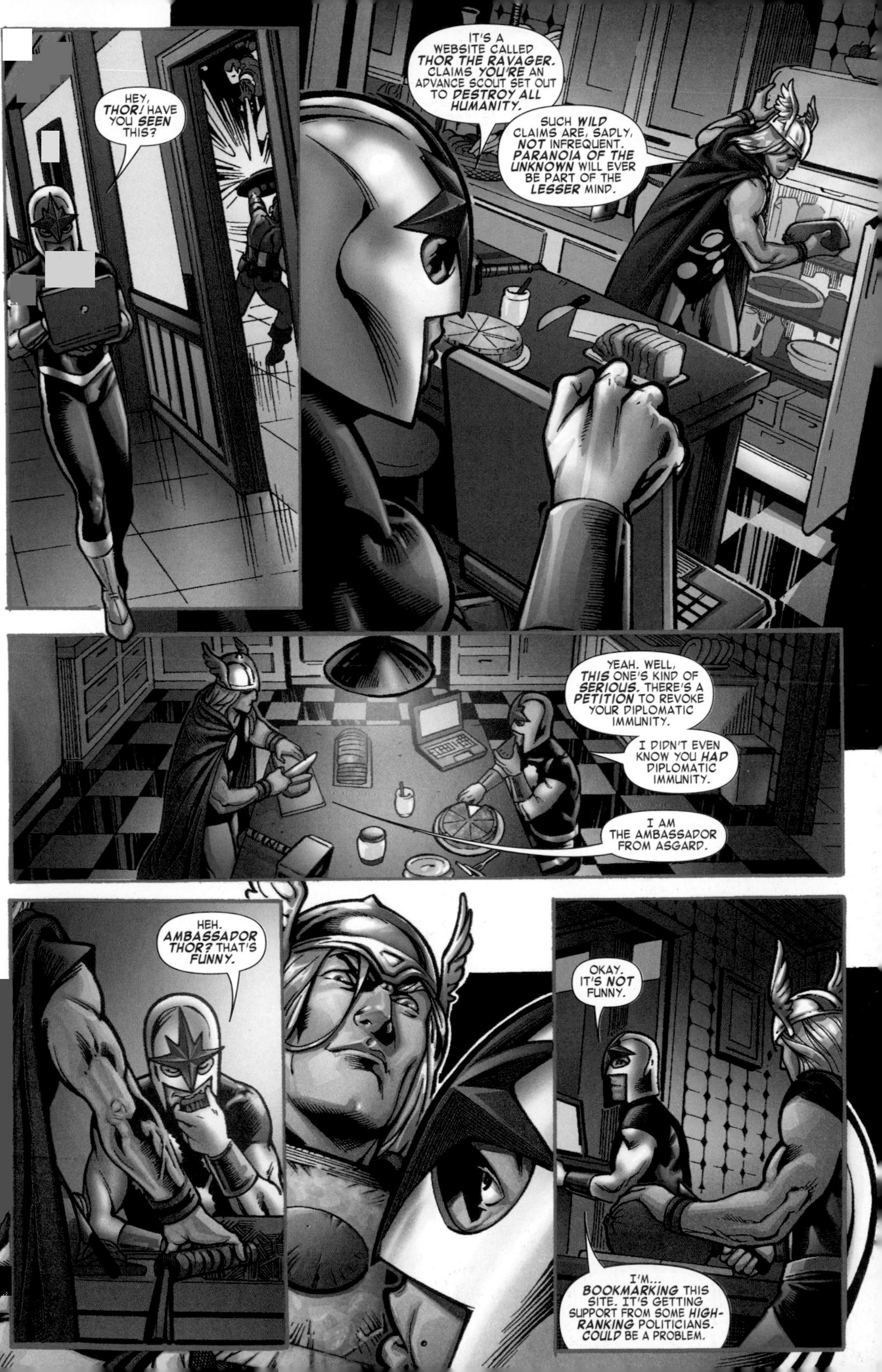
HEY, THOR! HAVE YOU SEEN THIS?
IT'S A WEBSITE CALLED THOR THE RAVAGER. CLAIMS YOU'RE AN ADVANCE SCOUT SET OUT TO DESTROY ALL HUMANITY.
SUCH WILD CLAIMS ARE, SADLY, NOT INFREQUENT. PARANOIA OF THE UNKNOWN WILL EVER BE PART OF THE LESSER MIND.
YEAH. WELL, THIS ONE'S KIND OF SERIOUS. THERE'S A PETITION TO REVOKE YOUR DIPLOMATIC IMMUNITY.
I DIDN'T EVEN KNOW YOU HAD DIPLOMATIC IMMUNITY.
I AM THE AMBASSADOR FROM ASGARD.
HEH. AMBASSADOR THOR? THAT'S FUNNY.
OKAY. IT'S NOT FUNNY.
I'M... BOOKMARKING THIS SITE. IT'S GETTING SUPPORT FROM SOME HIGH-RANKING POLITICIANS. COULD BE A PROBLEM.

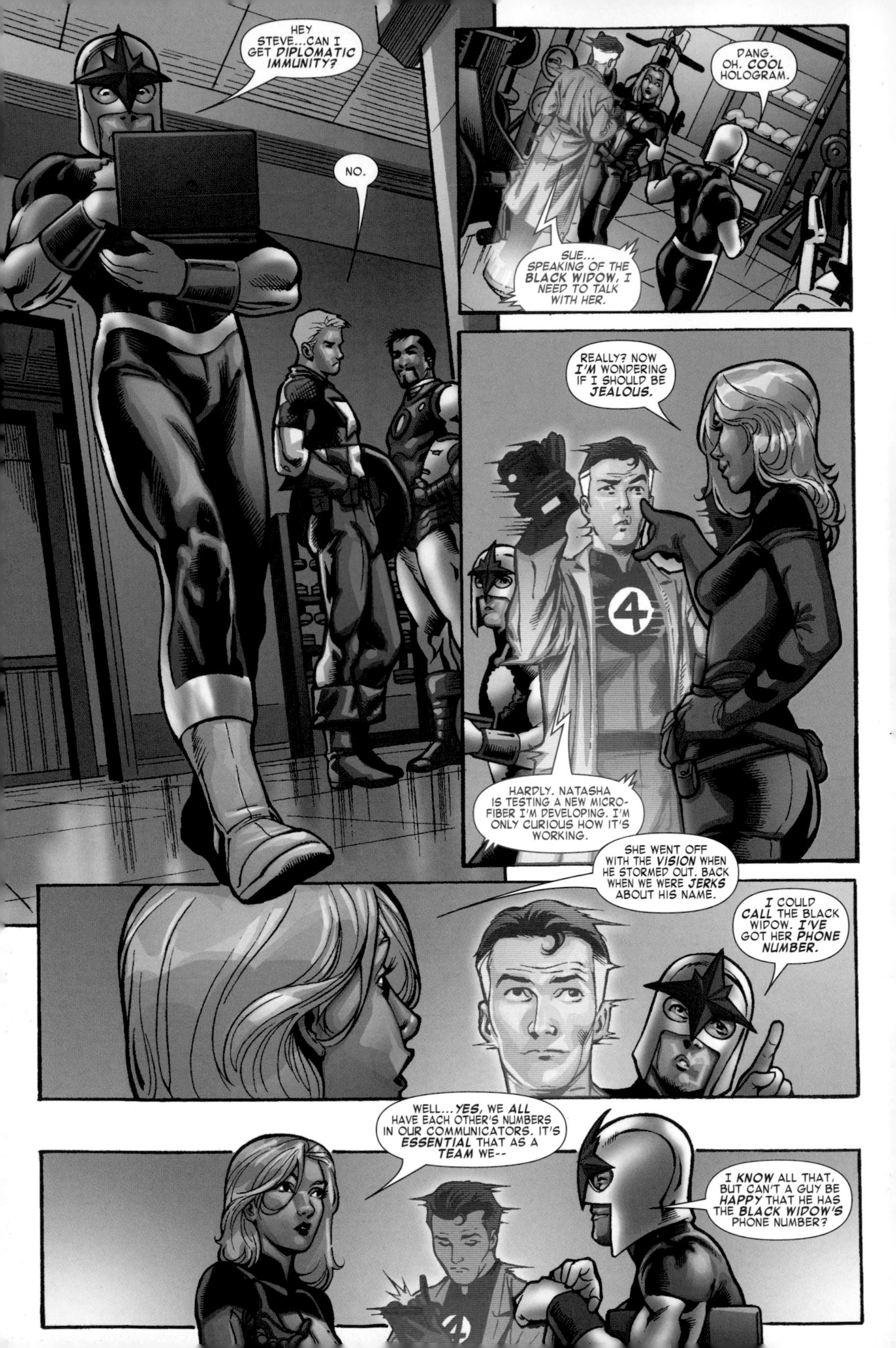
HEY STEVE...CAN I GET DIPLOMATIC IMMUNITY?
NO.
DANG. OH. COOL HOLOGRAM.
SUE... SPEAKING OF THE BLACK WIDOW, I NEED TO TALK WITH HER.
REALLY? NOW I'M WONDERING IF I SHOULD BE JEALOUS.
HARDLY. NATASHA IS TESTING A NEW MICRO-FIBER I'M DEVELOPING. I'M ONLY CURIOUS HOW IT'S WORKING.
SHE WENT OFF WITH THE VISION WHEN HE STORMED OUT. BACK WHEN WE WERE JERKS ABOUT HIS NAME.
I COULD CALL THE BLACK WIDOW. I'VE GOT HER PHONE NUMBER.
WELL... YES, WE ALL HAVE EACH OTHER'S NUMBERS IN OUR COMMUNICATORS. IT'S ESSENTIAL THAT AS A TEAM WE--
I KNOW ALL THAT, BUT CAN'T A GUY BE HAPPY THAT HE HAS THE BLACK WIDOW'S PHONE NUMBER?

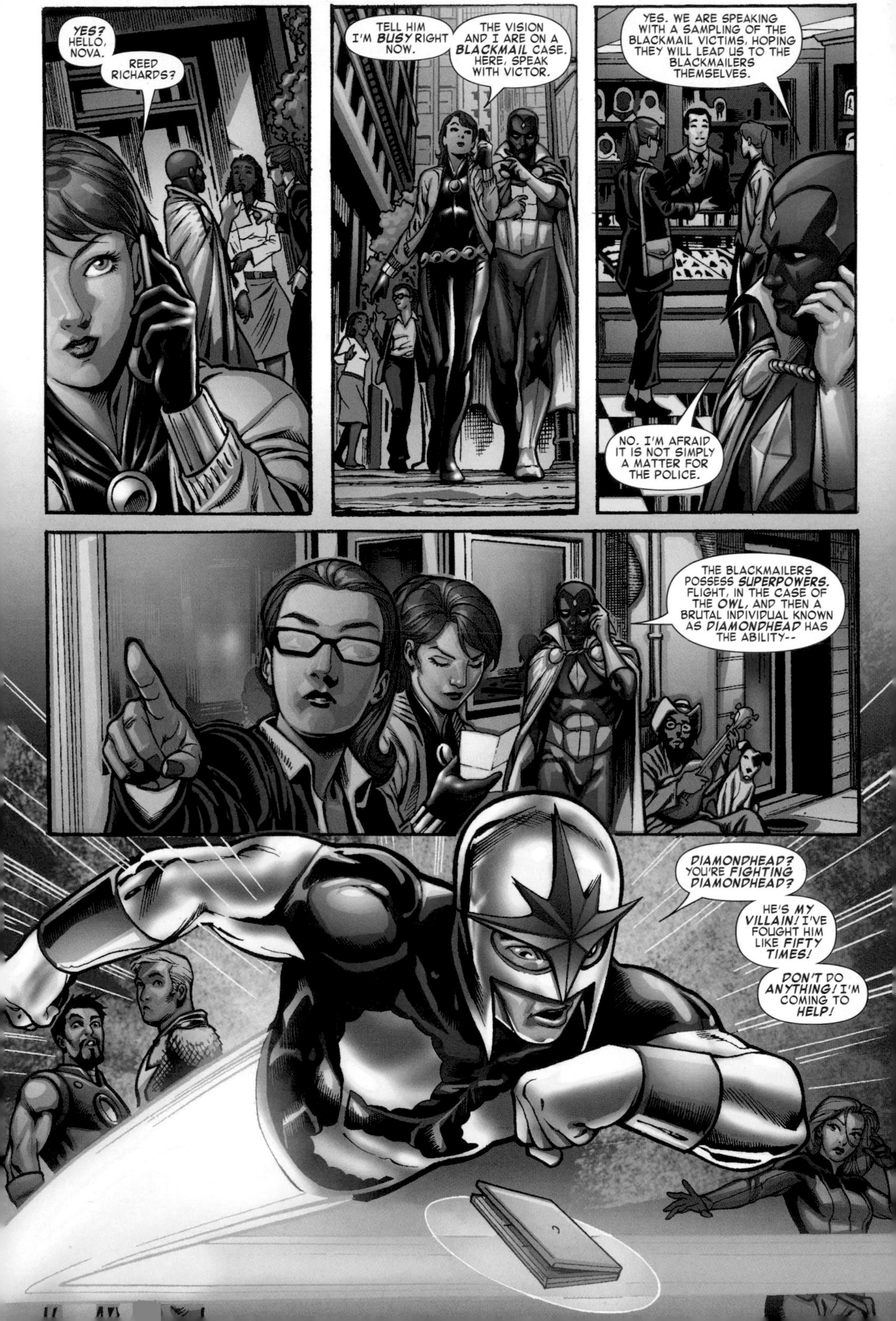
YES? HELLO, NOVA.
REED RICHARDS?
TELL HIM I'M BUSY RIGHT NOW.
THE VISION AND I ARE ON A BLACKMAIL CASE. HERE, SPEAK WITH VICTOR.
YES. WE ARE SPEAKING WITH A SAMPLING OF THE BLACKMAIL VICTIMS, HOPING THEY WILL LEAD US TO THE BLACKMAILERS THEMSELVES.
NO. I'M AFRAID IT IS NOT SIMPLY A MATTER FOR THE POLICE.
THE BLACKMAILERS POSSESS SUPERPOWERS. FLIGHT, IN THE CASE OF THE OWL, AND THEN A BRUTAL INDIVIDUAL KNOWN AS DIAMONDHEAD HAS THE ABILITY--
DIAMONDHEAD? YOU'RE FIGHTING DIAMONDHEAD?
HE'S MY VILLAIN! I'VE FOUGHT HIM LIKE FIFTY TIMES!
DON'T DO ANYTHING! I'M COMING TO HELP!

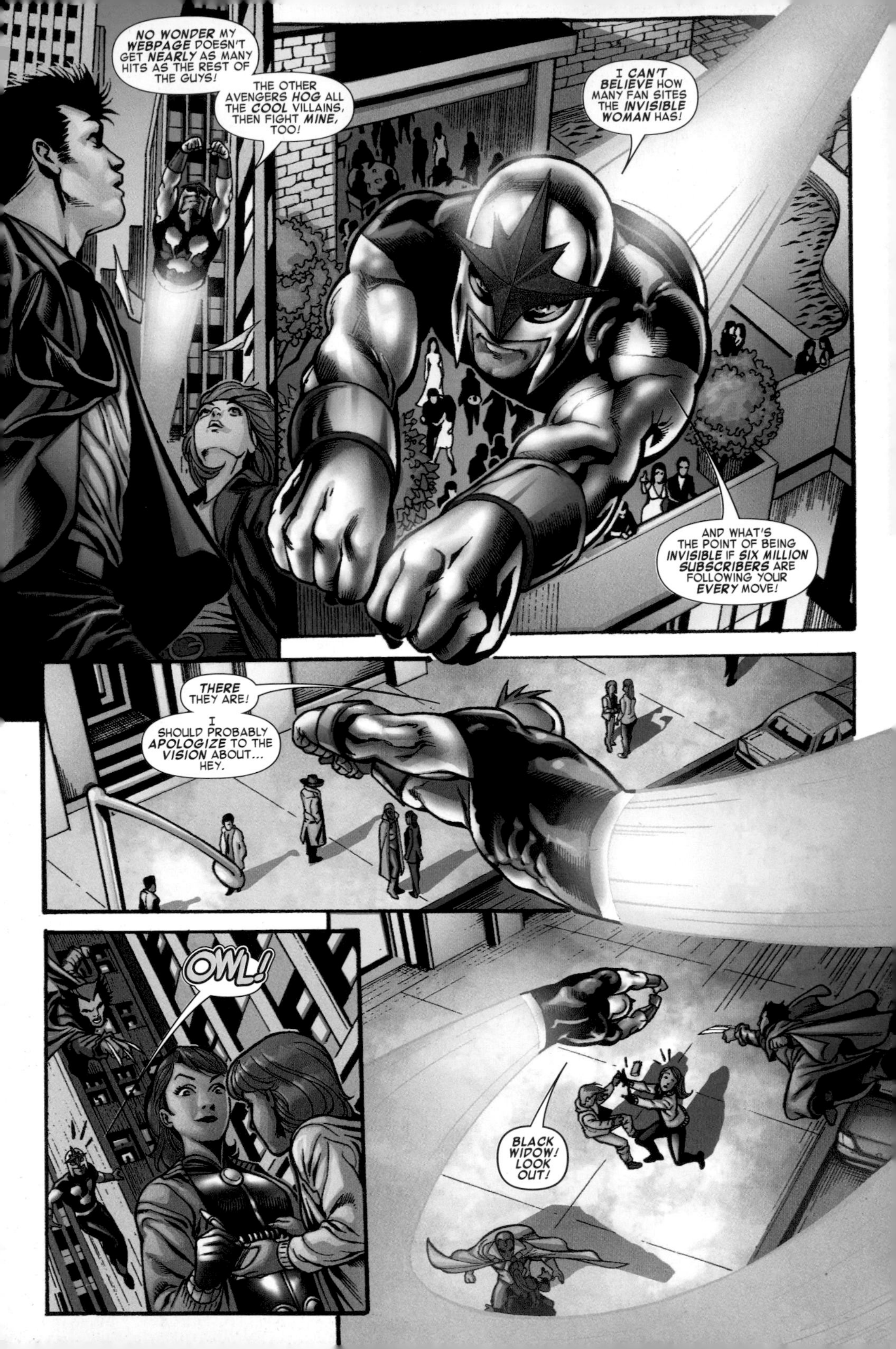
NO WONDER MY WEBPAGE DOESN'T GET NEARLY AS MANY HITS AS THE REST OF THE GUYS!
THE OTHER AVENGERS HOG ALL THE COOL VILLAINS, THEN FIGHT MINE, TOO!
I CAN'T BELIEVE HOW MANY FAN SITES THE INVISIBLE WOMAN HAS!
AND WHAT'S THE POINT OF BEING INVISIBLE IF SIX MILLION SUBSCRIBERS ARE FOLLOWING YOUR EVERY MOVE!
THERE THEY ARE!
I SHOULD PROBABLY APOLOGIZE TO THE VISION ABOUT... HEY.
OWL!
BLACK WIDOW! LOOK OUT!

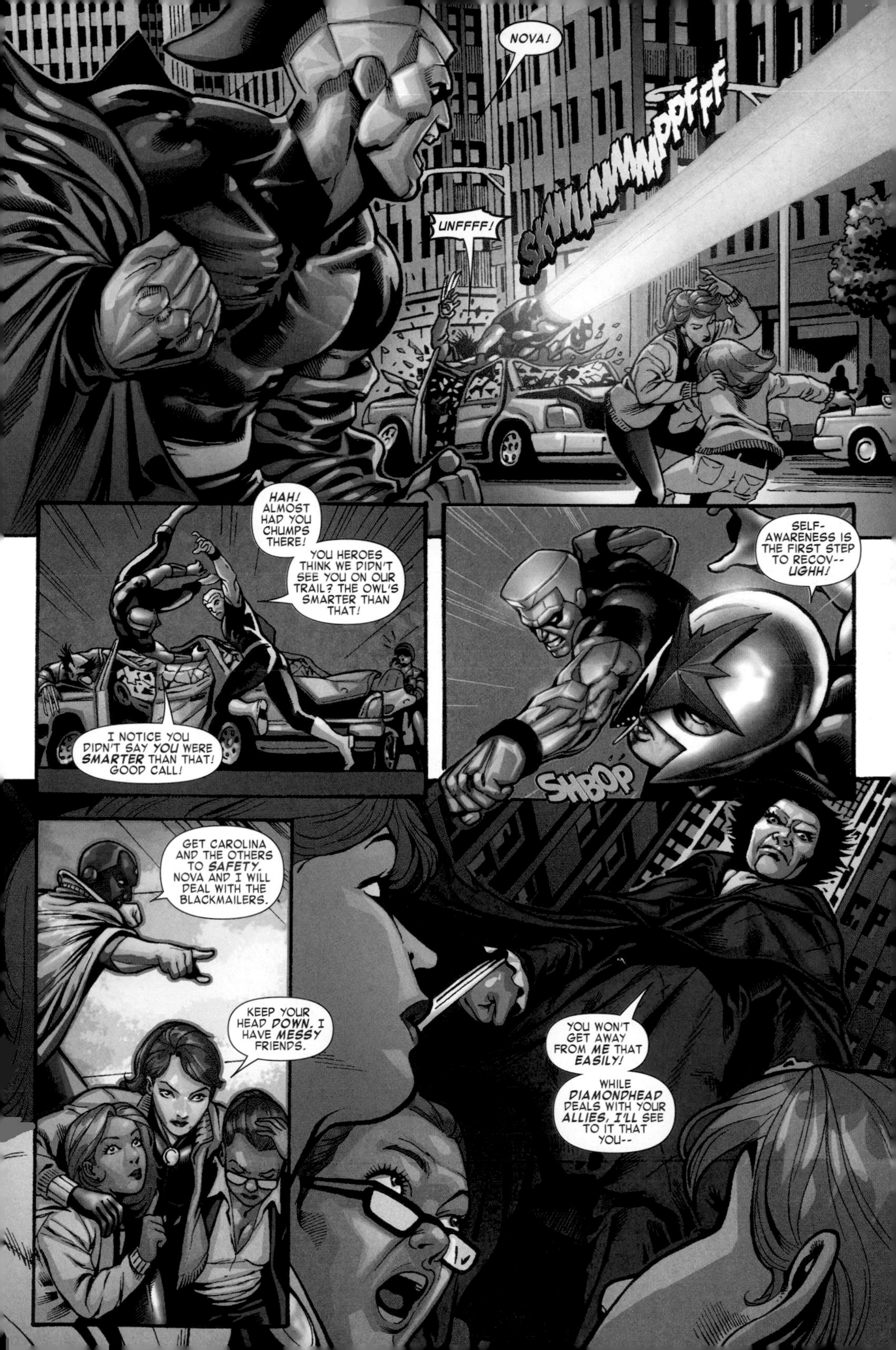
NOVA!
SKWUMMMMPFFF
UNFFFF!
HAH! ALMOST HAD YOU CHUMPS THERE!
YOU HEROES THINK WE DIDN'T SEE YOU ON OUR TRAIL? THE OWL'S SMARTER THAN THAT!
I NOTICE YOU DIDN'T SAY YOU WERE SMARTER THAN THAT! GOOD CALL!
SELF-AWARENESS IS THE FIRST STEP TO RECOV-- UGHH!
SHBOP
GET CAROLINA AND THE OTHERS TO SAFETY. NOVA AND I WILL DEAL WITH THE BLACKMAILERS.
KEEP YOUR HEAD DOWN. I HAVE MESSY FRIENDS.
YOU WON'T GET AWAY FROM ME THAT EASILY!
WHILE DIAMONDHEAD DEALS WITH YOUR ALLIES, I'LL SEE TO IT THAT YOU--

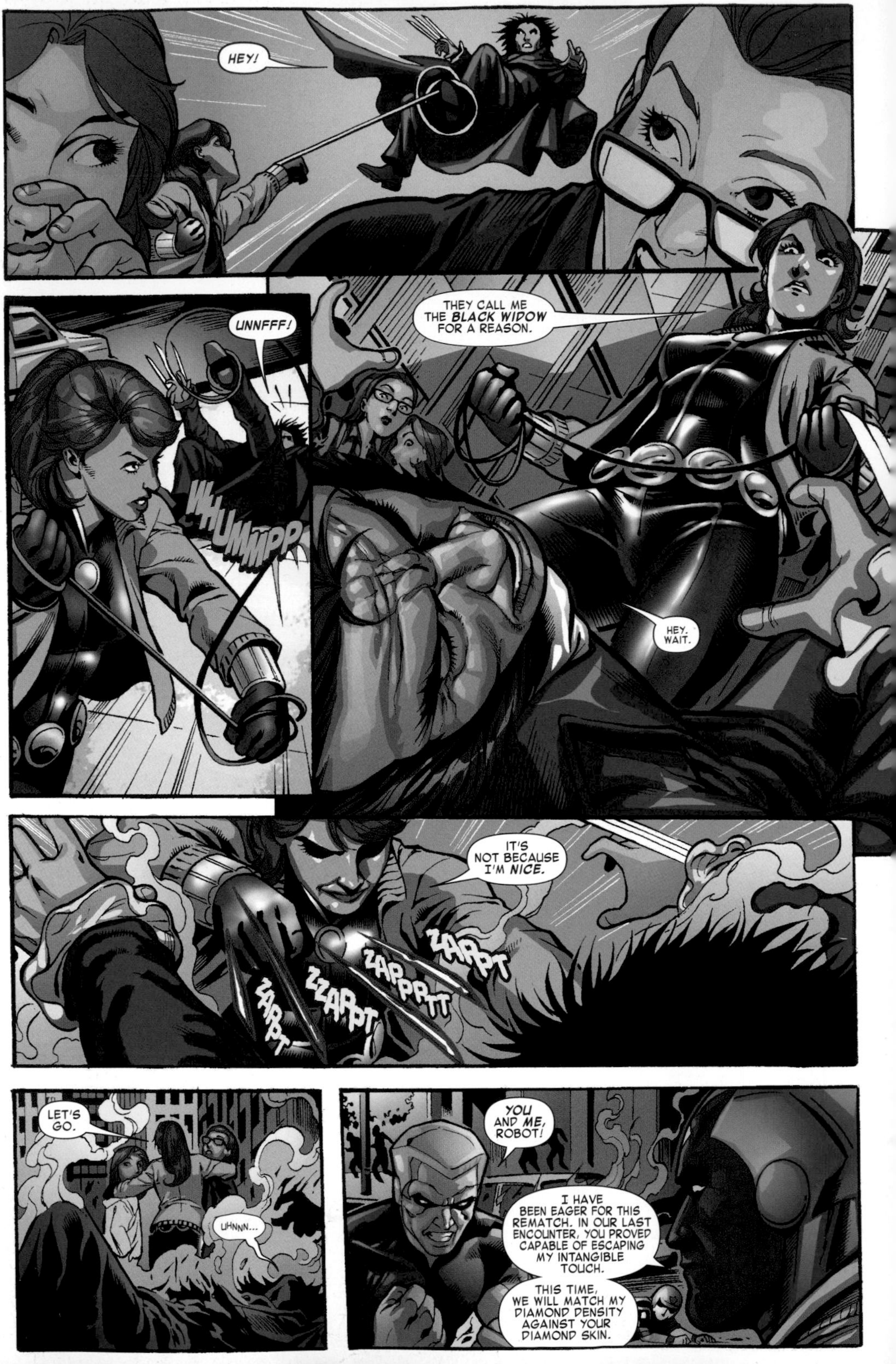
HEY!
UNNFFF!
WHUMMPP
THEY CALL ME THE BLACK WIDOW FOR A REASON.
HEY. WAIT.
IT'S NOT BECAUSE I'M NICE.
ZAPPT
ZZAPPT
ZAPPRTT
ZZAPPT
LET'S GO.
UHNNN...
YOU AND ME, ROBOT!
I HAVE BEEN EAGER FOR THIS REMATCH. IN OUR LAST ENCOUNTER, YOU PROVED CAPABLE OF ESCAPING MY INTANGIBLE TOUCH.
THIS TIME, WE WILL MATCH MY DIAMOND DENSITY AGAINST YOUR DIAMOND SKIN.

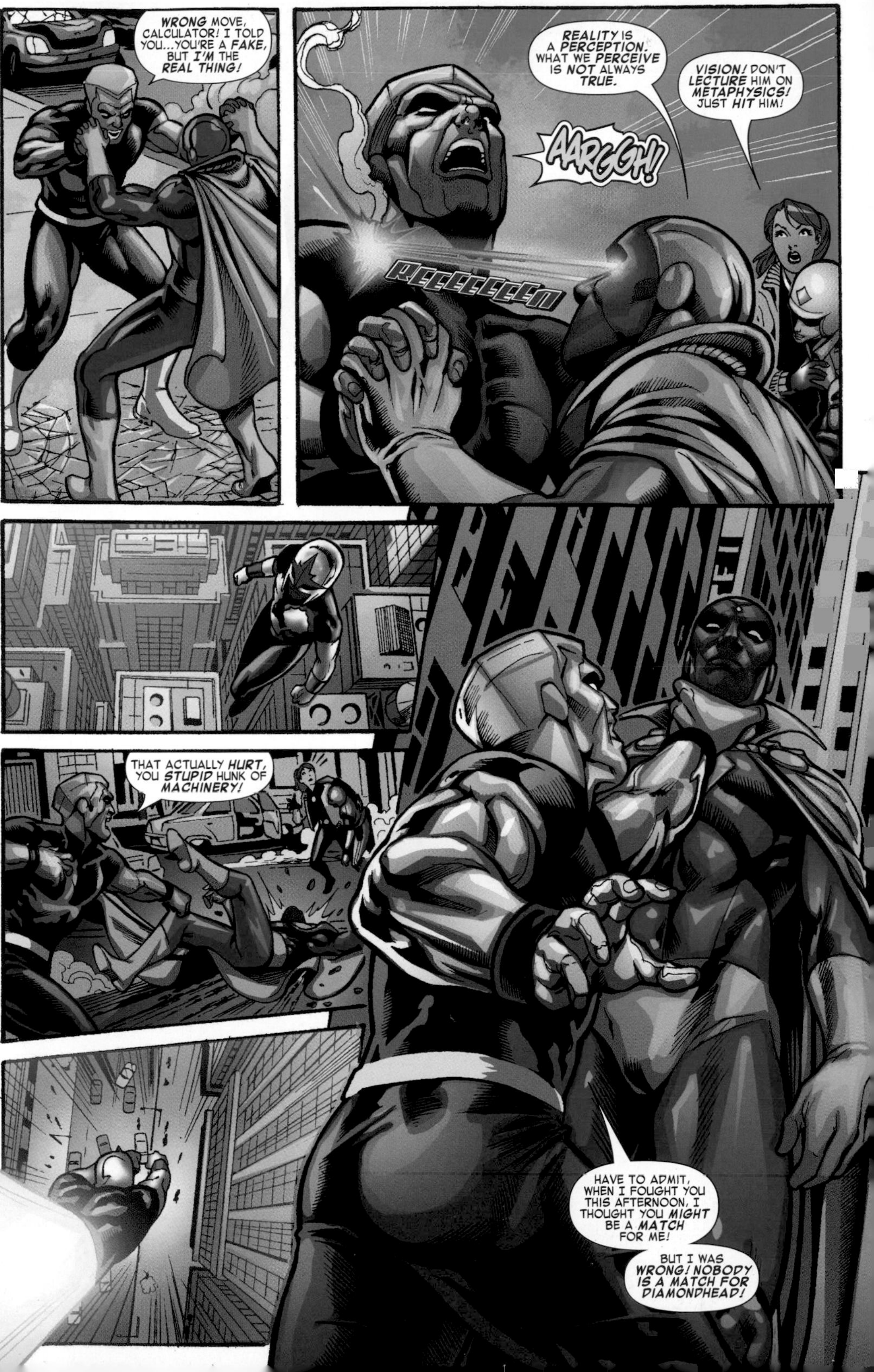

WRONG MOVE, CALCULATOR! I TOLD YOU...YOU'RE A FAKE, BUT I'M THE REAL THING!
REALITY IS A PERCEPTION. WHAT WE PERCEIVE IS NOT ALWAYS TRUE.
VISION! DON'T LECTURE HIM ON METAPHYSICS! JUST HIT HIM!
AARGGH!
REEEEEEEEN
THAT ACTUALLY HURT, YOU STUPID HUNK OF MACHINERY!
HAVE TO ADMIT, WHEN I FOUGHT YOU THIS AFTERNOON, I THOUGHT YOU MIGHT BE A MATCH FOR ME!
BUT I WAS WRONG! NOBODY IS A MATCH FOR DIAMONDHEAD!

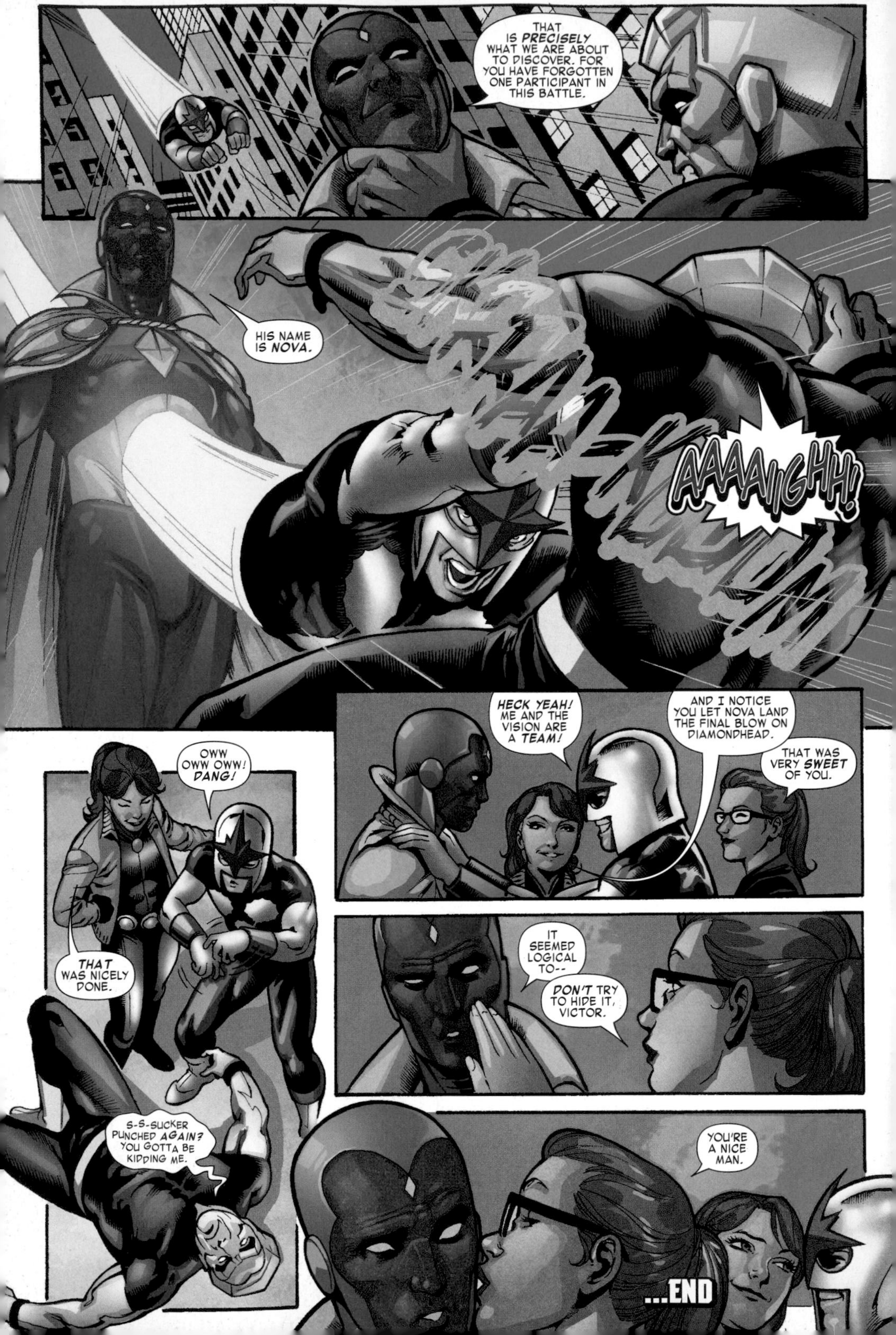
THAT IS PRECISELY WHAT WE ARE ABOUT TO DISCOVER. FOR YOU HAVE FORGOTTEN ONE PARTICIPANT IN THIS BATTLE.
HIS NAME IS NOVA.
AAAAIIGHH!
OWW OWW OWW! DANG!
THAT WAS NICELY DONE.
S-S-SUCKER PUNCHED AGAIN? YOU GOTTA BE KIDDING ME.
HECK YEAH! ME AND THE VISION ARE A TEAM!
AND I NOTICE YOU LET NOVA LAND THE FINAL BLOW ON DIAMONDHEAD.
THAT WAS VERY SWEET OF YOU.
IT SEEMED LOGICAL TO--
DON'T TRY TO HIDE IT, VICTOR.
YOU'RE A NICE MAN.
...END

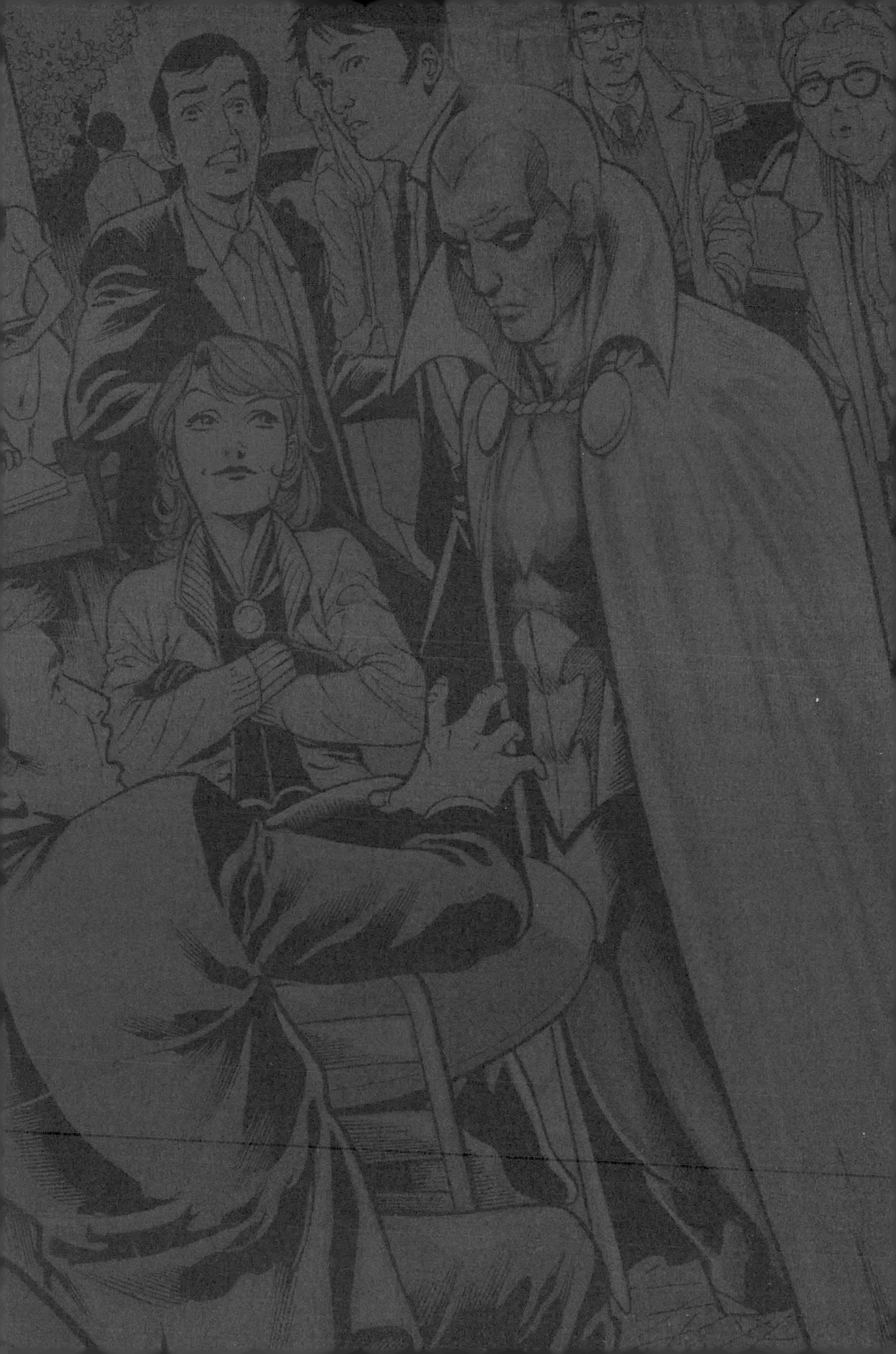

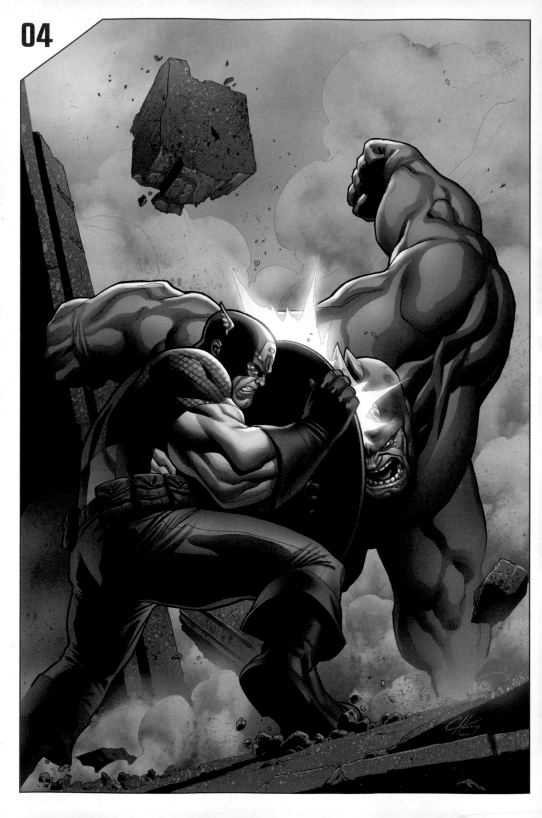

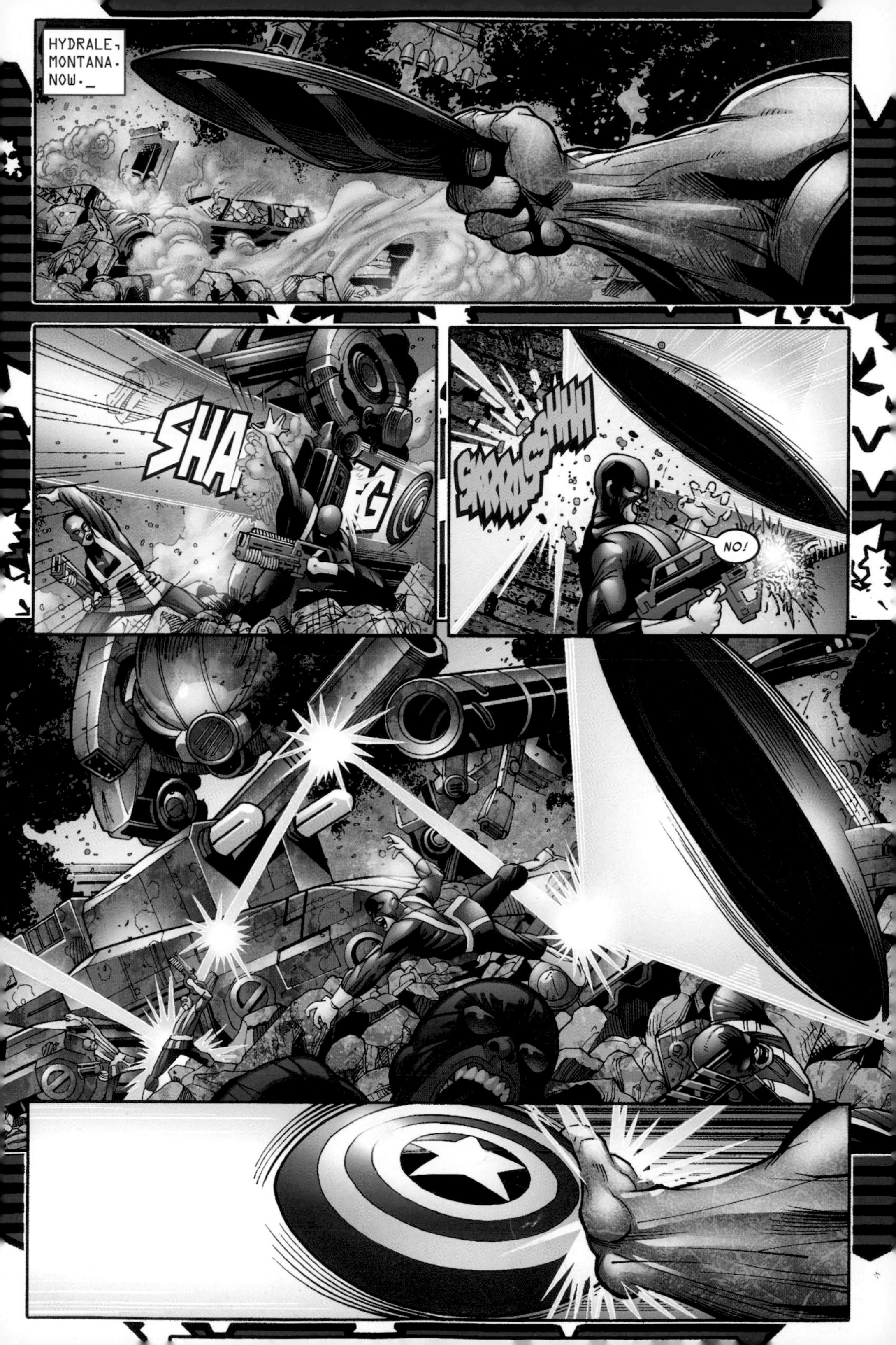

HYDRALE, MONTANA. NOW._
SHA
G
SKRRASSHHH
NO!

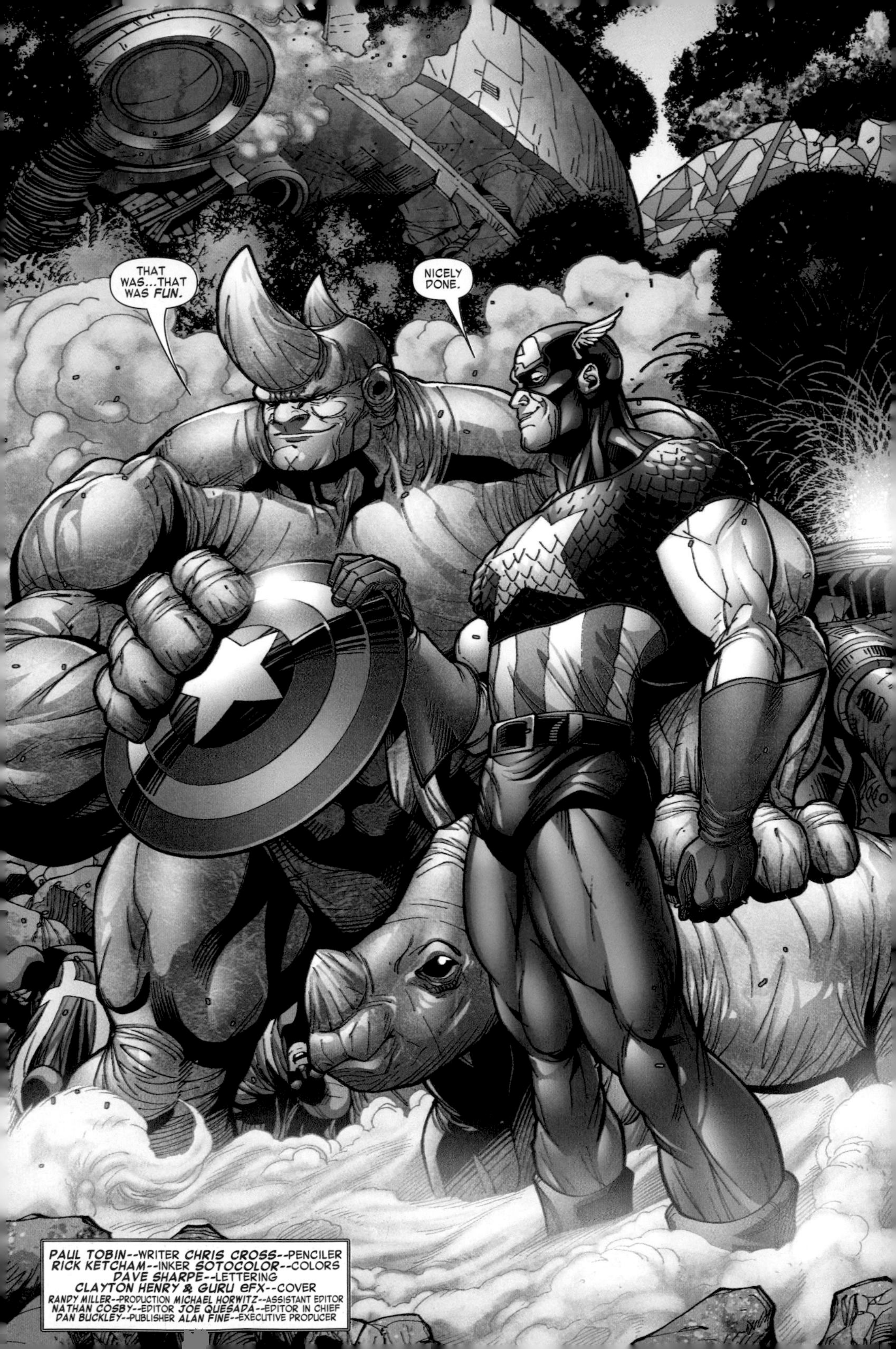

THAT WAS...THAT WAS FUN.
NICELY DONE.
PAUL TOBIN--WRITER CHRIS CROSS--PENCILER
RICK KETCHAM--INKER SOTOCOLOR--COLORS
DAVE SHARPE--LETTERING
CLAYTON HENRY & GURU eFX--COVER
RANDY MILLER--PRODUCTION MICHAEL HORWITZ--ASSISTANT EDITOR
NATHAN COSBY--EDITOR JOE QUESADA--EDITOR IN CHIEF
DAN BUCKLEY--PUBLISHER ALAN FINE--EXECUTIVE PRODUCER

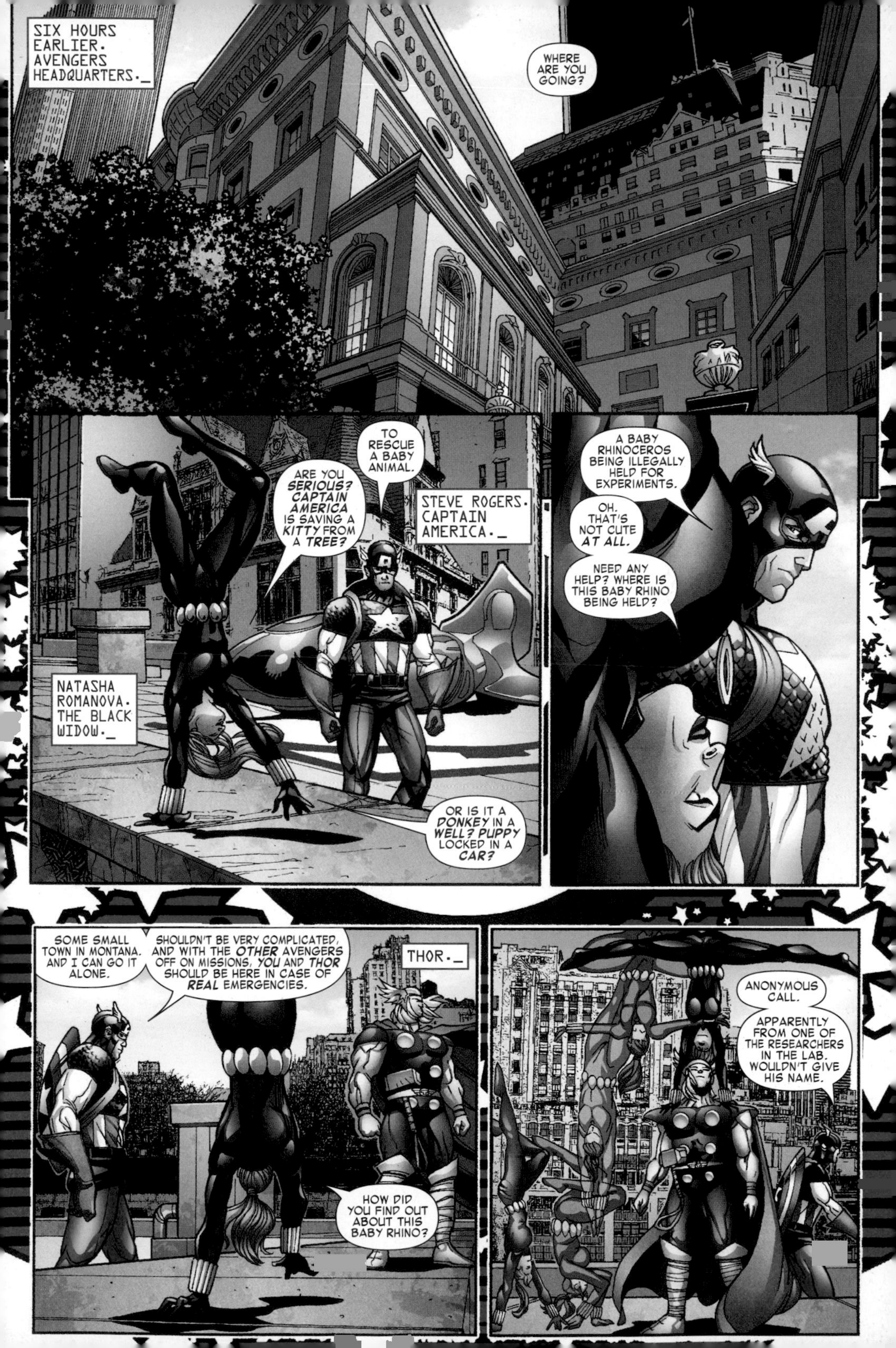
SIX HOURS EARLIER. AVENGERS HEADQUARTERS._
WHERE ARE YOU GOING?
TO RESCUE A BABY ANIMAL.
ARE YOU SERIOUS? CAPTAIN AMERICA IS SAVING A KITTY FROM A TREE?
STEVE ROGERS. CAPTAIN AMERICA._
NATASHA ROMANOVA. THE BLACK WIDOW._
OR IS IT A DONKEY IN A WELL? PUPPY LOCKED IN A CAR?
A BABY RHINOCEROS BEING ILLEGALLY HELD FOR EXPERIMENTS.
OH. THAT'S NOT CUTE AT ALL.
NEED ANY HELP? WHERE IS THIS BABY RHINO BEING HELD?
SOME SMALL TOWN IN MONTANA. AND I CAN GO IT ALONE.
SHOULDN'T BE VERY COMPLICATED, AND WITH THE OTHER AVENGERS OFF ON MISSIONS, YOU AND THOR SHOULD BE HERE IN CASE OF REAL EMERGENCIES.
THOR._
HOW DID YOU FIND OUT ABOUT THIS BABY RHINO?
ANONYMOUS CALL.
APPARENTLY FROM ONE OF THE RESEARCHERS IN THE LAB. WOULDN'T GIVE HIS NAME.

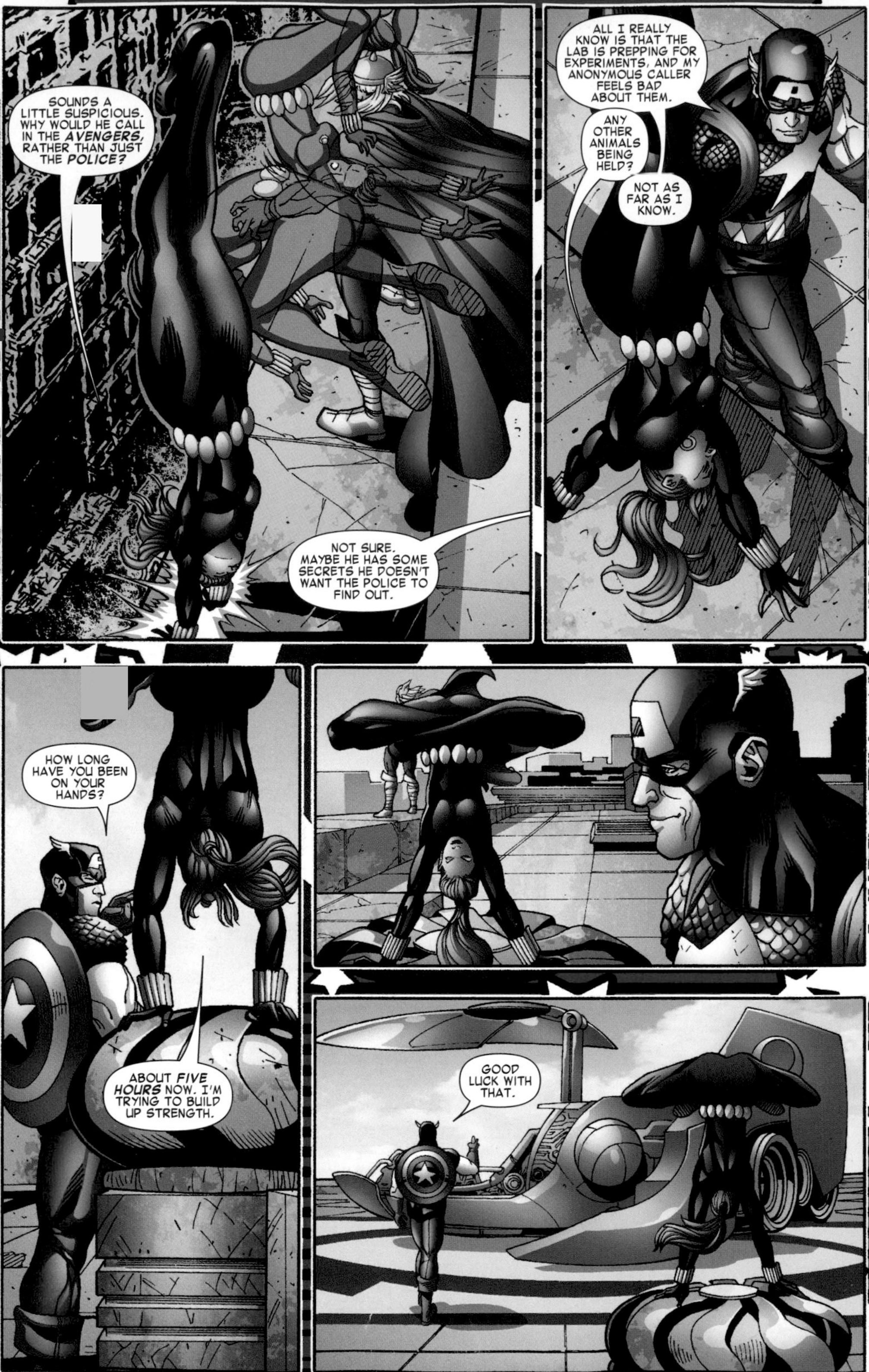
SOUNDS A LITTLE SUSPICIOUS. WHY WOULD HE CALL IN THE *AVENGERS,* RATHER THAN JUST THE *POLICE?*
NOT SURE. MAYBE HE HAS SOME SECRETS HE DOESN'T WANT THE POLICE TO FIND OUT.
ALL I REALLY KNOW IS THAT THE LAB IS PREPPING FOR EXPERIMENTS, AND MY ANONYMOUS CALLER FEELS BAD ABOUT THEM.
ANY OTHER ANIMALS BEING HELD?
NOT AS FAR AS I KNOW.
HOW LONG HAVE YOU BEEN ON YOUR HANDS?
ABOUT *FIVE HOURS* NOW. I'M TRYING TO BUILD UP STRENGTH.
GOOD LUCK WITH THAT.

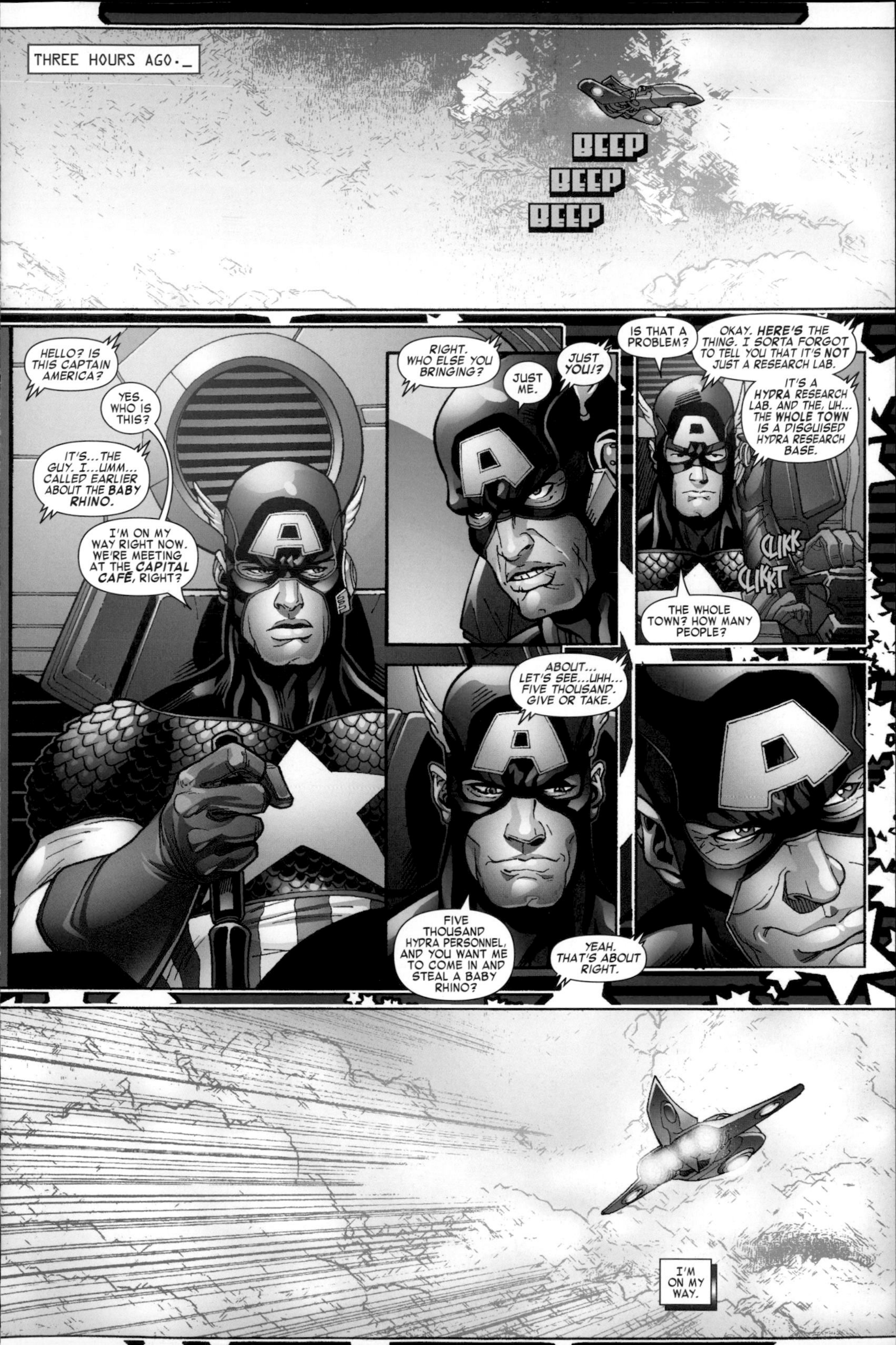
THREE HOURS AGO...
BEEP
BEEP
BEEP
HELLO? IS THIS CAPTAIN AMERICA?
YES. WHO IS THIS?
IT'S...THE GUY. I...UMM... CALLED EARLIER ABOUT THE BABY RHINO.
I'M ON MY WAY RIGHT NOW. WE'RE MEETING AT THE CAPITAL CAFÉ, RIGHT?
RIGHT. WHO ELSE YOU BRINGING?
JUST ME.
JUST YOU!?
IS THAT A PROBLEM?
OKAY. HERE'S THE THING. I SORTA FORGOT TO TELL YOU THAT IT'S NOT JUST A RESEARCH LAB.
IT'S A HYDRA RESEARCH LAB. AND THE, UH... THE WHOLE TOWN IS A DISGUISED HYDRA RESEARCH BASE.
CLIKK
CLIKKT
THE WHOLE TOWN? HOW MANY PEOPLE?
ABOUT... LET'S SEE...UHH... FIVE THOUSAND. GIVE OR TAKE.
FIVE THOUSAND HYDRA PERSONNEL, AND YOU WANT ME TO COME IN AND STEAL A BABY RHINO?
YEAH. THAT'S ABOUT RIGHT.
I'M ON MY WAY.

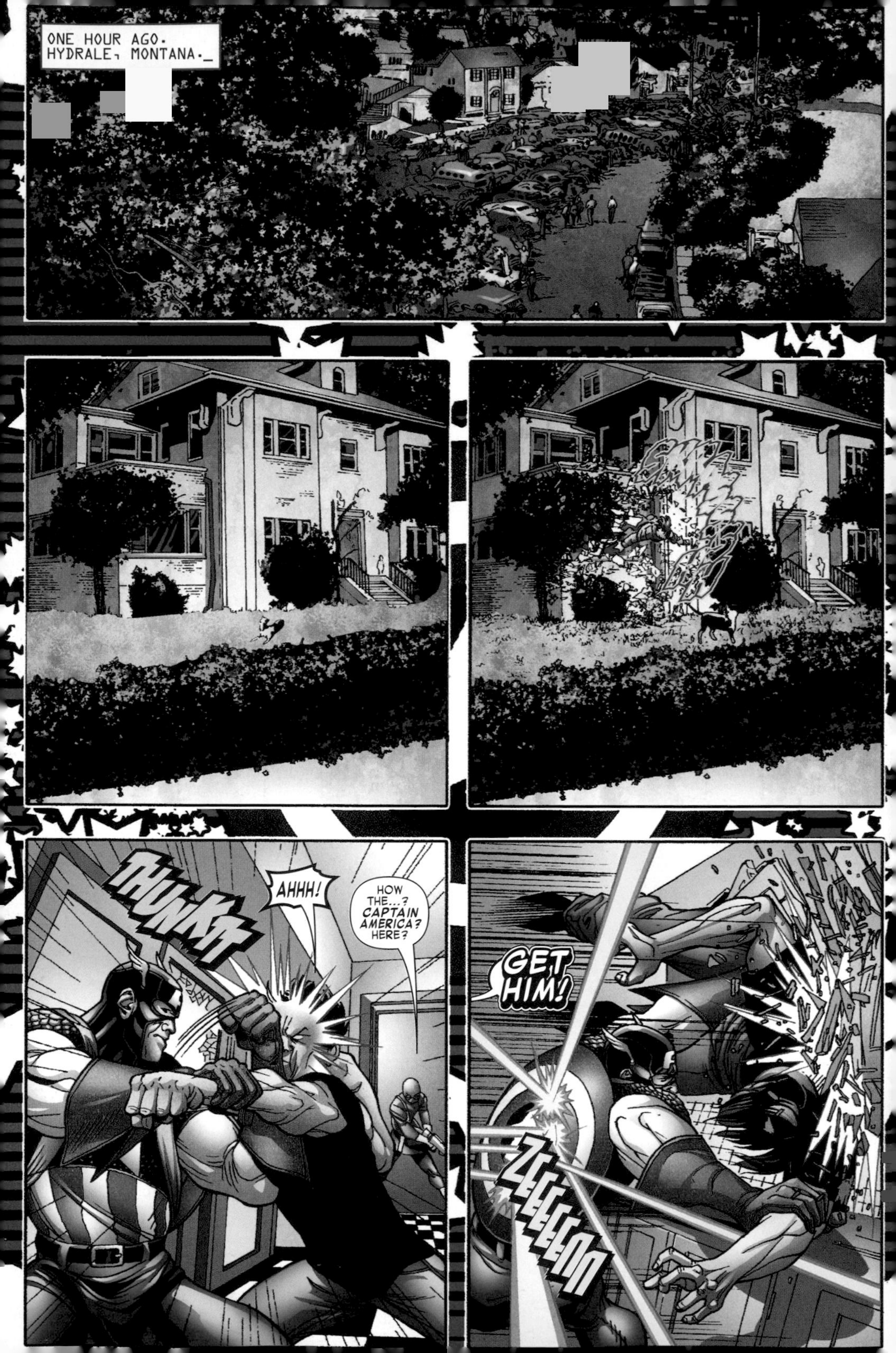
ONE HOUR AGO.
HYDRALE, MONTANA._
THUNKT
AHHH!
HOW THE...? CAPTAIN AMERICA? HERE?
GET HIM!

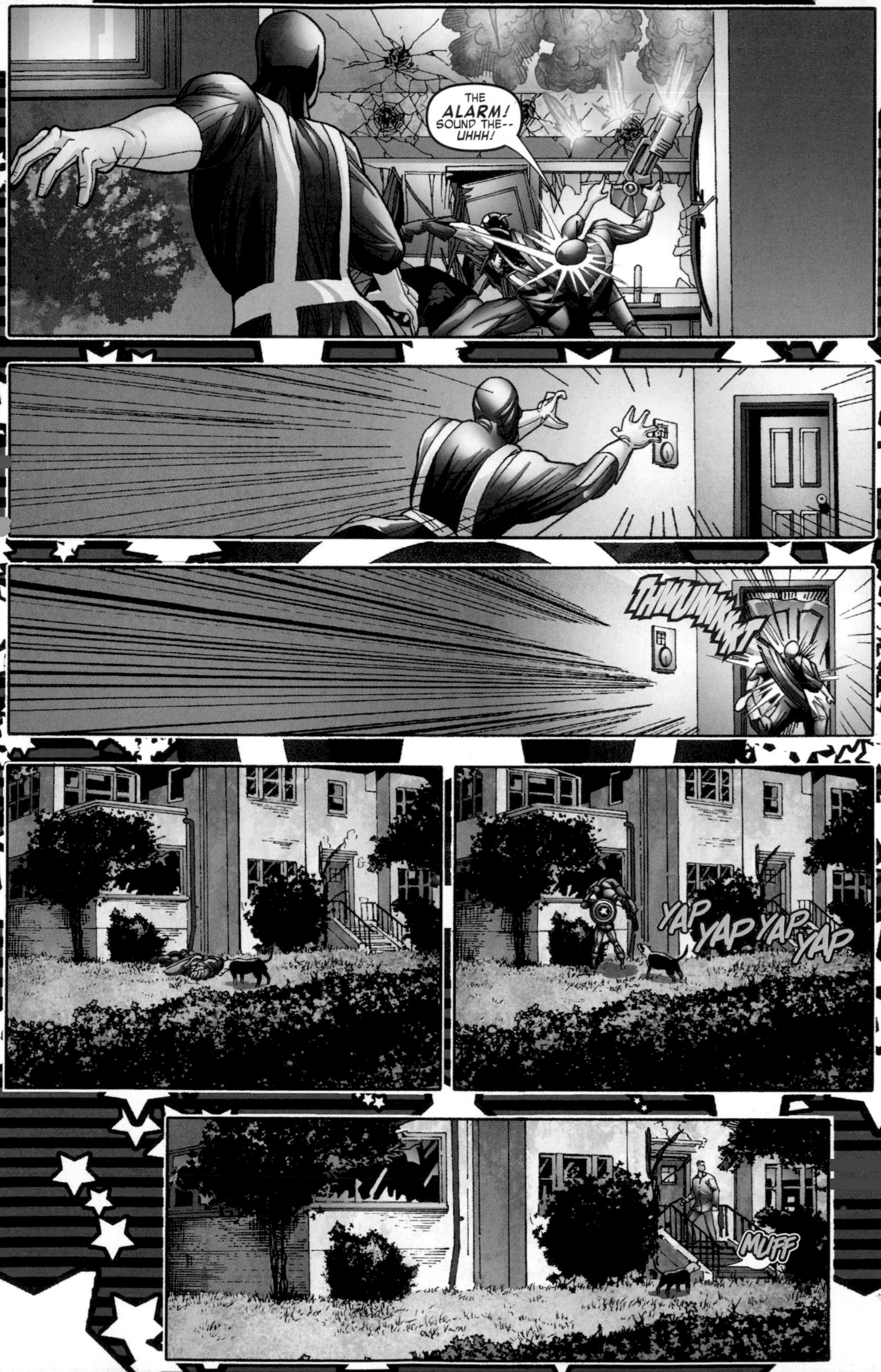
THE ALARM! SOUND THE-- UHHH!
THWUNNKKT
YAP YAP YAP YAP
MUFF

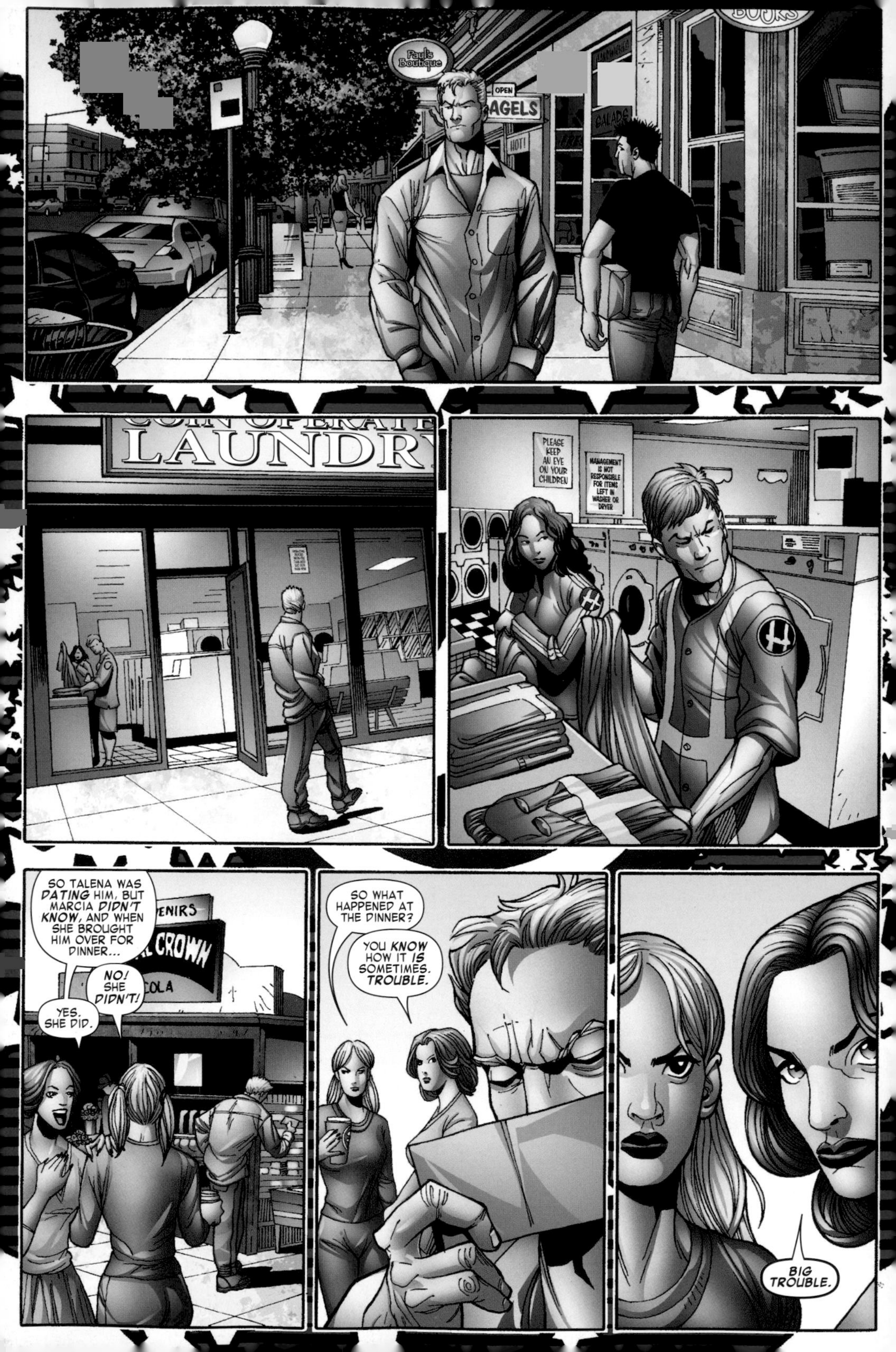

Paul's Boutique
OPEN
AGELS
HOT!
LAUNDRY
PLEASE KEEP AN EYE ON YOUR CHILDREN
MANAGEMENT IS NOT RESPONSIBLE FOR ITEMS LEFT IN WASHER OR DRYER
SO TALENA WAS *DATING* HIM, BUT MARCIA *DIDN'T KNOW*, AND WHEN SHE BROUGHT HIM OVER FOR DINNER...
*NO!* SHE *DIDN'T!*
YES. SHE DID.
CROWN
COLA
SO WHAT HAPPENED AT THE DINNER?
YOU *KNOW* HOW IT *IS* SOMETIMES. *TROUBLE.*
BIG TROUBLE.

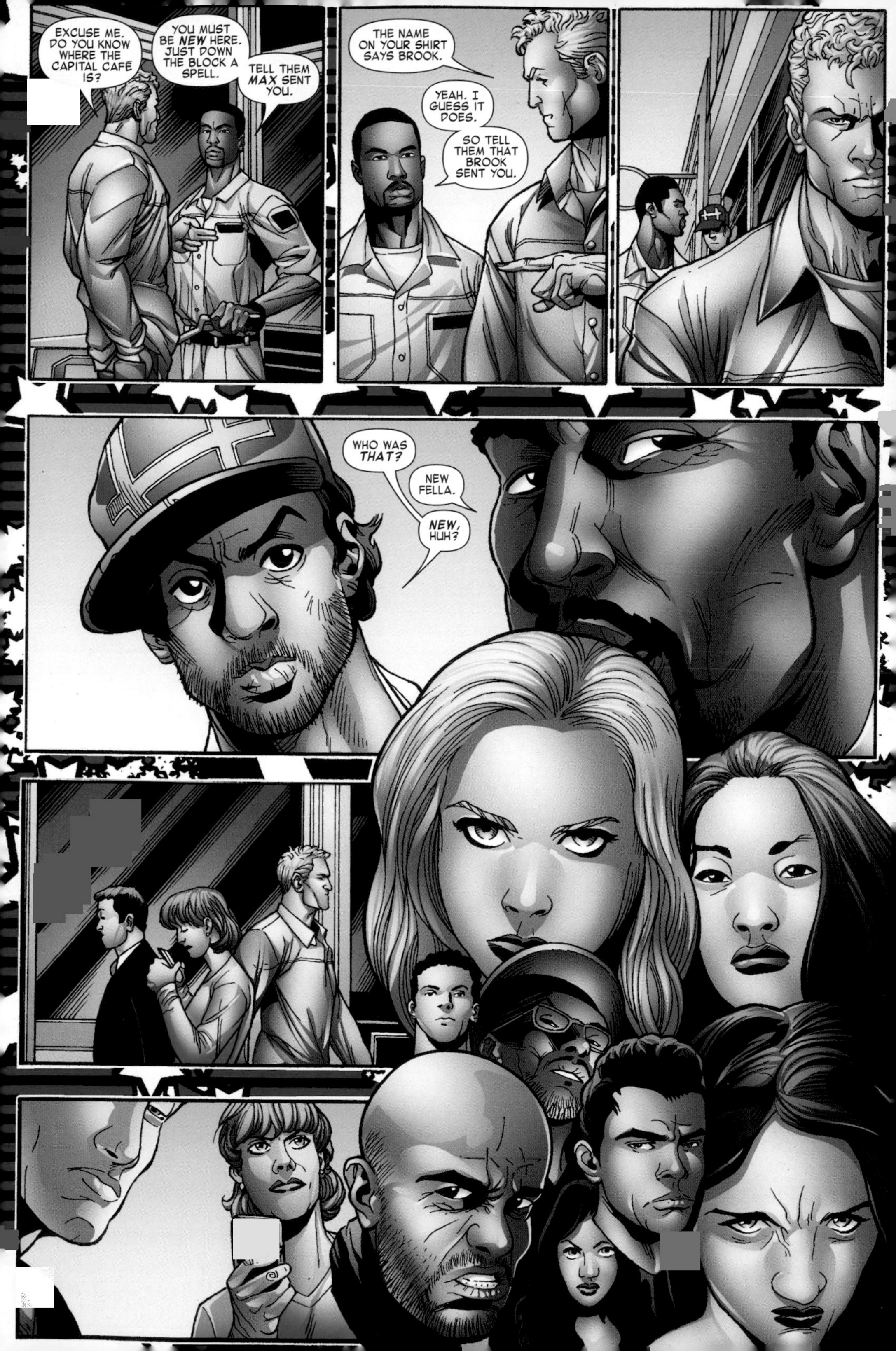
EXCUSE ME. DO YOU KNOW WHERE THE CAPITAL CAFÉ IS?
YOU MUST BE NEW HERE. JUST DOWN THE BLOCK A SPELL.
TELL THEM MAX SENT YOU.
THE NAME ON YOUR SHIRT SAYS BROOK.
YEAH. I GUESS IT DOES.
SO TELL THEM THAT BROOK SENT YOU.
WHO WAS THAT?
NEW FELLA.
NEW, HUH?

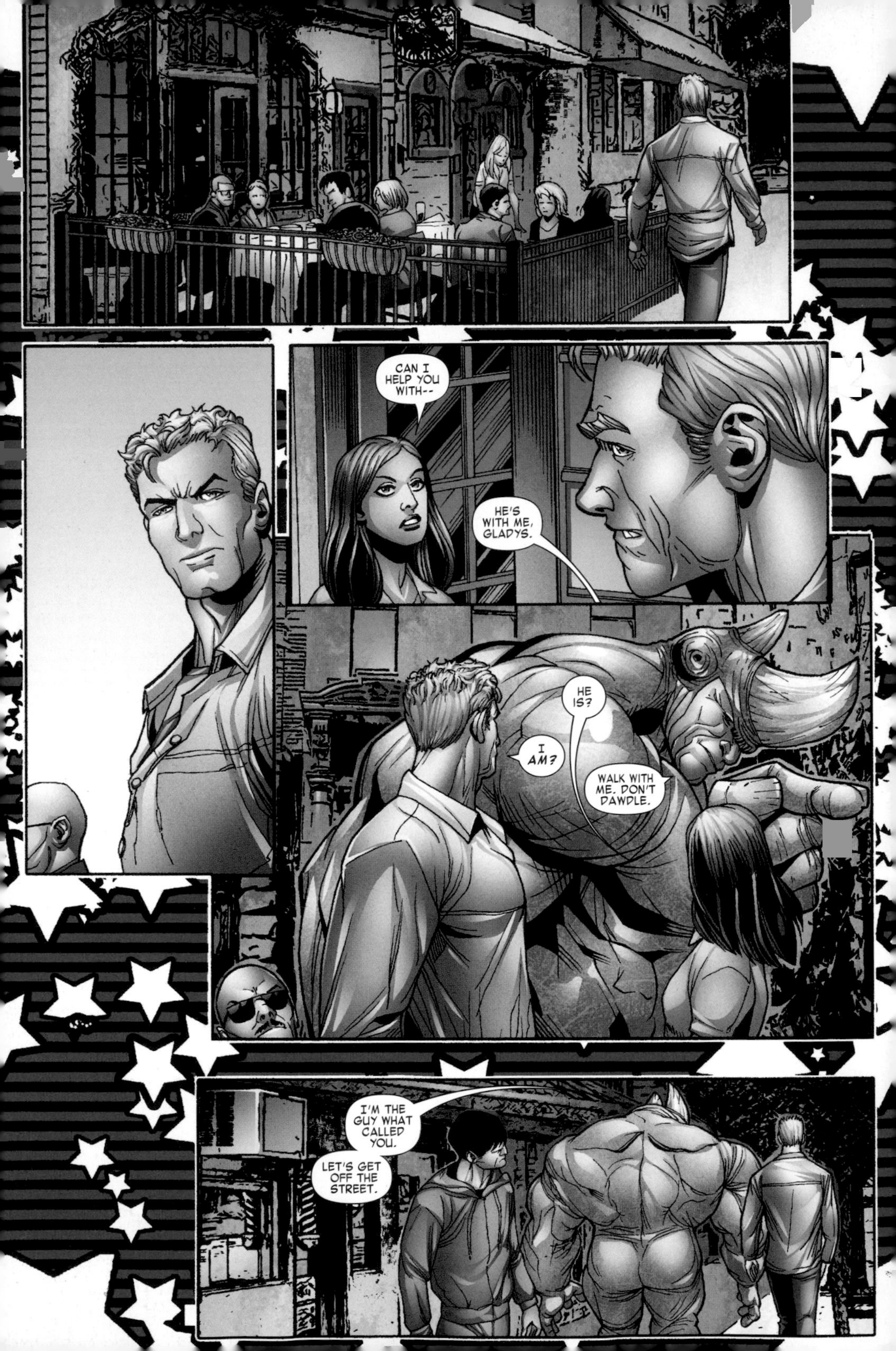
CAN I HELP YOU WITH--
HE'S WITH ME, GLADYS.
HE IS?
I AM?
WALK WITH ME. DON'T DAWDLE.
I'M THE GUY WHAT CALLED YOU.
LET'S GET OFF THE STREET.

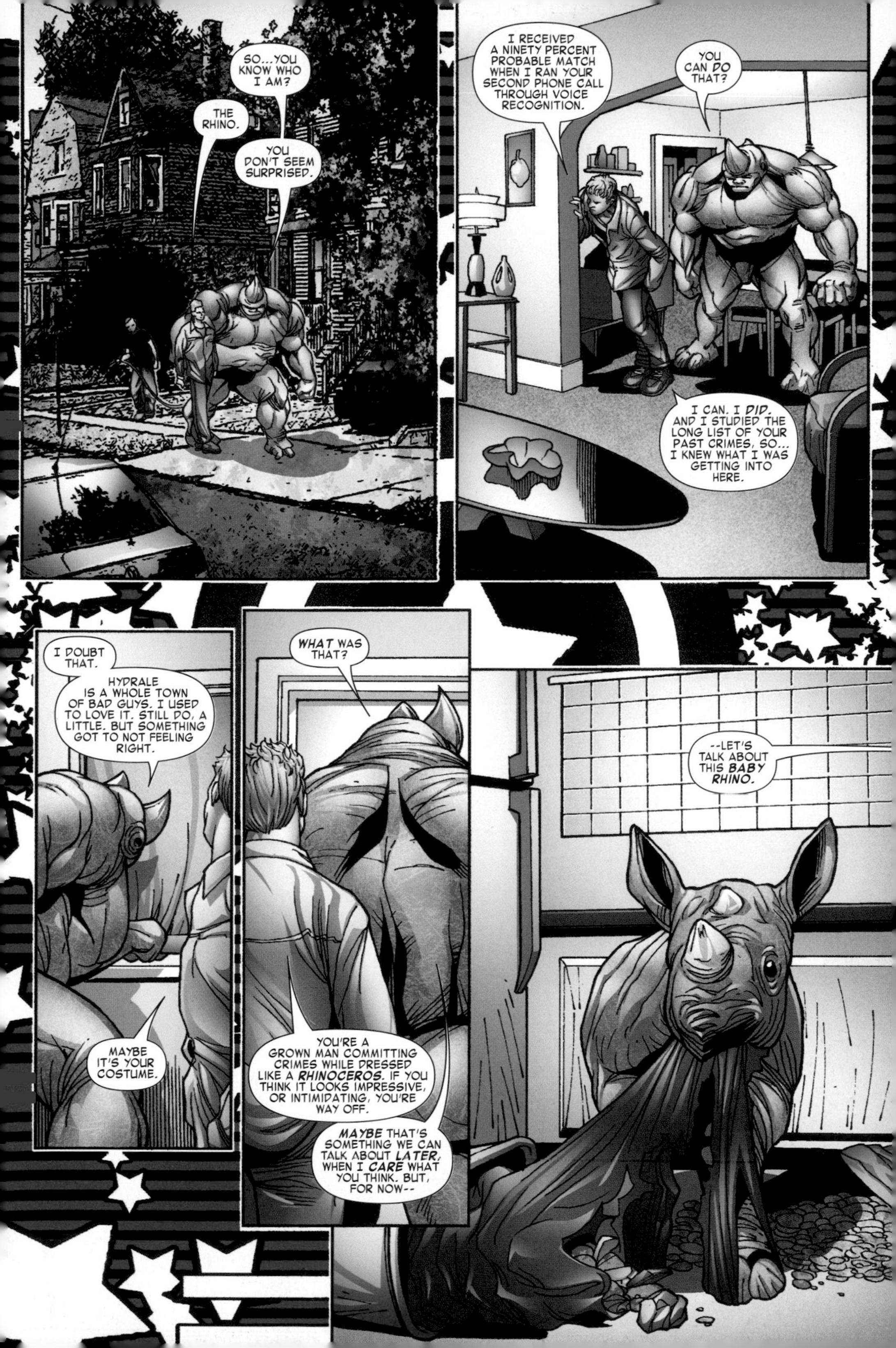
SO...YOU KNOW WHO I AM?
THE RHINO.
YOU DON'T SEEM SURPRISED.
I RECEIVED A NINETY PERCENT PROBABLE MATCH WHEN I RAN YOUR SECOND PHONE CALL THROUGH VOICE RECOGNITION.
YOU CAN DO THAT?
I CAN. I DID. AND I STUDIED THE LONG LIST OF YOUR PAST CRIMES, SO... I KNEW WHAT I WAS GETTING INTO HERE.
I DOUBT THAT.
HYDRALE IS A WHOLE TOWN OF BAD GUYS. I USED TO LOVE IT. STILL DO, A LITTLE. BUT SOMETHING GOT TO NOT FEELING RIGHT.
MAYBE IT'S YOUR COSTUME.
WHAT WAS THAT?
YOU'RE A GROWN MAN COMMITTING CRIMES WHILE DRESSED LIKE A RHINOCEROS. IF YOU THINK IT LOOKS IMPRESSIVE, OR INTIMIDATING, YOU'RE WAY OFF.
MAYBE THAT'S SOMETHING WE CAN TALK ABOUT LATER, WHEN I CARE WHAT YOU THINK. BUT, FOR NOW--
--LET'S TALK ABOUT THIS BABY RHINO.

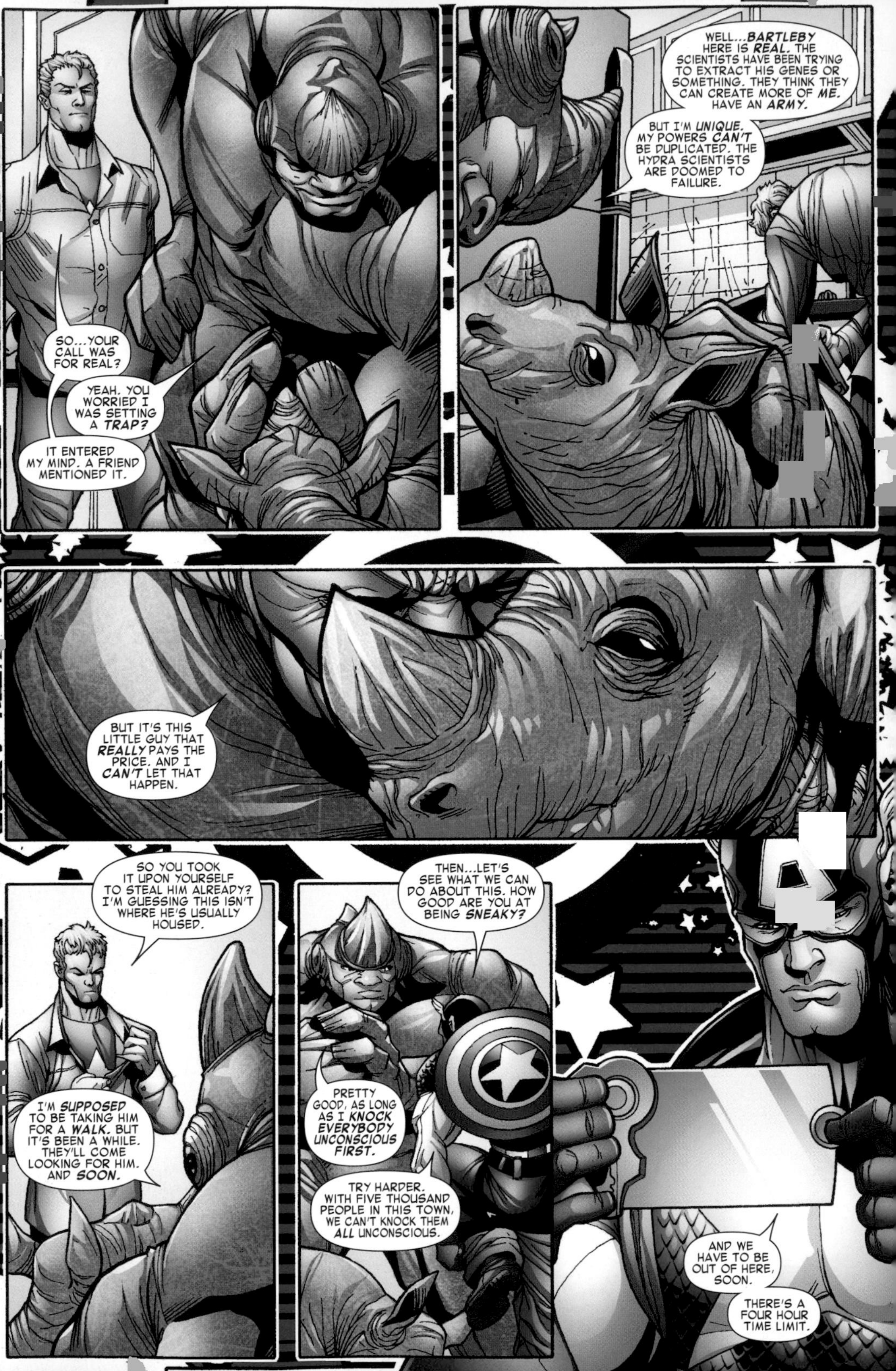

SO...YOUR CALL WAS FOR REAL?
YEAH. YOU WORRIED I WAS SETTING A *TRAP?*
IT ENTERED MY MIND. A FRIEND MENTIONED IT.
WELL...*BARTLEBY* HERE IS *REAL.* THE SCIENTISTS HAVE BEEN TRYING TO EXTRACT HIS GENES OR SOMETHING. THEY THINK THEY CAN CREATE MORE OF *ME.* HAVE AN *ARMY.*
BUT I'M *UNIQUE.* MY POWERS *CAN'T* BE DUPLICATED. THE HYDRA SCIENTISTS ARE DOOMED TO FAILURE.
BUT IT'S THIS LITTLE GUY THAT *REALLY* PAYS THE PRICE. AND I *CAN'T* LET THAT HAPPEN.
SO YOU TOOK IT UPON YOURSELF TO STEAL HIM ALREADY? I'M GUESSING THIS ISN'T WHERE HE'S USUALLY HOUSED.
I'M *SUPPOSED* TO BE TAKING HIM FOR A *WALK.* BUT IT'S BEEN A WHILE. THEY'LL COME LOOKING FOR HIM. AND *SOON.*
THEN...LET'S SEE WHAT WE CAN DO ABOUT THIS. HOW GOOD ARE YOU AT BEING *SNEAKY?*
PRETTY GOOD, AS LONG AS I *KNOCK EVERYBODY UNCONSCIOUS FIRST.*
TRY HARDER. WITH FIVE THOUSAND PEOPLE IN THIS TOWN, WE CAN'T KNOCK THEM *ALL* UNCONSCIOUS.
AND WE HAVE TO BE OUT OF HERE, SOON.
THERE'S A FOUR HOUR TIME LIMIT.

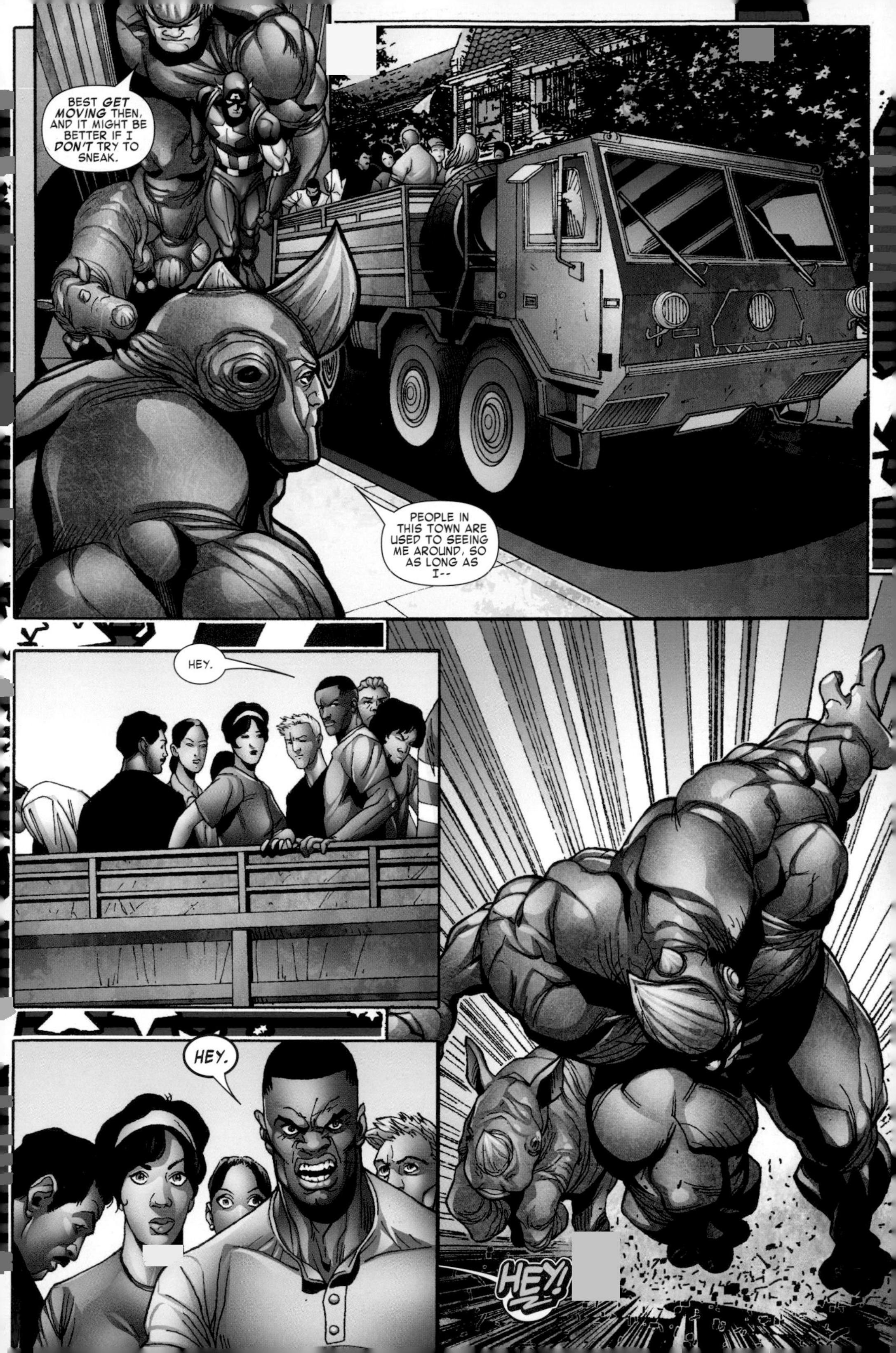
BEST GET MOVING THEN, AND IT MIGHT BE BETTER IF I DON'T TRY TO SNEAK.
PEOPLE IN THIS TOWN ARE USED TO SEEING ME AROUND, SO AS LONG AS I--
HEY.
HEY.
HEY!

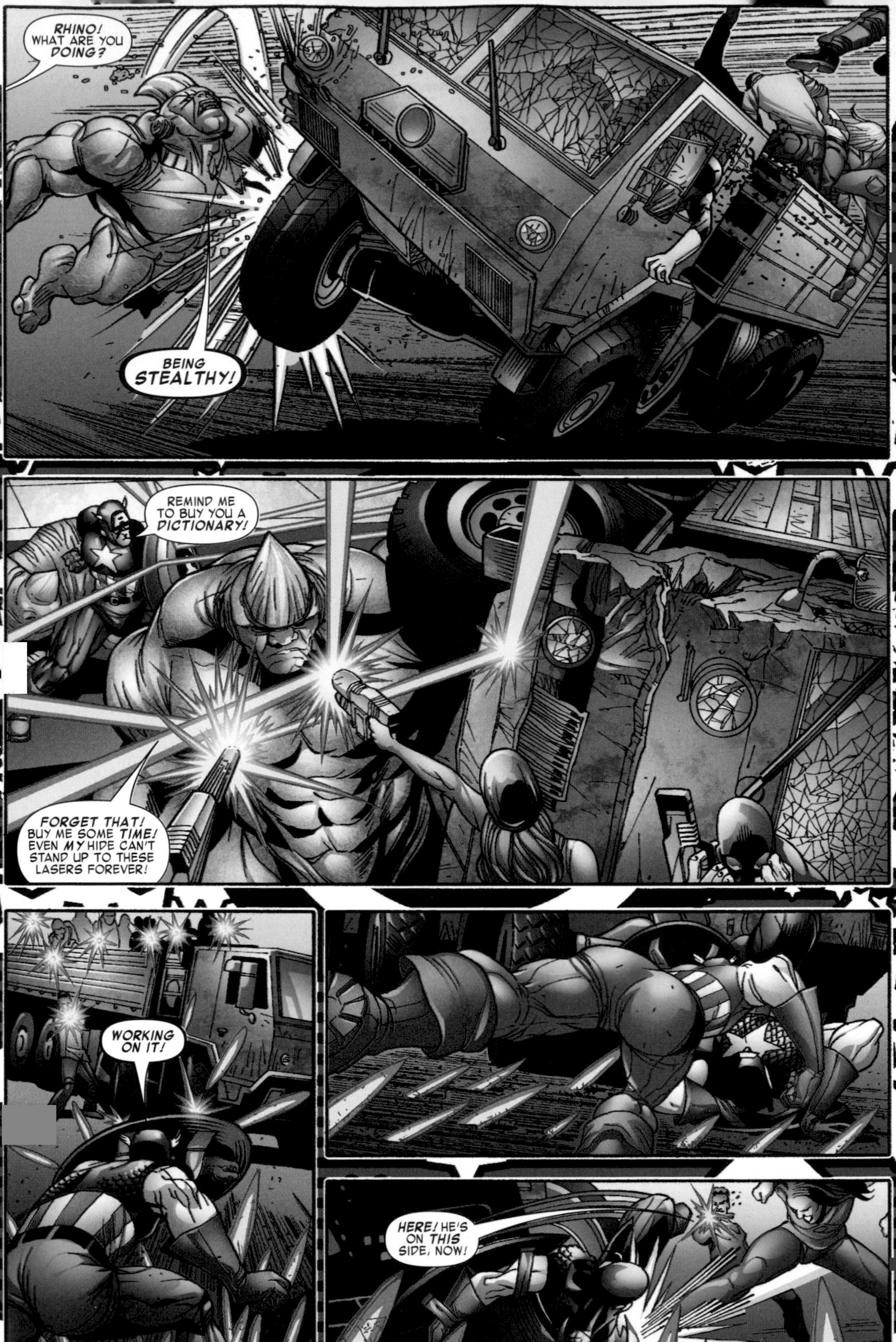
RHINO! WHAT ARE YOU DOING?
BEING STEALTHY!
REMIND ME TO BUY YOU A DICTIONARY!
FORGET THAT! BUY ME SOME TIME! EVEN MY HIDE CAN'T STAND UP TO THESE LASERS FOREVER!
WORKING ON IT!
HERE! HE'S ON THIS SIDE, NOW!
UNNHH!

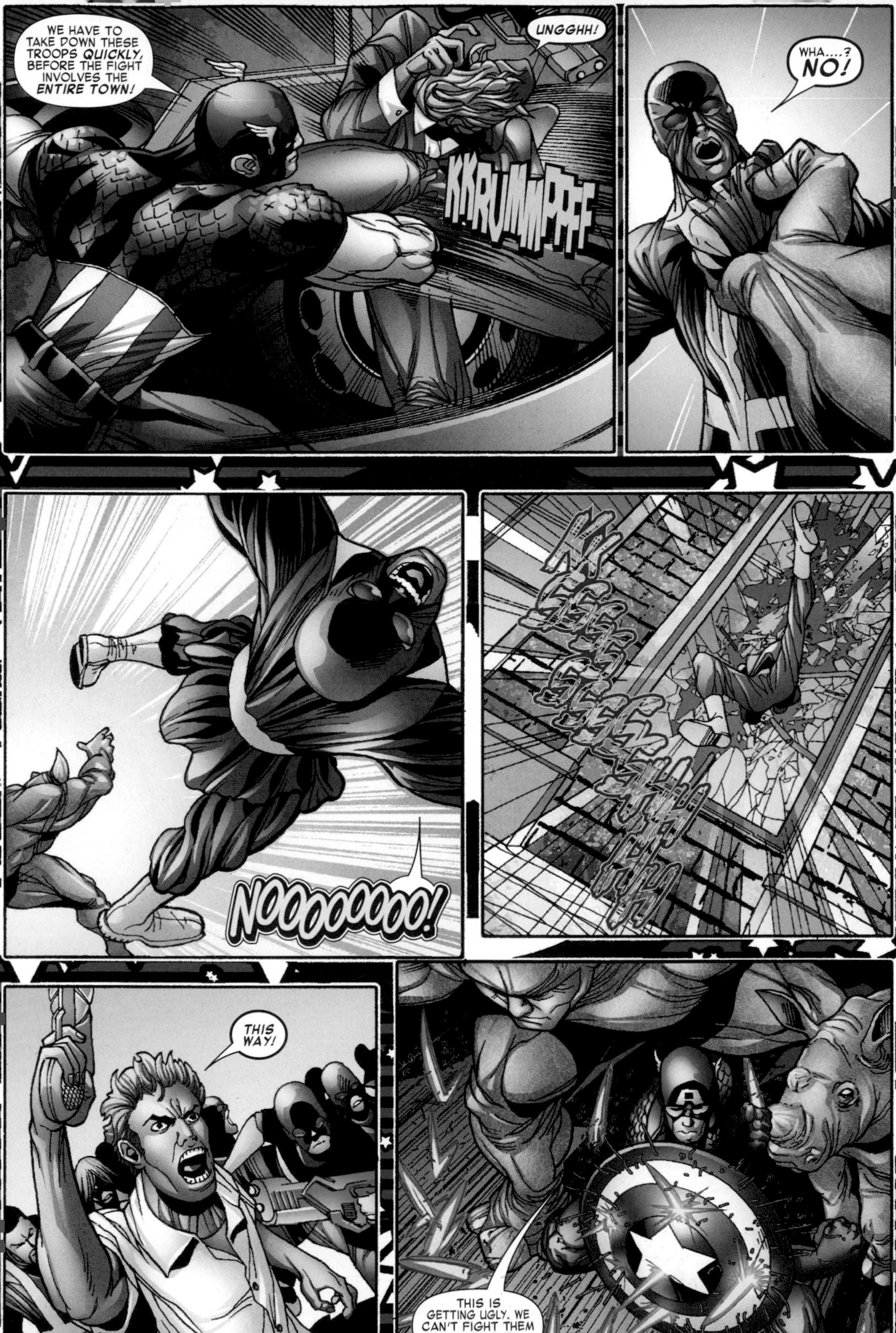
WE HAVE TO TAKE DOWN THESE TROOPS QUICKLY, BEFORE THE FIGHT INVOLVES THE ENTIRE TOWN!
UNGGHH!
KKRUMMPFF
WHA....? NO!
NOOOOOOOO!
THIS WAY!
THIS IS GETTING UGLY. WE CAN'T FIGHT THEM ALL. NOT EVEN WITH YOU.
GET US THROUGH THAT WALL.

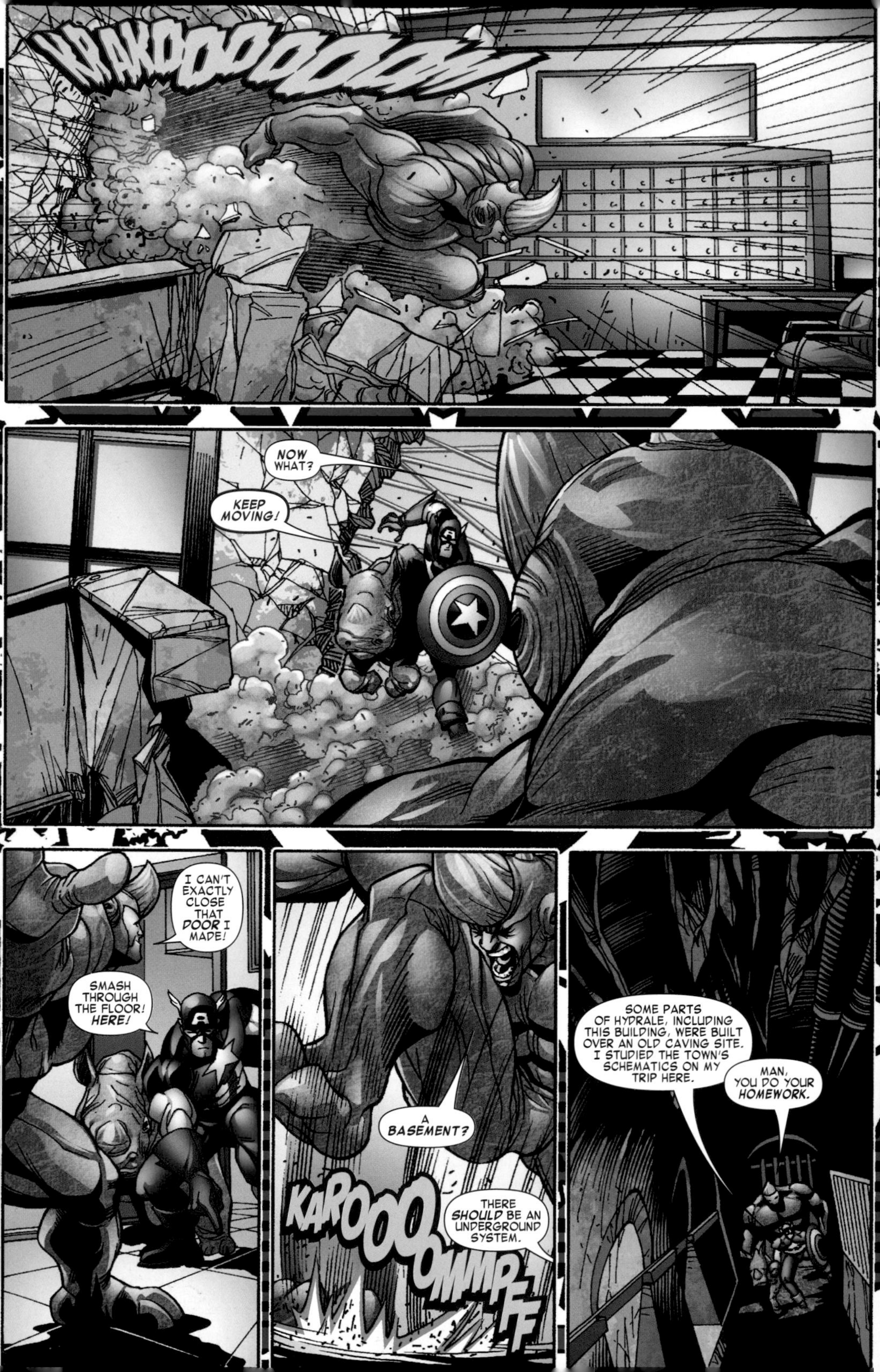
KRAKOOOOOOOM!
NOW WHAT?
KEEP MOVING!
I CAN'T EXACTLY CLOSE THAT DOOR I MADE!
SMASH THROUGH THE FLOOR! HERE!
A BASEMENT?
KAROOOOMMPFF
THERE SHOULD BE AN UNDERGROUND SYSTEM.
SOME PARTS OF HYDRALE, INCLUDING THIS BUILDING, WERE BUILT OVER AN OLD CAVING SITE. I STUDIED THE TOWN'S SCHEMATICS ON MY TRIP HERE.
MAN, YOU DO YOUR HOMEWORK.

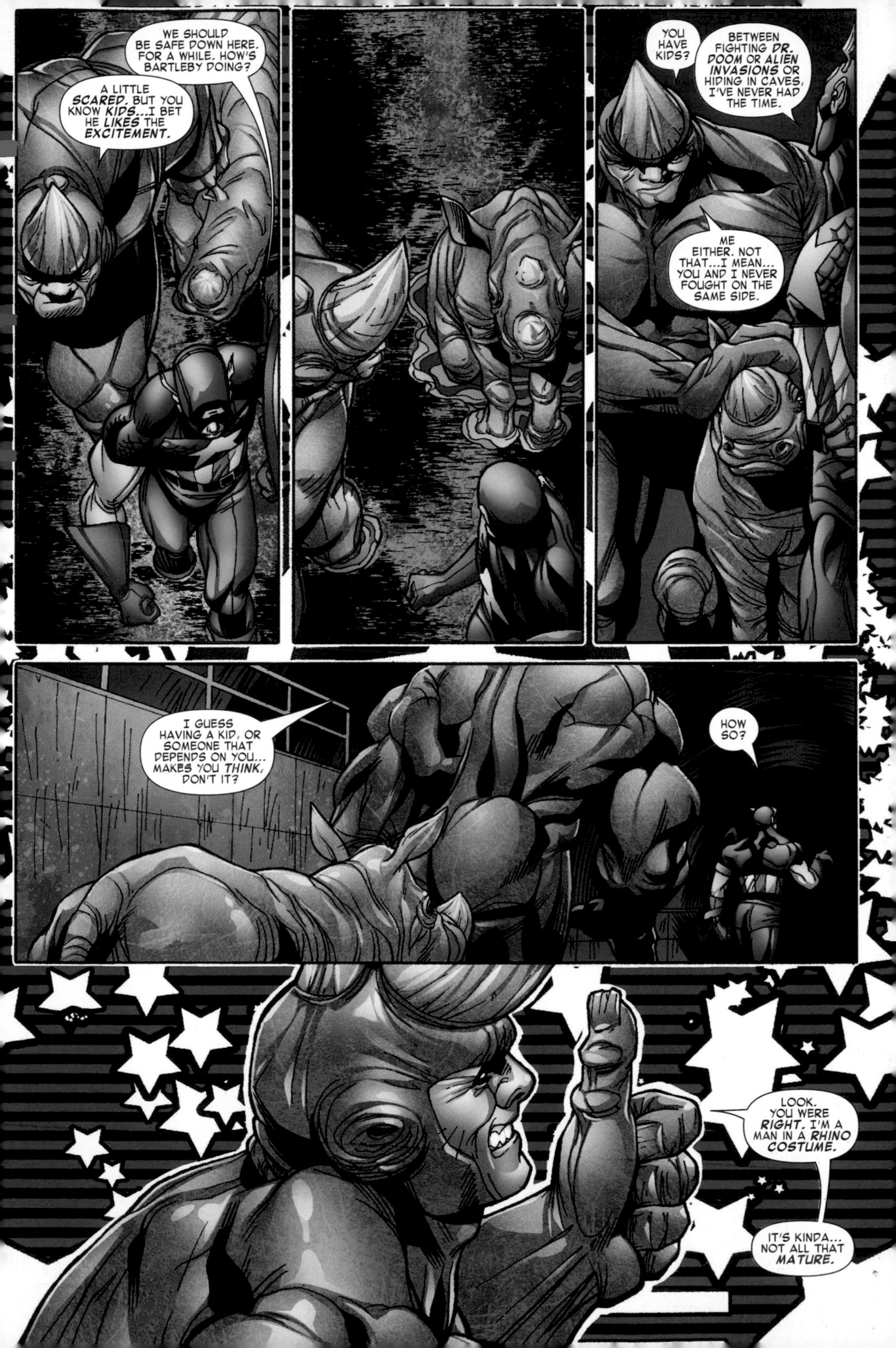
WE SHOULD BE SAFE DOWN HERE. FOR A WHILE. HOW'S BARTLEBY DOING?
A LITTLE SCARED. BUT YOU KNOW KIDS...I BET HE LIKES THE EXCITEMENT.
YOU HAVE KIDS?
BETWEEN FIGHTING DR. DOOM OR ALIEN INVASIONS OR HIDING IN CAVES, I'VE NEVER HAD THE TIME.
ME EITHER. NOT THAT...I MEAN... YOU AND I NEVER FOUGHT ON THE SAME SIDE.
I GUESS HAVING A KID, OR SOMEONE THAT DEPENDS ON YOU... MAKES YOU THINK, DON'T IT?
HOW SO?
LOOK. YOU WERE RIGHT. I'M A MAN IN A RHINO COSTUME.
IT'S KINDA... NOT ALL THAT MATURE.

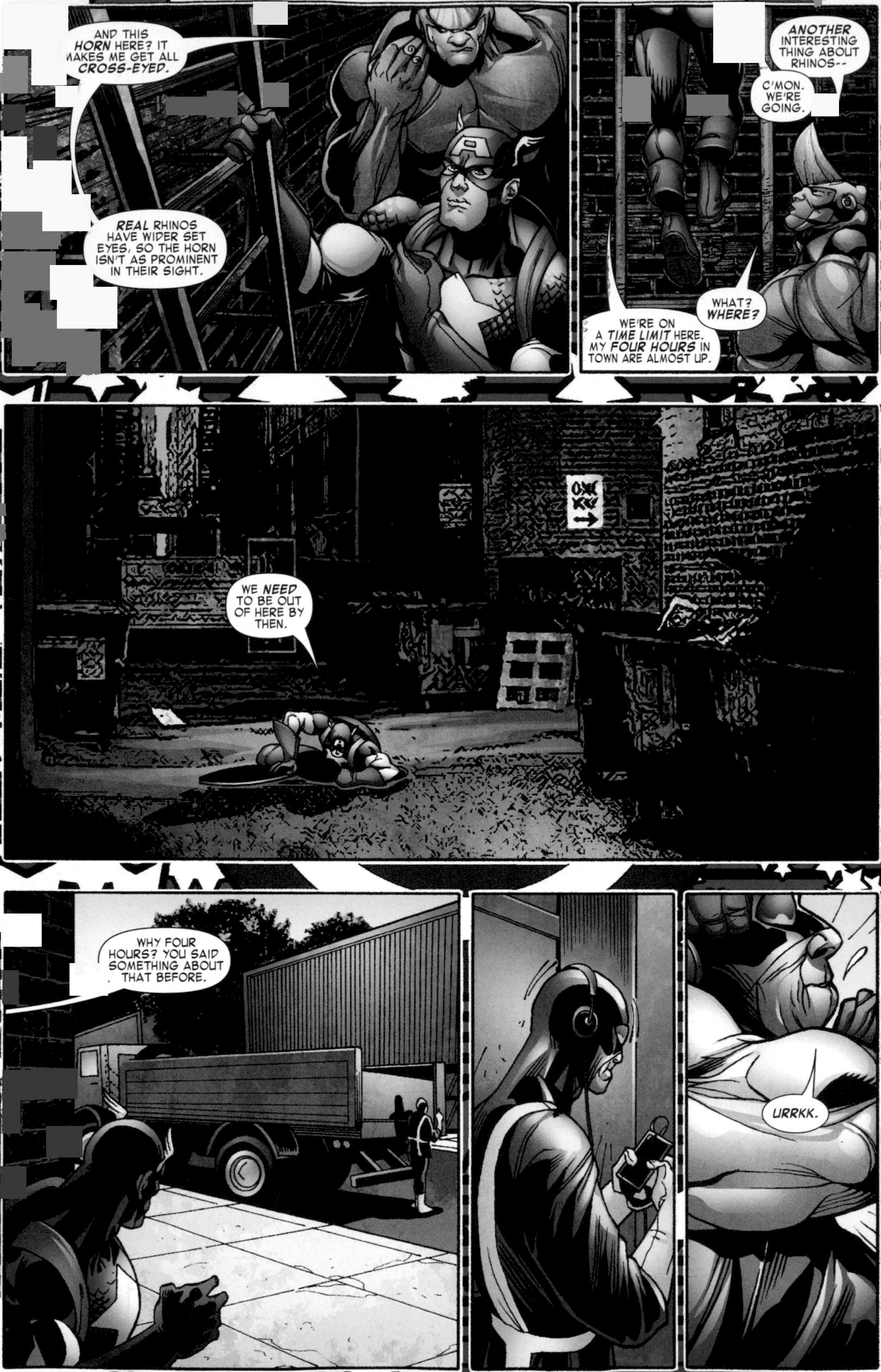
AND THIS HORN HERE? IT MAKES ME GET ALL CROSS-EYED.
REAL RHINOS HAVE WIDER SET EYES, SO THE HORN ISN'T AS PROMINENT IN THEIR SIGHT.
ANOTHER INTERESTING THING ABOUT RHINOS--
C'MON. WE'RE GOING.
WHAT? WHERE?
WE'RE ON A TIME LIMIT HERE. MY FOUR HOURS IN TOWN ARE ALMOST UP.
WE NEED TO BE OUT OF HERE BY THEN.
WHY FOUR HOURS? YOU SAID SOMETHING ABOUT THAT BEFORE.
URRKK.

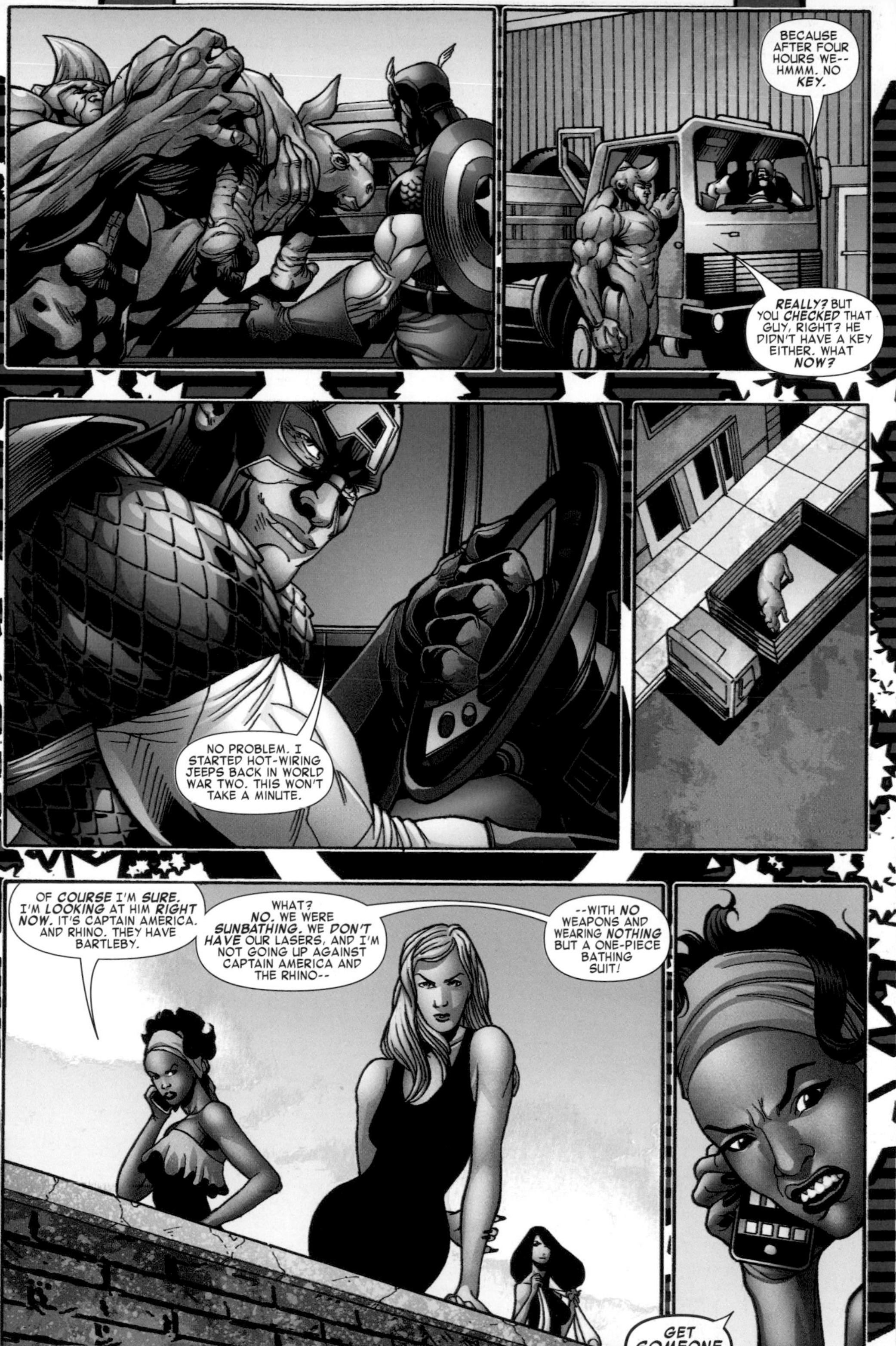
BECAUSE AFTER FOUR HOURS WE-- HMMM. NO KEY.
REALLY? BUT YOU CHECKED THAT GUY, RIGHT? HE DIDN'T HAVE A KEY EITHER. WHAT NOW?
NO PROBLEM. I STARTED HOT-WIRING JEEPS BACK IN WORLD WAR TWO. THIS WON'T TAKE A MINUTE.
OF COURSE I'M SURE. I'M LOOKING AT HIM RIGHT NOW. IT'S CAPTAIN AMERICA. AND RHINO. THEY HAVE BARTLEBY.
WHAT? NO. WE WERE SUNBATHING. WE DON'T HAVE OUR LASERS, AND I'M NOT GOING UP AGAINST CAPTAIN AMERICA AND THE RHINO--
--WITH NO WEAPONS AND WEARING NOTHING BUT A ONE-PIECE BATHING SUIT!
GET SOMEONE HERE!

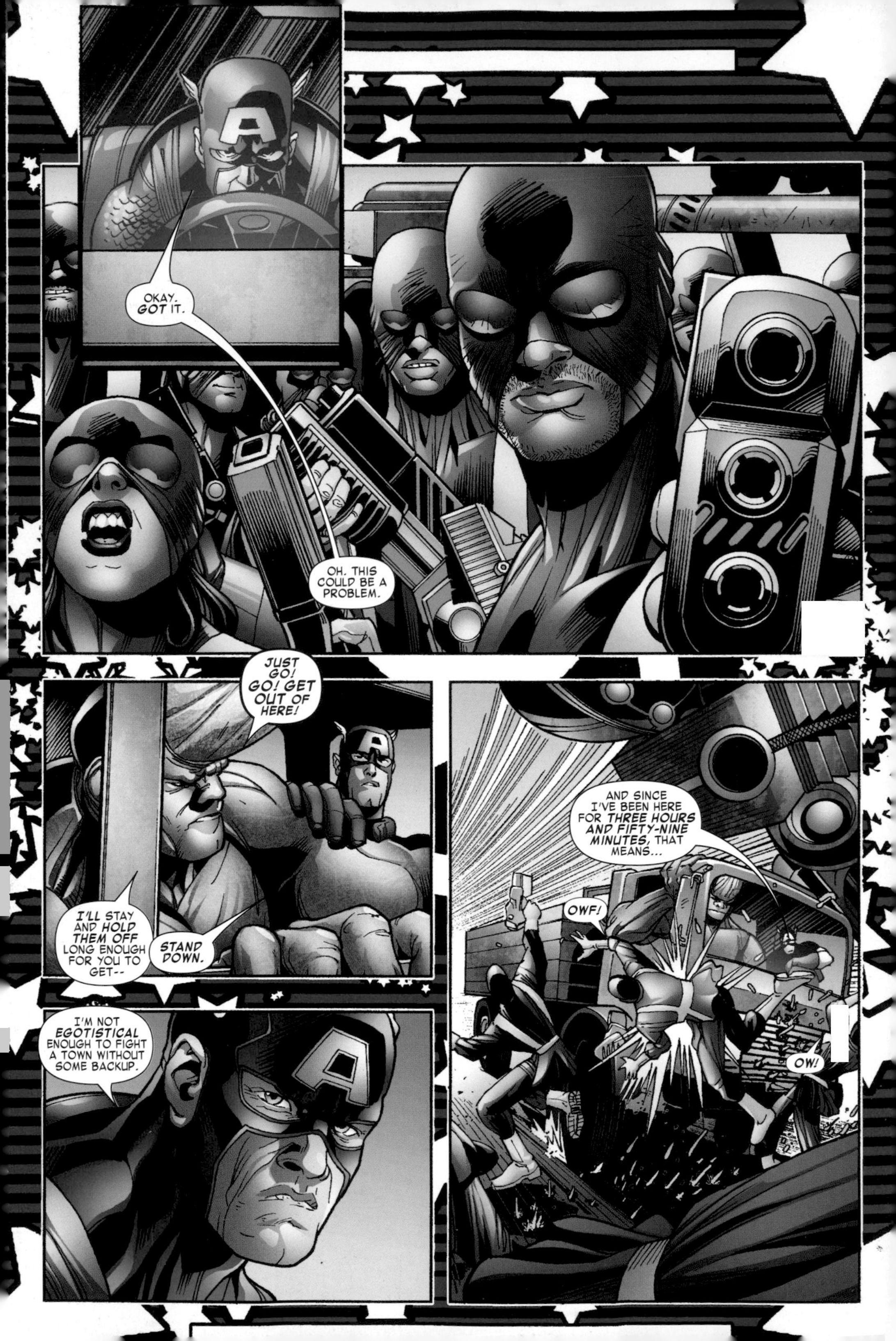
OKAY. GOT IT.
OH. THIS COULD BE A PROBLEM.
JUST GO! GO! GET OUT OF HERE!
I'LL STAY AND HOLD THEM OFF LONG ENOUGH FOR YOU TO GET--
STAND DOWN.
I'M NOT EGOTISTICAL ENOUGH TO FIGHT A TOWN WITHOUT SOME BACKUP.
AND SINCE I'VE BEEN HERE FOR THREE HOURS AND FIFTY-NINE MINUTES, THAT MEANS...
OWF!
OW!

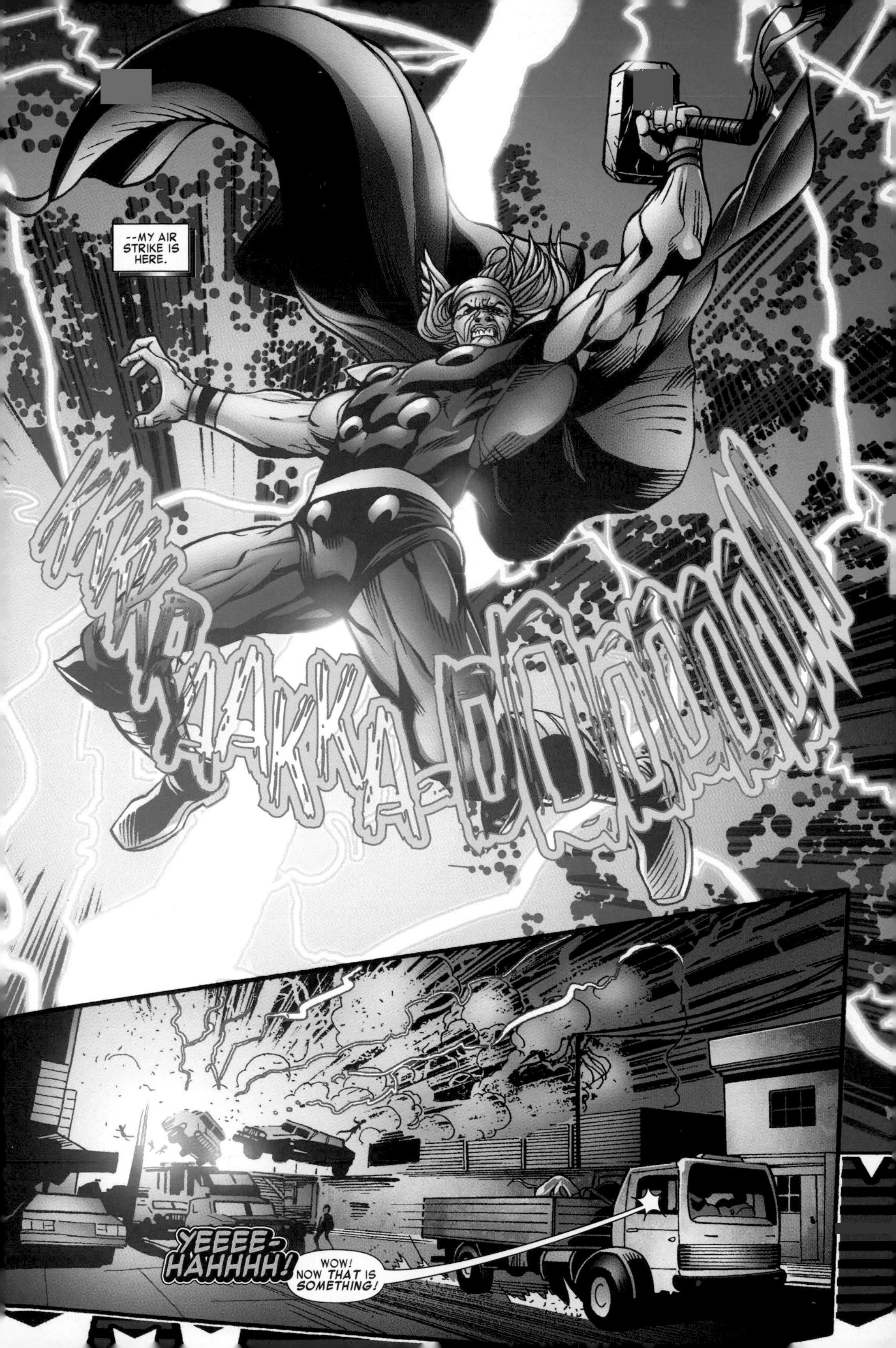
--MY AIR STRIKE IS HERE.
YEEEE-HAHHHH!
WOW! NOW THAT IS SOMETHING!

BUT...WHAT HAPPENS NOW?

YOU'RE STILL CAPTAIN AMERICA AND I'M... WHAT HAPPENS TO BARTLEBY?

HE GOES TO A RESERVE. I KNOW SOME PEOPLE. THEY'LL TAKE GOOD CARE OF HIM.

AS FOR YOU... YOU DID A GOOD THING TODAY, SO MAYBE I CAN LOOK THE OTHER WAY THIS ONCE.

HOPEFULLY THIS WILL CONVINCE YOU THERE'S A REWARD FOR DOING GOOD THINGS.

SO...I CAN GO FREE?

YES. GET OUT OF THE TRUCK. YOU CAN GO.

UMM... YOU GOING TO SLOW DOWN FIRST?

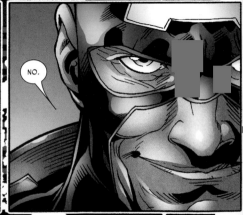

NO.

...END.

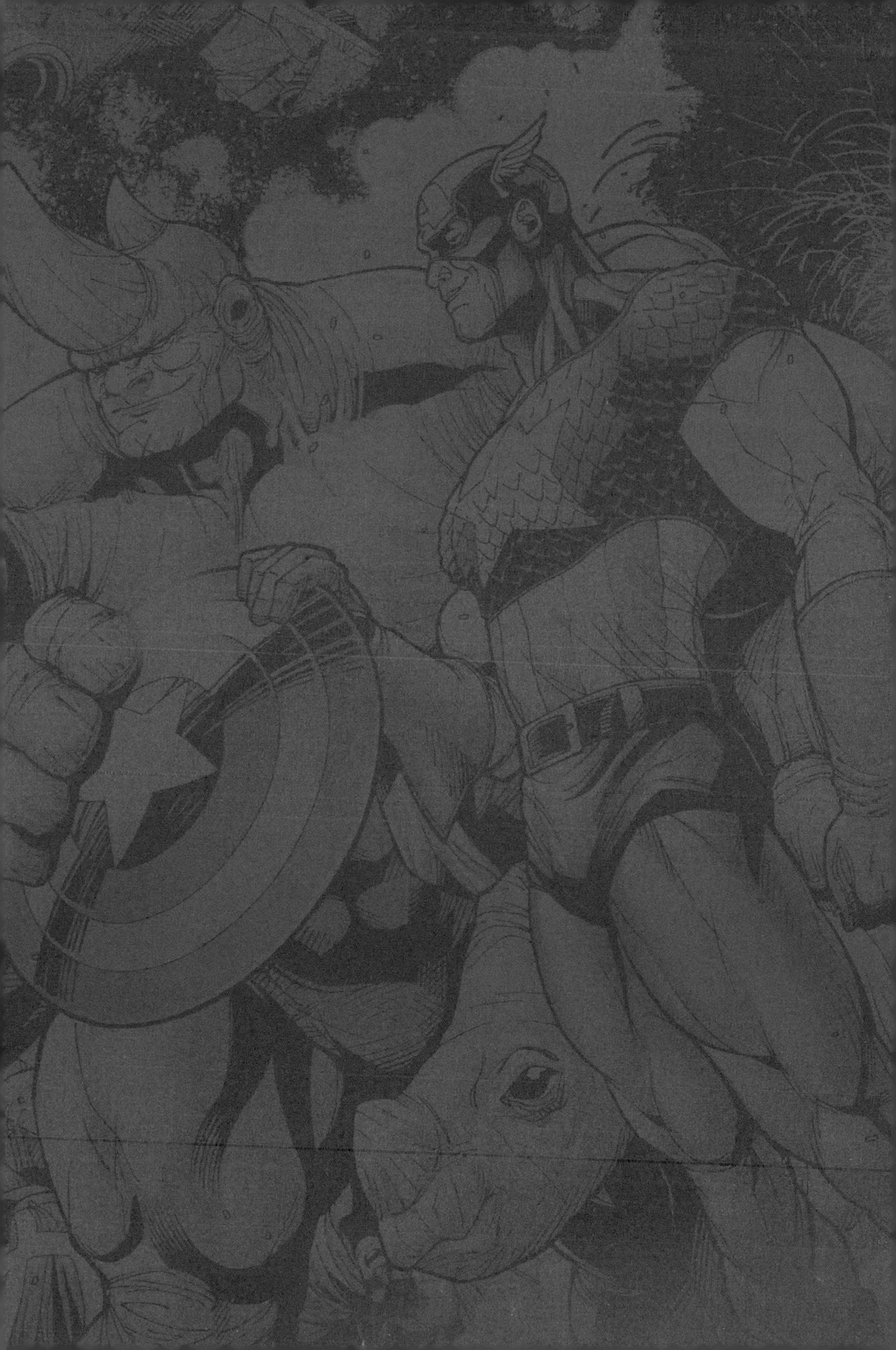

05

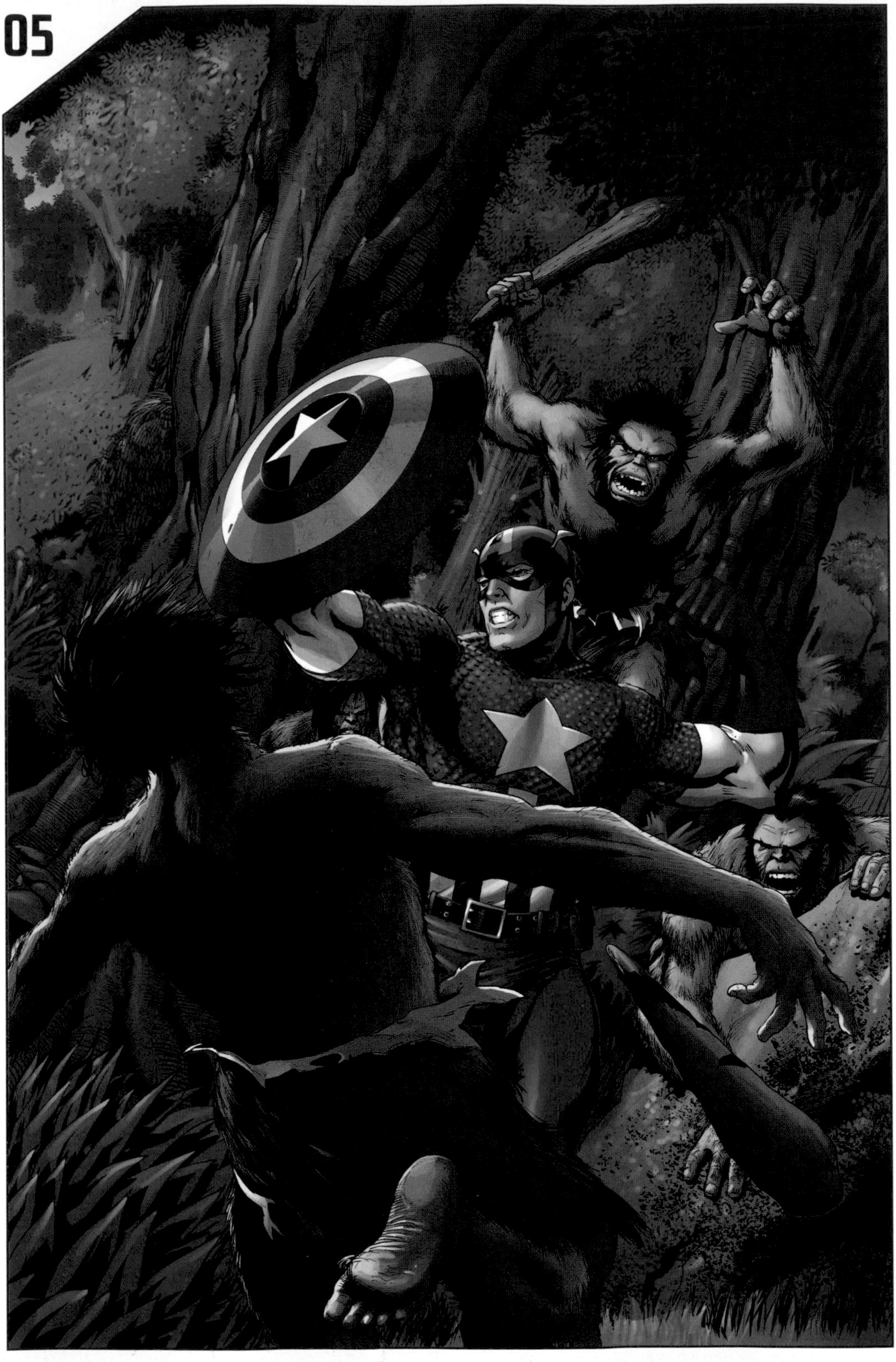

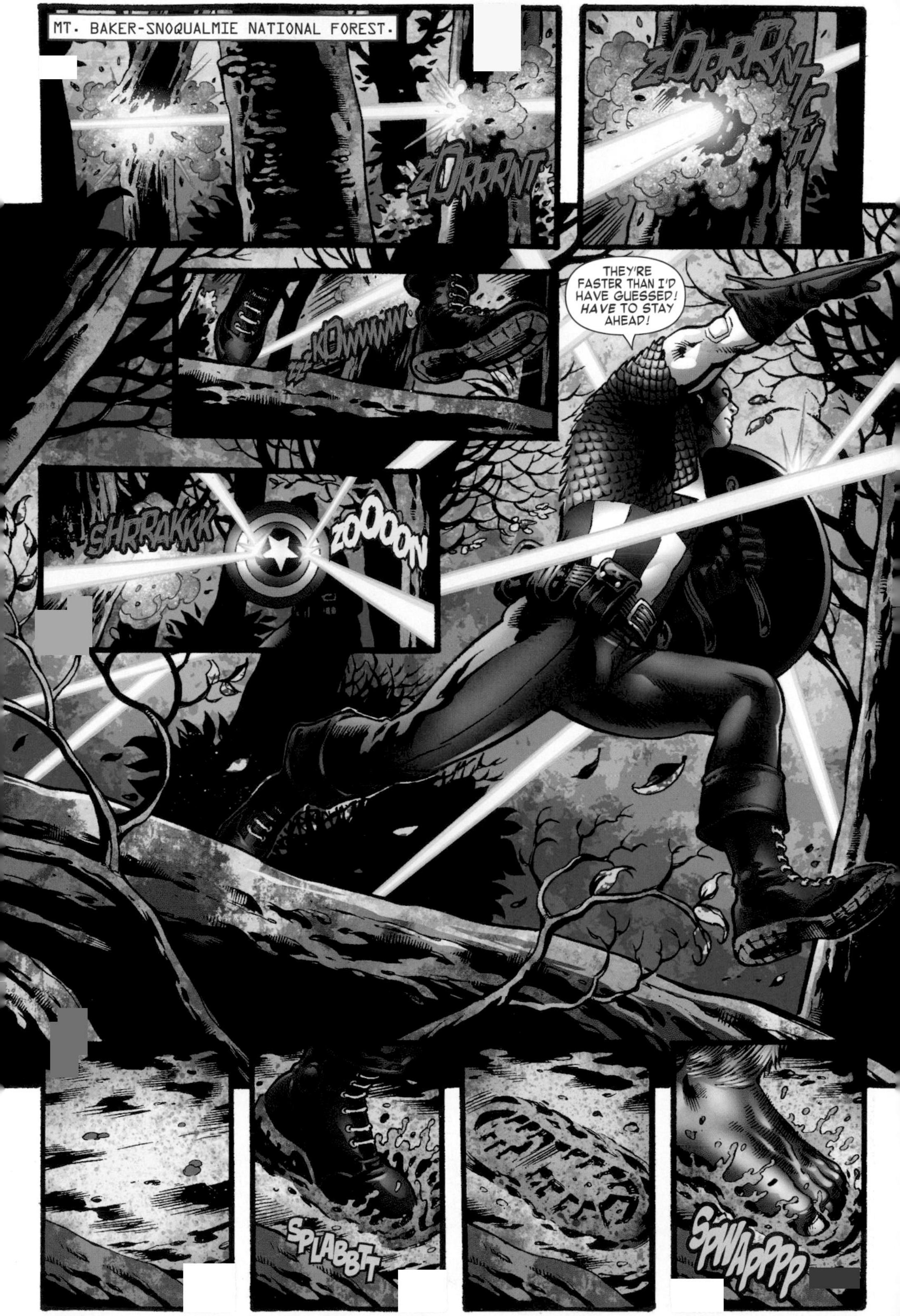
MT. BAKER-SNOQUALMIE NATIONAL FOREST.
ZORRRNT
ZORRRNTCH
THEY'RE FASTER THAN I'D HAVE GUESSED! *HAVE* TO STAY AHEAD!
SHRRAKKK
ZOOOON
SPLABBTT
SPWAPPPP

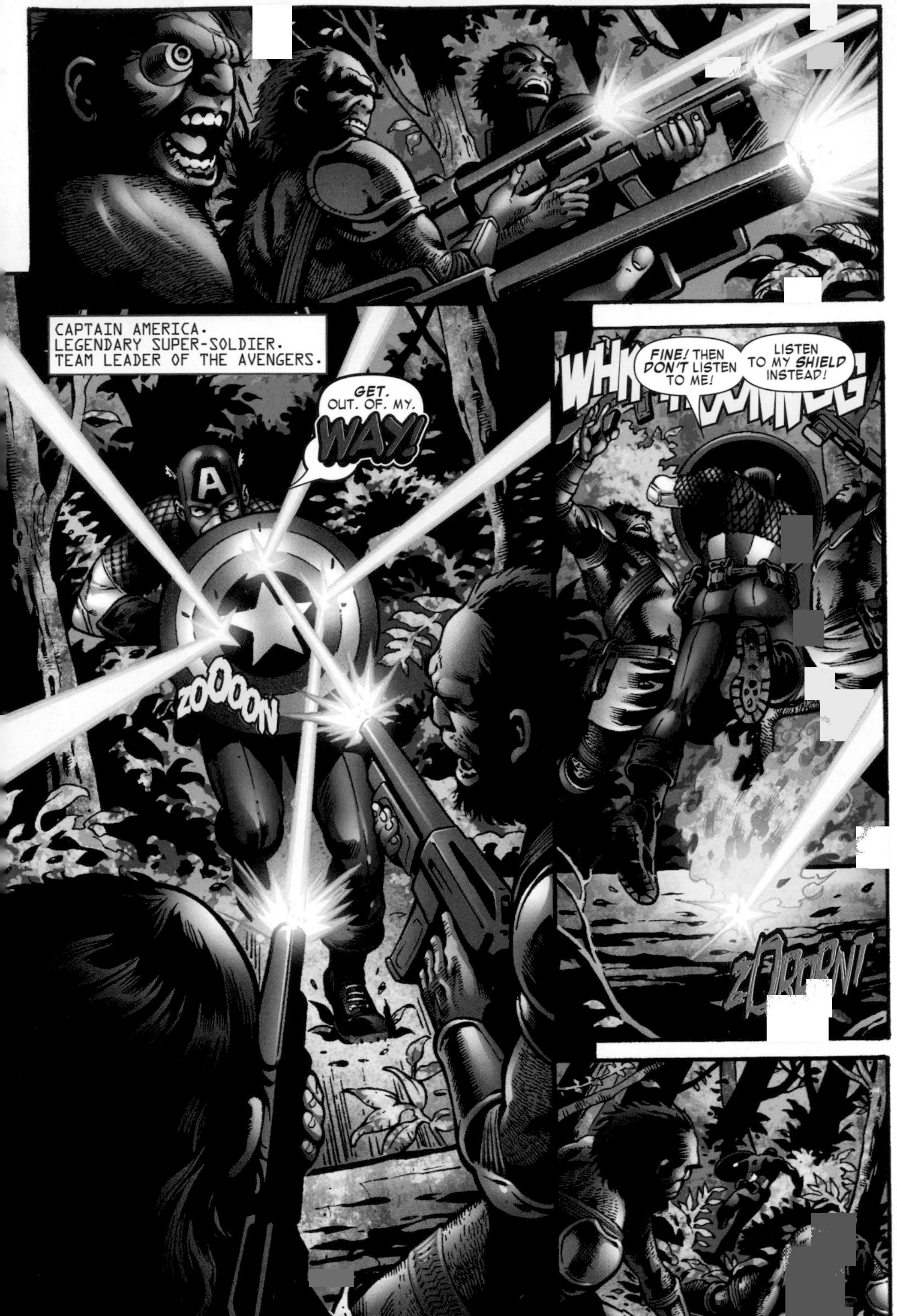

CAPTAIN AMERICA. LEGENDARY SUPER-SOLDIER. TEAM LEADER OF THE AVENGERS.
GET. OUT. OF. MY. WAY!
ZOOOON
FINE! THEN DON'T LISTEN TO ME!
LISTEN TO MY SHIELD INSTEAD!

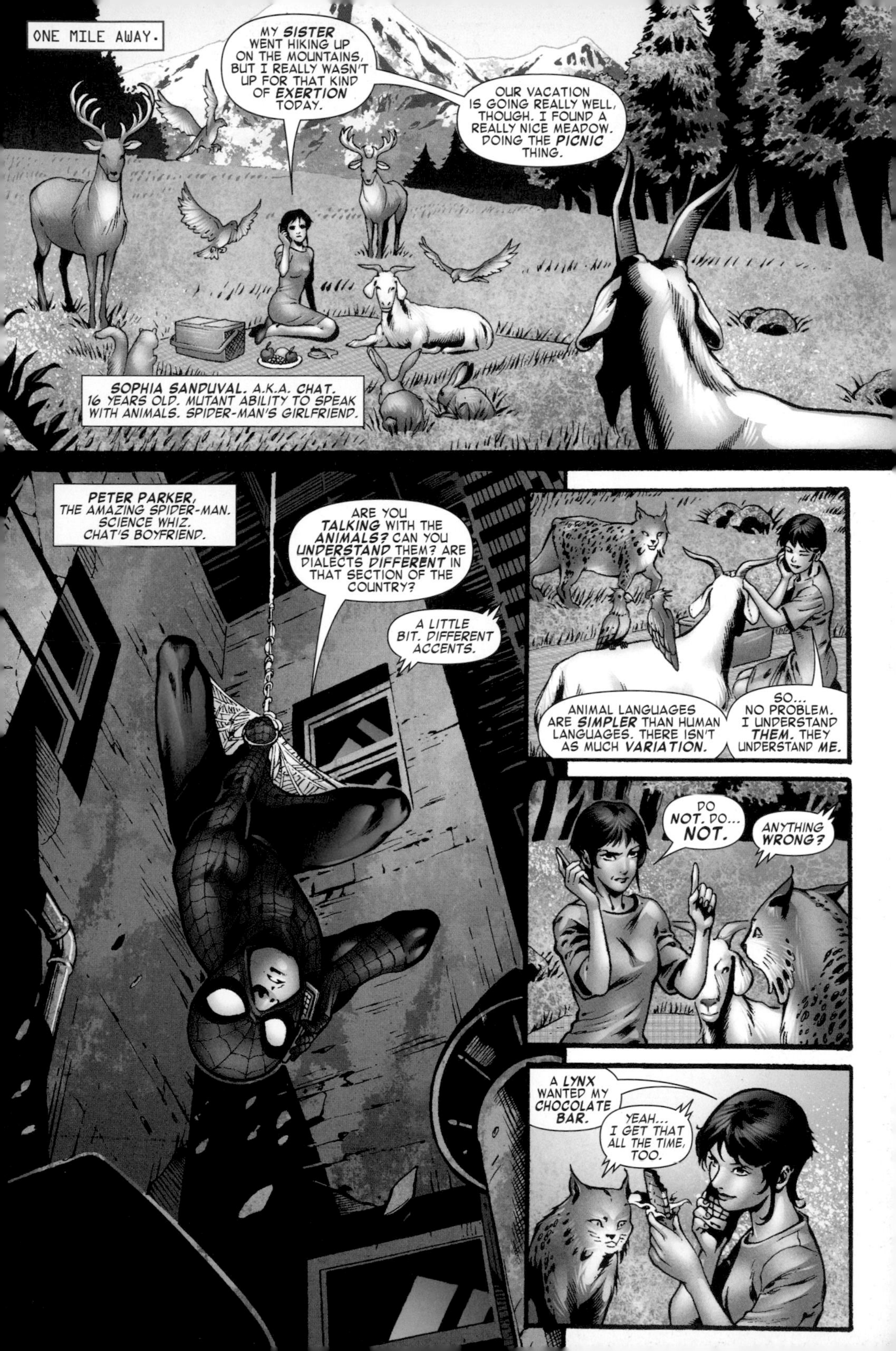
ONE MILE AWAY.
MY SISTER WENT HIKING UP ON THE MOUNTAINS, BUT I REALLY WASN'T UP FOR THAT KIND OF EXERTION TODAY.
OUR VACATION IS GOING REALLY WELL, THOUGH. I FOUND A REALLY NICE MEADOW. DOING THE PICNIC THING.
SOPHIA SANDUVAL. A.K.A. CHAT. 16 YEARS OLD. MUTANT ABILITY TO SPEAK WITH ANIMALS. SPIDER-MAN'S GIRLFRIEND.
PETER PARKER, THE AMAZING SPIDER-MAN. SCIENCE WHIZ. CHAT'S BOYFRIEND.
ARE YOU TALKING WITH THE ANIMALS? CAN YOU UNDERSTAND THEM? ARE DIALECTS DIFFERENT IN THAT SECTION OF THE COUNTRY?
A LITTLE BIT. DIFFERENT ACCENTS.
ANIMAL LANGUAGES ARE SIMPLER THAN HUMAN LANGUAGES. THERE ISN'T AS MUCH VARIATION.
SO... NO PROBLEM. I UNDERSTAND THEM. THEY UNDERSTAND ME.
DO NOT. DO... NOT.
ANYTHING WRONG?
A LYNX WANTED MY CHOCOLATE BAR.
YEAH... I GET THAT ALL THE TIME, TOO.

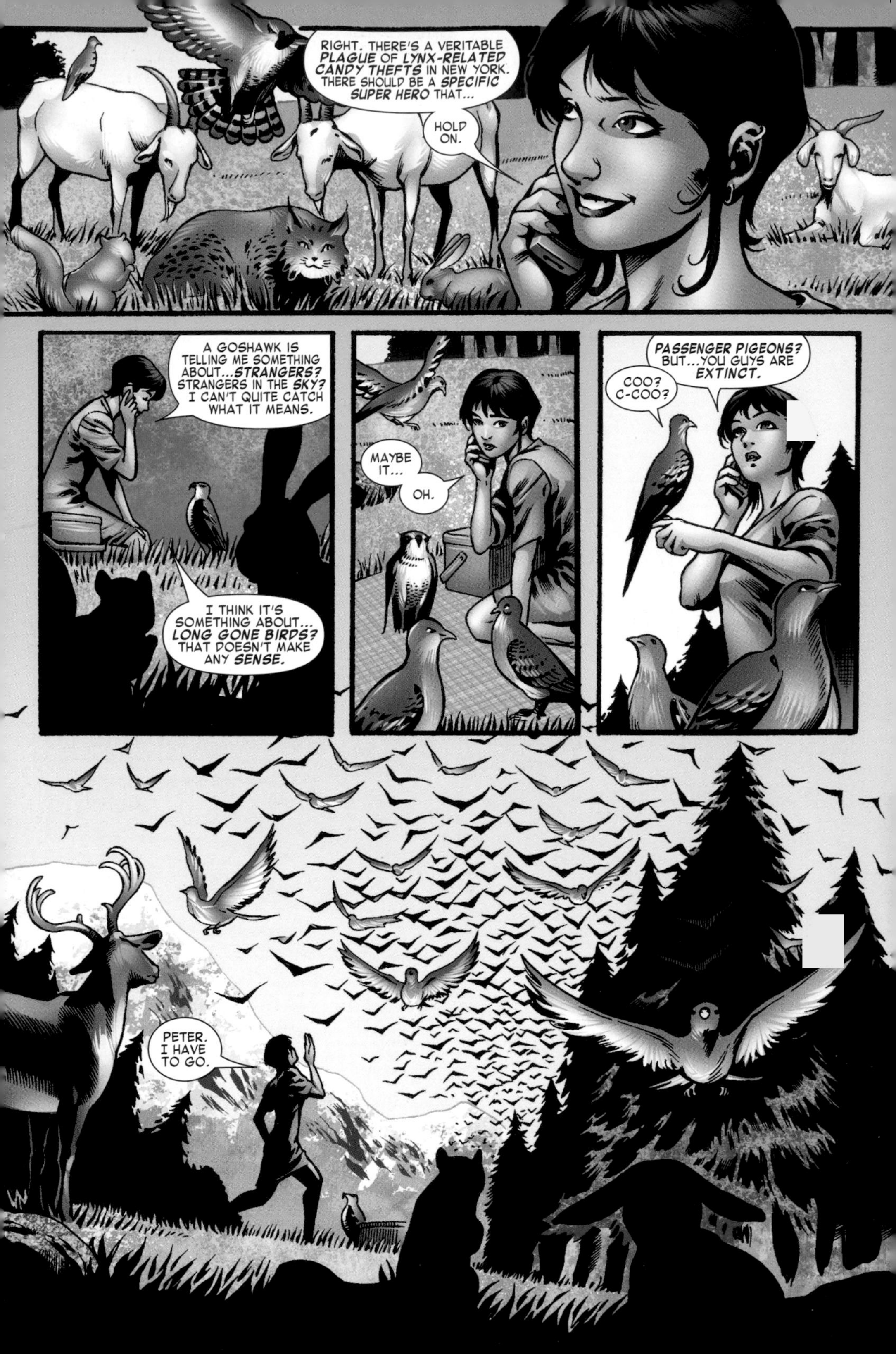
RIGHT. THERE'S A VERITABLE PLAGUE OF LYNX-RELATED CANDY THEFTS IN NEW YORK. THERE SHOULD BE A SPECIFIC SUPER HERO THAT...
HOLD ON.
A GOSHAWK IS TELLING ME SOMETHING ABOUT...STRANGERS? STRANGERS IN THE SKY? I CAN'T QUITE CATCH WHAT IT MEANS.
I THINK IT'S SOMETHING ABOUT... LONG GONE BIRDS? THAT DOESN'T MAKE ANY SENSE.
MAYBE IT...
OH.
PASSENGER PIGEONS? BUT...YOU GUYS ARE EXTINCT.
COO? C-COO?
PETER. I HAVE TO GO.

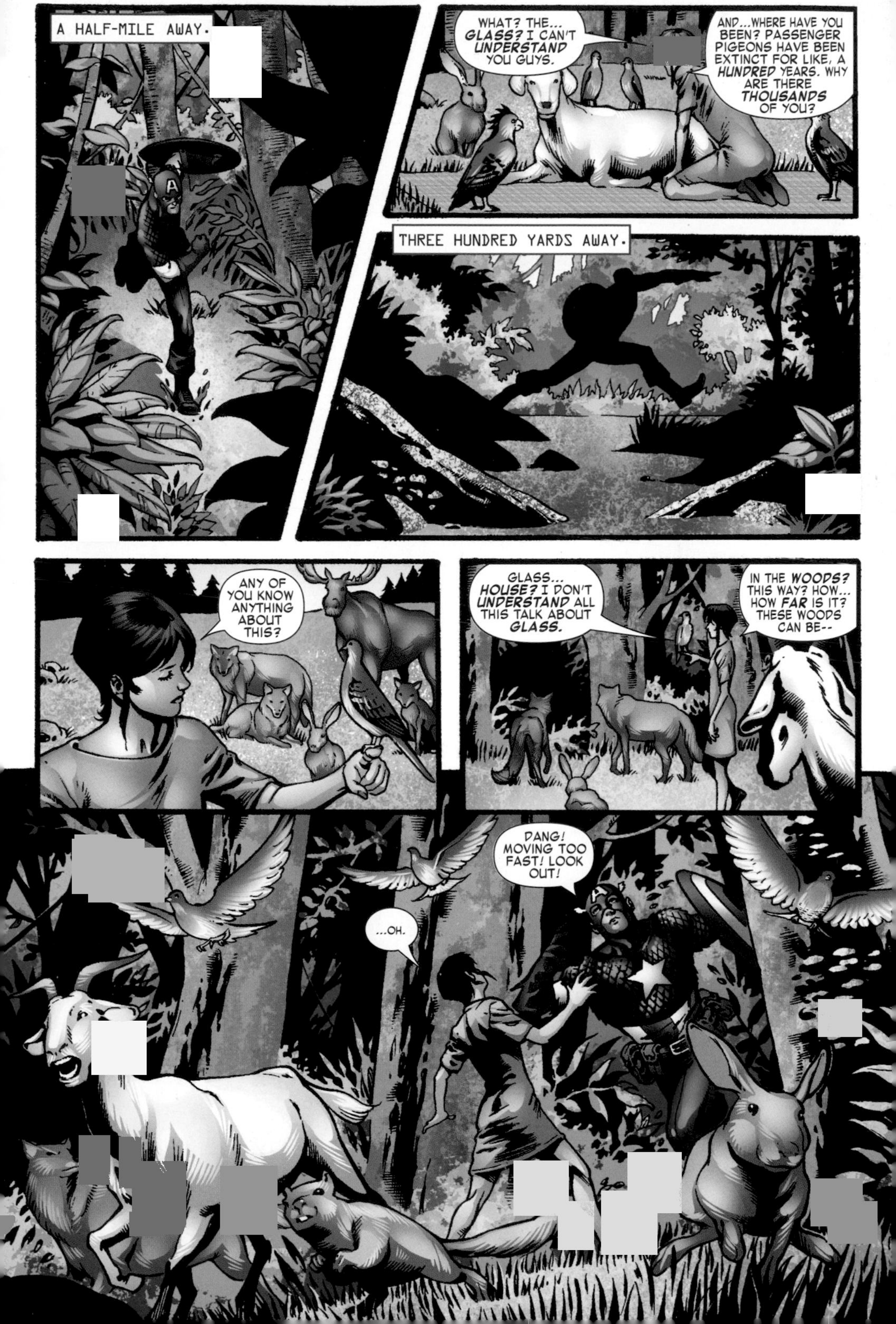
A HALF-MILE AWAY.
WHAT? THE... GLASS? I CAN'T UNDERSTAND YOU GUYS.
AND...WHERE HAVE YOU BEEN? PASSENGER PIGEONS HAVE BEEN EXTINCT FOR LIKE, A HUNDRED YEARS. WHY ARE THERE THOUSANDS OF YOU?
THREE HUNDRED YARDS AWAY.
ANY OF YOU KNOW ANYTHING ABOUT THIS?
GLASS... HOUSE? I DON'T UNDERSTAND ALL THIS TALK ABOUT GLASS.
IN THE WOODS? THIS WAY? HOW... HOW FAR IS IT? THESE WOODS CAN BE--
DANG! MOVING TOO FAST! LOOK OUT!
...OH.

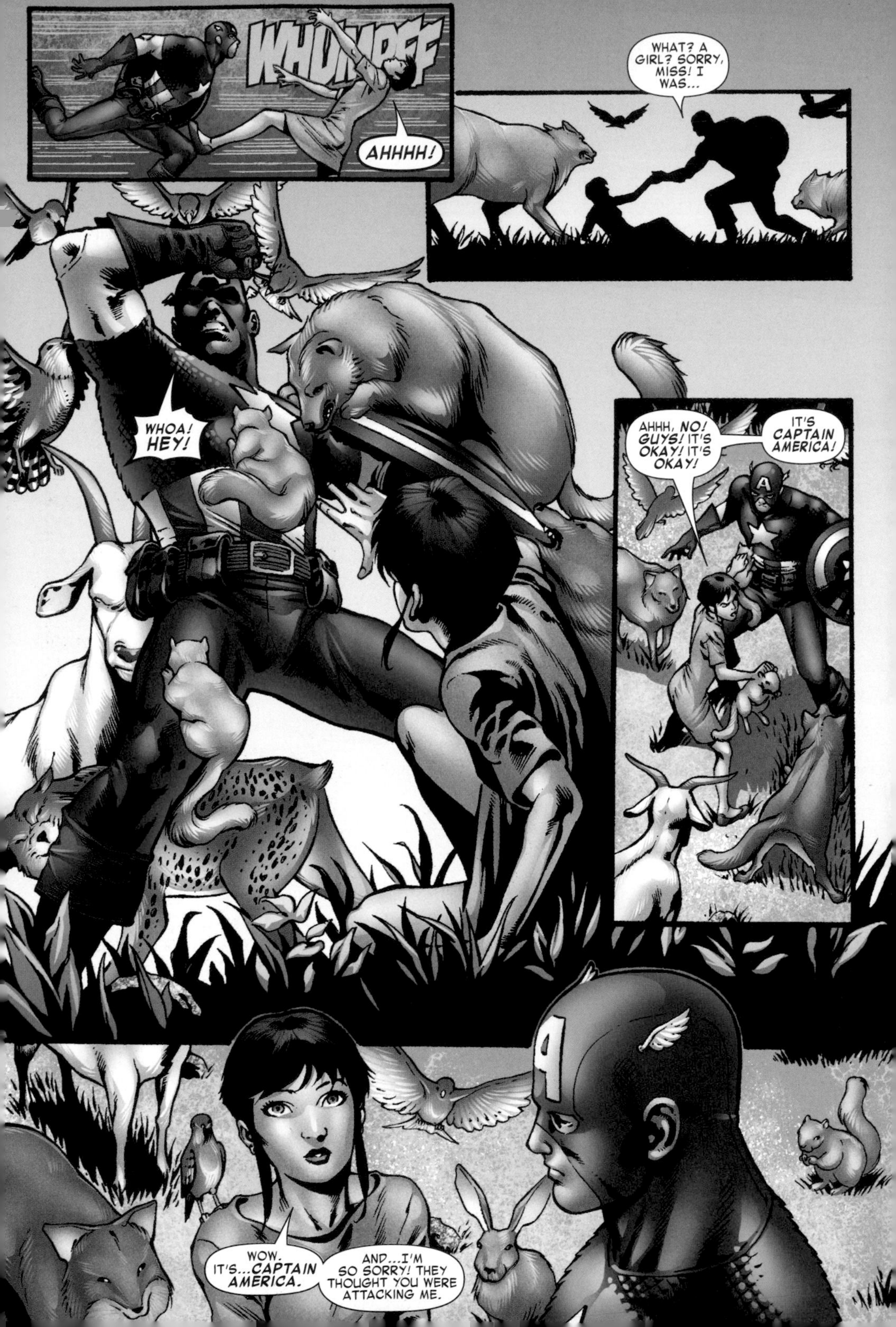
WHUMPFF
AHHHH!
WHAT? A GIRL? SORRY, MISS! I WAS...
WHOA! HEY!
AHHH, NO! GUYS! IT'S OKAY! IT'S OKAY!
IT'S CAPTAIN AMERICA!
WOW. IT'S...CAPTAIN AMERICA.
AND...I'M SO SORRY! THEY THOUGHT YOU WERE ATTACKING ME.

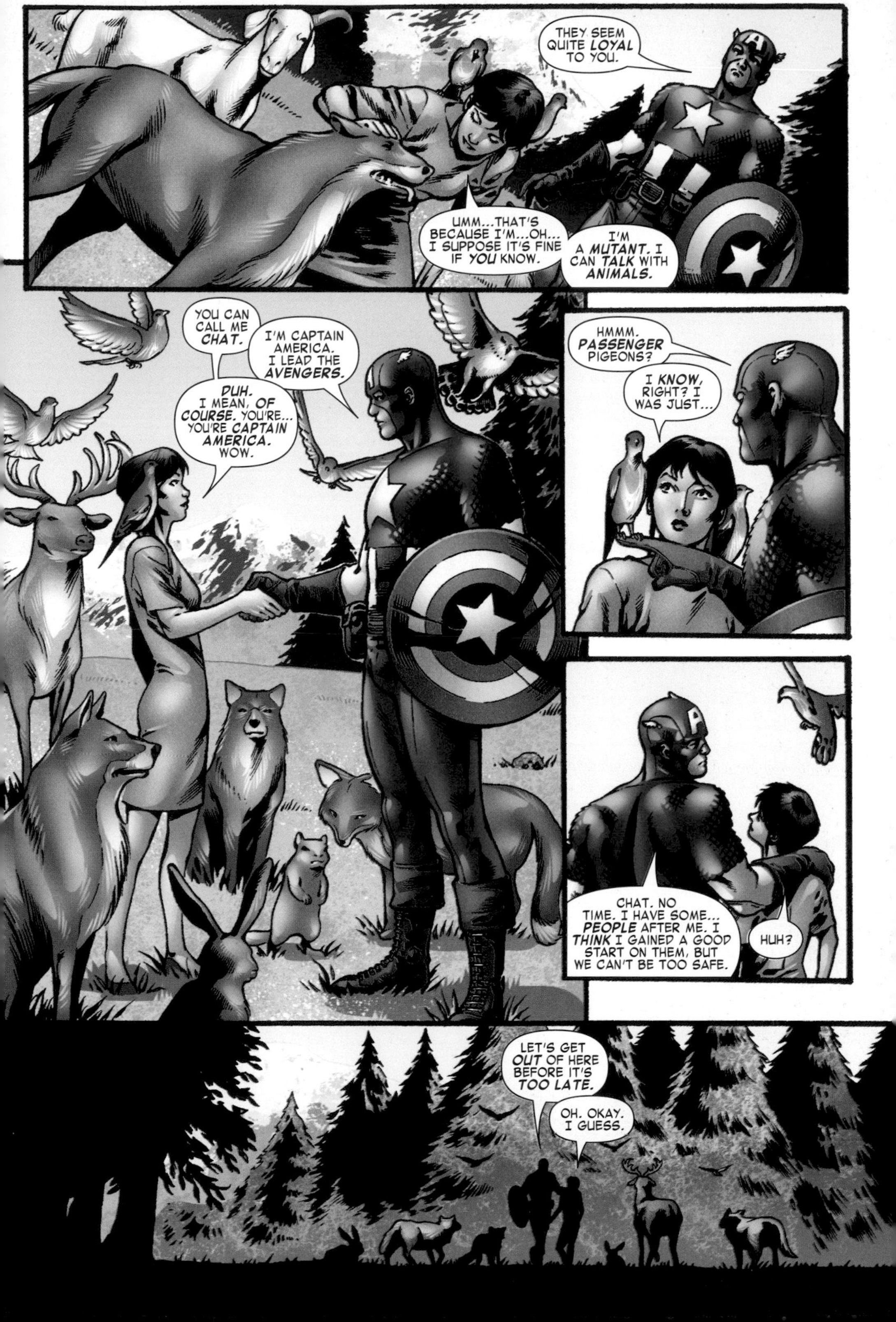
THEY SEEM QUITE LOYAL TO YOU.
UMM...THAT'S BECAUSE I'M...OH... I SUPPOSE IT'S FINE IF YOU KNOW.
I'M A MUTANT. I CAN TALK WITH ANIMALS.
I'M CAPTAIN AMERICA. I LEAD THE AVENGERS.
YOU CAN CALL ME CHAT.
DUH. I MEAN, OF COURSE. YOU'RE... YOU'RE CAPTAIN AMERICA. WOW.
HMMM. PASSENGER PIGEONS?
I KNOW, RIGHT? I WAS JUST...
CHAT. NO TIME. I HAVE SOME... PEOPLE AFTER ME. I THINK I GAINED A GOOD START ON THEM, BUT WE CAN'T BE TOO SAFE.
HUH?
LET'S GET OUT OF HERE BEFORE IT'S TOO LATE.
OH. OKAY. I GUESS.

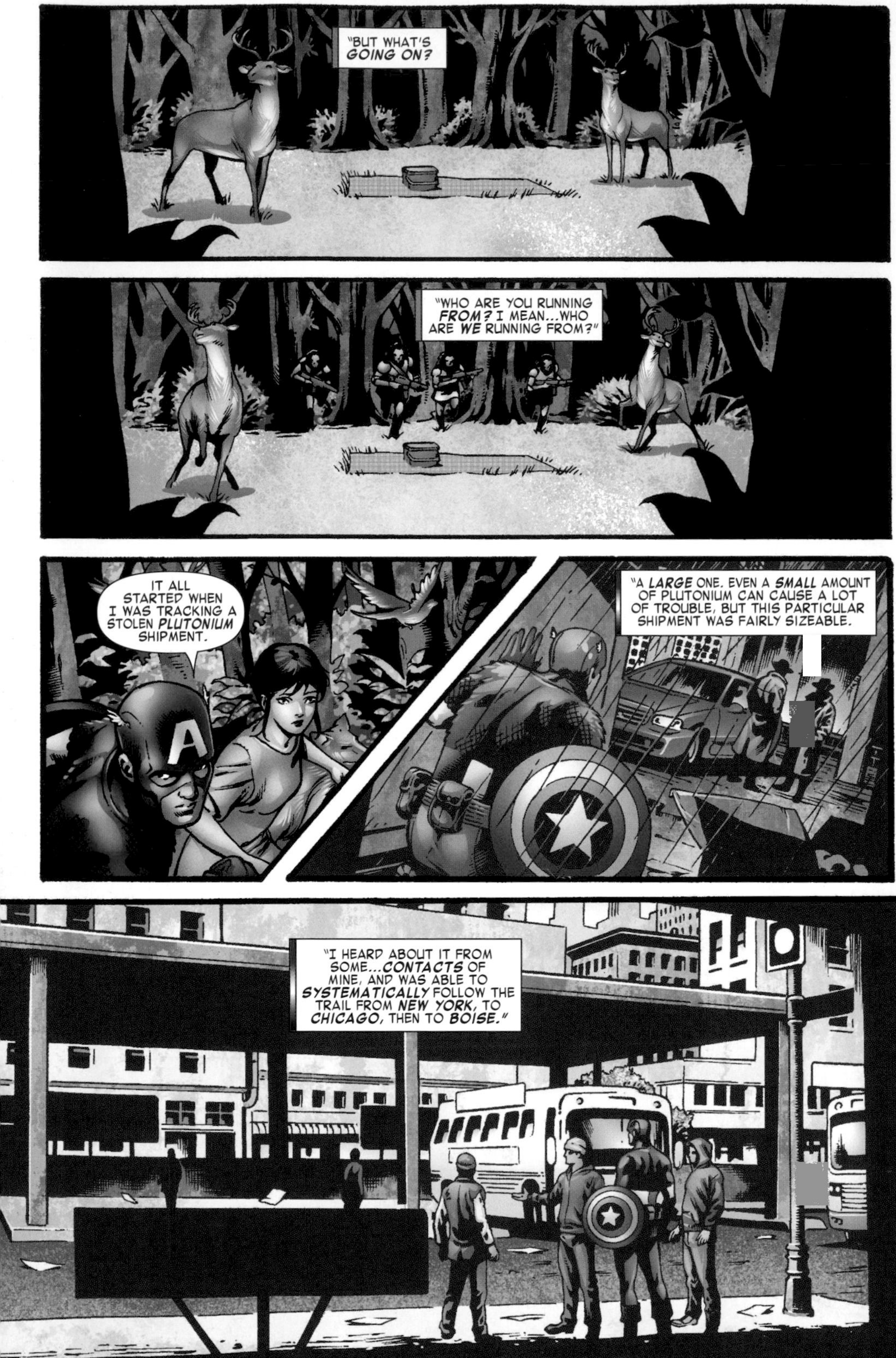
"BUT WHAT'S GOING ON?
"WHO ARE YOU RUNNING FROM? I MEAN...WHO ARE WE RUNNING FROM?"
IT ALL STARTED WHEN I WAS TRACKING A STOLEN PLUTONIUM SHIPMENT.
"A LARGE ONE. EVEN A SMALL AMOUNT OF PLUTONIUM CAN CAUSE A LOT OF TROUBLE, BUT THIS PARTICULAR SHIPMENT WAS FAIRLY SIZEABLE.
"I HEARD ABOUT IT FROM SOME...CONTACTS OF MINE, AND WAS ABLE TO SYSTEMATICALLY FOLLOW THE TRAIL FROM NEW YORK, TO CHICAGO, THEN TO BOISE."

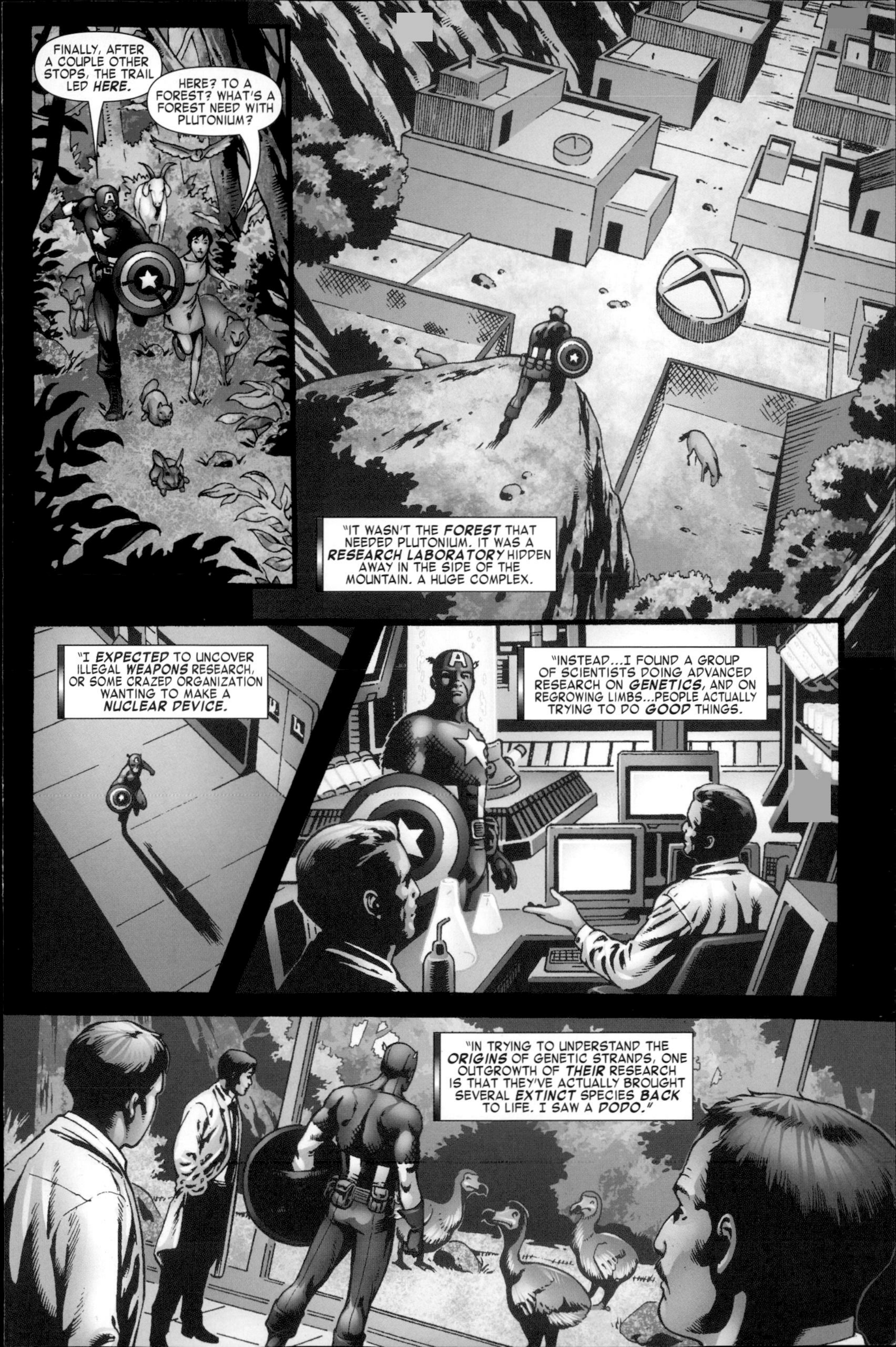

FINALLY, AFTER A COUPLE OTHER STOPS, THE TRAIL LED HERE.
HERE? TO A FOREST? WHAT'S A FOREST NEED WITH PLUTONIUM?
"IT WASN'T THE FOREST THAT NEEDED PLUTONIUM. IT WAS A RESEARCH LABORATORY HIDDEN AWAY IN THE SIDE OF THE MOUNTAIN. A HUGE COMPLEX.
"I EXPECTED TO UNCOVER ILLEGAL WEAPONS RESEARCH, OR SOME CRAZED ORGANIZATION WANTING TO MAKE A NUCLEAR DEVICE.
"INSTEAD...I FOUND A GROUP OF SCIENTISTS DOING ADVANCED RESEARCH ON GENETICS, AND ON REGROWING LIMBS...PEOPLE ACTUALLY TRYING TO DO GOOD THINGS.
"IN TRYING TO UNDERSTAND THE ORIGINS OF GENETIC STRANDS, ONE OUTGROWTH OF THEIR RESEARCH IS THAT THEY'VE ACTUALLY BROUGHT SEVERAL EXTINCT SPECIES BACK TO LIFE. I SAW A DODO."

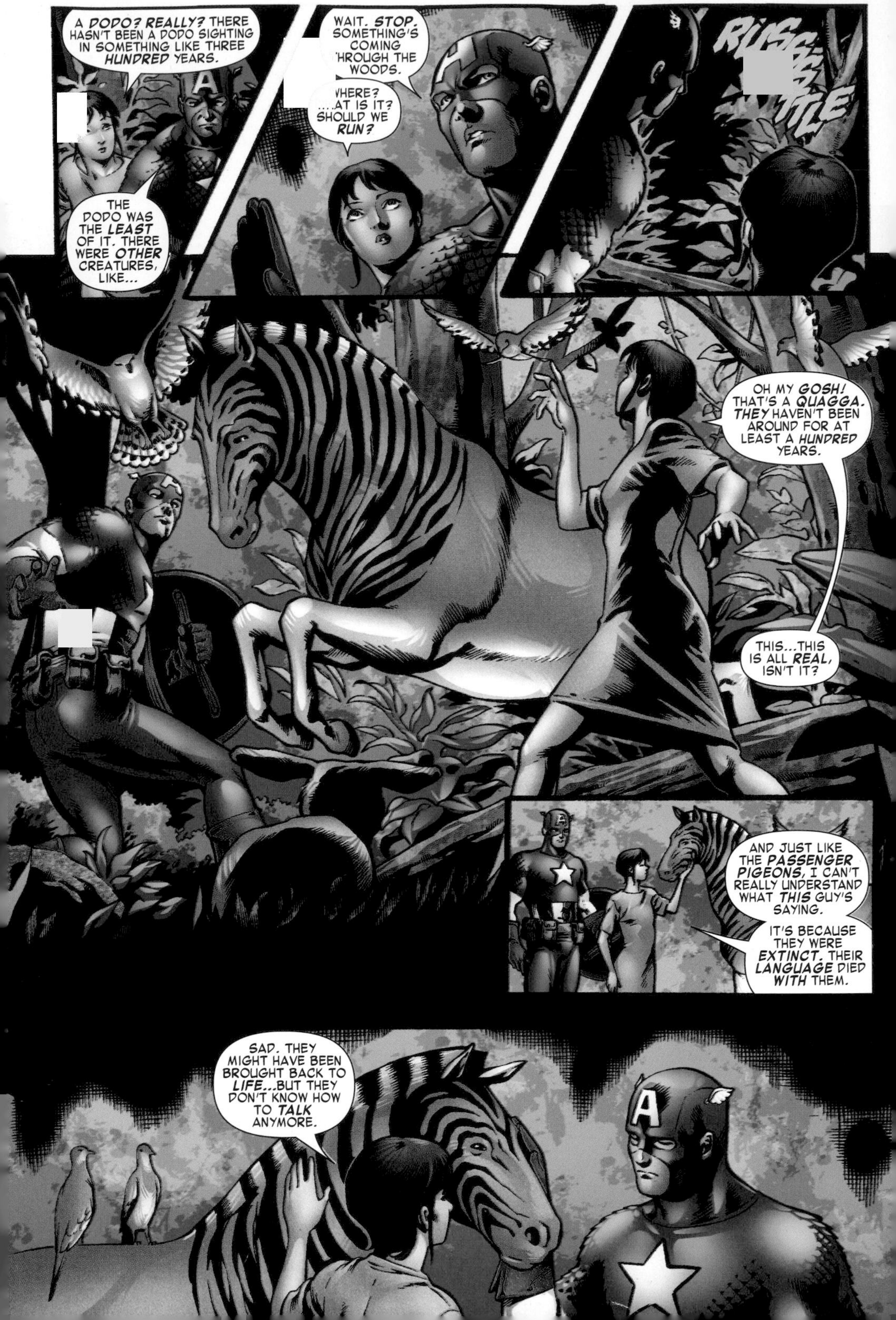
A DODO? REALLY? THERE HASN'T BEEN A DODO SIGHTING IN SOMETHING LIKE THREE HUNDRED YEARS.
THE DODO WAS THE LEAST OF IT. THERE WERE OTHER CREATURES, LIKE...
WAIT. STOP. SOMETHING'S COMING THROUGH THE WOODS.
WHERE? ...AT IS IT? SHOULD WE RUN?
OH MY GOSH! THAT'S A QUAGGA. THEY HAVEN'T BEEN AROUND FOR AT LEAST A HUNDRED YEARS.
THIS...THIS IS ALL REAL, ISN'T IT?
AND JUST LIKE THE PASSENGER PIGEONS, I CAN'T REALLY UNDERSTAND WHAT THIS GUY'S SAYING.
IT'S BECAUSE THEY WERE EXTINCT. THEIR LANGUAGE DIED WITH THEM.
SAD. THEY MIGHT HAVE BEEN BROUGHT BACK TO LIFE...BUT THEY DON'T KNOW HOW TO TALK ANYMORE.

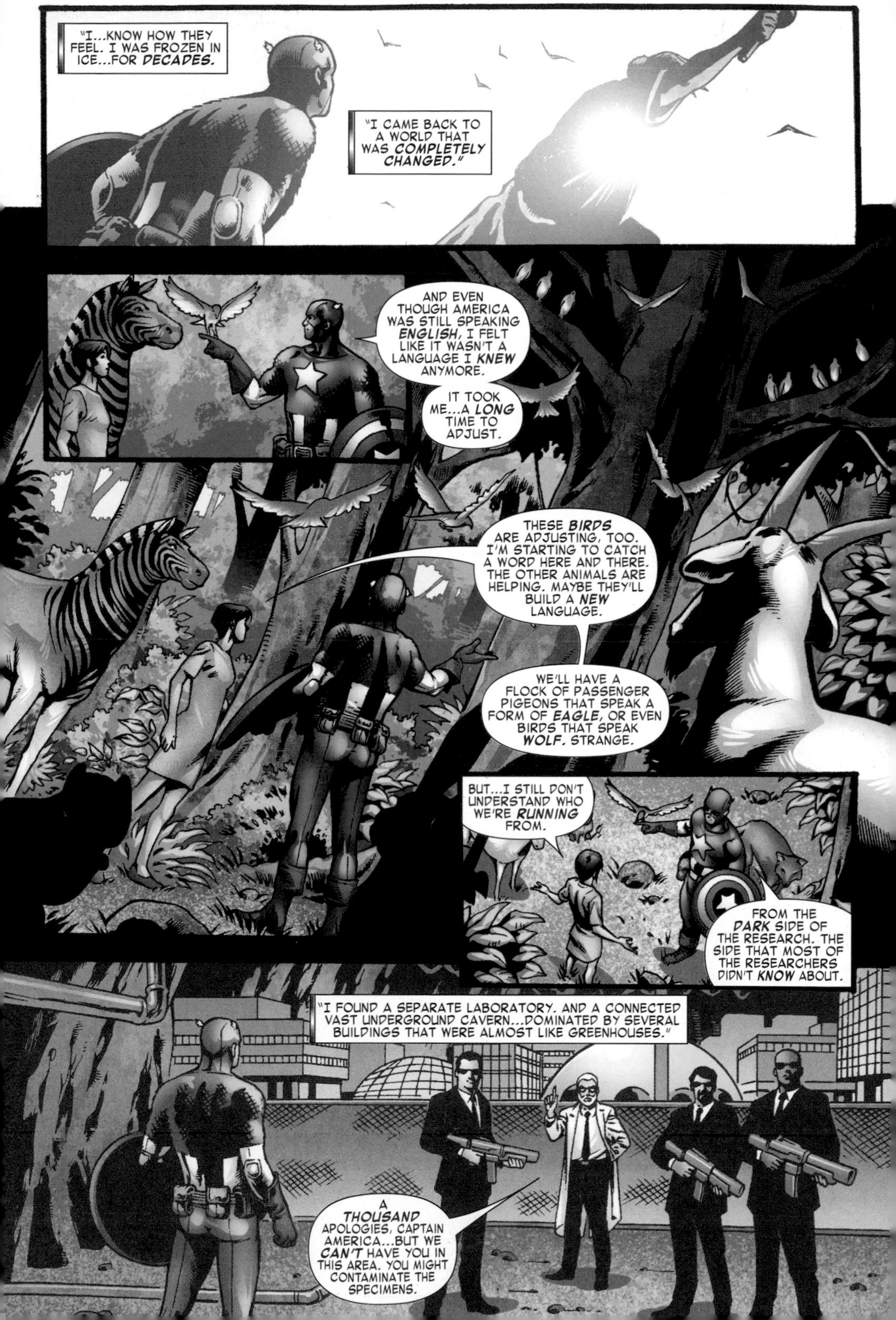
"I...KNOW HOW THEY FEEL. I WAS FROZEN IN ICE...FOR DECADES.
"I CAME BACK TO A WORLD THAT WAS COMPLETELY CHANGED."
AND EVEN THOUGH AMERICA WAS STILL SPEAKING ENGLISH, I FELT LIKE IT WASN'T A LANGUAGE I KNEW ANYMORE.
IT TOOK ME...A LONG TIME TO ADJUST.
THESE BIRDS ARE ADJUSTING, TOO. I'M STARTING TO CATCH A WORD HERE AND THERE. THE OTHER ANIMALS ARE HELPING. MAYBE THEY'LL BUILD A NEW LANGUAGE.
WE'LL HAVE A FLOCK OF PASSENGER PIGEONS THAT SPEAK A FORM OF EAGLE, OR EVEN BIRDS THAT SPEAK WOLF. STRANGE.
BUT...I STILL DON'T UNDERSTAND WHO WE'RE RUNNING FROM.
FROM THE DARK SIDE OF THE RESEARCH. THE SIDE THAT MOST OF THE RESEARCHERS DIDN'T KNOW ABOUT.
"I FOUND A SEPARATE LABORATORY. AND A CONNECTED VAST UNDERGROUND CAVERN...DOMINATED BY SEVERAL BUILDINGS THAT WERE ALMOST LIKE GREENHOUSES."
A THOUSAND APOLOGIES, CAPTAIN AMERICA...BUT WE CAN'T HAVE YOU IN THIS AREA. YOU MIGHT CONTAMINATE THE SPECIMENS.

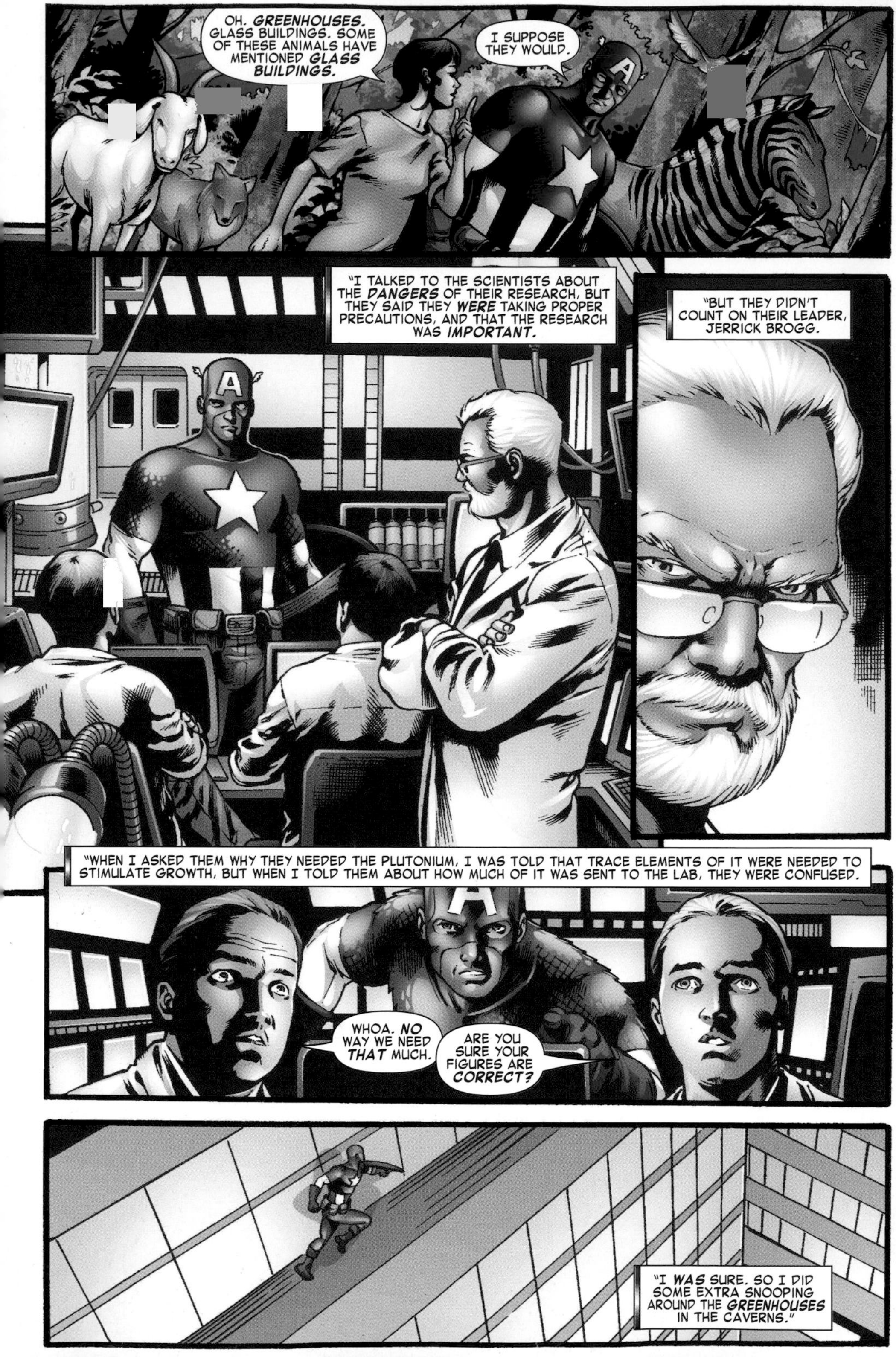
OH. GREENHOUSES. GLASS BUILDINGS. SOME OF THESE ANIMALS HAVE MENTIONED GLASS BUILDINGS.
I SUPPOSE THEY WOULD.
"I TALKED TO THE SCIENTISTS ABOUT THE DANGERS OF THEIR RESEARCH, BUT THEY SAID THEY WERE TAKING PROPER PRECAUTIONS, AND THAT THE RESEARCH WAS IMPORTANT.
"BUT THEY DIDN'T COUNT ON THEIR LEADER, JERRICK BROGG.
"WHEN I ASKED THEM WHY THEY NEEDED THE PLUTONIUM, I WAS TOLD THAT TRACE ELEMENTS OF IT WERE NEEDED TO STIMULATE GROWTH, BUT WHEN I TOLD THEM ABOUT HOW MUCH OF IT WAS SENT TO THE LAB, THEY WERE CONFUSED.
WHOA. NO WAY WE NEED THAT MUCH.
ARE YOU SURE YOUR FIGURES ARE CORRECT?
"I WAS SURE. SO I DID SOME EXTRA SNOOPING AROUND THE GREENHOUSES IN THE CAVERNS."

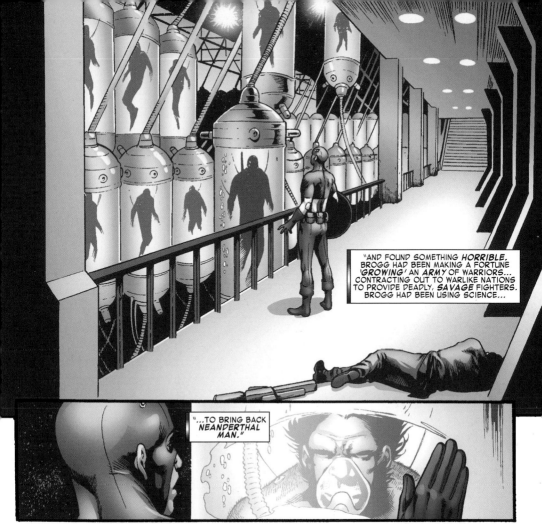

"AND FOUND SOMETHING *HORRIBLE.* BROGG HAD BEEN MAKING A FORTUNE *'GROWING'* AN *ARMY* OF WARRIORS... CONTRACTING OUT TO WARLIKE NATIONS TO PROVIDE DEADLY, *SAVAGE* FIGHTERS. BROGG HAD BEEN USING SCIENCE..."

"...TO BRING BACK *NEANDERTHAL MAN.*"

BUT...THAT'S *INSANE.* NEANDERTHALS ARE A LONG *EXTINCT* SUB-SPECIES OF TODAY'S HUMANS. HOW WOULD THEY FIT INTO *TODAY'S* WORLD?

THEY *WOULDN'T.* NOT IN ANY WAY EXCEPT AS *SOLDIERS.* BROGG PLANNED TO CREATE *ARMIES* THAT...

HOLD ON A SECOND, CAP.

WHY? WHAT'S...?

THE *BIRDS.* THEY SAY...THERE ARE *STRANGE MEN* IN THE WOODS.

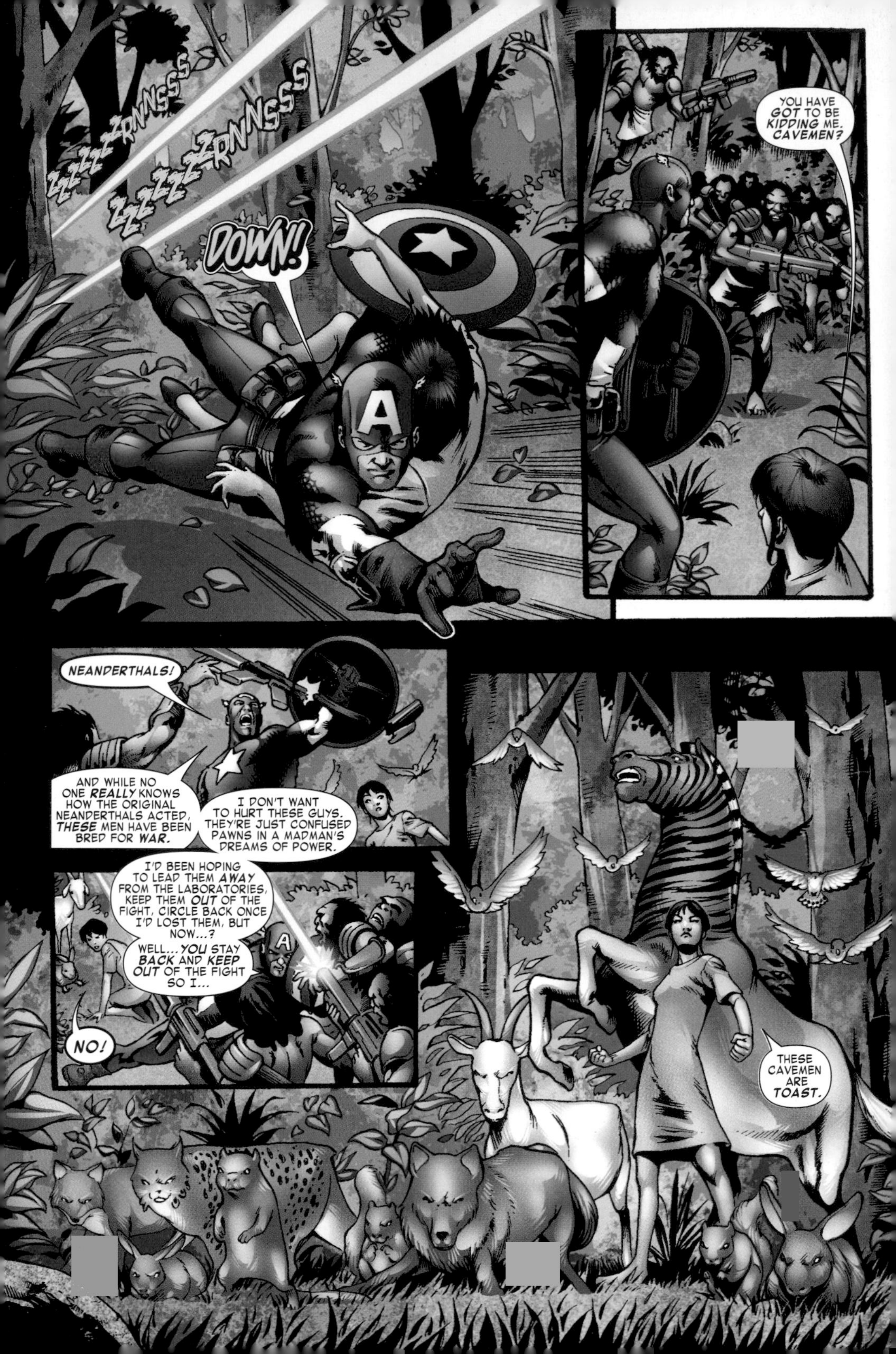
ZZZZZZRNNSSS
ZZZZZZZRNNSSS
DOWN!
YOU HAVE GOT TO BE KIDDING ME. CAVEMEN?
NEANDERTHALS!
AND WHILE NO ONE REALLY KNOWS HOW THE ORIGINAL NEANDERTHALS ACTED, THESE MEN HAVE BEEN BRED FOR WAR.
I DON'T WANT TO HURT THESE GUYS. THEY'RE JUST CONFUSED PAWNS IN A MADMAN'S DREAMS OF POWER.
I'D BEEN HOPING TO LEAD THEM AWAY FROM THE LABORATORIES, KEEP THEM OUT OF THE FIGHT, CIRCLE BACK ONCE I'D LOST THEM, BUT NOW...?
WELL... YOU STAY BACK AND KEEP OUT OF THE FIGHT SO I...
NO!
THESE CAVEMEN ARE TOAST.

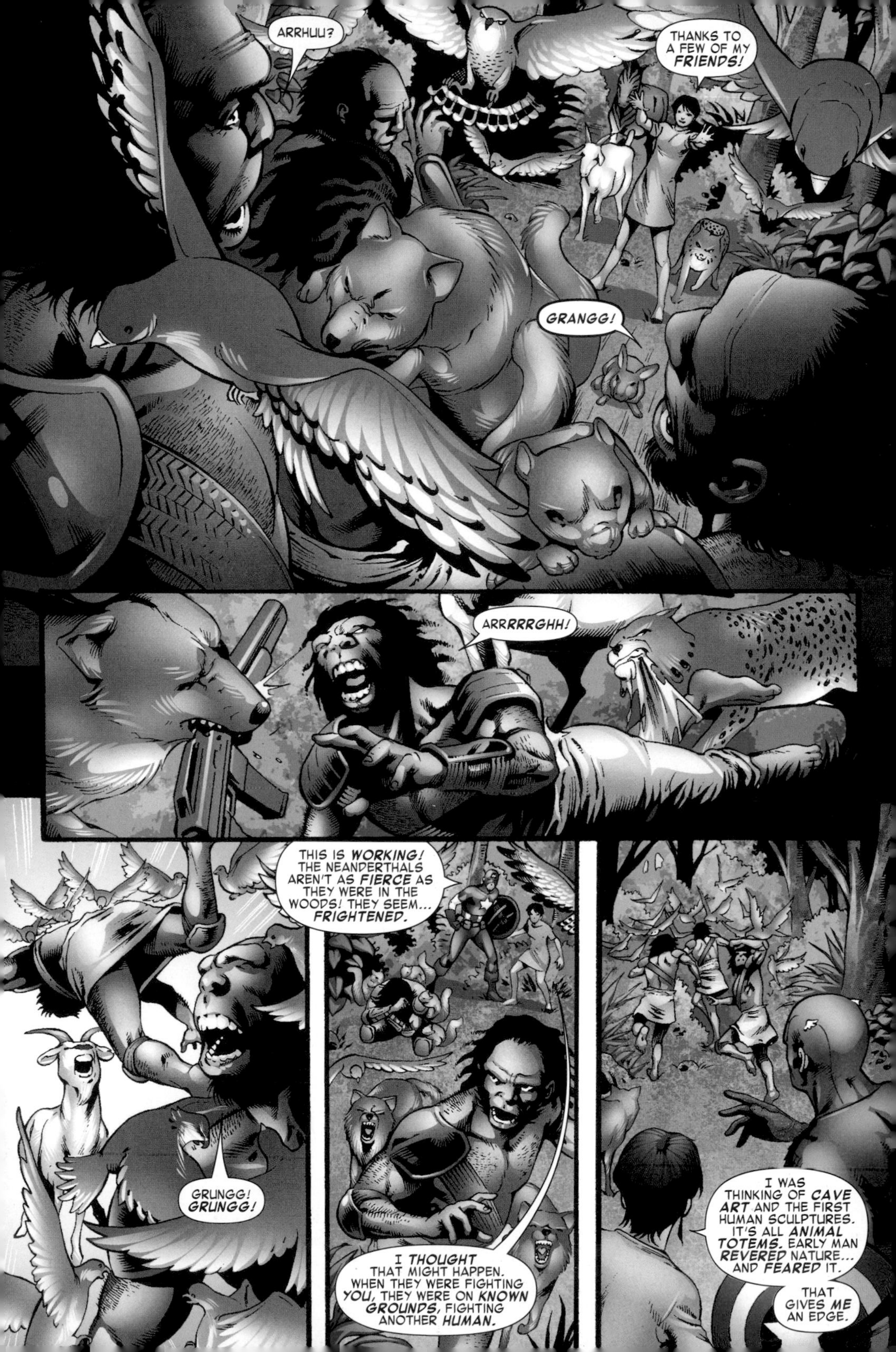
ARRHUU?
THANKS TO A FEW OF MY FRIENDS!
GRANGG!
ARRRRRGHH!
THIS IS WORKING! THE NEANDERTHALS AREN'T AS FIERCE AS THEY WERE IN THE WOODS! THEY SEEM... FRIGHTENED.
GRUNGG! GRUNGG!
I THOUGHT THAT MIGHT HAPPEN. WHEN THEY WERE FIGHTING YOU, THEY WERE ON KNOWN GROUNDS, FIGHTING ANOTHER HUMAN.
I WAS THINKING OF CAVE ART AND THE FIRST HUMAN SCULPTURES. IT'S ALL ANIMAL TOTEMS. EARLY MAN REVERED NATURE... AND FEARED IT.
THAT GIVES ME AN EDGE.

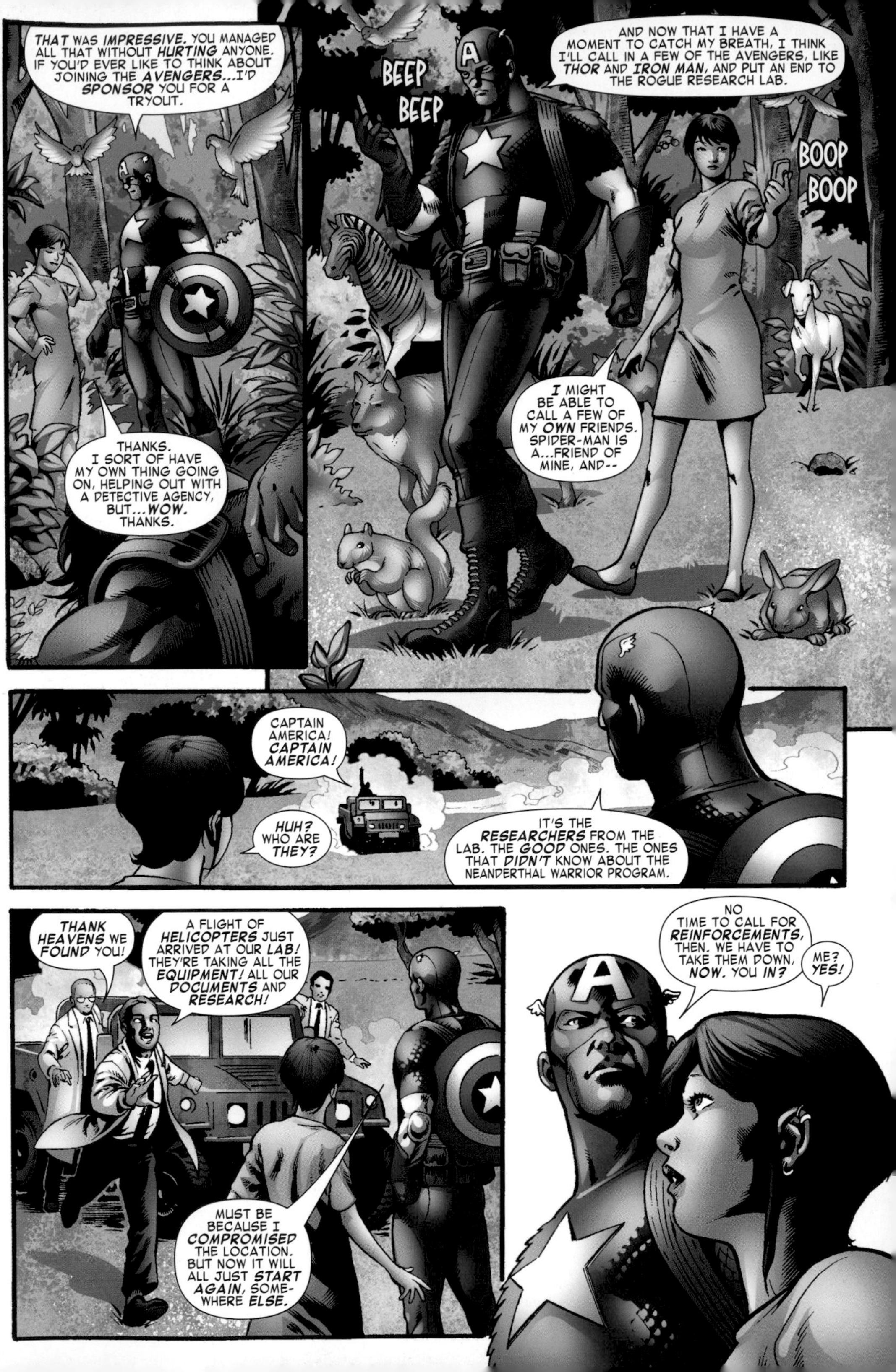
THAT WAS IMPRESSIVE. YOU MANAGED ALL THAT WITHOUT HURTING ANYONE. IF YOU'D EVER LIKE TO THINK ABOUT JOINING THE AVENGERS...I'D SPONSOR YOU FOR A TRYOUT.
THANKS. I SORT OF HAVE MY OWN THING GOING ON, HELPING OUT WITH A DETECTIVE AGENCY, BUT...WOW. THANKS.
BEEP
BEEP
AND NOW THAT I HAVE A MOMENT TO CATCH MY BREATH, I THINK I'LL CALL IN A FEW OF THE AVENGERS, LIKE THOR AND IRON MAN, AND PUT AN END TO THE ROGUE RESEARCH LAB.
BOOP
BOOP
I MIGHT BE ABLE TO CALL A FEW OF MY OWN FRIENDS. SPIDER-MAN IS A...FRIEND OF MINE, AND--
CAPTAIN AMERICA! CAPTAIN AMERICA!
HUH? WHO ARE THEY?
IT'S THE RESEARCHERS FROM THE LAB. THE GOOD ONES. THE ONES THAT DIDN'T KNOW ABOUT THE NEANDERTHAL WARRIOR PROGRAM.
THANK HEAVENS WE FOUND YOU!
A FLIGHT OF HELICOPTERS JUST ARRIVED AT OUR LAB! THEY'RE TAKING ALL THE EQUIPMENT! ALL OUR DOCUMENTS AND RESEARCH!
MUST BE BECAUSE I COMPROMISED THE LOCATION. BUT NOW IT WILL ALL JUST START AGAIN, SOME-WHERE ELSE.
NO TIME TO CALL FOR REINFORCEMENTS, THEN. WE HAVE TO TAKE THEM DOWN, NOW. YOU IN?
ME? YES!

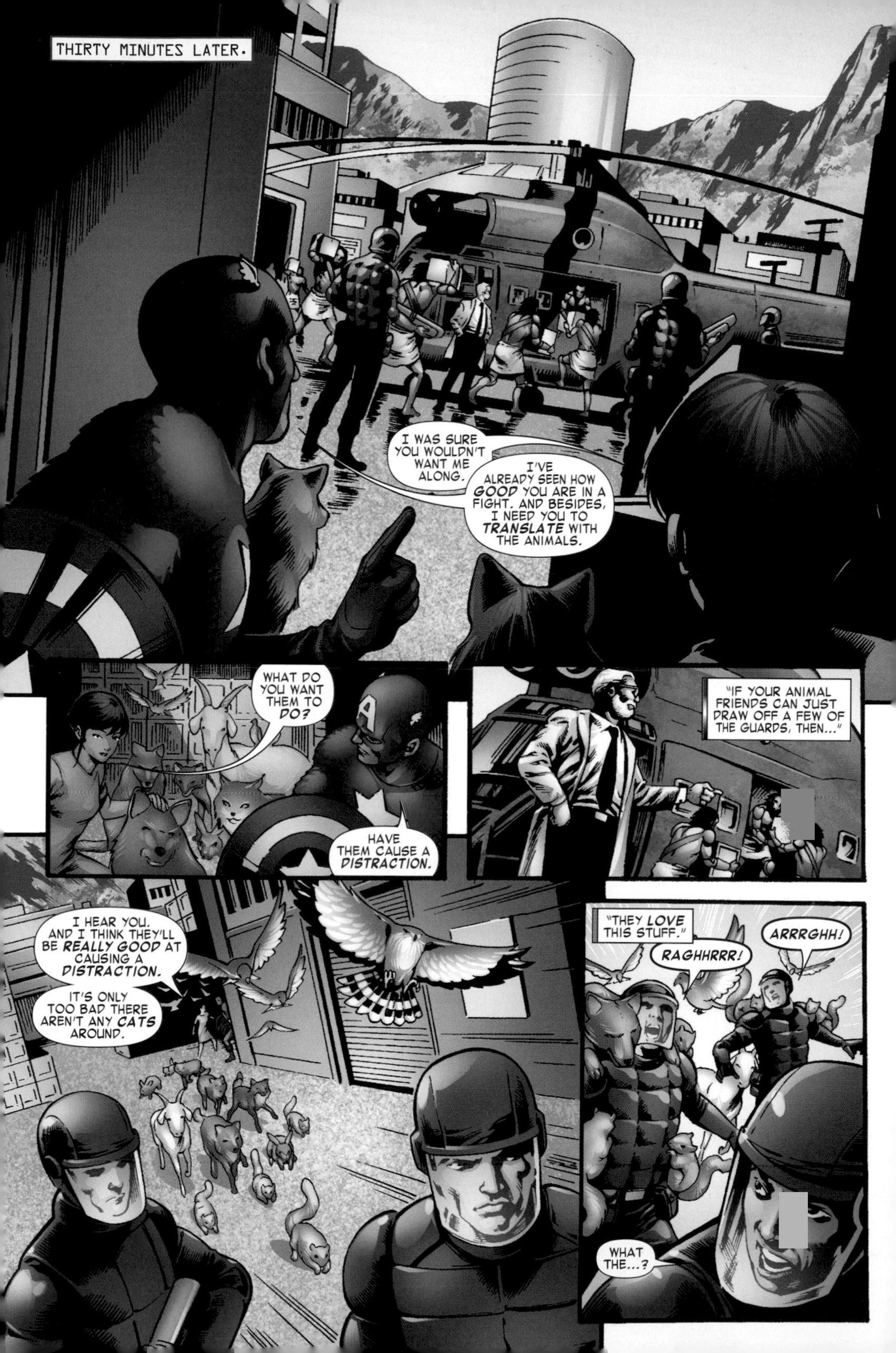
THIRTY MINUTES LATER.
I WAS SURE YOU WOULDN'T WANT ME ALONG.
I'VE ALREADY SEEN HOW GOOD YOU ARE IN A FIGHT. AND BESIDES, I NEED YOU TO TRANSLATE WITH THE ANIMALS.
WHAT DO YOU WANT THEM TO DO?
HAVE THEM CAUSE A DISTRACTION.
"IF YOUR ANIMAL FRIENDS CAN JUST DRAW OFF A FEW OF THE GUARDS, THEN..."
I HEAR YOU. AND I THINK THEY'LL BE REALLY GOOD AT CAUSING A DISTRACTION.
IT'S ONLY TOO BAD THERE AREN'T ANY CATS AROUND.
"THEY LOVE THIS STUFF."
RAGHHRRR!
ARRRGHH!
WHAT THE...?

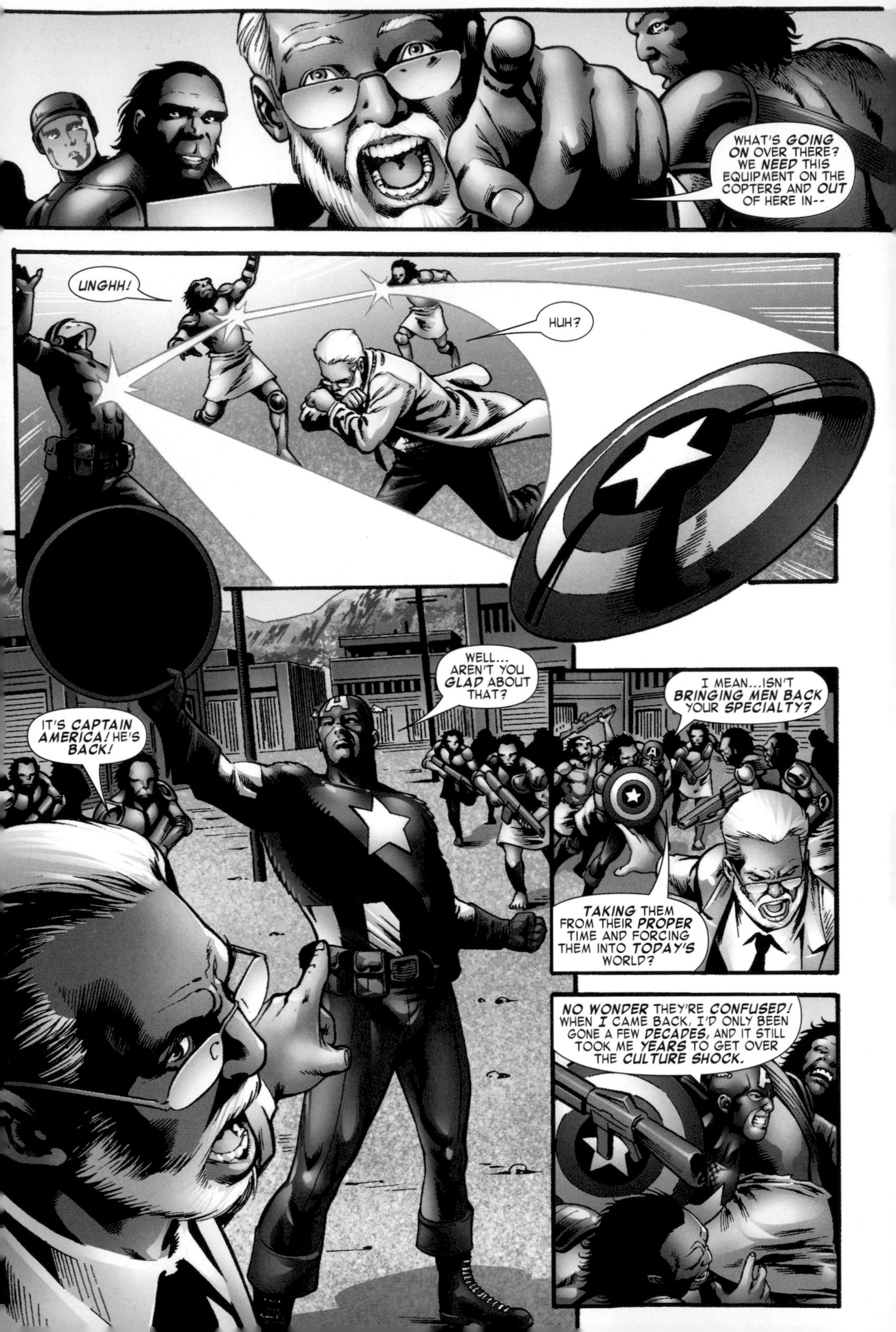
WHAT'S GOING ON OVER THERE? WE NEED THIS EQUIPMENT ON THE COPTERS AND OUT OF HERE IN--
UNGHH!
HUH?
IT'S CAPTAIN AMERICA! HE'S BACK!
WELL... AREN'T YOU GLAD ABOUT THAT?
I MEAN...ISN'T BRINGING MEN BACK YOUR SPECIALTY?
TAKING THEM FROM THEIR PROPER TIME AND FORCING THEM INTO TODAY'S WORLD?
NO WONDER THEY'RE CONFUSED! WHEN I CAME BACK, I'D ONLY BEEN GONE A FEW DECADES, AND IT STILL TOOK ME YEARS TO GET OVER THE CULTURE SHOCK.

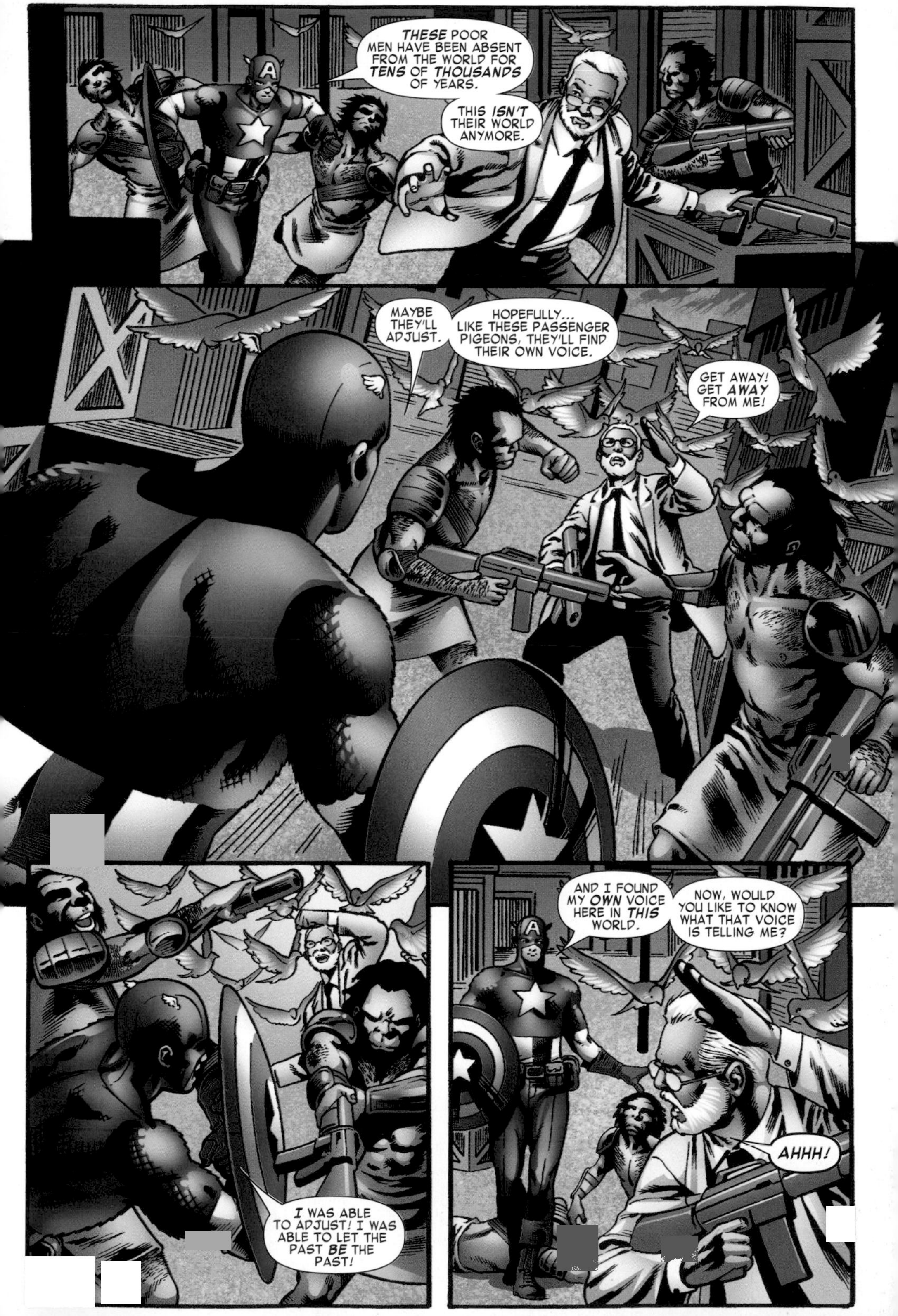
THESE POOR MEN HAVE BEEN ABSENT FROM THE WORLD FOR TENS OF THOUSANDS OF YEARS.
THIS ISN'T THEIR WORLD ANYMORE.
MAYBE THEY'LL ADJUST.
HOPEFULLY... LIKE THESE PASSENGER PIGEONS, THEY'LL FIND THEIR OWN VOICE.
GET AWAY! GET AWAY FROM ME!
I WAS ABLE TO ADJUST! I WAS ABLE TO LET THE PAST BE THE PAST!
AND I FOUND MY OWN VOICE HERE IN THIS WORLD.
NOW, WOULD YOU LIKE TO KNOW WHAT THAT VOICE IS TELLING ME?
AHHH!

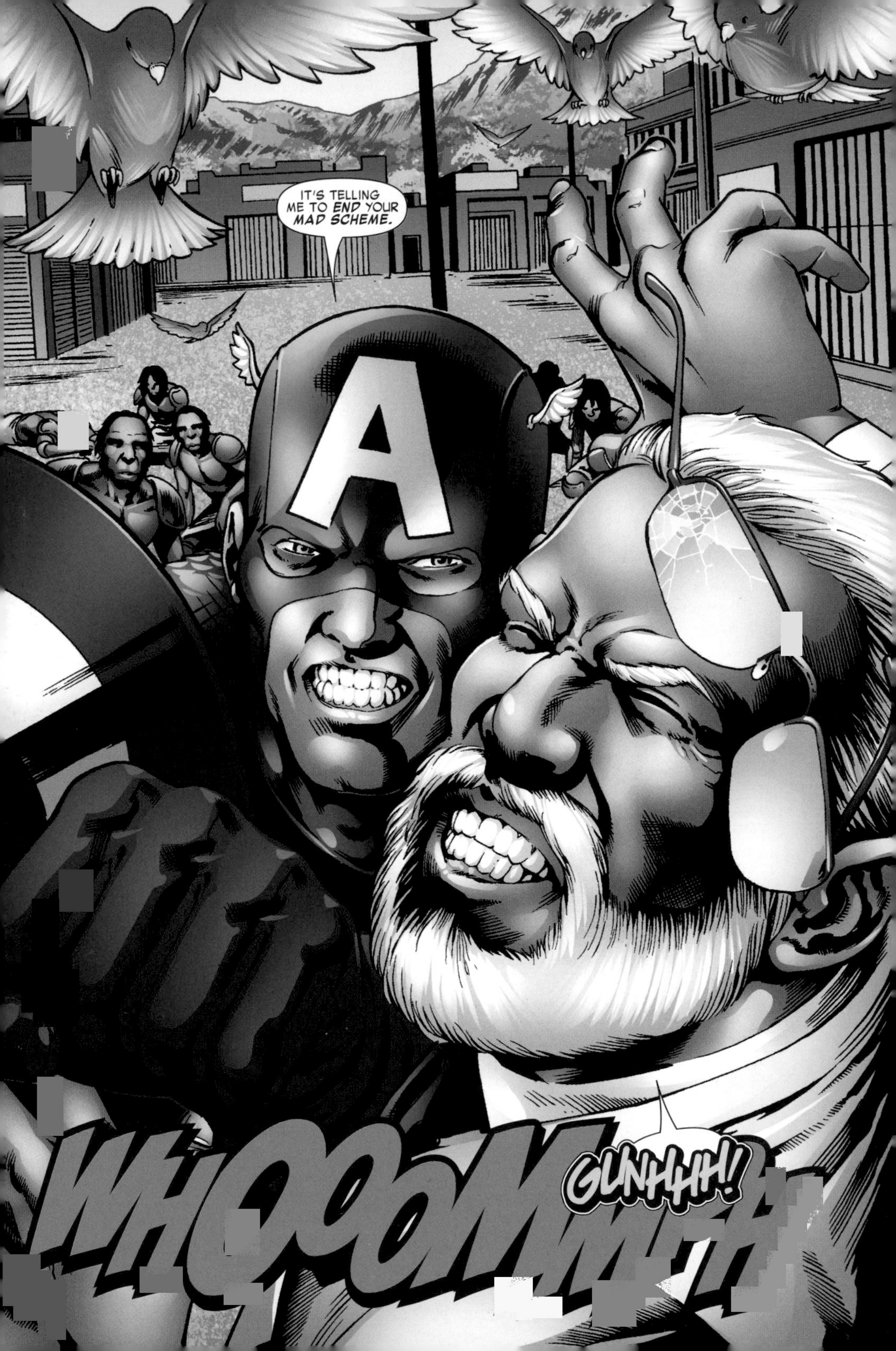
IT'S TELLING ME TO END YOUR MAD SCHEME.
WHOOOMMM
GUNHHH!

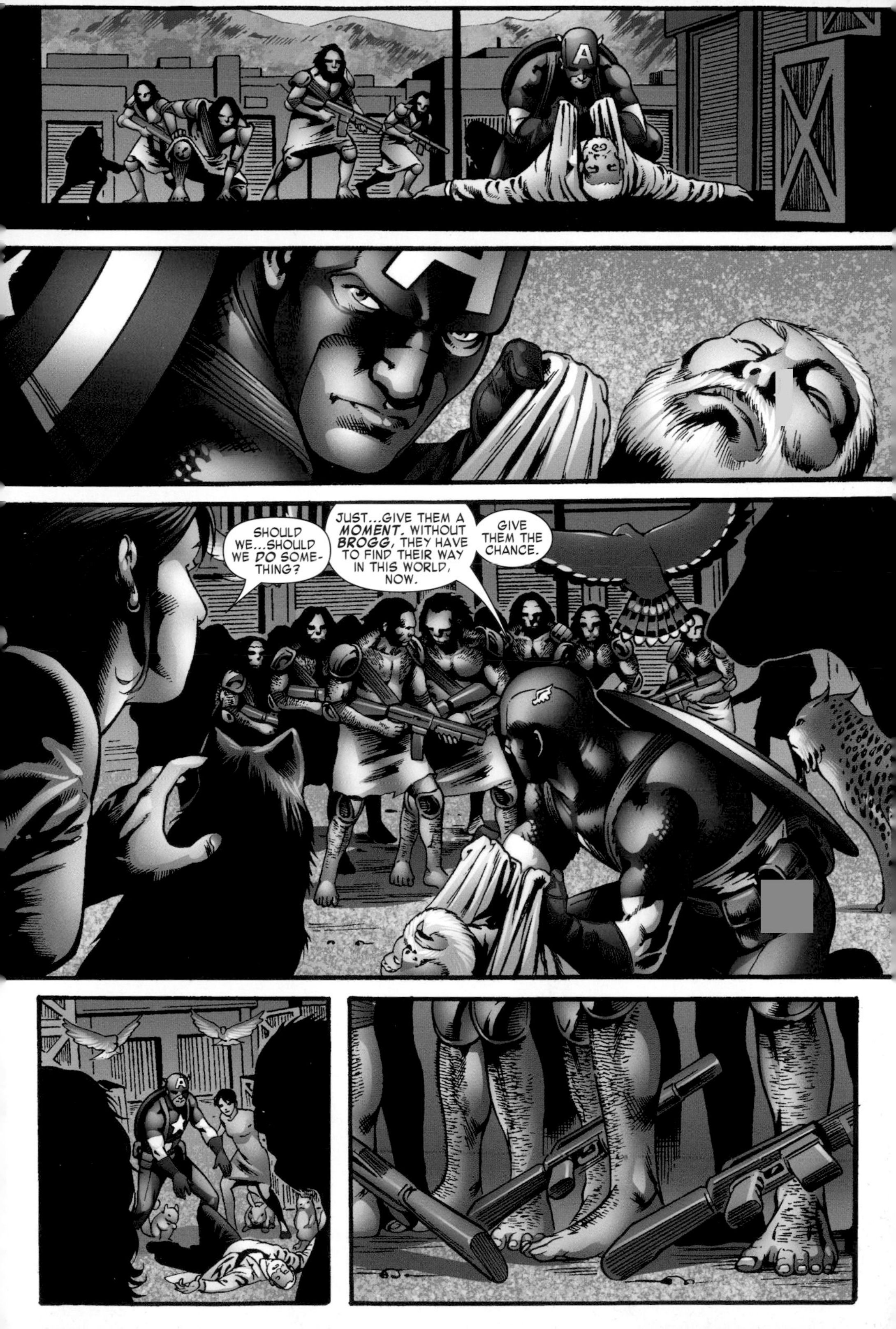
SHOULD WE...SHOULD WE DO SOME-THING?
JUST...GIVE THEM A MOMENT. WITHOUT BROGG, THEY HAVE TO FIND THEIR WAY IN THIS WORLD, NOW.
GIVE THEM THE CHANCE.

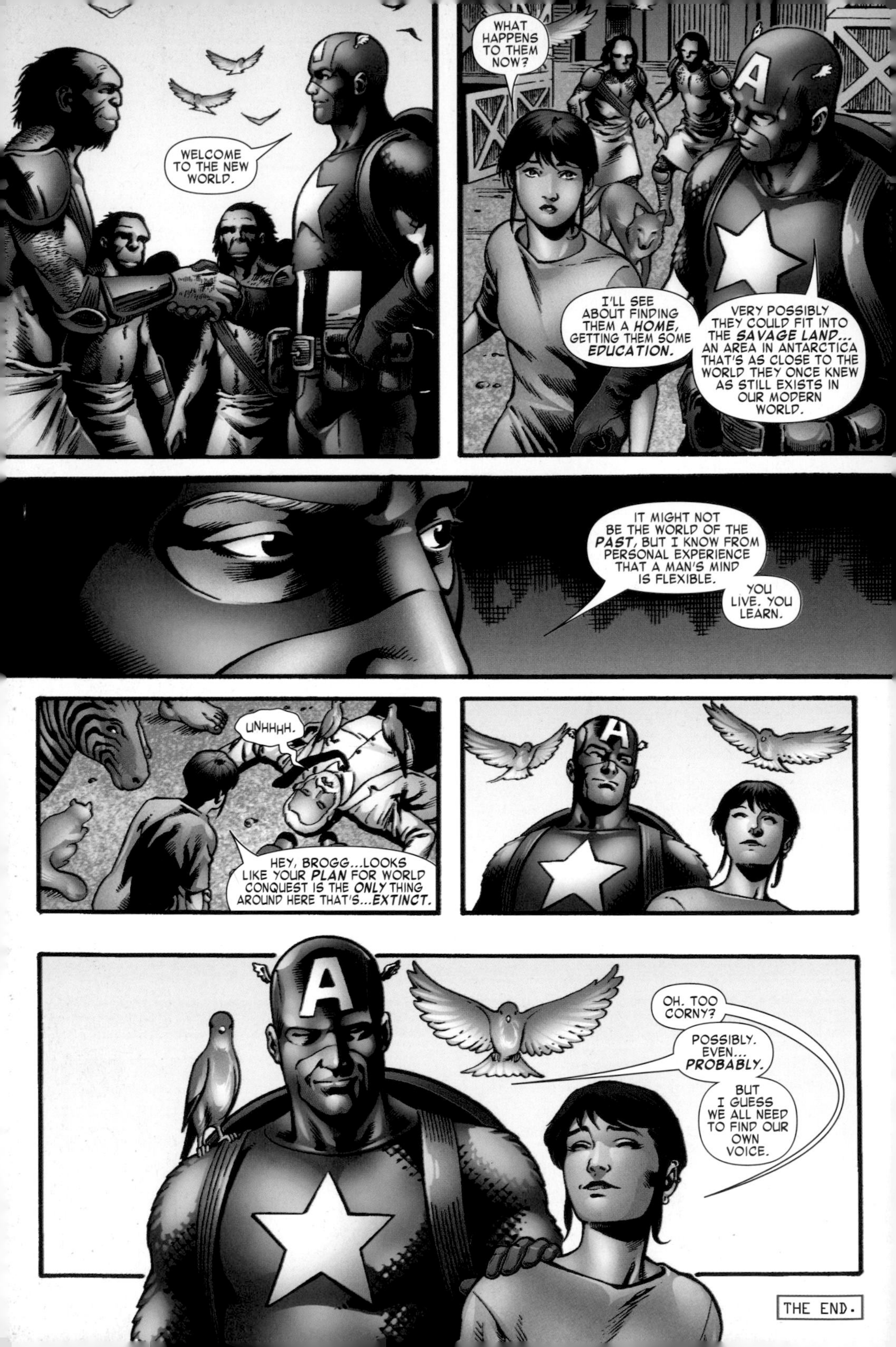
WELCOME TO THE NEW WORLD.
WHAT HAPPENS TO THEM NOW?
I'LL SEE ABOUT FINDING THEM A HOME, GETTING THEM SOME EDUCATION.
VERY POSSIBLY THEY COULD FIT INTO THE SAVAGE LAND... AN AREA IN ANTARCTICA THAT'S AS CLOSE TO THE WORLD THEY ONCE KNEW AS STILL EXISTS IN OUR MODERN WORLD.
IT MIGHT NOT BE THE WORLD OF THE PAST, BUT I KNOW FROM PERSONAL EXPERIENCE THAT A MAN'S MIND IS FLEXIBLE.
YOU LIVE. YOU LEARN.
UNHHHH.
HEY, BROGG...LOOKS LIKE YOUR PLAN FOR WORLD CONQUEST IS THE ONLY THING AROUND HERE THAT'S...EXTINCT.
OH. TOO CORNY?
POSSIBLY. EVEN... PROBABLY.
BUT I GUESS WE ALL NEED TO FIND OUR OWN VOICE.
THE END.

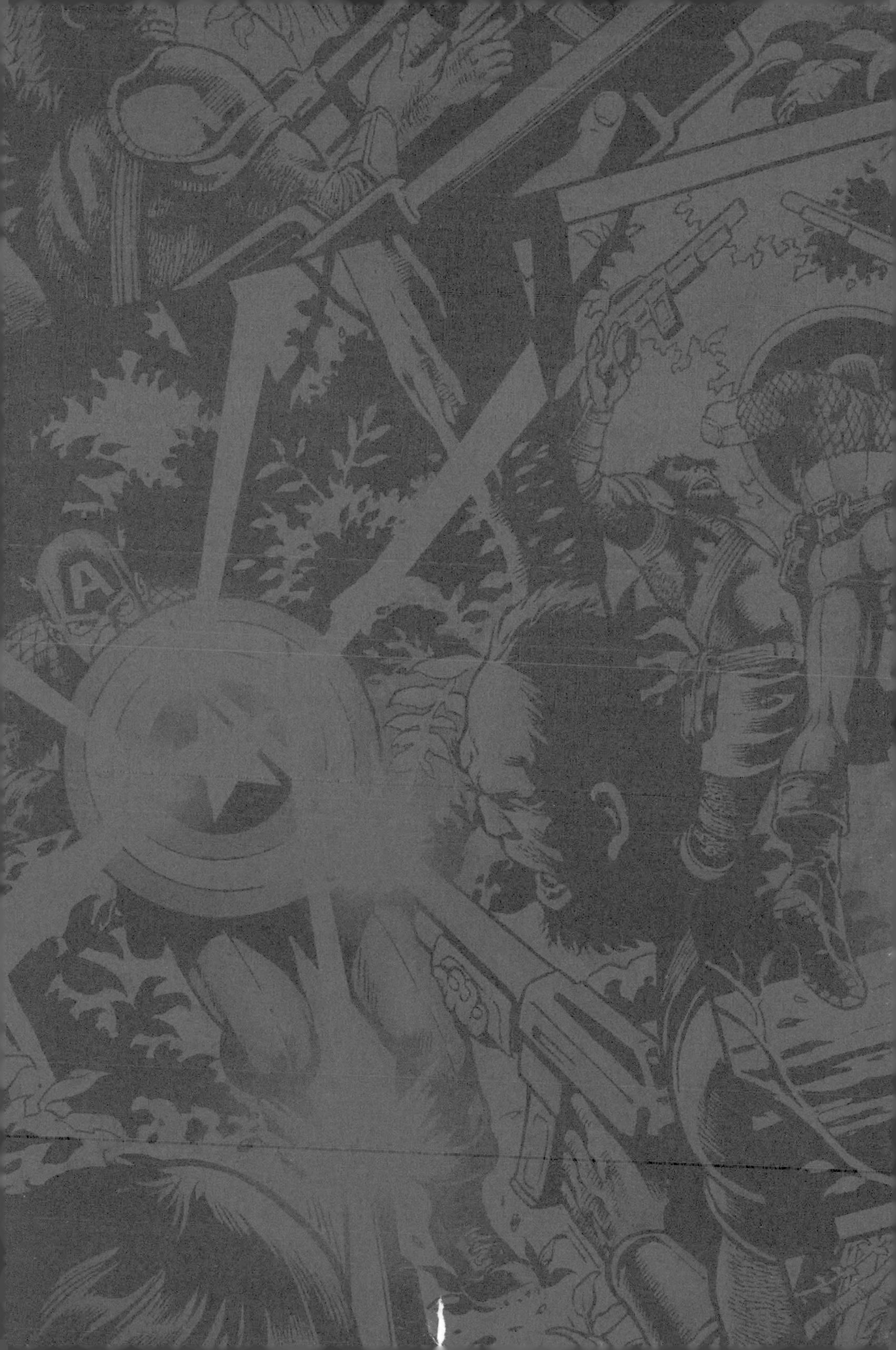

06

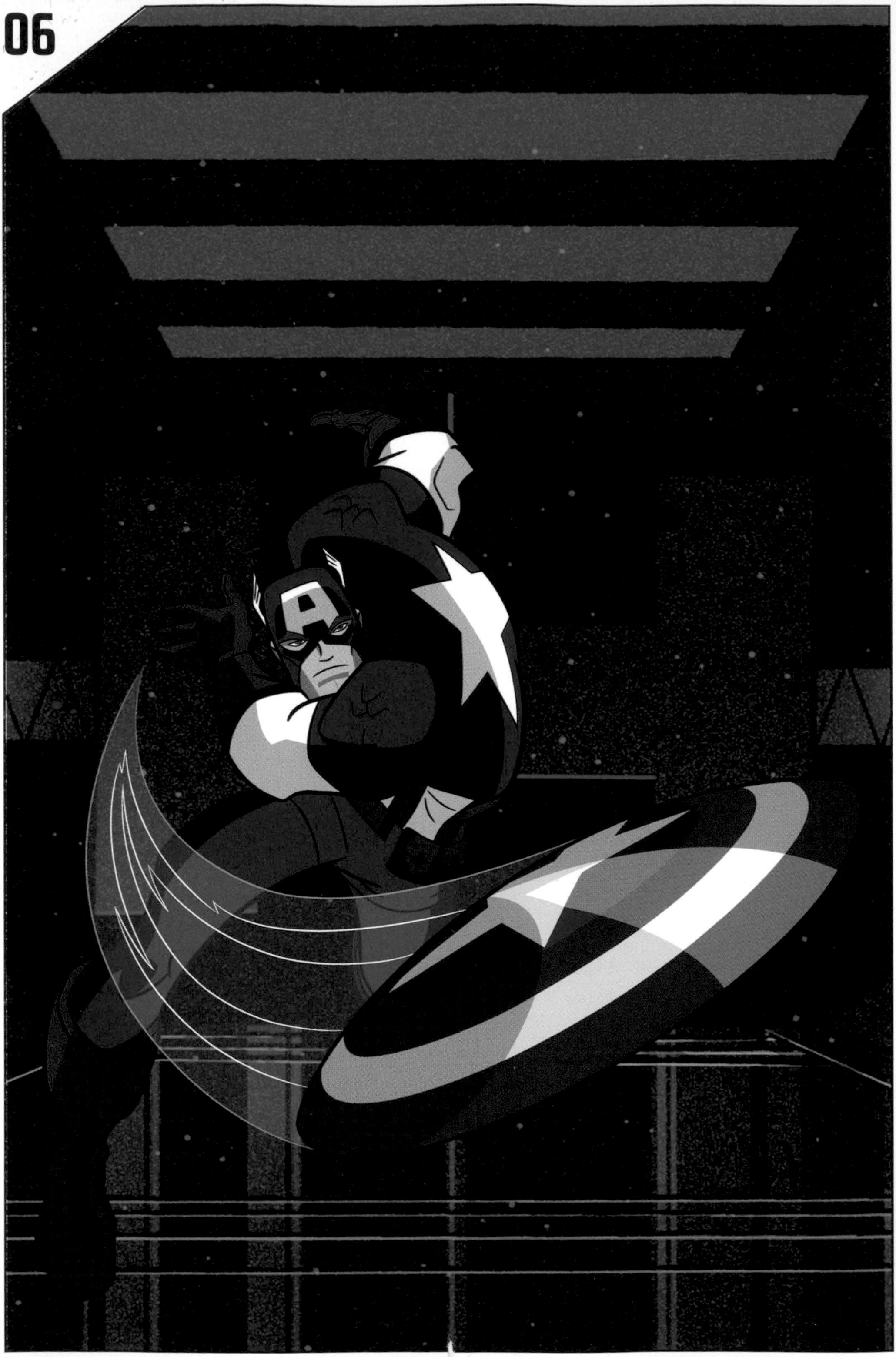

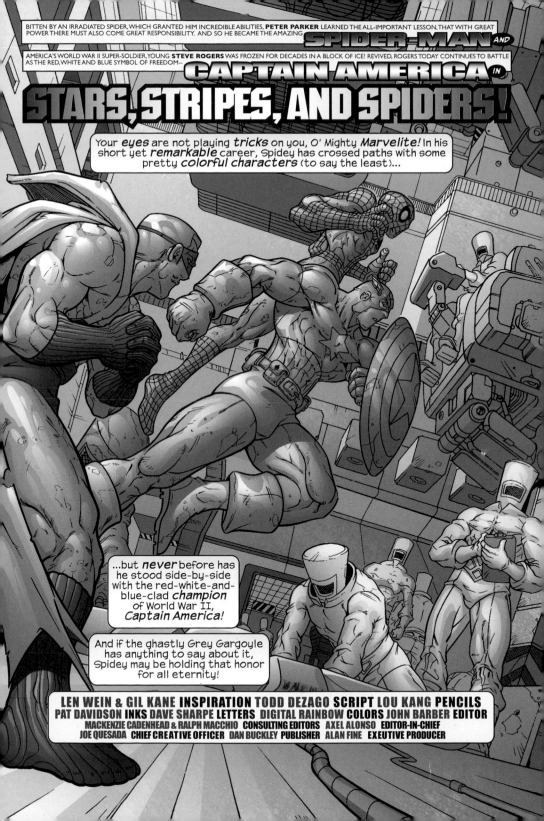

BITTEN BY AN IRRADIATED SPIDER, WHICH GRANTED HIM INCREDIBLE ABILITIES, **PETER PARKER** LEARNED THE ALL-IMPORTANT LESSON, THAT WITH GREAT POWER THERE MUST ALSO COME GREAT RESPONSIBILITY. AND SO HE BECAME THE AMAZING **SPIDER-MAN** AND

AMERICA'S WORLD WAR II SUPER-SOLDIER, YOUNG **STEVE ROGERS** WAS FROZEN FOR DECADES IN A BLOCK OF ICE! REVIVED, ROGERS CONTINUES TO BATTLE AS THE RED, WHITE AND BLUE SYMBOL OF FREEDOM-- **CAPTAIN AMERICA** IN

# STARS, STRIPES, AND SPIDERS!

Your *eyes* are not playing *tricks* on you, O' Mighty *Marvelite!* In his short yet *remarkable* career, Spidey has crossed paths with some pretty *colorful characters* (to say the least)...

...but *never* before has he stood side-by-side with the red-white-and-blue-clad *champion* of World War II, Captain America!

And if the ghastly Grey Gargoyle has anything to say about it, Spidey may be holding that honor for all eternity!

LEN WEIN & GIL KANE INSPIRATION  TODD DEZAGO SCRIPT  LOU KANG PENCILS
PAT DAVIDSON INKS  DAVE SHARPE LETTERS  DIGITAL RAINBOW COLORS  JOHN BARBER EDITOR
MACKENZIE CADENHEAD & RALPH MACCHIO CONSULTING EDITORS  AXEL ALONSO EDITOR-IN-CHIEF
JOE QUESADA CHIEF CREATIVE OFFICER  DAN BUCKLEY PUBLISHER  ALAN FINE EXEUTIVE PRODUCER

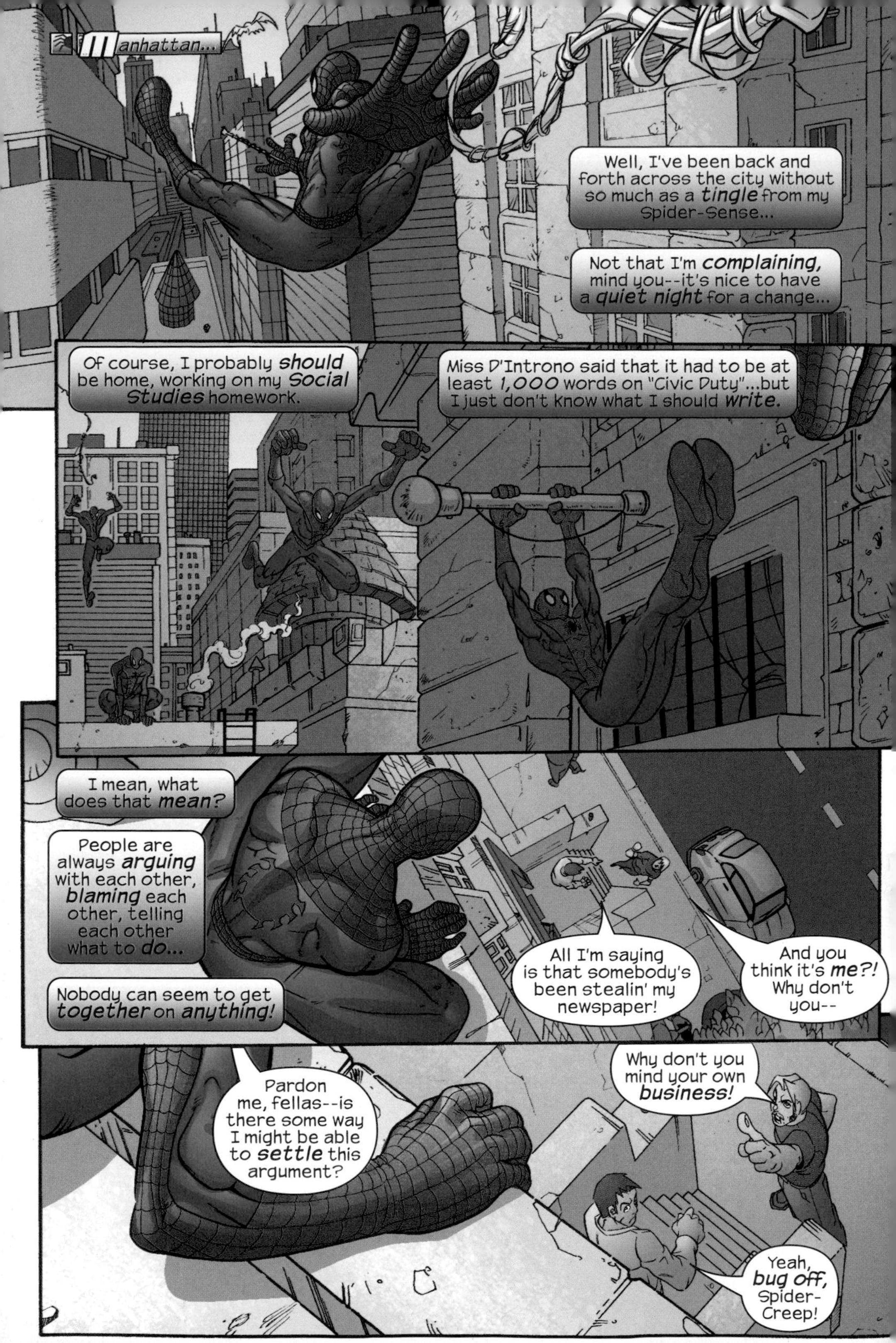

Manhattan...
Well, I've been back and forth across the city without so much as a tingle from my Spider-Sense...
Not that I'm complaining, mind you--it's nice to have a quiet night for a change...
Of course, I probably should be home, working on my Social Studies homework.
Miss D'Introno said that it had to be at least 1,000 words on "Civic Duty"...but I just don't know what I should write.
I mean, what does that mean?
People are always arguing with each other, blaming each other, telling each other what to do...
Nobody can seem to get together on anything!
All I'm saying is that somebody's been stealin' my newspaper!
And you think it's me?! Why don't you--
Pardon me, fellas--is there some way I might be able to settle this argument?
Why don't you mind your own business!
Yeah, bug off, Spider-Creep!

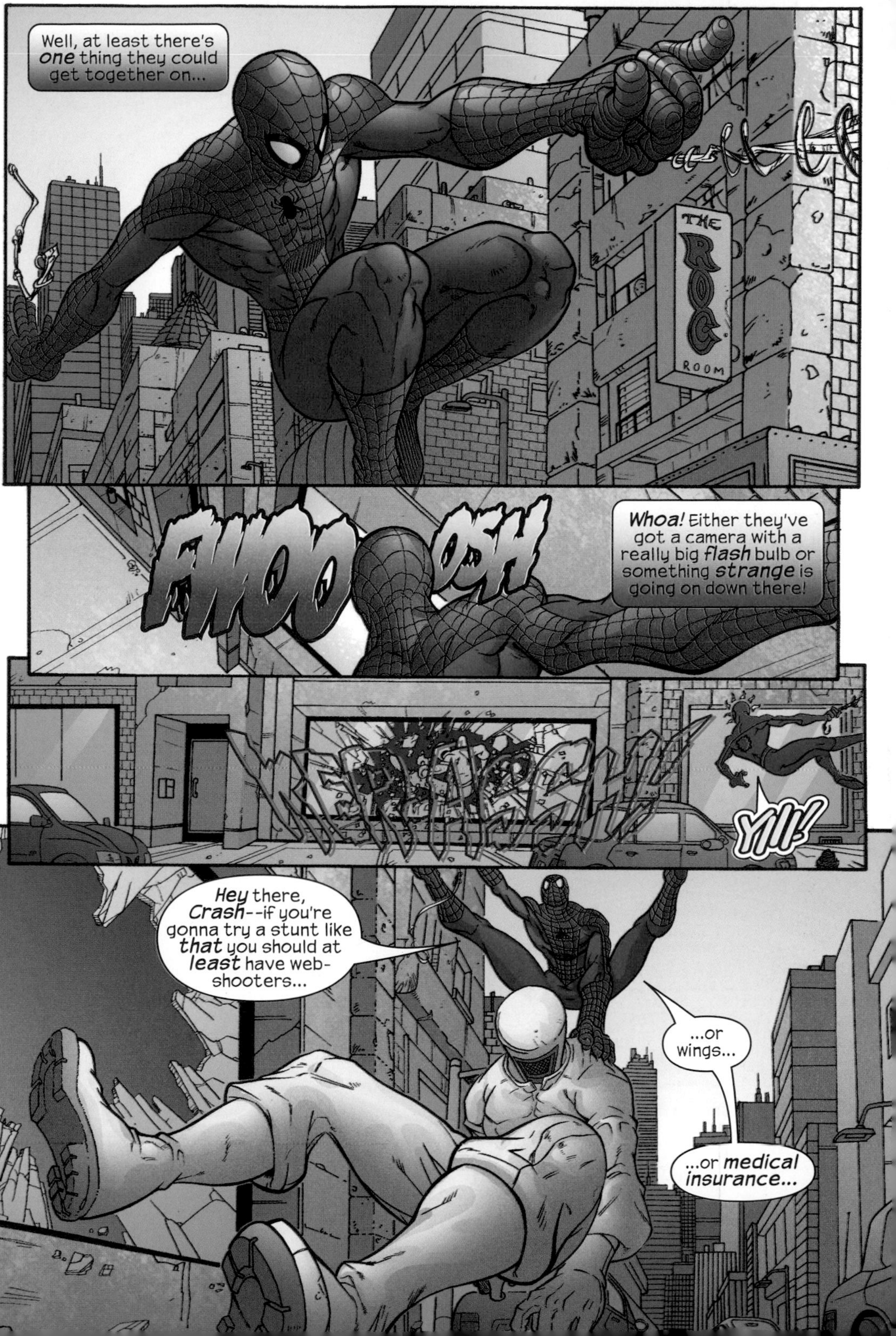

Well, at least there's *one* thing they could get together on...
THE ROC ROOM
FWOO OSH
*Whoa!* Either they've got a camera with a really big *flash* bulb or something *strange* is going on down there!
YIII!
*Hey* there, *Crash*--if you're gonna try a stunt like *that* you should at *least* have web-shooters...
...or wings...
...or *medical insurance*...

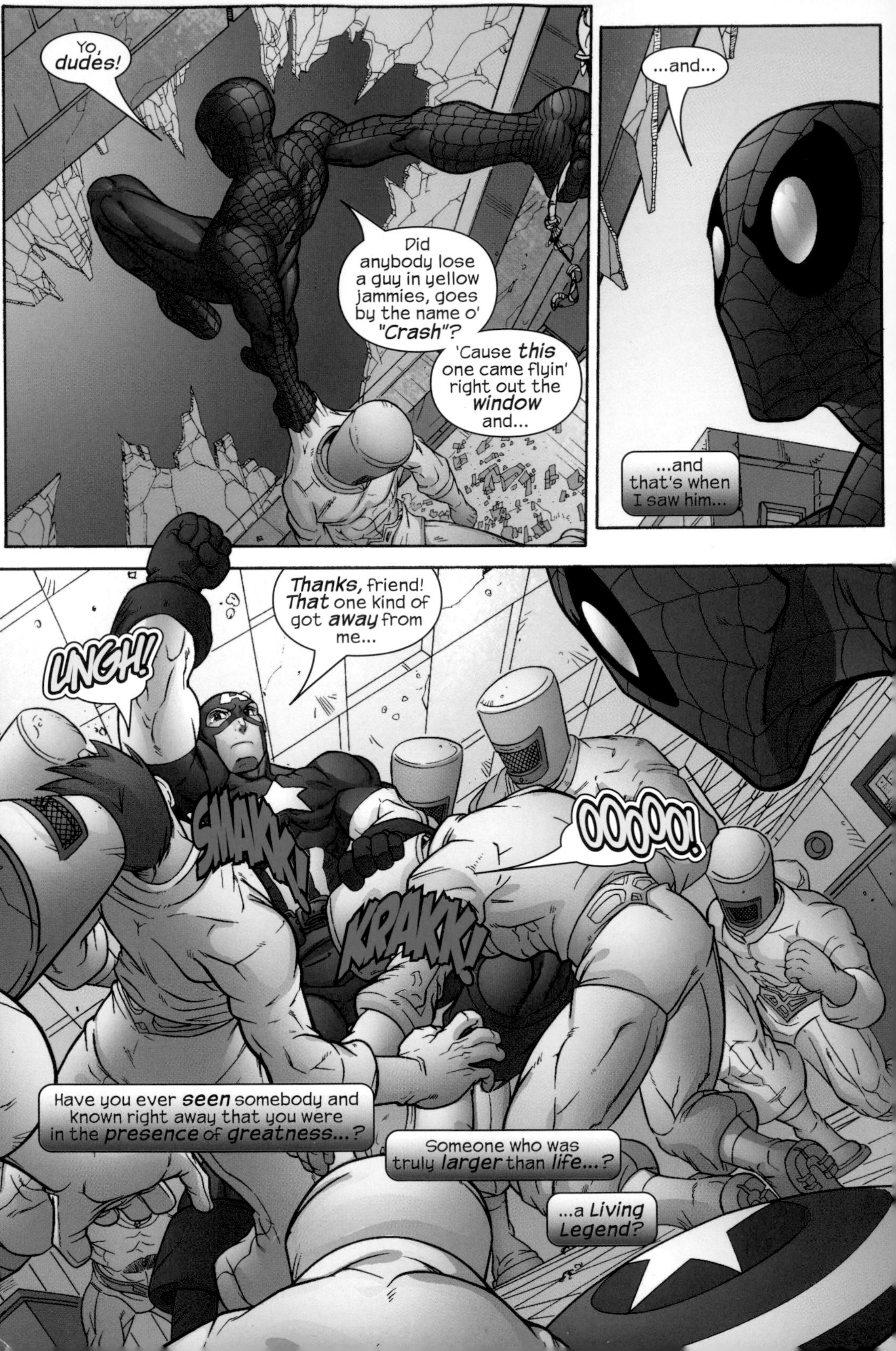
Yo, dudes!
Did anybody lose a guy in yellow jammies, goes by the name o' "Crash"?
'Cause this one came flyin' right out the window and...
...and...
...and that's when I saw him...
UNGH!
Thanks, friend! That one kind of got away from me...
SMAKK!
OOOOO!
KRAKK!
Have you ever seen somebody and known right away that you were in the presence of greatness...?
Someone who was truly larger than life...?
...a Living Legend?

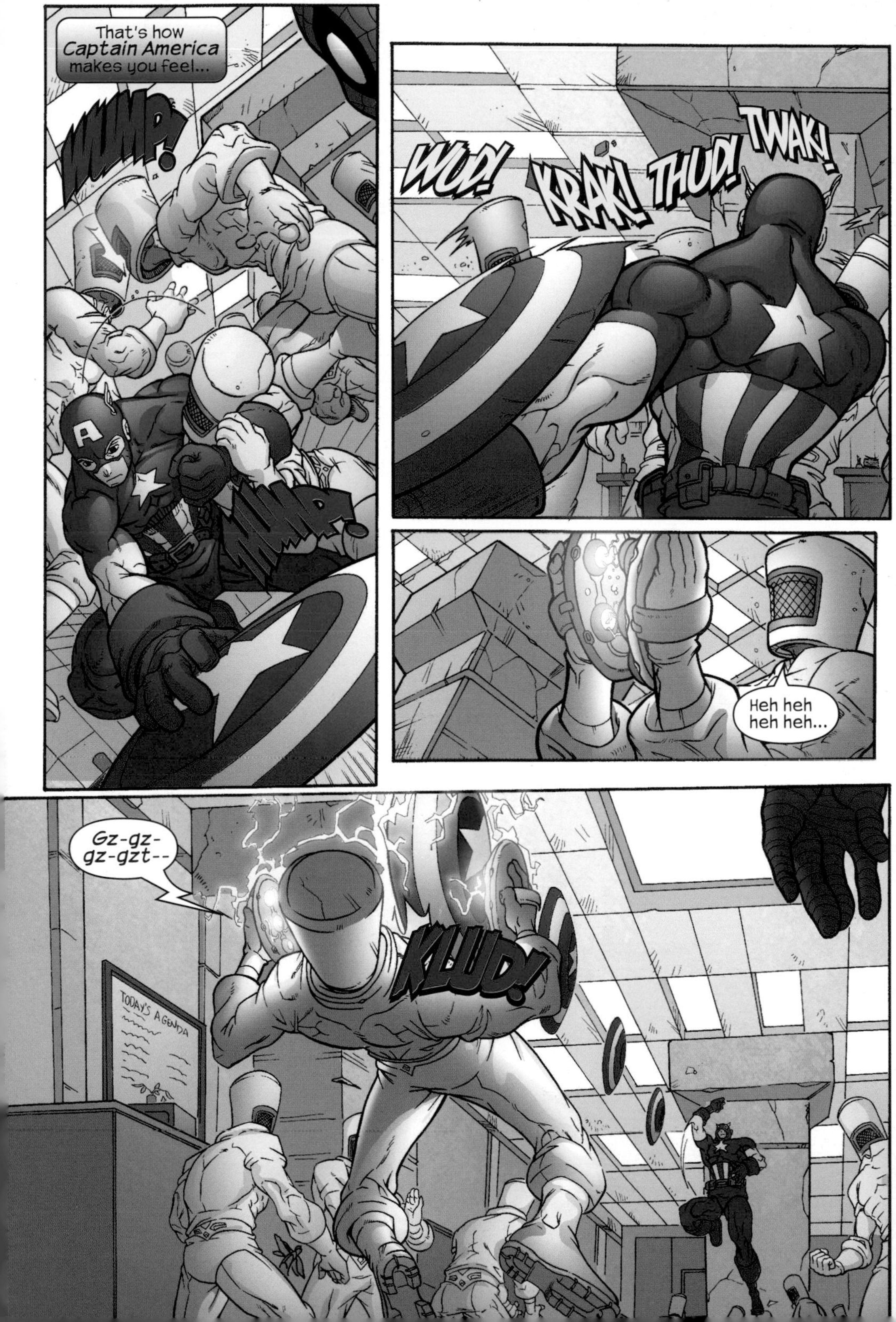
That's how Captain America makes you feel...
WUMP!
WUMP!
WUD!
KRAK!
THUD!
TWAK!
Heh heh heh heh...
Gz-gz-gz-gzt--
KLUD!
TODAY'S AGENDA

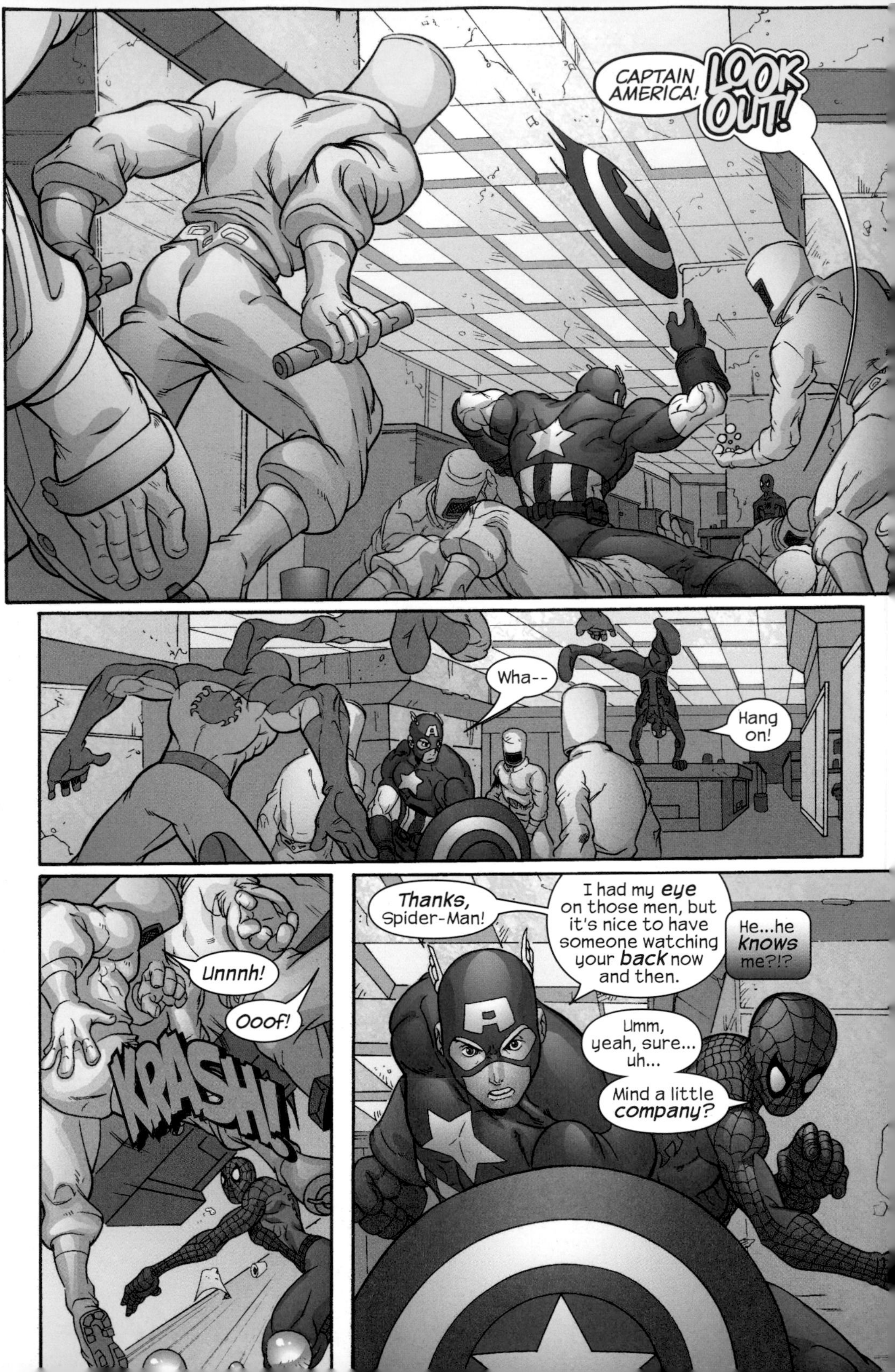
CAPTAIN AMERICA! LOOK OUT!
Wha--
Hang on!
Unnnh!
Ooof!
KRASH!
Thanks, Spider-Man!
I had my eye on those men, but it's nice to have someone watching your back now and then.
He...he knows me?!?
Umm, yeah, sure... uh...
Mind a little company?

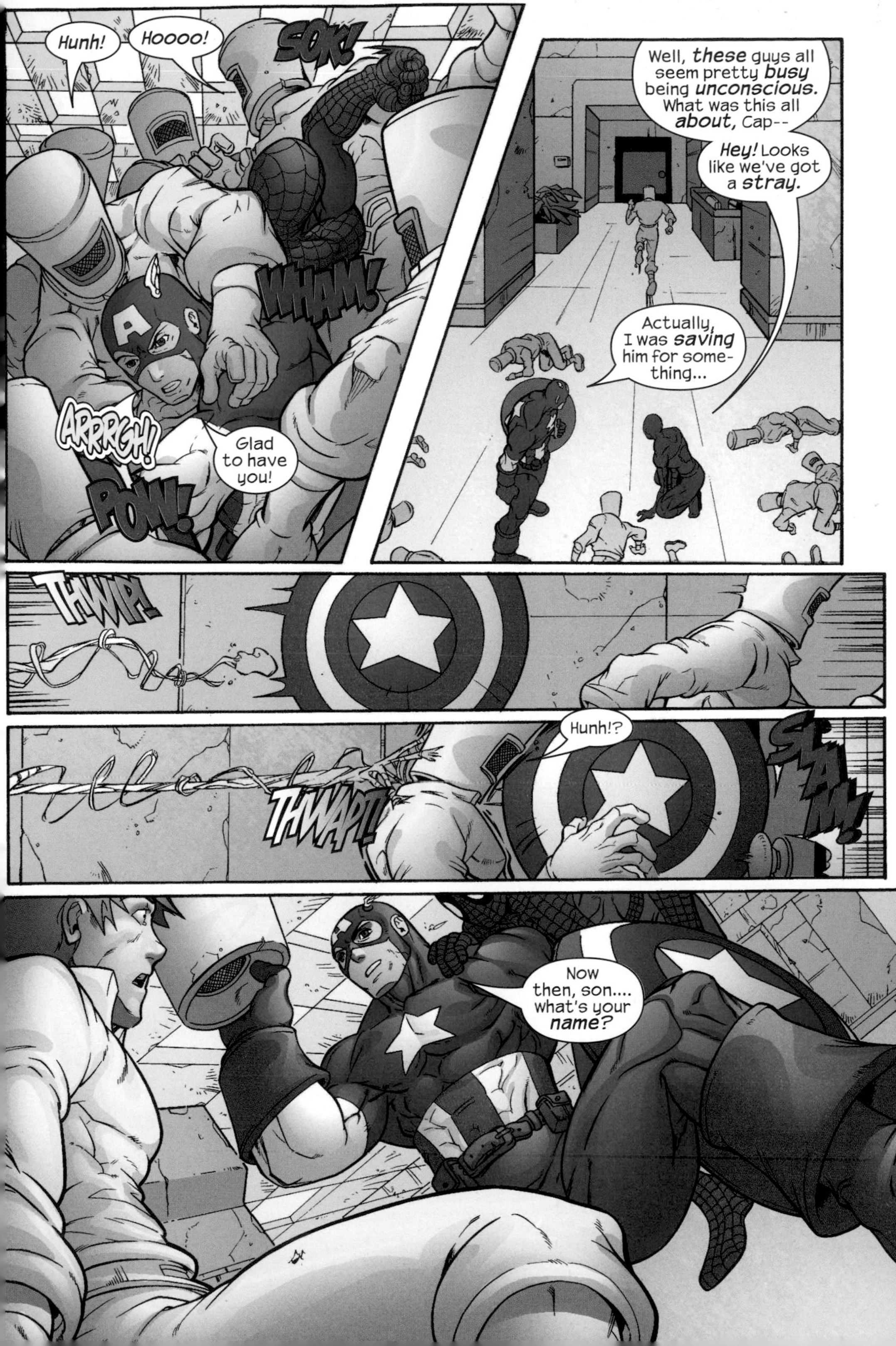
Hunh!
Hoooo!
SOK!
WHAM!
ARRRGH!
Glad to have you!
POW!
Well, these guys all seem pretty busy being unconscious. What was this all about, Cap--
Hey! Looks like we've got a stray.
Actually, I was saving him for some-thing...
THWIP!
Hunh!?
THWAP!!
SLAM!
Now then, son.... what's your name?

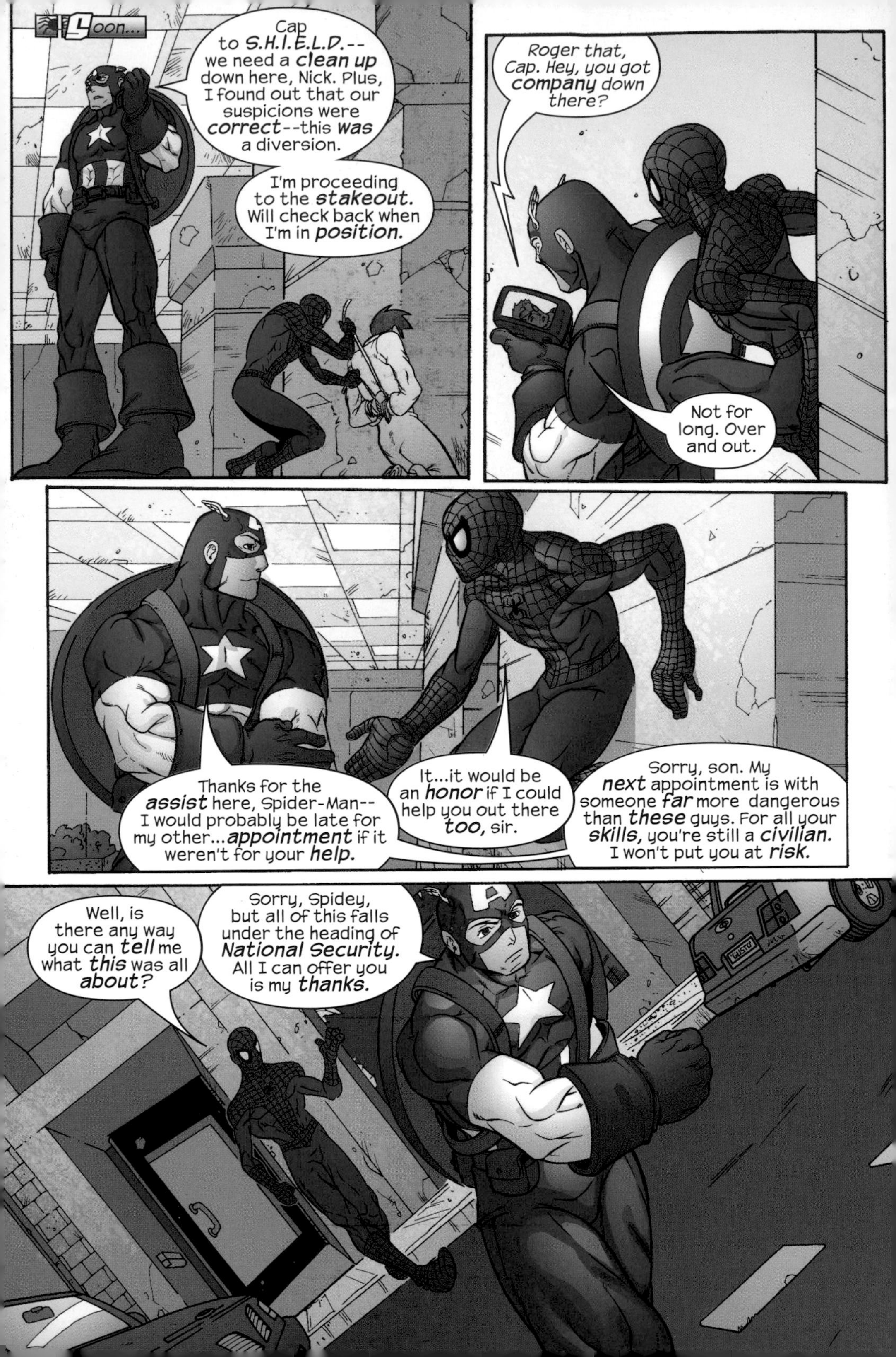
Soon...
Cap to S.H.I.E.L.D.-- we need a clean up down here, Nick. Plus, I found out that our suspicions were correct--this was a diversion.
I'm proceeding to the stakeout. Will check back when I'm in position.
Roger that, Cap. Hey, you got company down there?
Not for long. Over and out.
Thanks for the assist here, Spider-Man-- I would probably be late for my other...appointment if it weren't for your help.
It...it would be an honor if I could help you out there too, sir.
Sorry, son. My next appointment is with someone far more dangerous than these guys. For all your skills, you're still a civilian. I won't put you at risk.
Well, is there any way you can tell me what this was all about?
Sorry, Spidey, but all of this falls under the heading of National Security. All I can offer you is my thanks.

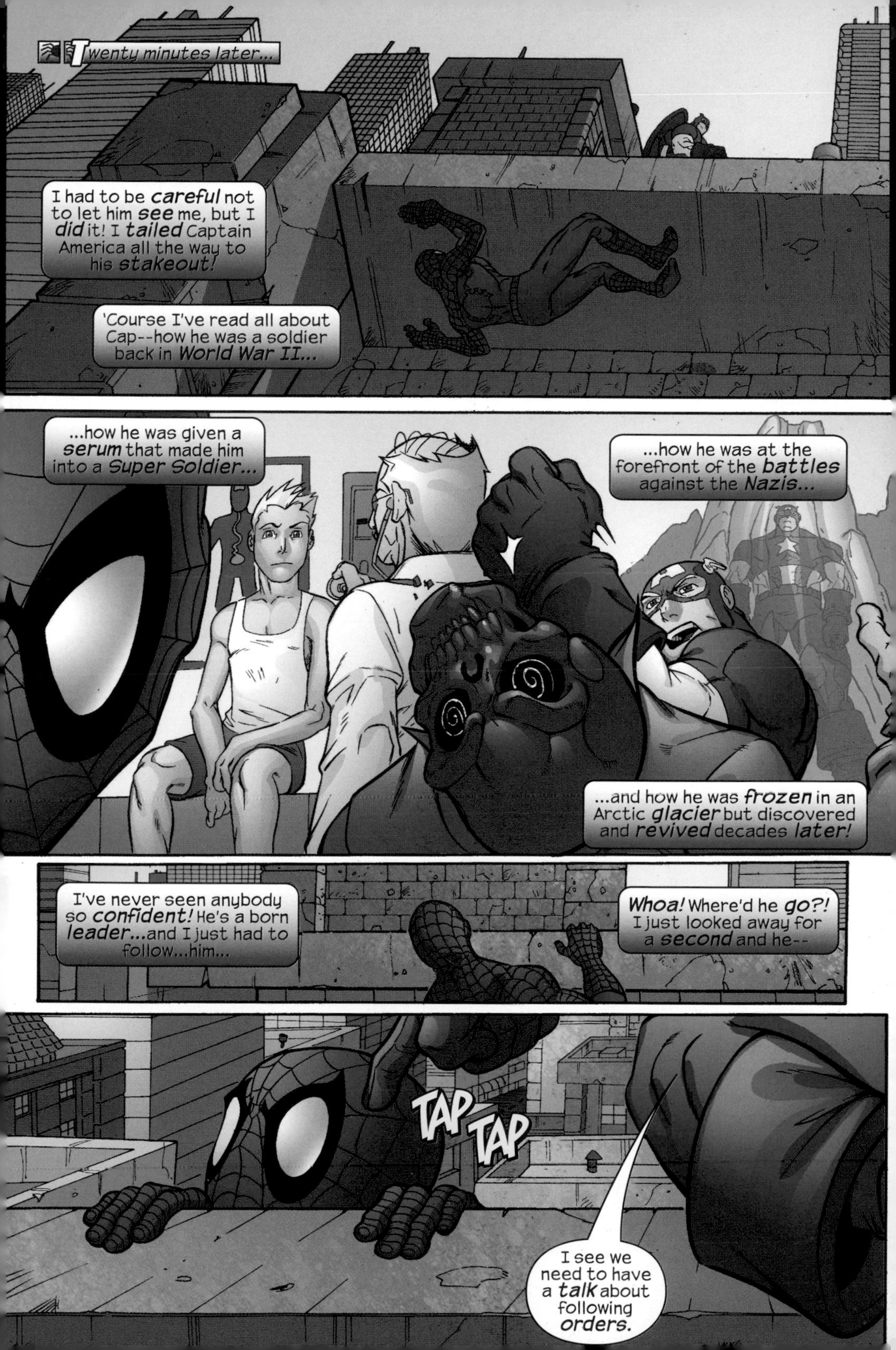
Twenty minutes later...
I had to be careful not to let him see me, but I did it! I tailed Captain America all the way to his stakeout!
'Course I've read all about Cap--how he was a soldier back in World War II...
...how he was given a serum that made him into a Super Soldier...
...how he was at the forefront of the battles against the Nazis...
...and how he was frozen in an Arctic glacier but discovered and revived decades later!
I've never seen anybody so confident! He's a born leader...and I just had to follow...him...
Whoa! Where'd he go?! I just looked away for a second and he--
TAP TAP
I see we need to have a talk about following orders.

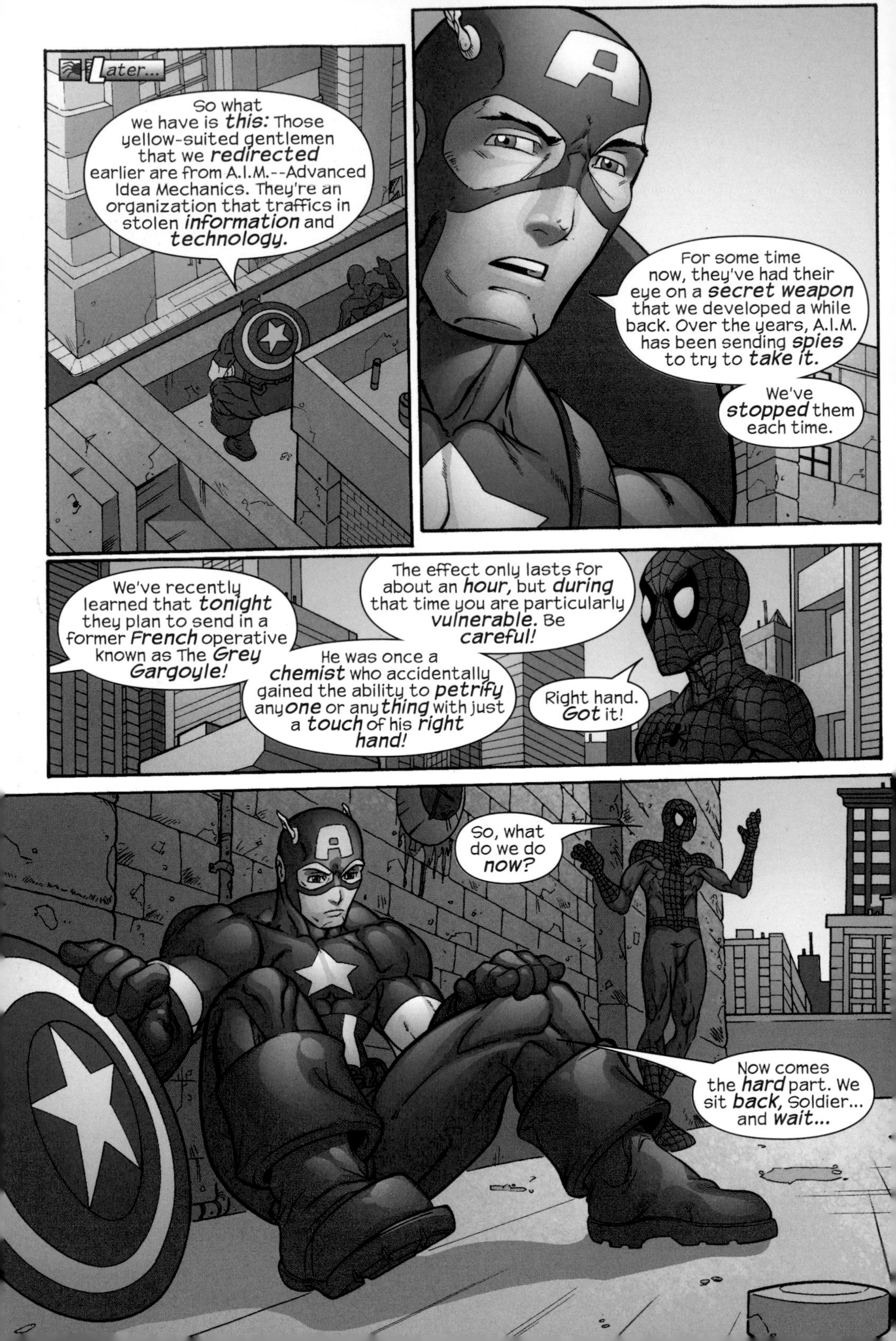
Later...
So what we have is this: Those yellow-suited gentlemen that we redirected earlier are from A.I.M.--Advanced Idea Mechanics. They're an organization that traffics in stolen information and technology.
For some time now, they've had their eye on a secret weapon that we developed a while back. Over the years, A.I.M. has been sending spies to try to take it.
We've stopped them each time.
We've recently learned that tonight they plan to send in a former French operative known as The Grey Gargoyle!
He was once a chemist who accidentally gained the ability to petrify anyone or anything with just a touch of his right hand!
The effect only lasts for about an hour, but during that time you are particularly vulnerable. Be careful!
Right hand. Got it!
So, what do we do now?
Now comes the hard part. We sit back, Soldier... and wait...

And so we do...

Minutes become hours...

Cap...? You were in World War II, *right?* I always wondered--how come they didn't give the Super-Soldier Serum to *other* guys in the Army?

I was the only one to receive the formula before its creator, *Dr. Erskine,* died...it was a *true* secret... and the formula died *with* him.

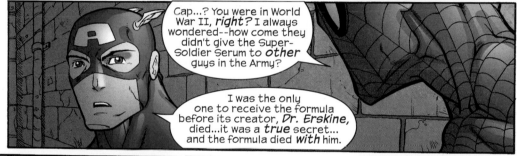

Oh. Still it must've been a lot *easier* back then, huh? My *Uncle* used to call World War II the last *good war...*

*No* war is ever *good,* son. I saw a lot of men lose their *lives* in that war--most of them not much older than *you.* But I know what you *mean...*

Looking back, things *do* seem like they were much clearer then. It was *easy* to tell right from wrong.

We were the *good* guys and we were fighting against a horrible *evil!* We *believed* in what we were fighting for.

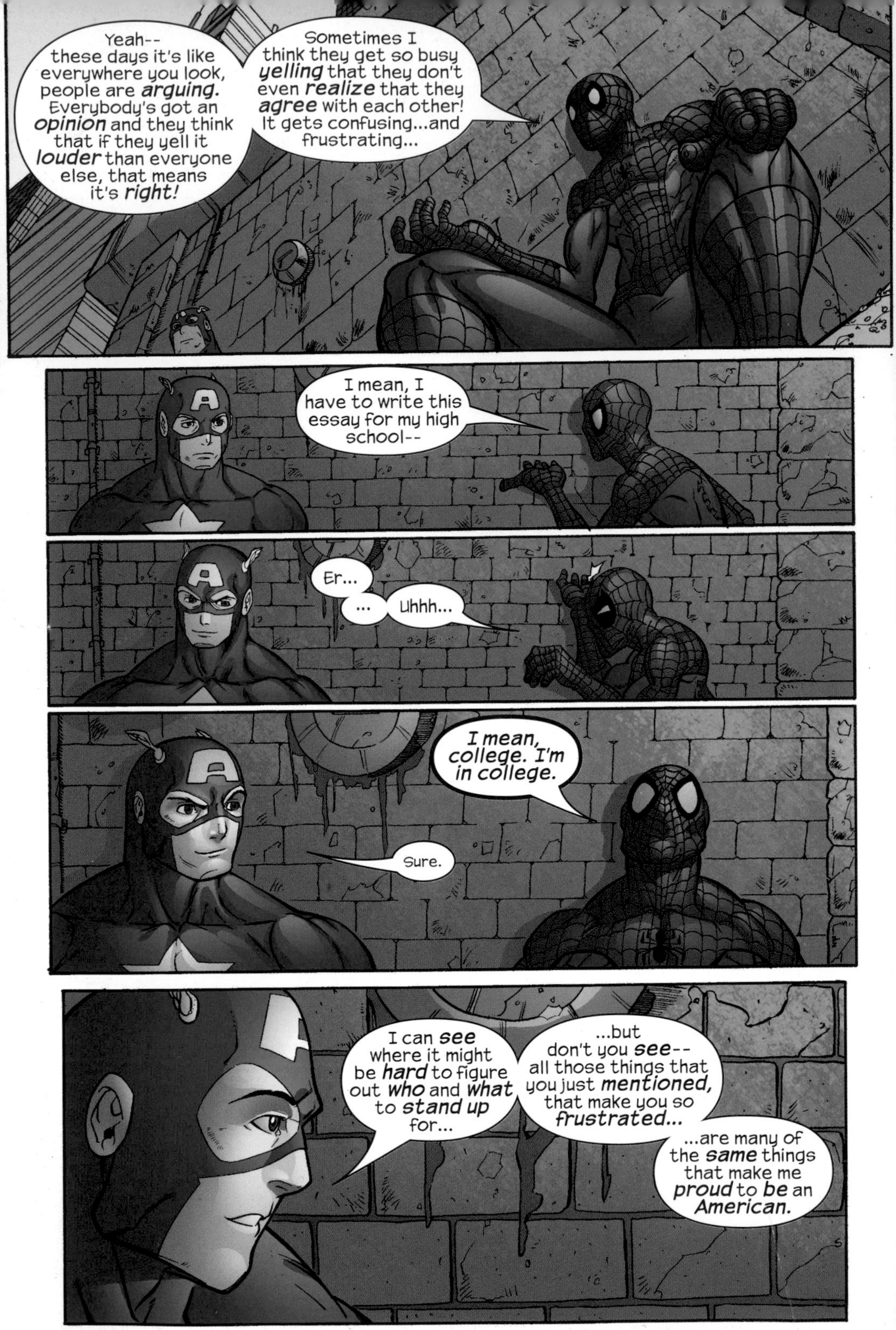

Yeah-- these days it's like everywhere you look, people are *arguing.* Everybody's got an *opinion* and they think that if they yell it *louder* than everyone else, that means it's *right!*
Sometimes I think they get so busy *yelling* that they don't even *realize* that they *agree* with each other! It gets confusing...and frustrating...
I mean, I have to write this essay for my high school--
Er...
...
Uhhh...
*I mean, college. I'm in college.*
Sure.
I can *see* where it might be *hard* to figure out *who* and *what* to *stand up* for...
...but don't you *see*-- all those things that you just *mentioned,* that make you so *frustrated...*
...are many of the *same* things that make me *proud* to *be* an *American.*

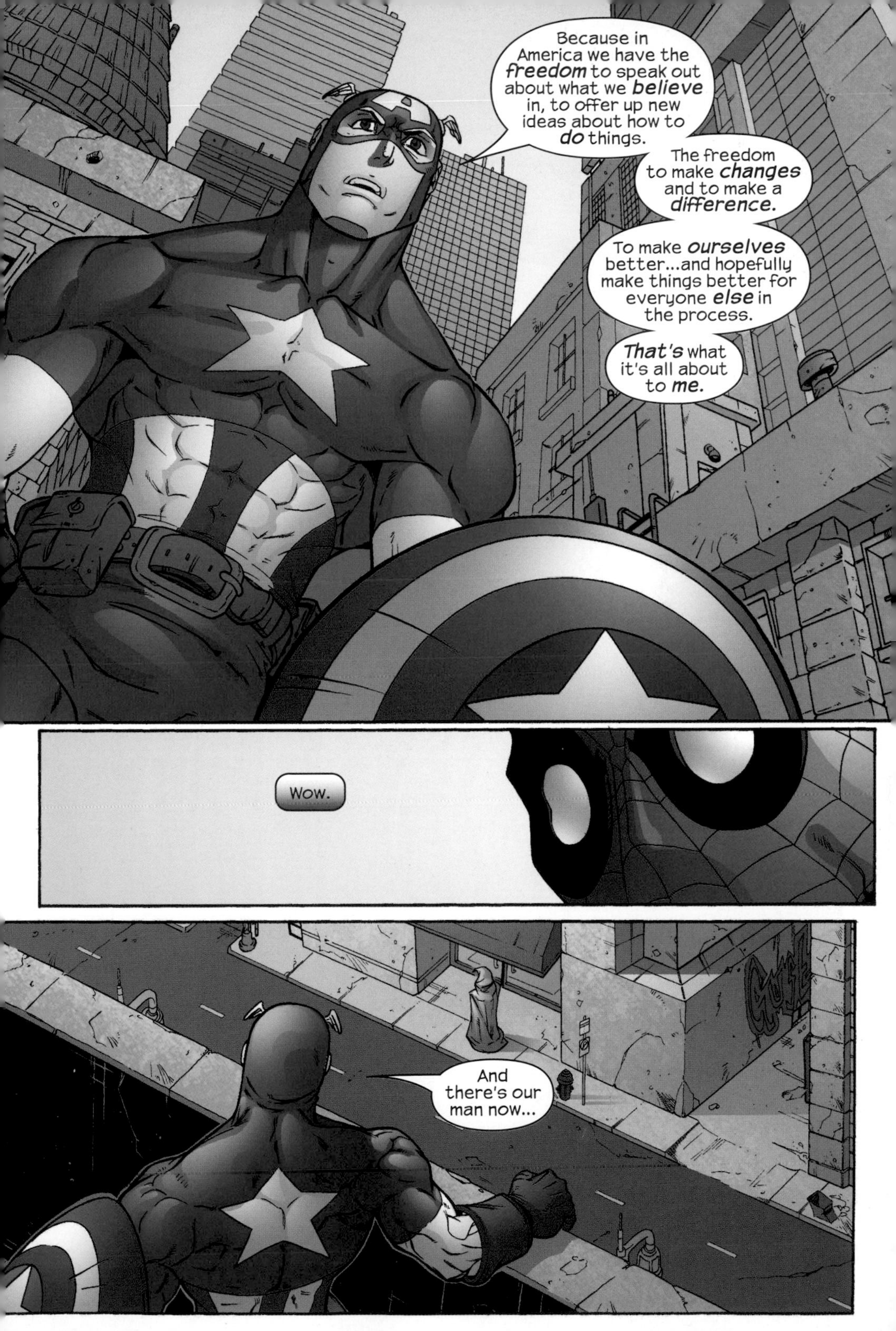
Because in America we have the freedom to speak out about what we believe in, to offer up new ideas about how to do things.
The freedom to make changes and to make a difference.
To make ourselves better...and hopefully make things better for everyone else in the process.
That's what it's all about to me.
Wow.
And there's our man now...

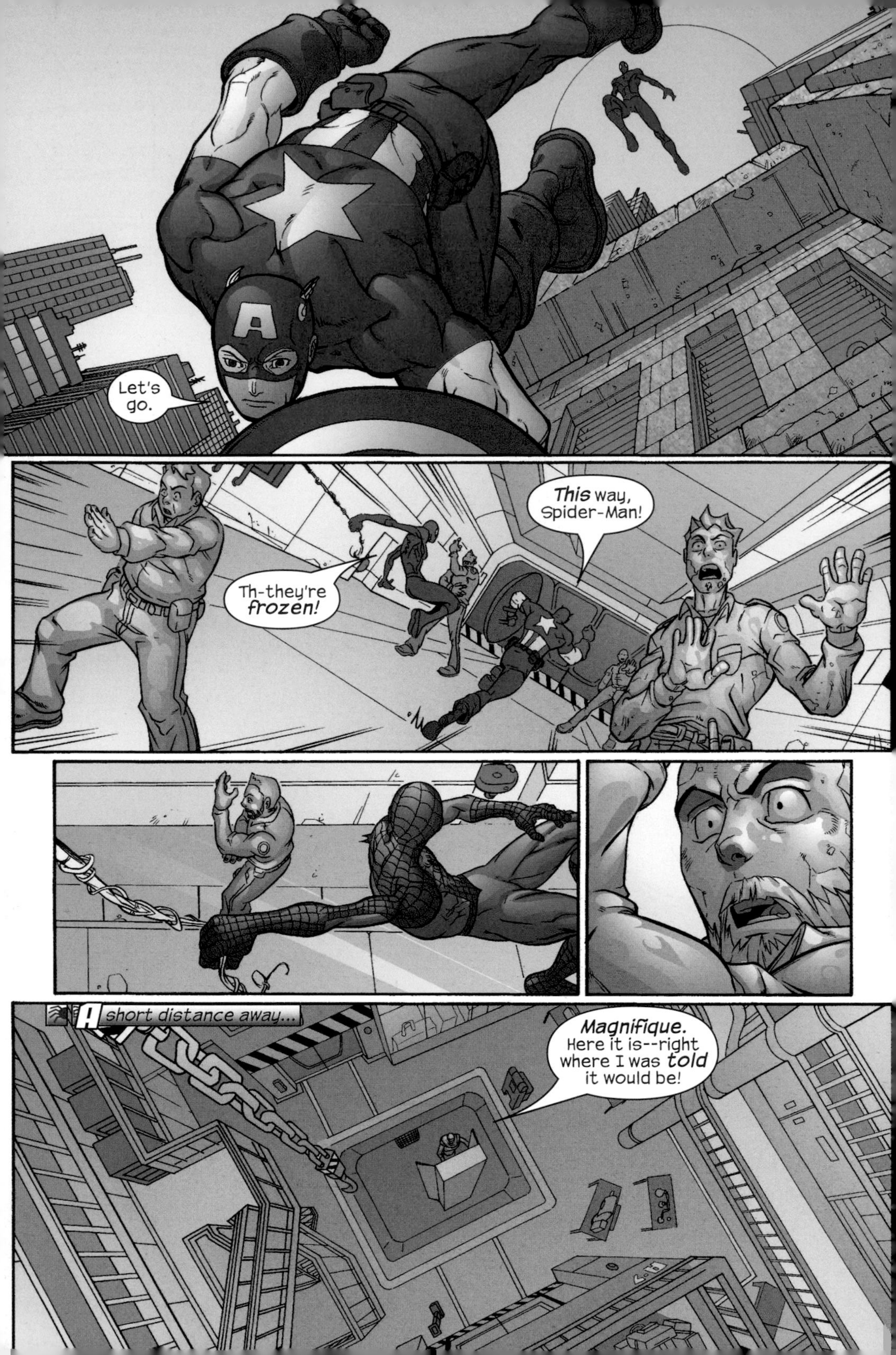
Let's go.
This way, Spider-Man!
Th-they're frozen!
A short distance away...
Magnifique. Here it is--right where I was told it would be!

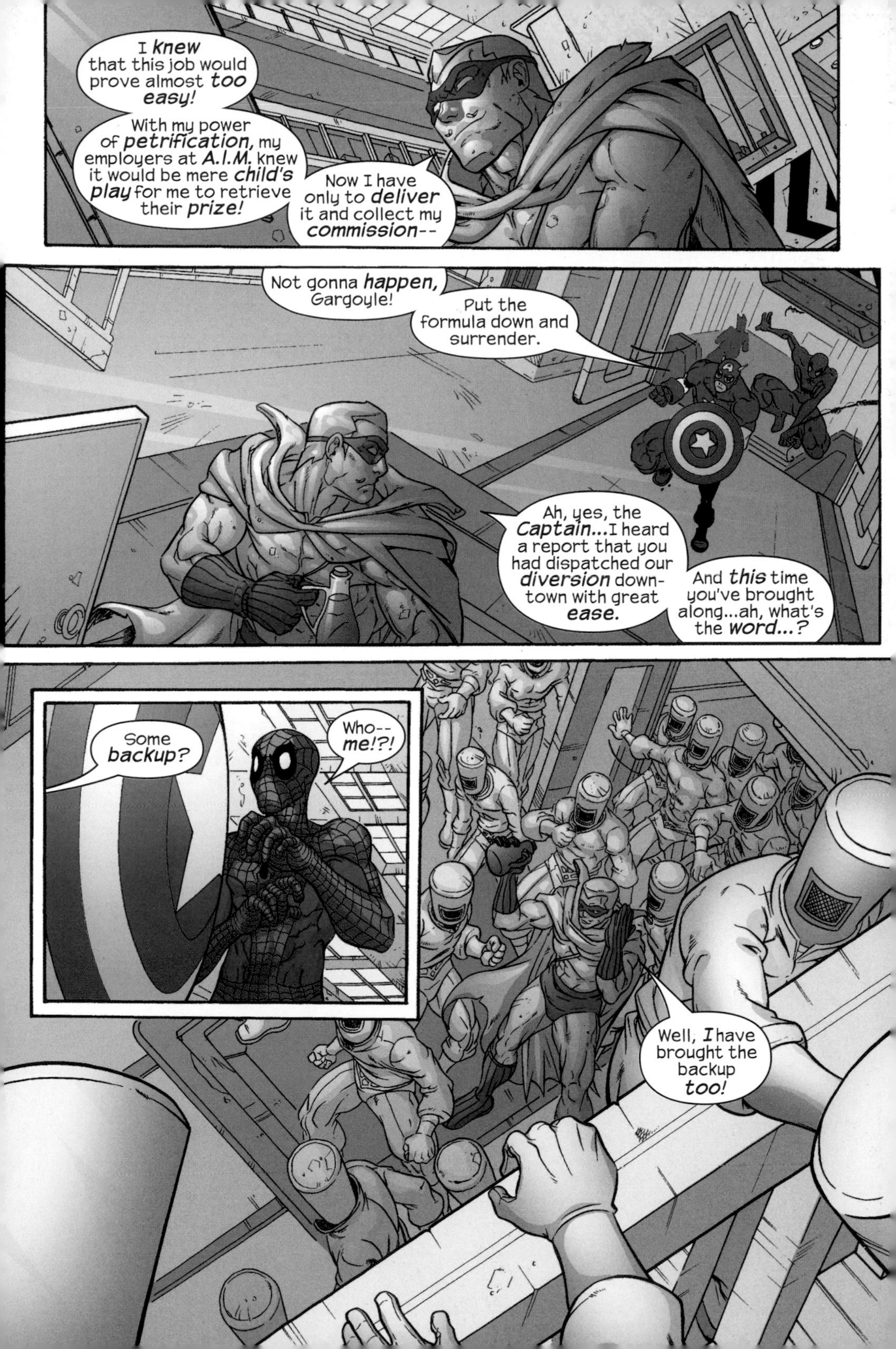
I knew that this job would prove almost too easy!
With my power of petrification, my employers at A.I.M. knew it would be mere child's play for me to retrieve their prize!
Now I have only to deliver it and collect my commission--
Not gonna happen, Gargoyle!
Put the formula down and surrender.
Ah, yes, the Captain...I heard a report that you had dispatched our diversion downtown with great ease.
And this time you've brought along...ah, what's the word...?
Some backup?
Who--me!?!
Well, I have brought the backup too!

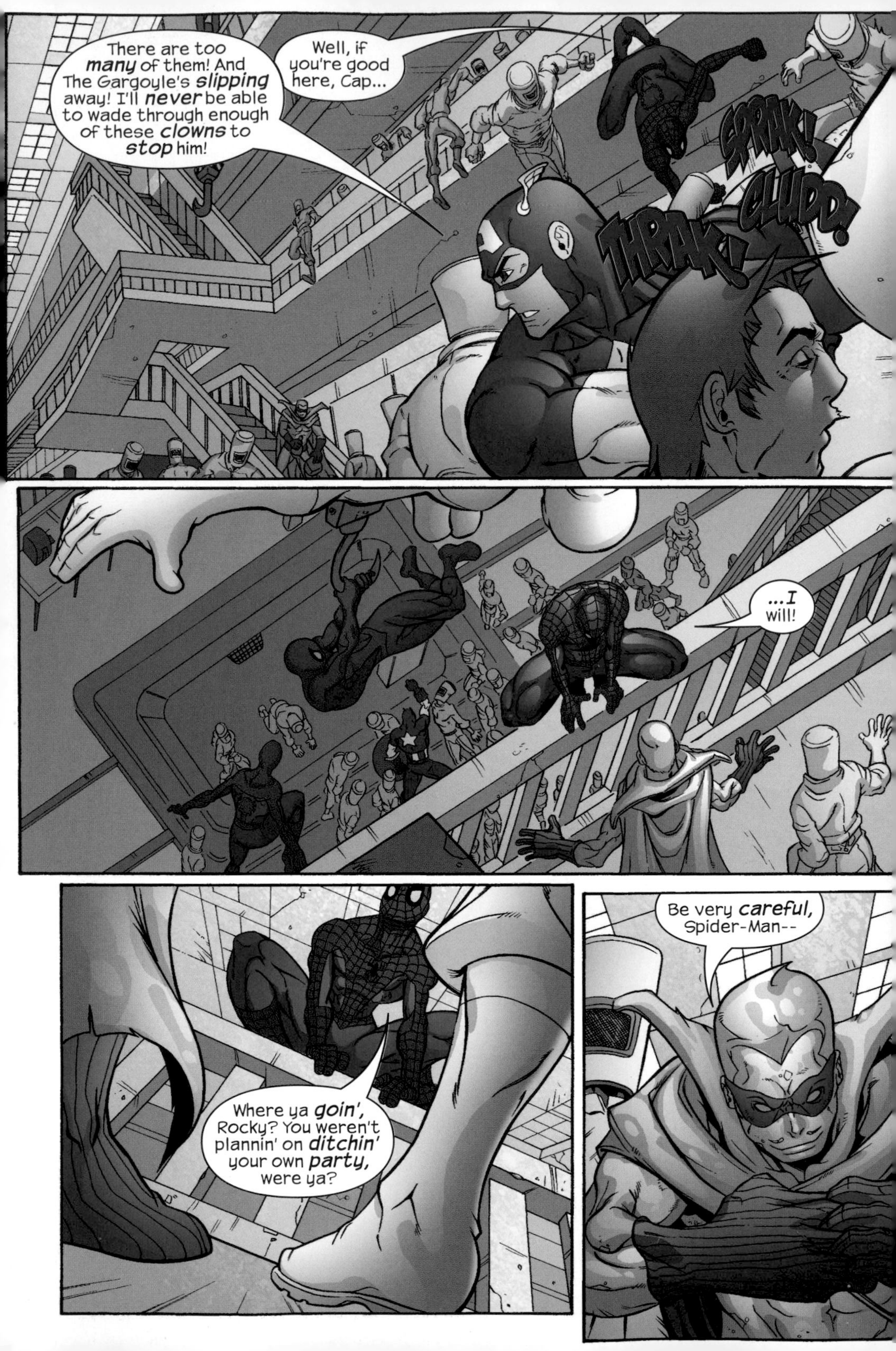
There are too many of them! And The Gargoyle's slipping away! I'll never be able to wade through enough of these clowns to stop him!
Well, if you're good here, Cap...
SPRAK!
THRAK!
CLUDD!
...I will!
Where ya goin', Rocky? You weren't plannin' on ditchin' your own party, were ya?
Be very careful, Spider-Man--

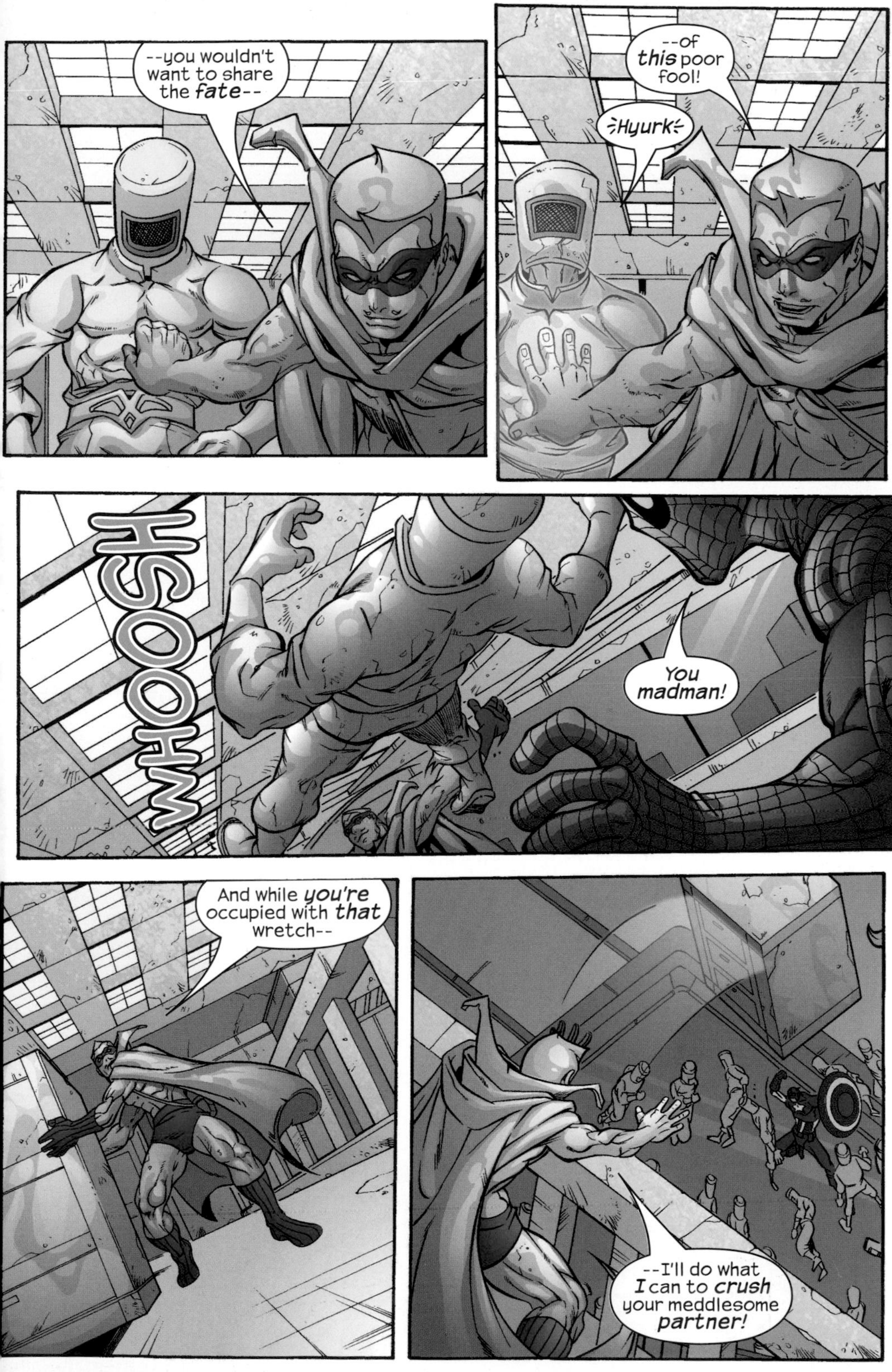
--you wouldn't want to share the *fate*--
--of *this* poor fool!
Hyurk
WHOOSH
You madman!
And while *you're* occupied with *that* wretch--
--I'll do what *I* can to *crush* your meddlesome *partner*!

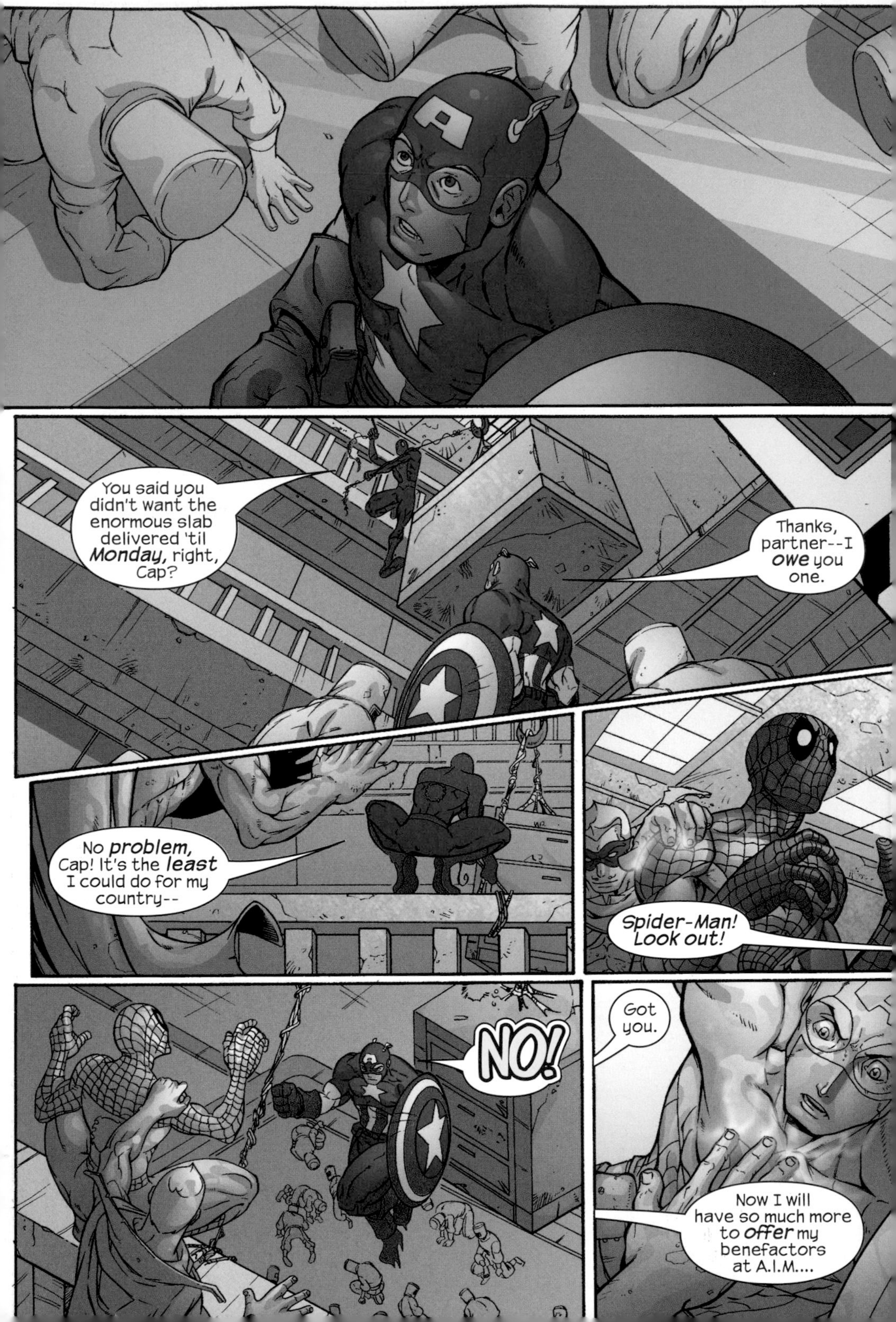
You said you didn't want the enormous slab delivered 'til Monday, right, Cap?
Thanks, partner--I owe you one.
No problem, Cap! It's the least I could do for my country--
Spider-Man! Look out!
NO!
Got you.
Now I will have so much more to offer my benefactors at A.I.M....

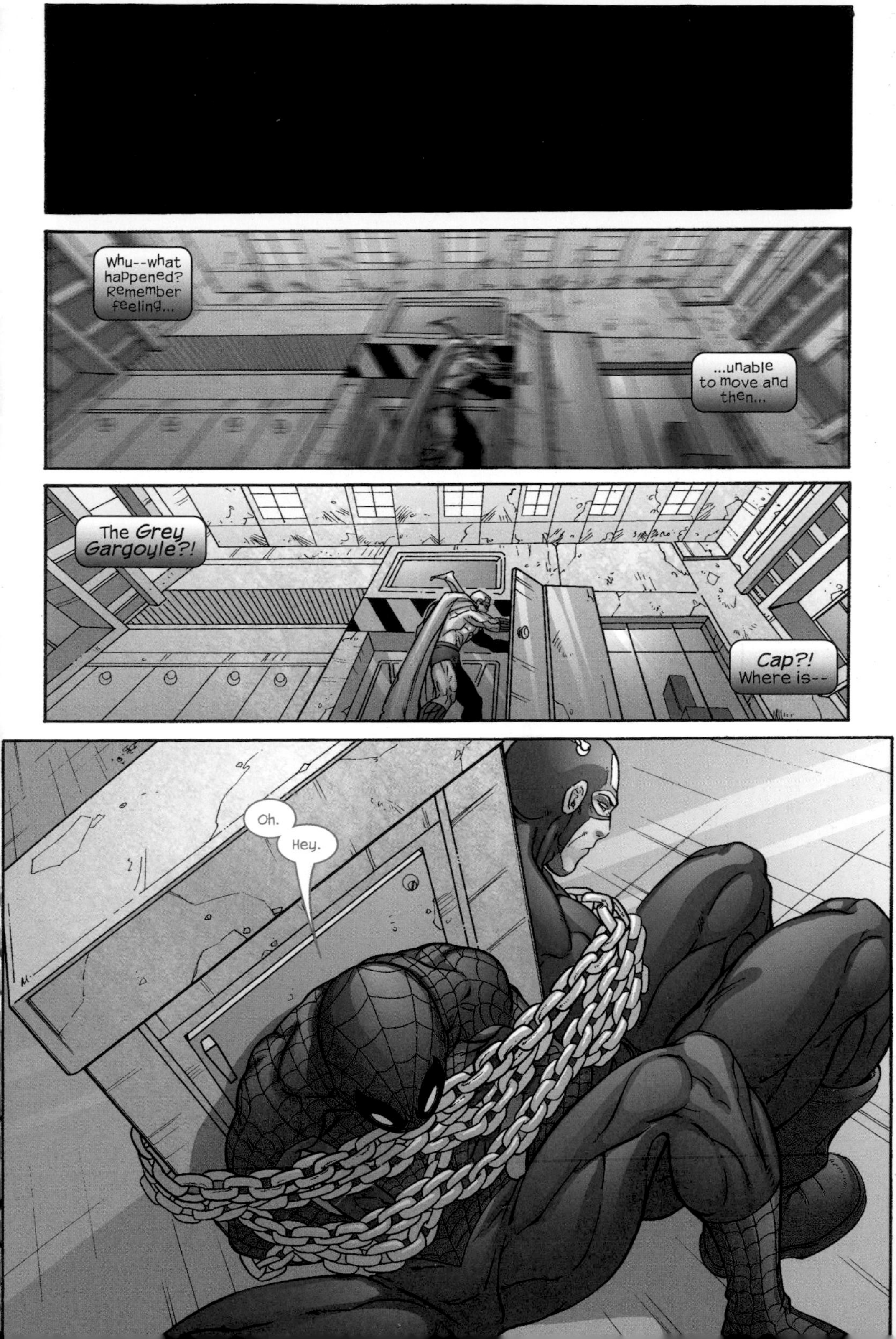
Whu--what happened? Remember feeling...
...unable to move and then...
The Grey Gargoyle?!
Cap?! Where is--
Oh.
Hey.

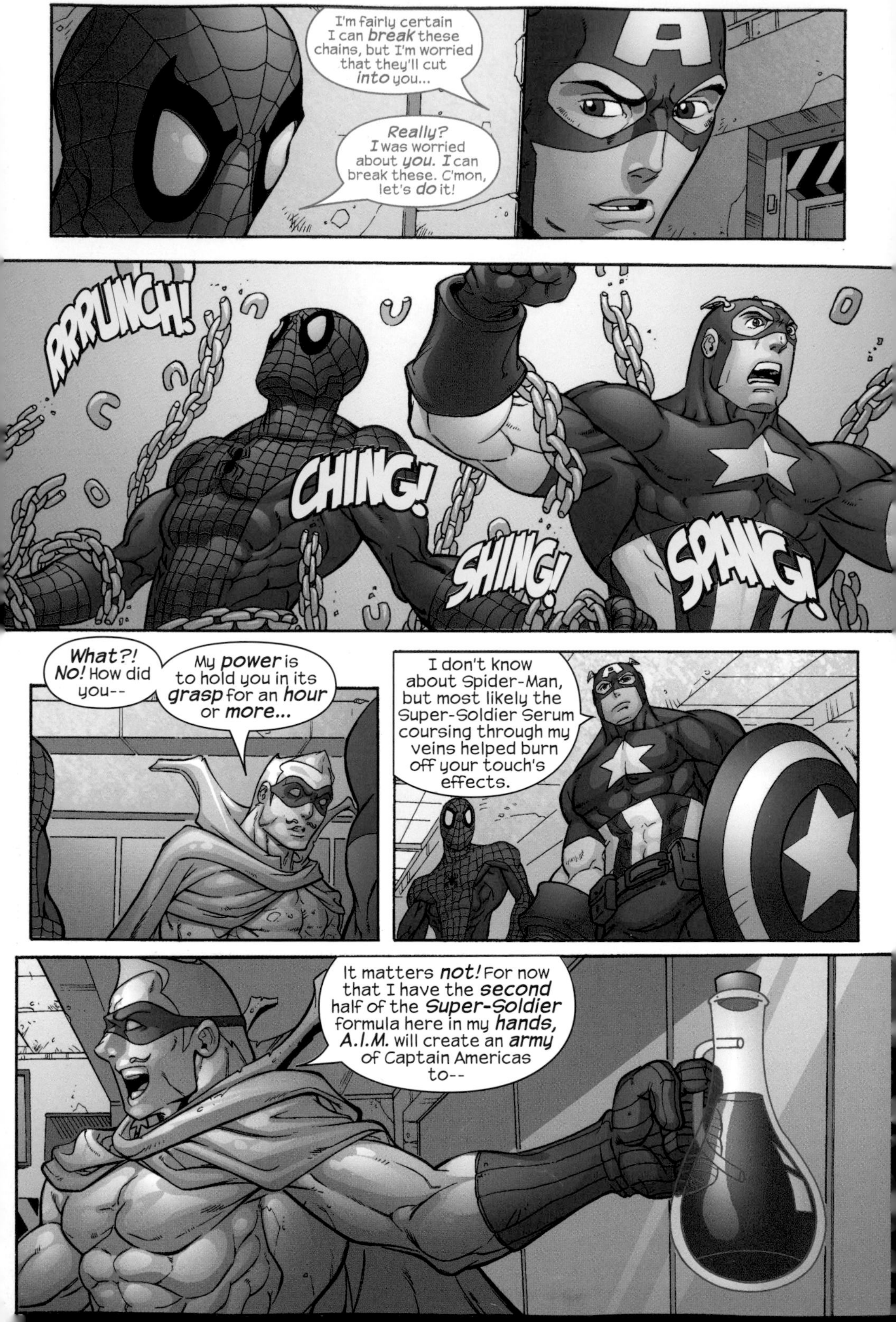
I'm fairly certain I can break these chains, but I'm worried that they'll cut into you...
Really? I was worried about you. I can break these. C'mon, let's do it!
RRRUNCH!
CHING!
SHING!
SPANG!
What?! No! How did you--
My power is to hold you in its grasp for an hour or more...
I don't know about Spider-Man, but most likely the Super-Soldier Serum coursing through my veins helped burn off your touch's effects.
It matters not! For now that I have the second half of the Super-Soldier formula here in my hands, A.I.M. will create an army of Captain Americas to--

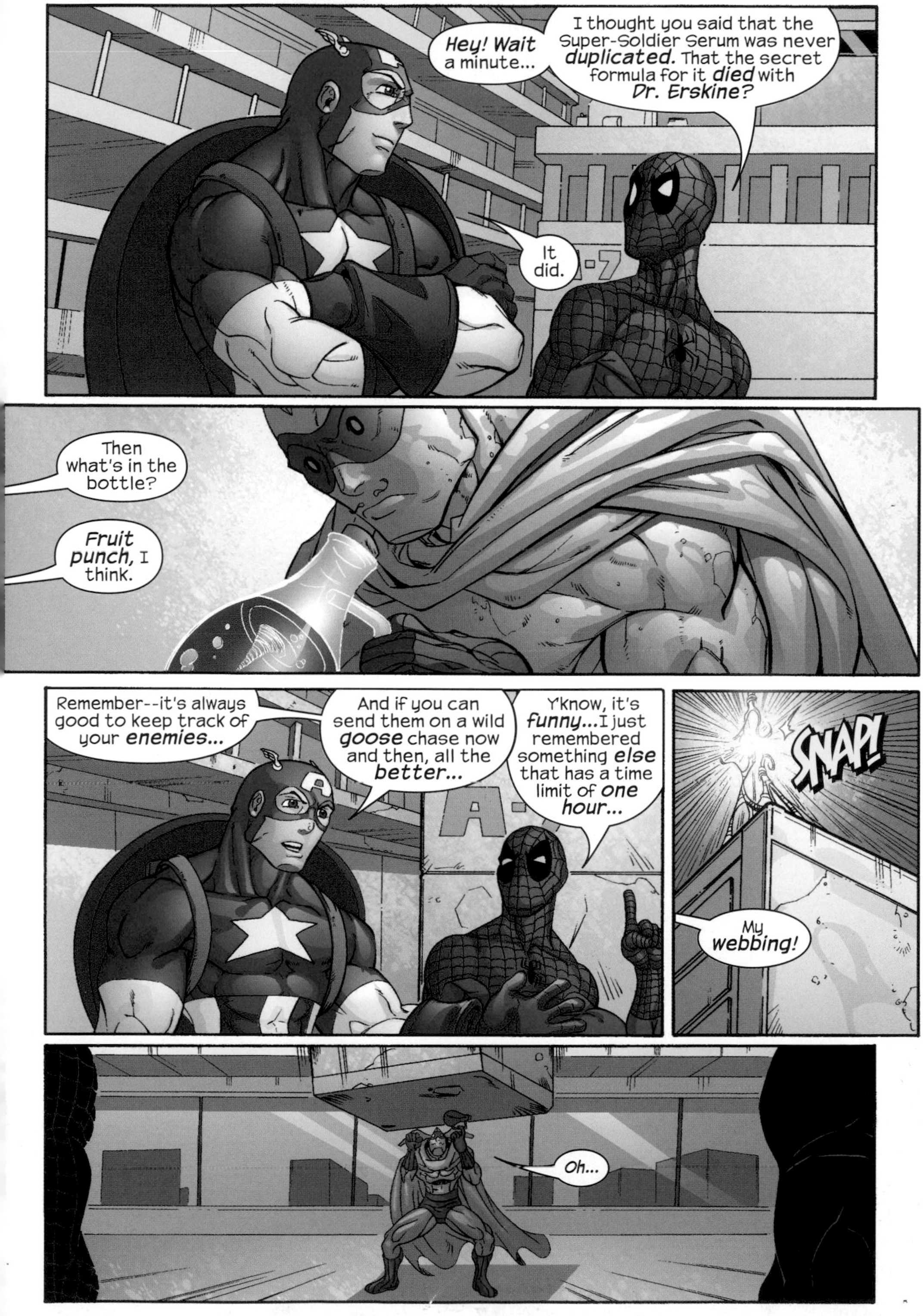
Hey! Wait a minute...
I thought you said that the Super-Soldier Serum was never duplicated. That the secret formula for it died with Dr. Erskine?
It did.
Then what's in the bottle?
Fruit punch, I think.
Remember--it's always good to keep track of your enemies...
And if you can send them on a wild goose chase now and then, all the better...
Y'know, it's funny...I just remembered something else that has a time limit of one hour...
SNAP!
My webbing!
Oh...

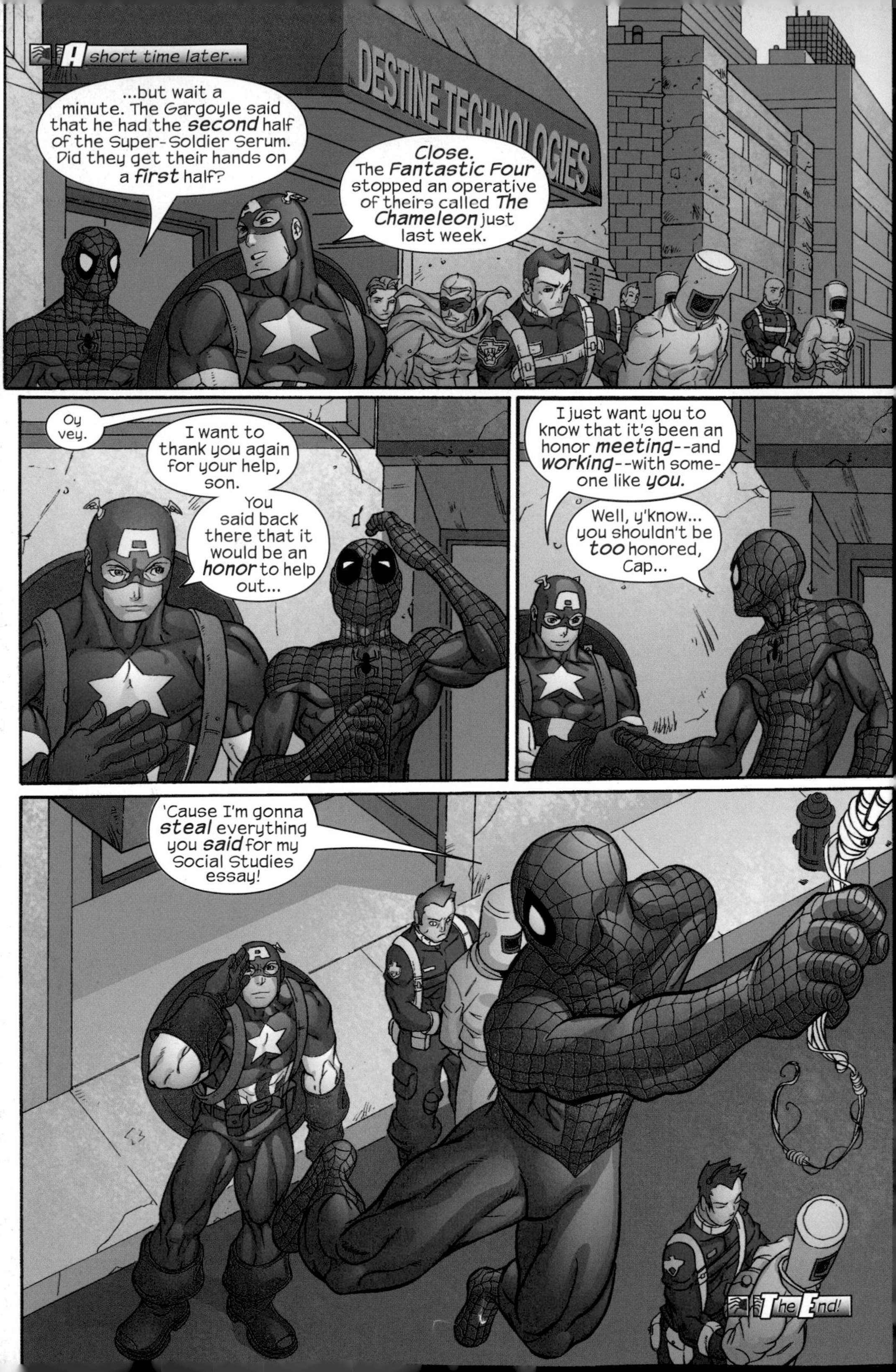
A short time later...
...but wait a minute. The Gargoyle said that he had the second half of the Super-Soldier Serum. Did they get their hands on a first half?
Close. The Fantastic Four stopped an operative of theirs called The Chameleon just last week.
DESTINE TECHNOLOGIES
I want to thank you again for your help, son.
You said back there that it would be an honor to help out...
Oy vey.
I just want you to know that it's been an honor meeting--and working--with someone like you.
Well, y'know... you shouldn't be too honored, Cap...
'Cause I'm gonna steal everything you said for my Social Studies essay!
The End!

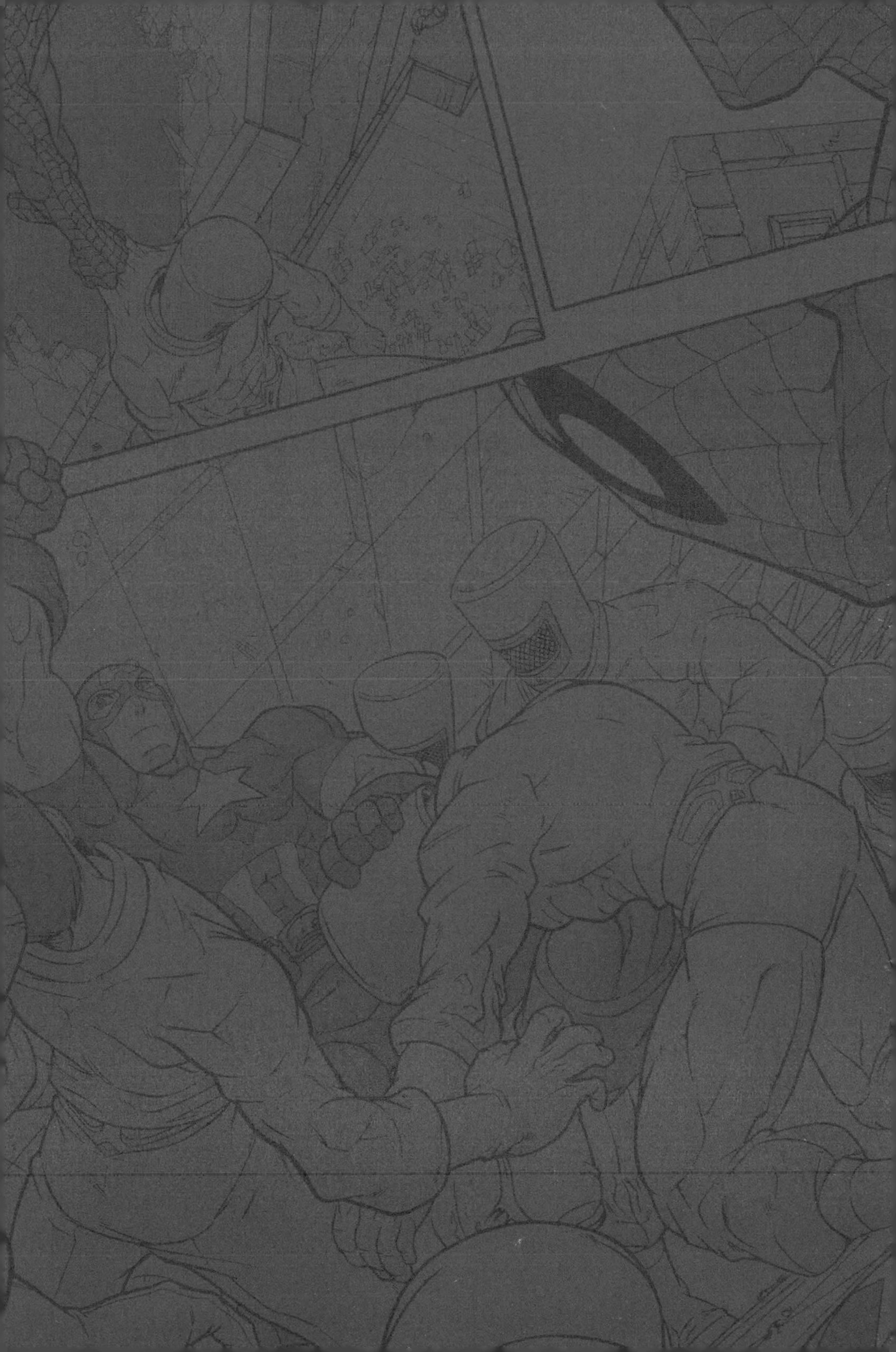

07

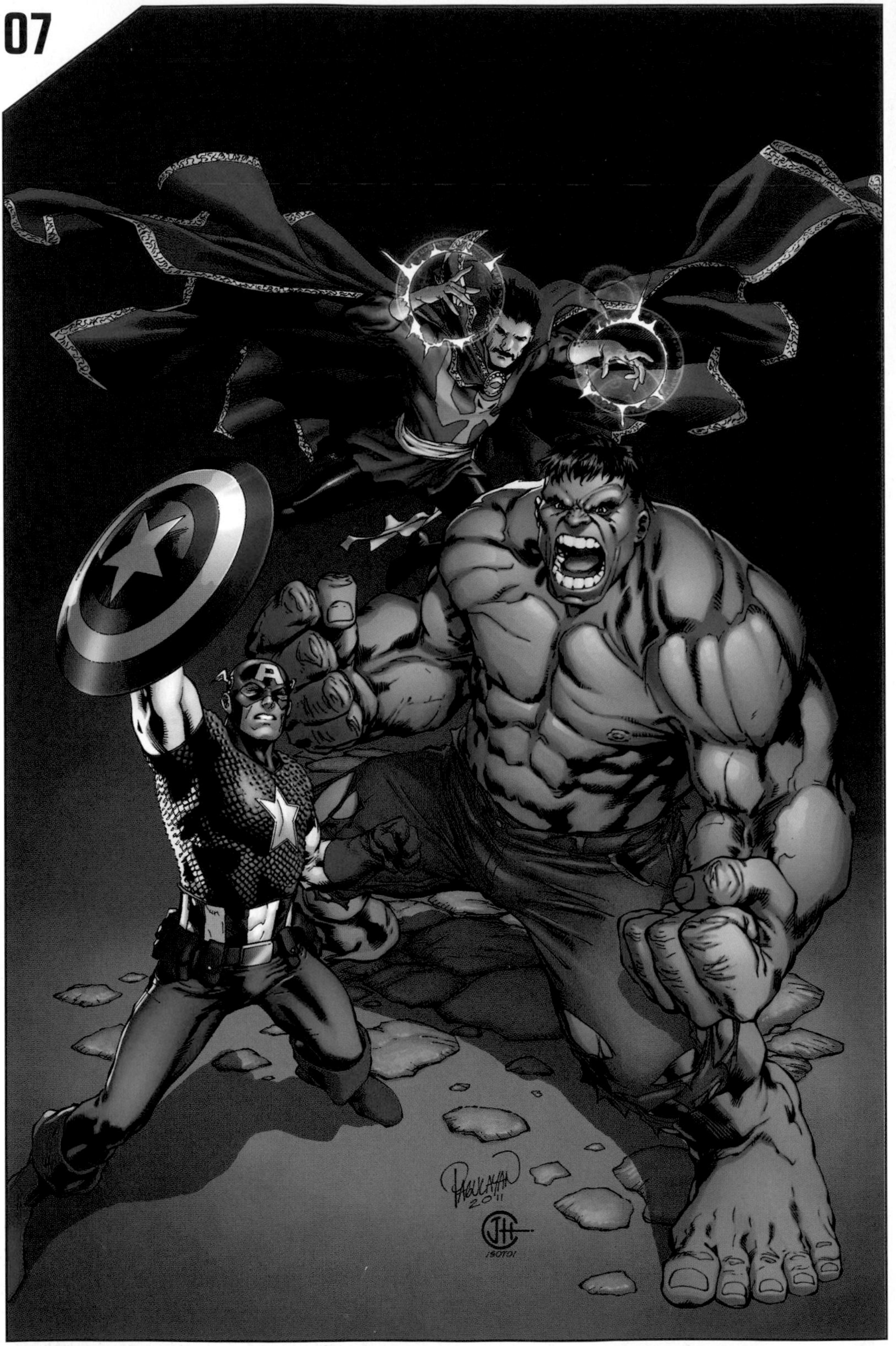

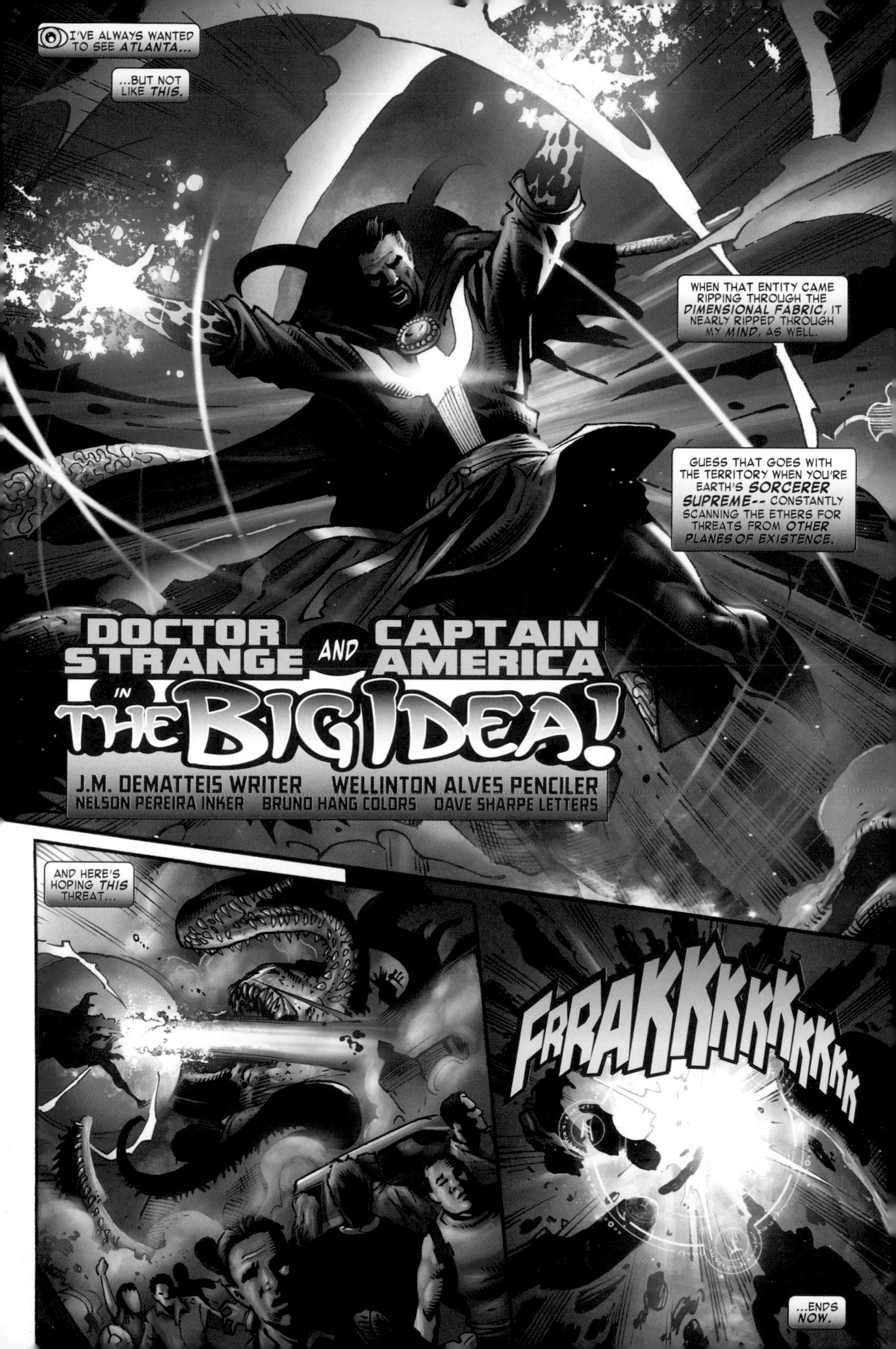
I'VE ALWAYS WANTED TO SEE ATLANTA...
...BUT NOT LIKE THIS.
WHEN THAT ENTITY CAME RIPPING THROUGH THE DIMENSIONAL FABRIC, IT NEARLY RIPPED THROUGH MY MIND, AS WELL.
GUESS THAT GOES WITH THE TERRITORY WHEN YOU'RE EARTH'S SORCERER SUPREME-- CONSTANTLY SCANNING THE ETHERS FOR THREATS FROM OTHER PLANES OF EXISTENCE.
DOCTOR STRANGE AND CAPTAIN AMERICA
IN THE BIG IDEA!
J.M. DEMATTEIS WRITER WELLINTON ALVES PENCILER
NELSON PEREIRA INKER BRUNO HANG COLORS DAVE SHARPE LETTERS
AND HERE'S HOPING THIS THREAT...
FRRAKKKKKKKKK
...ENDS NOW.

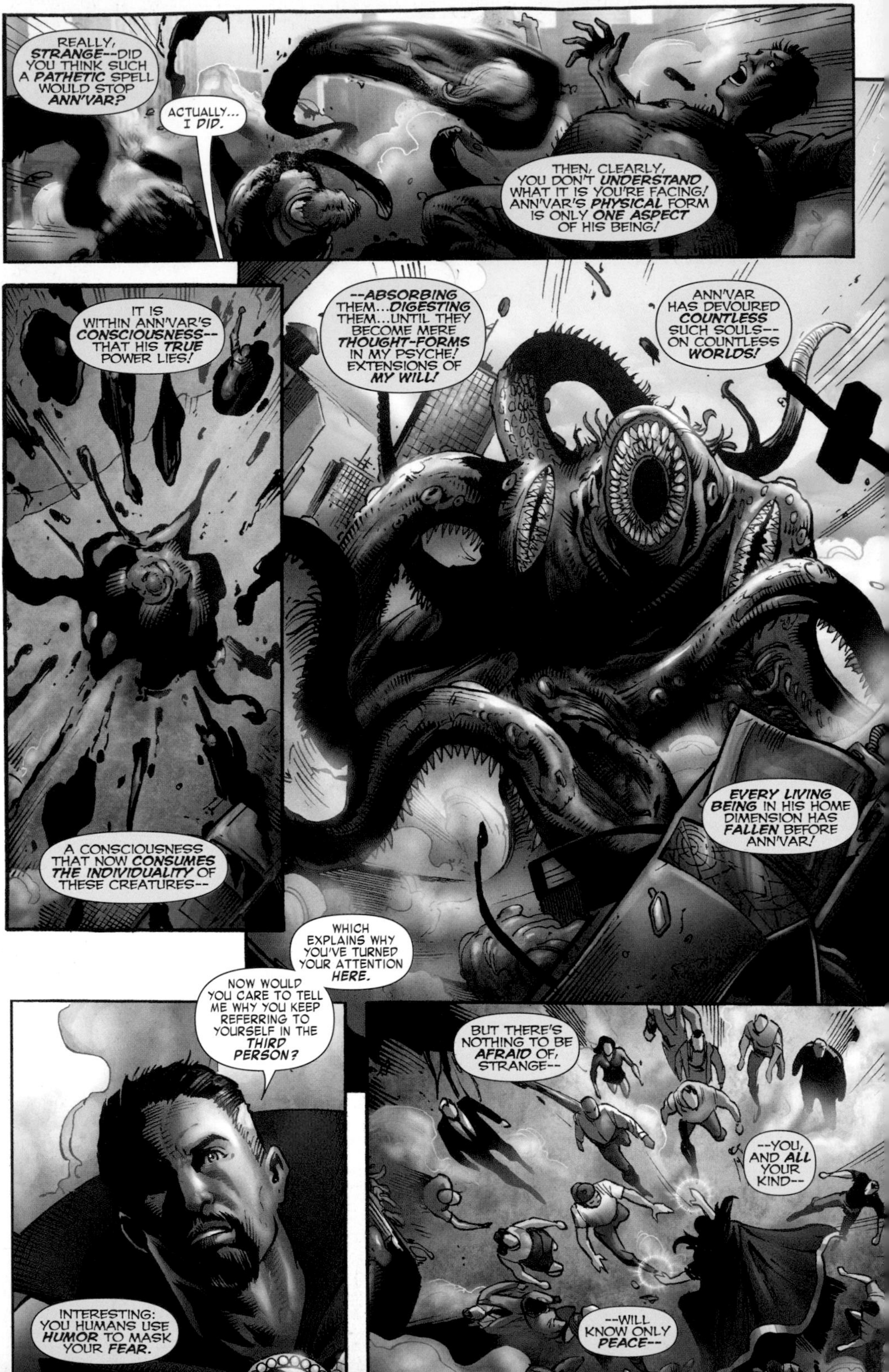
REALLY, STRANGE--DID YOU THINK SUCH A PATHETIC SPELL WOULD STOP ANN'VAR?
ACTUALLY... I DID.
THEN, CLEARLY, YOU DON'T UNDERSTAND WHAT IT IS YOU'RE FACING! ANN'VAR'S PHYSICAL FORM IS ONLY ONE ASPECT OF HIS BEING!
IT IS WITHIN ANN'VAR'S CONSCIOUSNESS--THAT HIS TRUE POWER LIES!
A CONSCIOUSNESS THAT NOW CONSUMES THE INDIVIDUALITY OF THESE CREATURES--
--ABSORBING THEM...DIGESTING THEM...UNTIL THEY BECOME MERE THOUGHT-FORMS IN MY PSYCHE! EXTENSIONS OF MY WILL!
ANN'VAR HAS DEVOURED COUNTLESS SUCH SOULS--ON COUNTLESS WORLDS!
EVERY LIVING BEING IN HIS HOME DIMENSION HAS FALLEN BEFORE ANN'VAR!
WHICH EXPLAINS WHY YOU'VE TURNED YOUR ATTENTION HERE.
NOW WOULD YOU CARE TO TELL ME WHY YOU KEEP REFERRING TO YOURSELF IN THE THIRD PERSON?
INTERESTING: YOU HUMANS USE HUMOR TO MASK YOUR FEAR.
BUT THERE'S NOTHING TO BE AFRAID OF, STRANGE--
--YOU, AND ALL YOUR KIND--
--WILL KNOW ONLY PEACE--

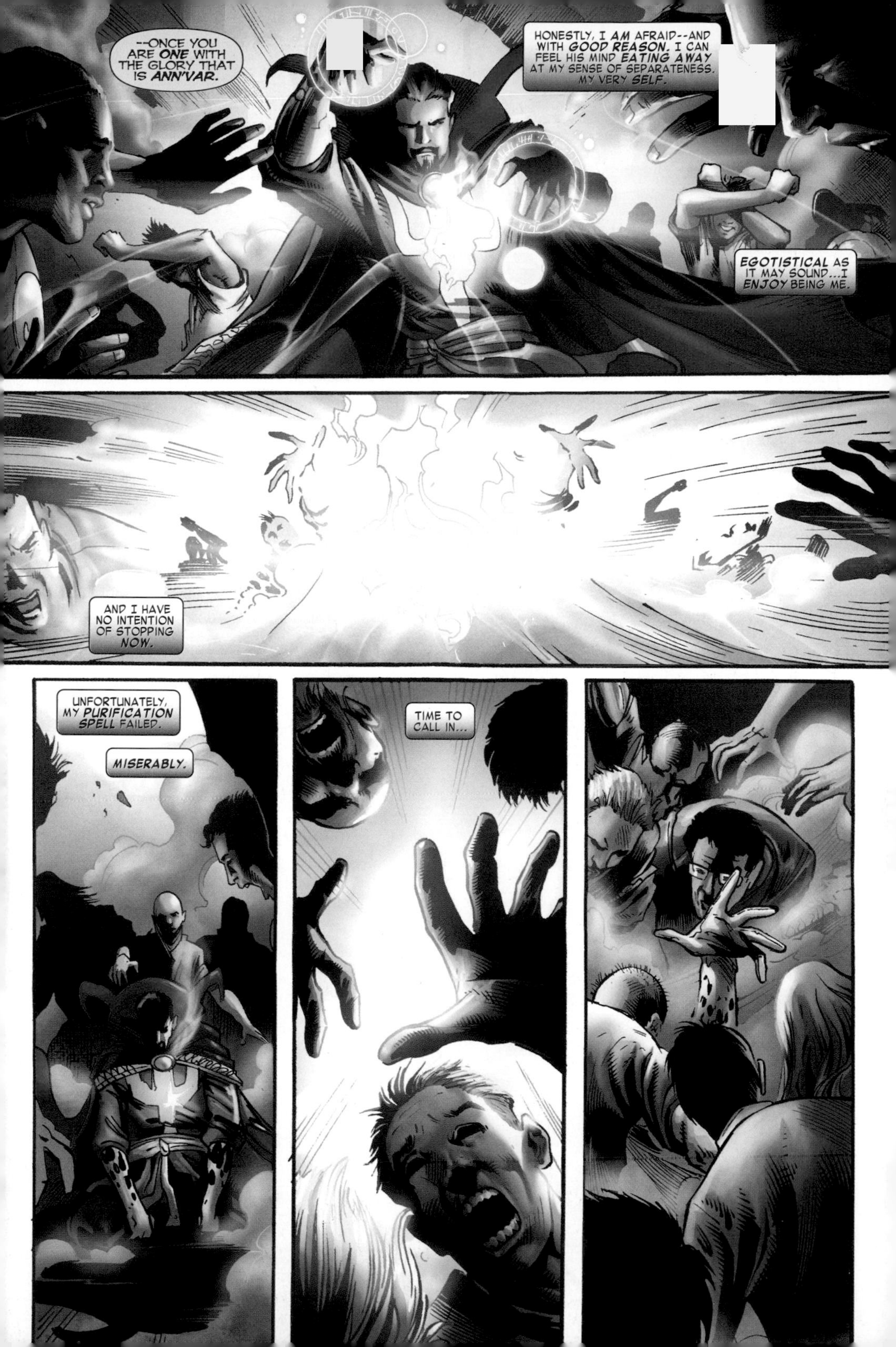
--ONCE YOU ARE ONE WITH THE GLORY THAT IS ANN'VAR.
HONESTLY, I AM AFRAID--AND WITH GOOD REASON. I CAN FEEL HIS MIND EATING AWAY AT MY SENSE OF SEPARATENESS. MY VERY SELF.
EGOTISTICAL AS IT MAY SOUND...I ENJOY BEING ME.
AND I HAVE NO INTENTION OF STOPPING NOW.
UNFORTUNATELY, MY PURIFICATION SPELL FAILED.
MISERABLY.
TIME TO CALL IN...

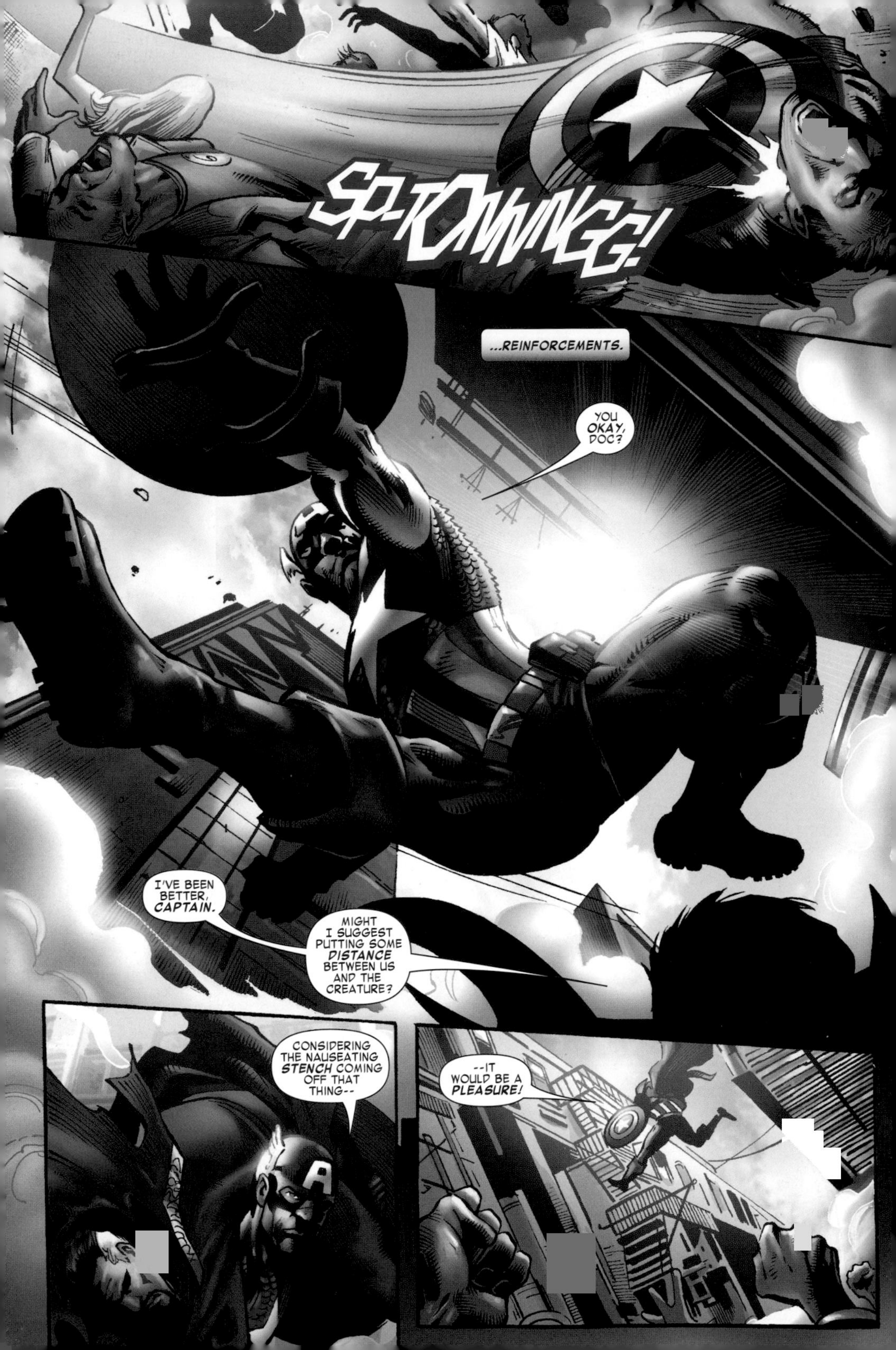
SP-KOWWNGG!
...REINFORCEMENTS.
YOU OKAY, DOC?
I'VE BEEN BETTER, CAPTAIN.
MIGHT I SUGGEST PUTTING SOME DISTANCE BETWEEN US AND THE CREATURE?
CONSIDERING THE NAUSEATING STENCH COMING OFF THAT THING--
--IT WOULD BE A PLEASURE!

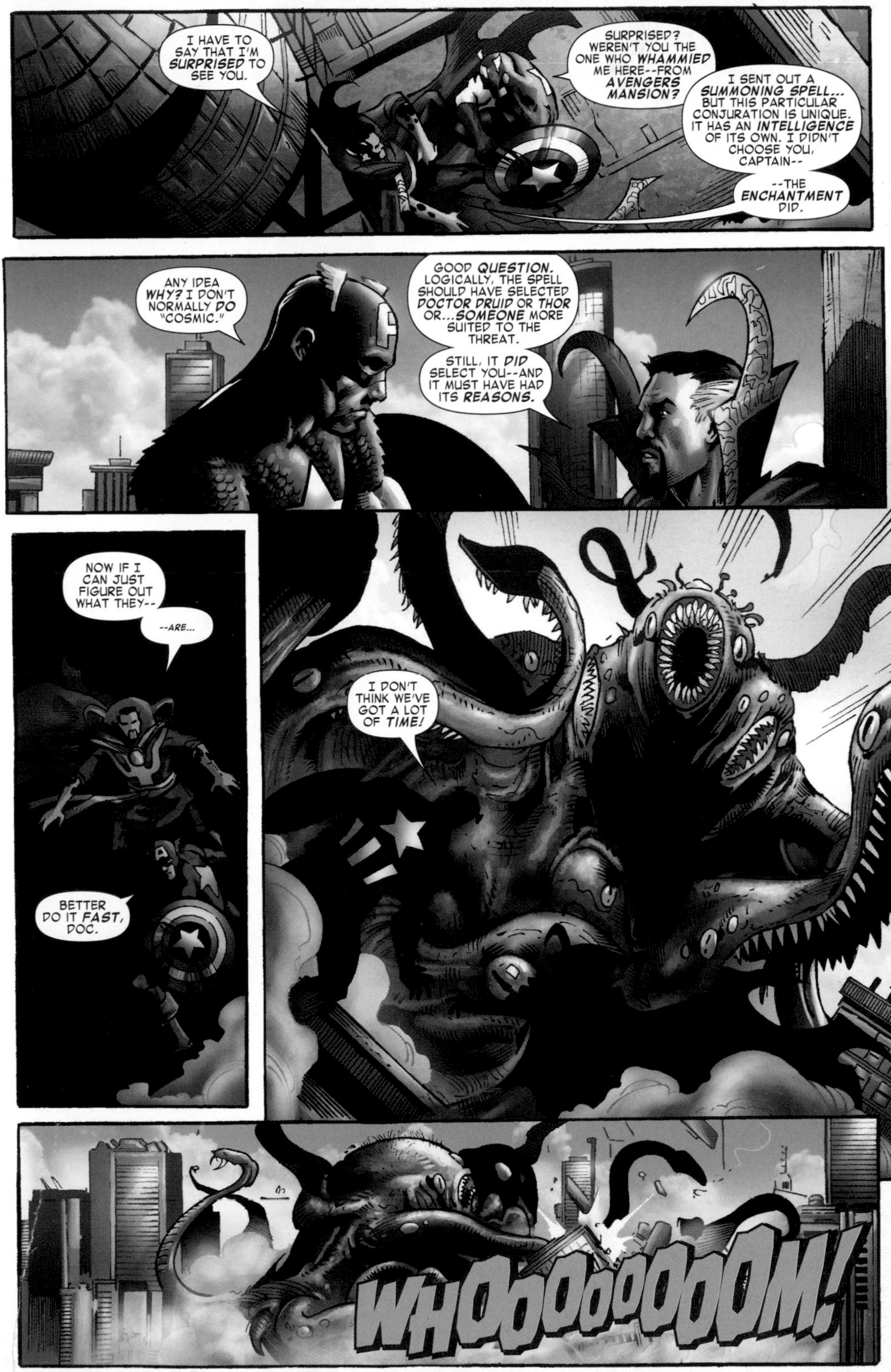
I HAVE TO SAY THAT I'M SURPRISED TO SEE YOU.
SURPRISED? WEREN'T YOU THE ONE WHO WHAMMIED ME HERE--FROM AVENGERS MANSION?
I SENT OUT A SUMMONING SPELL... BUT THIS PARTICULAR CONJURATION IS UNIQUE. IT HAS AN INTELLIGENCE OF ITS OWN. I DIDN'T CHOOSE YOU, CAPTAIN--
--THE ENCHANTMENT DID.
ANY IDEA WHY? I DON'T NORMALLY DO "COSMIC."
GOOD QUESTION. LOGICALLY, THE SPELL SHOULD HAVE SELECTED DOCTOR DRUID OR THOR OR...SOMEONE MORE SUITED TO THE THREAT.
STILL, IT DID SELECT YOU--AND IT MUST HAVE HAD ITS REASONS.
NOW IF I CAN JUST FIGURE OUT WHAT THEY--
--ARE...
BETTER DO IT FAST, DOC.
I DON'T THINK WE'VE GOT A LOT OF TIME!
WHOOOOOOOOOM!

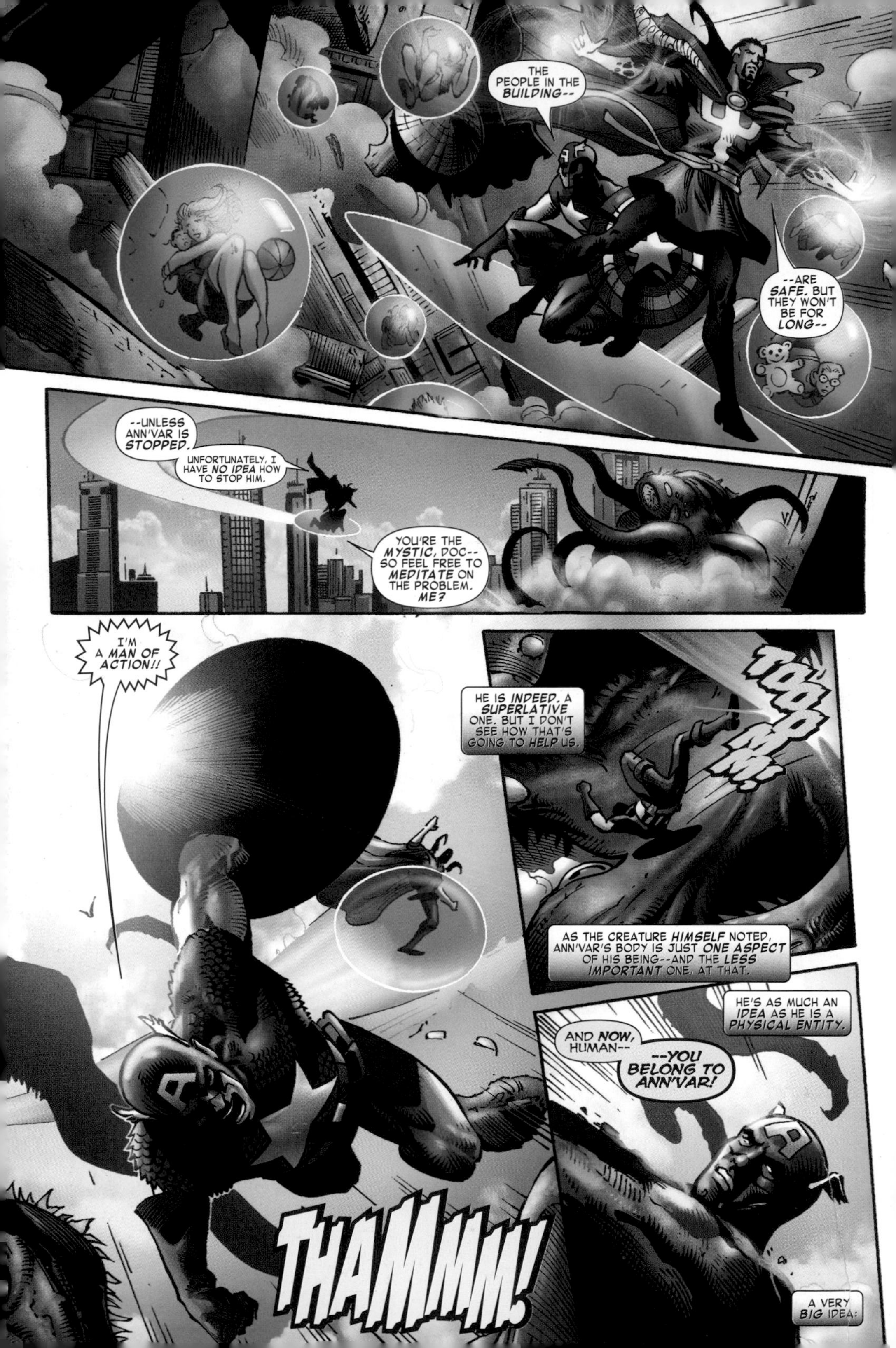
THE PEOPLE IN THE BUILDING--
--ARE SAFE. BUT THEY WON'T BE FOR LONG--
--UNLESS ANN'VAR IS STOPPED.
UNFORTUNATELY, I HAVE NO IDEA HOW TO STOP HIM.
YOU'RE THE MYSTIC, DOC--SO FEEL FREE TO MEDITATE ON THE PROBLEM. ME?
I'M A MAN OF ACTION!!
HE IS INDEED. A SUPERLATIVE ONE. BUT I DON'T SEE HOW THAT'S GOING TO HELP US.
TOOOMM!
AS THE CREATURE HIMSELF NOTED, ANN'VAR'S BODY IS JUST ONE ASPECT OF HIS BEING--AND THE LESS IMPORTANT ONE, AT THAT.
HE'S AS MUCH AN IDEA AS HE IS A PHYSICAL ENTITY.
AND NOW, HUMAN--
--YOU BELONG TO ANN'VAR!
THAMMM!
A VERY BIG IDEA.

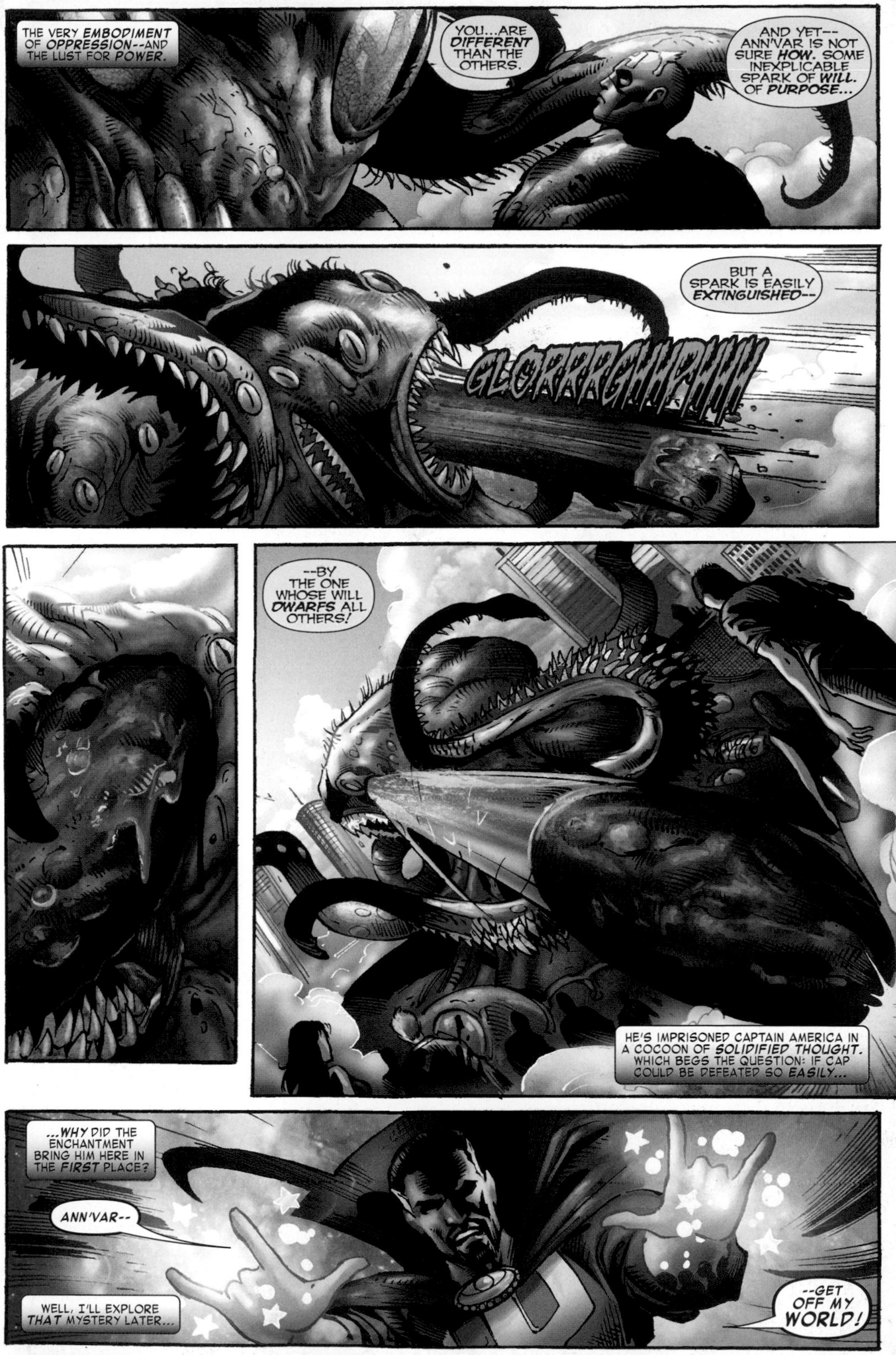
THE VERY EMBODIMENT OF OPPRESSION--AND THE LUST FOR POWER.
YOU...ARE DIFFERENT THAN THE OTHERS.
AND YET-- ANN'VAR IS NOT SURE HOW. SOME INEXPLICABLE SPARK OF WILL. OF PURPOSE...
BUT A SPARK IS EASILY EXTINGUISHED--
GLORRRGHHPHHH
--BY THE ONE WHOSE WILL DWARFS ALL OTHERS!
HE'S IMPRISONED CAPTAIN AMERICA IN A COCOON OF SOLIDIFIED THOUGHT. WHICH BEGS THE QUESTION: IF CAP COULD BE DEFEATED SO EASILY...
...WHY DID THE ENCHANTMENT BRING HIM HERE IN THE FIRST PLACE?
ANN'VAR--
WELL, I'LL EXPLORE THAT MYSTERY LATER...
--GET OFF MY WORLD!

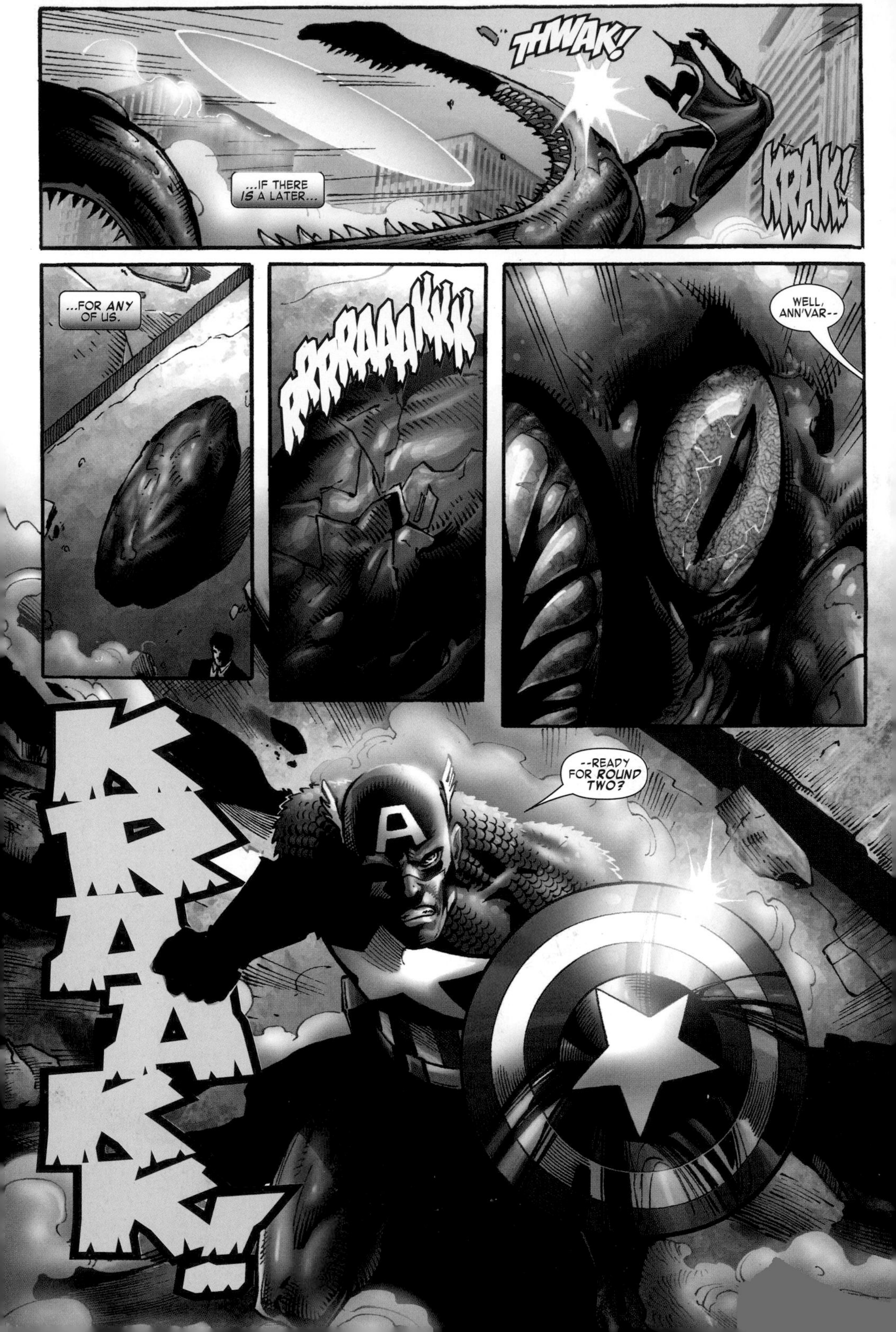
THWAK!
...IF THERE IS A LATER...
KRAK!
...FOR ANY OF US.
RRRRAAAKKK
WELL, ANN'VAR--
--READY FOR ROUND TWO?
KRAAK!

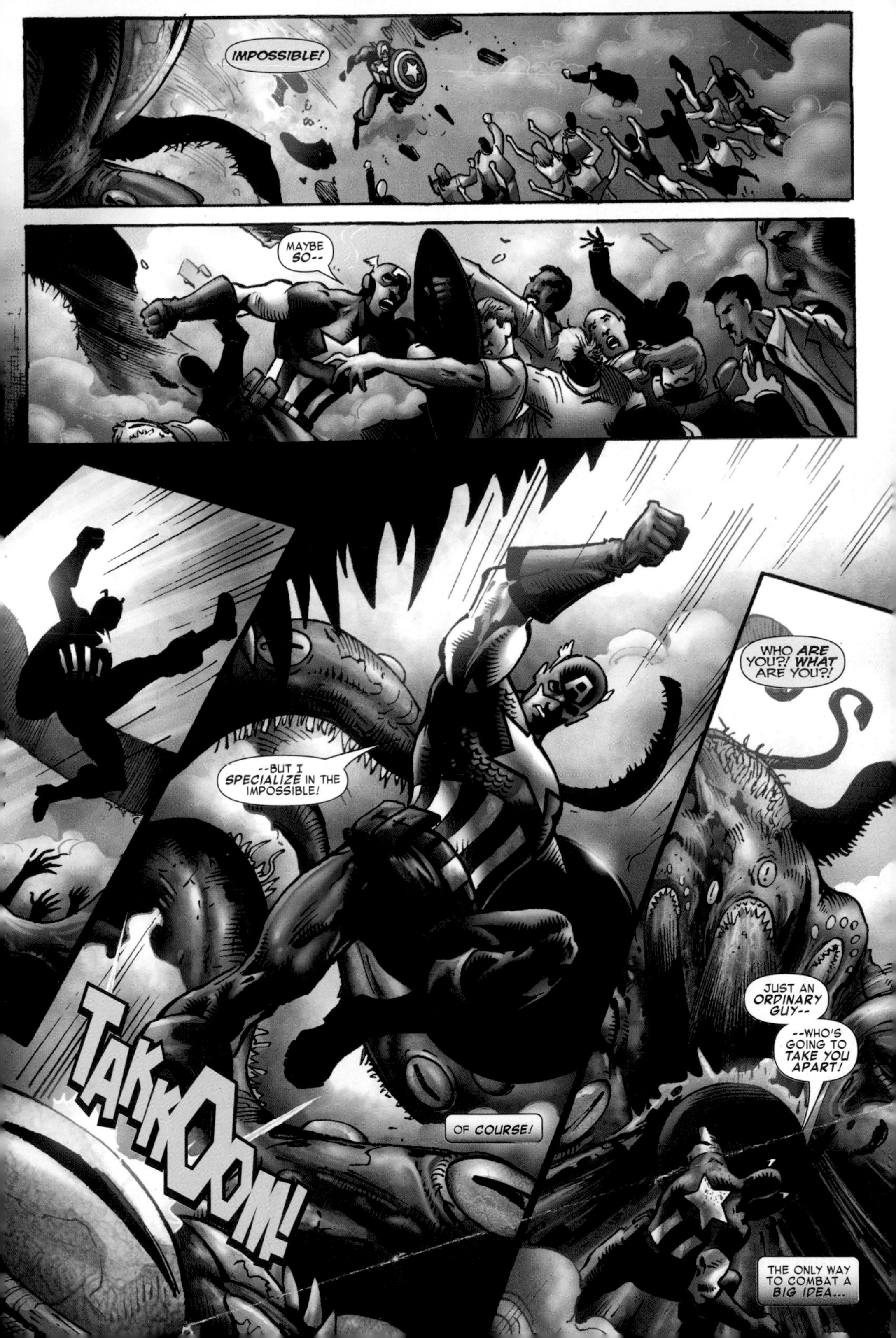
IMPOSSIBLE!
MAYBE SO--
--BUT I SPECIALIZE IN THE IMPOSSIBLE!
WHO ARE YOU?! WHAT ARE YOU?!
JUST AN ORDINARY GUY--
--WHO'S GOING TO TAKE YOU APART!
TAKKOOM!
OF COURSE!
THE ONLY WAY TO COMBAT A BIG IDEA...

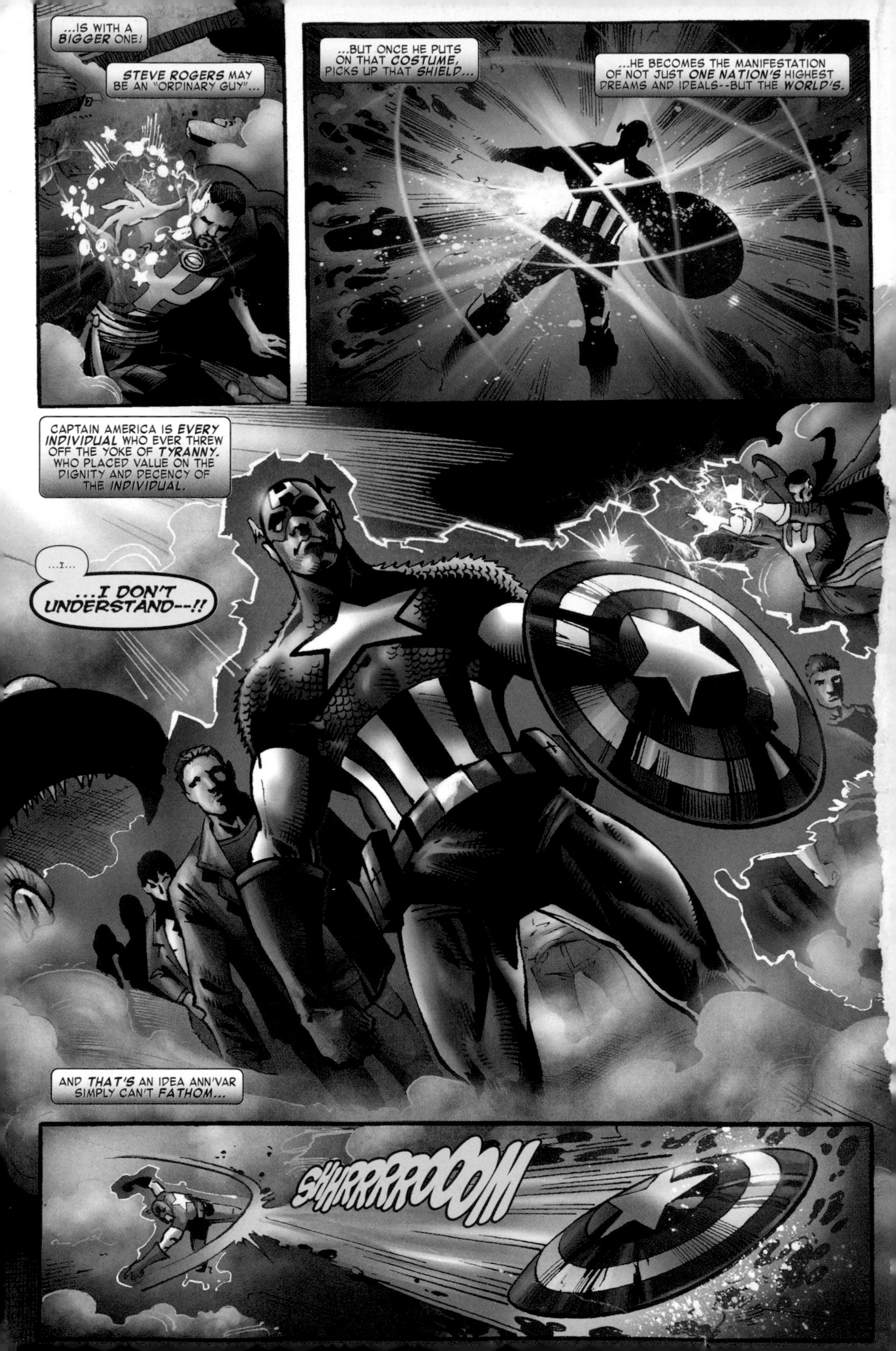
...IS WITH A BIGGER ONE!
STEVE ROGERS MAY BE AN "ORDINARY GUY"...
...BUT ONCE HE PUTS ON THAT COSTUME, PICKS UP THAT SHIELD...
...HE BECOMES THE MANIFESTATION OF NOT JUST ONE NATION'S HIGHEST DREAMS AND IDEALS--BUT THE WORLD'S.
CAPTAIN AMERICA IS EVERY INDIVIDUAL WHO EVER THREW OFF THE YOKE OF TYRANNY. WHO PLACED VALUE ON THE DIGNITY AND DECENCY OF THE INDIVIDUAL.
...I...
...I DON'T UNDERSTAND--!!
AND THAT'S AN IDEA ANN'VAR SIMPLY CAN'T FATHOM...
SHRRRROOOM

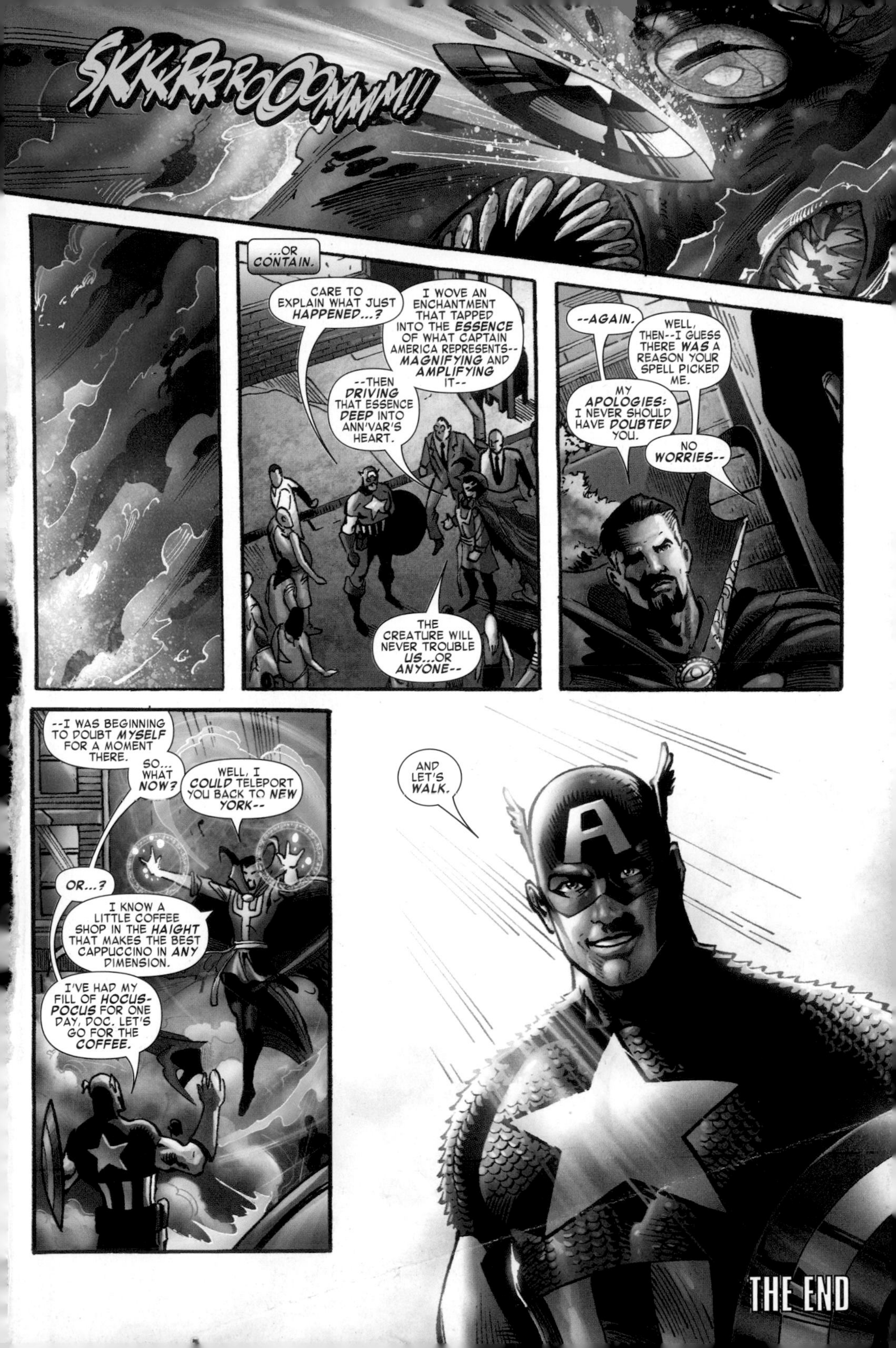
SKKRRROOOMMM!!
...OR CONTAIN.
CARE TO EXPLAIN WHAT JUST HAPPENED...?
I WOVE AN ENCHANTMENT THAT TAPPED INTO THE ESSENCE OF WHAT CAPTAIN AMERICA REPRESENTS-- MAGNIFYING AND AMPLIFYING IT--
--THEN DRIVING THAT ESSENCE DEEP INTO ANN'VAR'S HEART.
THE CREATURE WILL NEVER TROUBLE US...OR ANYONE--
--AGAIN.
WELL, THEN--I GUESS THERE WAS A REASON YOUR SPELL PICKED ME.
MY APOLOGIES: I NEVER SHOULD HAVE DOUBTED YOU.
NO WORRIES--
--I WAS BEGINNING TO DOUBT MYSELF FOR A MOMENT THERE.
SO... WHAT NOW?
WELL, I COULD TELEPORT YOU BACK TO NEW YORK--
OR...?
I KNOW A LITTLE COFFEE SHOP IN THE HAIGHT THAT MAKES THE BEST CAPPUCCINO IN ANY DIMENSION.
I'VE HAD MY FILL OF HOCUS-POCUS FOR ONE DAY, DOC. LET'S GO FOR THE COFFEE.
AND LET'S WALK.
THE END

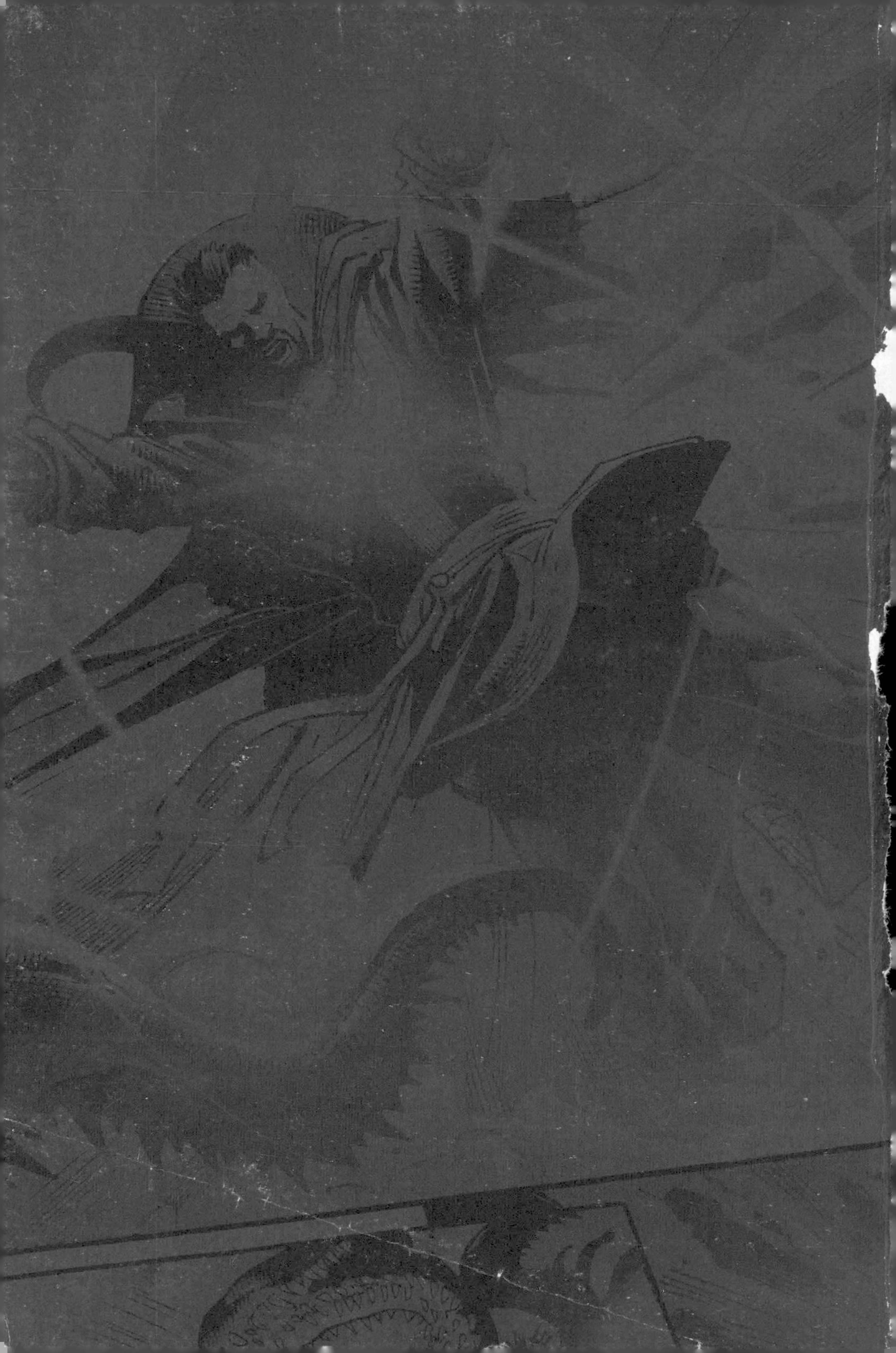